The JILLS

The JILLS

A Novel

KAREN PARKMAN

BALLANTINE BOOKS
NEW YORK

Ballantine Books
An imprint of Random House
A division of Penguin Random House LLC
1745 Broadway, New York, NY 10019
randomhousebooks.com
penguinrandomhouse.com

LIBRARY OF CONGRESS CATALOGING-IN-PUBLICATION DATA
Names: Parkman, Karen, author.
Title: The Jills: a novel / Karen Parkman.
Description: First edition. | New York: Ballantine Books, 2026. |
Identifiers: LCCN 2025032262 (print) | LCCN 2025032263 (ebook) |
ISBN 9780593982921 hardcover | ISBN 9780593982938 ebook
Subjects: LCSH: Cheerleaders—Fiction | Missing persons—Fiction |
LCGFT: Detective and mystery fiction | Novels
Classification: LCC PS3616.A75516 J55 2026 (print) | LCC PS3616.A75516 (ebook) |
DDC 813/.6—dc23/eng/20250716
LC record available at https://lccn.loc.gov/2025032262
LC ebook record available at https://lccn.loc.gov/2025032263

Printed in the United States of America on acid-free paper

1st Printing

First Edition

BOOK TEAM: Production editor: Michelle Daniel • Managing editor: Pamela Alders • Production manager: Jane Sankner • Copy editor: Bonnie Thompson • Proofreaders: Alissa Fitzgerald, Lawrence Krauser, and Taylor Teague

Book design by Diane Hobbing

The authorized representative in the EU for product safety and compliance is Penguin Random House Ireland, Morrison Chambers, 32 Nassau Street, Dublin D02 YH68, Ireland. https://eu-contact.penguin.ie

For my parents

Part 1

Chapter 1

ON SUNDAYS, JEANINE and I got ready for games together. We'd trade off whose apartment we met at. My place had the smaller bathroom, but in my bedroom was a big vanity mirror where we could smear on makeup, outline our lips and eyes with slick crayons, and watch our faces brighten and sharpen without bumping elbows. Jeanine's apartment had the bigger bathroom, complete with double sinks to clutter with our makeup and appliances, the air growing humid and close from the heat of our curling irons. These were the conditions under which we labored, piling on products until we looked like we were supposed to, until we looked like Jills.

It was better to get ready together. We could laugh and fret through our pregame nerves, reassure each other and fix each other's hair, and exclaim about how hot we were becoming in front of our own eyes. Alone, I was more aware of the shakiness of my hands and the churn in my stomach. I'd been dancing in competitions or on football fields since I was four years old. I loved the fear, I cherished it, but I wanted to share it with another person. It was so astoundingly affirming to meet your teammate's gaze and see your fear on her face, too. You could fall in love with someone that way, and you could fall in love with yourself, by sharing the fear of what you were about to do and knowing you were going to do it anyway.

But today, the only face in the mirror was mine. It was seven-thirty A.M., five and a half hours till kickoff. I grabbed my phone. **I'm driving you, right?** The screen turned grainy and slick from the foundation on my fingers as I typed. I sent Jeanine a picture of my hair. **Do you see this volume? The hair gods are with me today.**

I squeezed into my tights and typed again: **Are you at your place? Getting a ride from Bobby? Have you been struck dumb by post-coital bliss?** My body was alight with adrenaline, energy searching for an emotion as an outlet—annoyance, panic, anticipation, ecstatic glee. Jeanine's silence was making my nerves collapse in on themselves. I stalled, checking the contents of my monogrammed Jills duffel for the third time, waiting for her to respond. After five minutes there was nothing to do but leave.

When Jeanine went AWOL for a night or a weekend, it meant she was with Bobby Paladino. Bobby had a brownstone in Park Meadow, as well as a condo in Tampa. He'd flown Jeanine down there a few times, as well as to Tulum, Los Angeles, New Orleans, and San Marco. Back in February, they went skiing in Lake Tahoe. This wouldn't be the first time she'd sprinted straight from the airport to a game or practice at the last minute.

On my way to the stadium, I stopped by her apartment, an impressive one-bedroom in a freshly built complex two blocks off Chippewa. The building towered over Main Street near the intersection with Pearl, all faux brick and gleaming windows absorbing the gray morning light. I double-parked and shimmied into the small glass vestibule to lay on her buzzer.

It was a damp fall morning and the vestibule was muggy, like a cooled sauna. I hit the buzzer again and practiced the turn from bar eight of our opening number, teetering on the business-casual pumps I wore to walk into the stadium. The temperature was perfect for dancing, but our hair would be deflated by halftime.

After four turns I teetered to a stop. I looked back at my car, illegally parked. At this point I had just enough time to drive to Orchard

Park, navigate tailgating traffic, go through security, and make the winding journey through the stadium's inner corridors to the Jills' locker room. Not enough time, certainly, to ride up nine stories to Jeanine's unit to see if she was in there.

I tried not to be annoyed as I ducked back into my car, gesturing at a massive honking Ford truck to go around me. I almost texted her, **Don't be late or Suzanna will murder you.** The word *murder* glared up at me like a dare. Probably, she was rushing from Bobby's brownstone at that very moment, her phone tangled in the bedsheets or balanced on the edge of his sink. Or she'd swung home to pick up her uniform and I'd just missed her.

How many nights had I lain awake picturing the various ways in which my sister, Laura, might be attacked or murdered or kidnapped or run off the road or left in a ditch? I'd imagined each scenario in as much detail as possible, in a perverse attempt to protect her from these potential fates—surely they couldn't happen *while* I was thinking about them. But I never would have joked about these possibilities or put them in writing. That wasn't how the spell worked.

Obviously, I understood that the worst could and often did happen, whether you thought of it or not. Still, I erased the text, dropped my phone into the cupholder, and drove. I just didn't want to have sent it.

THE SMELL OF feet and hairspray nearly knocked me over, flooding my system with dopamine. It was four hours to kickoff, and the locker room at Ralph Wilson Stadium was crammed full of Jills.

I stood on the bench to scan the crowd for Jeanine. We got ready in the former referees' locker room, which featured three walls of lighted mirrors and a row of defunct urinals. Every inch of this tiny space we filled with the glorious mess of girls: tumbleweeds of hair, deflated ribbons of ripped pantyhose, sports bras browned at the armpits, athletic socks stained with blood from popped blisters, hair ties and bobby pins and spilled glitter littering the carpet, the air thick with aerosol. Girls sat at their assigned mirrors or cross-legged in groups on the floor, compacts propped up on the benches, squinting at their makeup—MAC products exclusively, which were provided at a discount from Edges Salon, one of our newest sponsors. They fought over outlets to plug in hair curlers and dryers. They practiced choreography and fussed over hair and eyebrows and emerging zits. One of the youngest girls on the squad, Maria, had brought some ridiculous little instrument, a recorder or a piccolo, on which she was loopily tootling out the notes to our opening number, Pitbull's "I Know You Want Me." The girls around her dissolved into fits of laughter and begged her to stop, wiping at their makeup. Beneath a muggy layer of jasmine and coconut, the locker room reeked—of dried BO and something deeper, the metallic scent of concealed fluids: blood, urine. The mess, the stink of it, made me dizzy with love and elation. It was the only proof we had of how hard we worked to appear shiny and perfect and effortless. I was so happy to be in this place, with these girls. My unease shrank to a dull twinge and retreated.

I clambered down from the bench and bumped into Lana from Line 2. "Help," she begged, fanning her face, false eyelashes drooping from her left eye. "Did I smudge my eyeliner?"

Scattered around her feet was a pile of dropped cotton balls smeared with foundation and mascara. Our required makeup ran when we danced, but substituting other products was strictly verboten.

"Let me fix it," I said. She pointed her gaze to the floor while I patted her falsies back into place. "Have you seen Jeanine? She wasn't checked off the roster at the door."

"Uh-oh," said Lana. "Think she got held up on the beach with Robbie Richboy?"

"Bobby," I corrected, as she studied her lashes in her compact mirror. Her face smelled waxy and greasy, like a fresh crayon.

"If she's coked up at a resort while we're here in the chicken coop, I swear to God." Lana said this without judgment; Jeanine knew where to get drugs of all kinds—coke, Adderall, illegal diet pills—and Lana had purchased them off her many times. She snapped the mirror shut and glanced pointedly at the digital clock on the wall above our heads. "I'm sure she's sprinting across the parking lot as we speak. She's got exactly twenty minutes before Suzanna starts breathing fire."

We jumped as Sharrice kicked open the door behind us, brandishing a bag of ice above her head like a trophy. The room erupted in cheers. She emptied the bag into two urinals, forming twin mounds of ice into which the girls shoved champagne, wine, cans of Diet Coke.

I joined my Line 4 girls—Sharrice, Gina, and Alicia, minus Jeanine—and took a swig from a bottle of white wine Sharrice handed me. I was overcome by the full-body nausea that preceded every game and wanted to be close to the girls I'd be dancing with for most of the day. After performing as a big group for our opening number, we split into six lines to dance on the sidelines facing the crowds. Together, we five would be sweating and moving the entire game. We moved more than half the football players, who sat around on the bench while we jumped and kicked and swerved for hours on end. My line was, basically, my platoon.

Gina crouched in the corner, elbows propped on her spread knees, forehead wrinkled in discomfort. "Yeast infection," she muttered in response to my look.

Sharrice was warning Alicia, the rookie of our group, about Steelers fans.

"They're the ones you have to watch out for. They yell the worst stuff at us."

"Like what?" said Alicia, as she spritzed a new pair of pantyhose with hairspray, a trick to prevent runs.

"Oh, like names. Or 'Take your top off.' They're also more likely to throw things."

Alicia's eyes widened, pantyhose dangling from her hand. "Like *what*?"

"The usual—snowballs, beer cans," said Sharrice. "Batteries."

"You lost a chicken cutlet," said Gina from her deep squat position, her head even with my hip.

She handed me the gel insert that had slipped out of my bra, and I shoved it back in. Once you made it on the squad you got a free—meaning, mandatory—consultation with a local plastic surgeon, a Jills sponsor, who offered discounts on procedures. I was complimented on the slope of my nose but strongly advised to augment my breasts, which don't quite fill a C-cup. I told him thank you but opted for inserts and other optical illusions to make them look bigger.

Sharrice turned to me. "Where's Jeanine? Didn't you drive together?" Her eyes darted to the digital clock on the wall overhead, its red numbers glaring, and her hand flew to her mouth. "Oh my God, she's officially late. Oh my God. She's going to get benched. We're already a girl down today. What the heck? Does Suzanna know? What are we going to do?"

"I'm here ready to dance all day with a bum vagina, and Jeanine can't even be bothered to show up on time?" Gina exclaimed from the floor.

"Be careful not to strain your Kegel muscles," said Alicia, with complete earnestness, dousing her pantyhose with another spray.

We collapsed into fits.

"*Alicia*!" Sharrice shrieked. "That's the name of the exercise, there are no *Kegel* muscles, oh my gosh—"

Alicia covered her face, overcome with giggles, while Gina gestured weakly for us to stop, clutching her lower abdomen.

Sharrice wiped her eyes and liberally applied setting spray to her stomach, which she'd contoured with blush to enhance her abs.

"I needed one more laugh," she said, "before you tell Suzanna and the ceiling comes down on us all."

WE DIDN'T DO it for the money. For game-day activities, we were paid in comped tickets and free parking passes. Charitable appearances and mandatory events for the Bills and our sponsors went unpaid, as did our six to eight hours of practice each week. We got free swag from sponsors, free gym and tanning salon memberships, and discounts on teeth whitening, and you could sign up for paid corporate appearances at thirty-five bucks an hour, but that didn't come close to covering our hair, nail, and tanning appointments for the month, even with the discounts.

But none of this was why we showed up. The real reason you never missed a game was because dancing at games was the best part. It was the *point*. Between pre- and regular season, plus the Toronto game, we were guaranteed ten home games per season, plus more if the Bills made the playoffs, which wasn't likely—the Jills hadn't had a chance to cheer in the postseason since 1999, and we were under no illusions that Chan Gailey or Ryan Fitzpatrick would end the twelve-year drought this year. So every week we counted down our remaining games, our last chances to perform. We were here to dance. That was why we sprinted from our day jobs to make it to practice and appearances week after week, why we dieted and sweated and lost sleep. That was why we went through two weeks of grueling tryouts every spring, and endured a brutal training camp every summer, and survived conditioning throughout the season: to be here, at the stadium, to dance. What was it for if you didn't show up to dance?

Three hours to showtime, Suzanna clapped her hands and the locker room went silent. "I'm not seeing that," she said, pointing to Sharrice, who hid the wine bottle behind her back.

Behind Suzanna stood Terry Fitzsimmons, the lanky, balding man who owned the broadcasting company that owned the Jills. He surveyed us happily, as though we had all been arranged according to his specifications.

"I was hoping you wouldn't all be so decent," he said, and waited for us to laugh. "I wanted to say go break a leg out there, ladies. You are the glue holding the Bills community together. I think I speak for all of us when I say—being a Bills fan is special. When I think about football . . ."

He paused with feigned gravitas and we all went still, gripping our hair and makeup products, wondering how long this was going to take. I was fond of the Bills, but football was, for me, more of an accessory to cheerleading rather than the other way around. My dad, before he died, was as ardent a fan as any. He'd drag me and Laura to games, rant to us about Jim Kelly's stats, explain Marv Levy's strategies in excruciating detail, and send himself into conniptions over each failed attempt at a down. Meanwhile, I took refuge in the constancy of the Jills—who were always smiling, always happy to be there—and spent games watching them through a pair of binoculars, trying to memorize the dance moves. Now I memorized flash cards of facts about the current players and stats from the previous game so I could talk about them at appearances.

"When I think about football," Terry went on, "I can't help but think about evolution. Thousands of years to create this team of men in top physical condition. Each generation perfecting on the mistakes of the past, to bring us to today. Football is men doing exceptional feats. And cheerleading—that's women doing their own exceptional feats. In this stadium we have gathered together the best men and women to represent the fighting spirit of Buffalo. But looking at you girls, I realize: this is not just the best of Buffalo I see here in front of me. This may be the best goddamn group of girls on the planet."

Suzanna stood next to him, arms folded, the curve from her chin to her collarbone deep as a cave. Even in her forties she kept her hair platinum, feathered bangs teased high over her forehead, with her cleavage propped up beneath a well-moisturized clavicle. Her white tracksuit practically gleamed. Her face, as always, was beautifully made up. Currently, it was arranged in a look of rapidly diminishing tolerance.

Terry finished, "I guess what I'm trying to say is, I'm proud to be a Bills fan and I'm proud to root for the Jills, too. Let's go, Buffalo!"

We shouted, "Let's go, Buffalo!" and launched into applause before he could start talking again. Terry backed out of the room, clapping for himself.

I found Suzanna with Sara, the Line 1 captain, huddled over the giant white three-ring binder where Suzanna kept track of all our faults.

I broke the news swiftly: "Jeanine isn't here."

Suzanna lifted her gaze, her headset crackling softly. From the way her eyes darted, she seemed to be making a set of rapid calculations. Over Suzanna's shoulder, Sara clenched her teeth in terror and ran her index finger across her throat.

There was a terrible silence, which I tried to endure with poise. Girls got benched all the time, for showing up a minute late to practice or failing uniform check. It was one of the most embarrassing things you could endure as a Jill, to be found so lacking you weren't even allowed to step foot on the field. It also brought the most collective shame, because of the stress and inconvenience it caused the other girls—when a Jill got benched, we all had to deal with the fallout by reconfiguring our lines, dancing one girl down. But for someone to simply not show up for a game, without warning, was completely unheard of, and it was a girl on my line, a girl *I* was responsible for.

"You." Suzanna snapped her fingers at Sophie, a rookie standing nearby, awaiting instructions. Sophie'd been benched earlier in the week for being photographed at an appearance with her bra strap showing. Even benched girls had to show up on game day to provide support, hand out supplies for autograph signings, or follow whatever orders Suzanna barked at them.

"I saw you lugging in your uniform bag. Did you pack everything you need to dance today?"

"Yes!" Sophie said, leaping to attention. She was lean and muscular, Korean American—the only Asian girl on the squad. "I didn't know what you'd need from me, so I brought everything just in case."

"We can't redo the lines this late. There's not enough time. This is your lucky day, Sophie. You're off the bench, on Virginia's line, Line 4. This will *never* happen again."

"Thank you, Suzanna." Sophie's eyes glistened with tears.

"Get your girls organized," Suzanna said to me. "Do *not* put Sophie in the front row. Go."

I led Sophie, who was gripping her face and chanting, "Oh my God, oh my God," back to our corner. There was no time to think: we had to run through the steps with Sophie, we had field rehearsal, then pregame appearances, and photos, and more hair and makeup back in the locker room while we scarfed down protein bars and room-temperature yogurt cups to fuel us for the game. We had to hydrate and stay upright and not pass out.

Thirty minutes to kickoff. We gathered into a wide circle, elbows linked, poms gripped in our sweating palms. It was Sara's turn to pray. She prayed that God would protect the players on the field, and the fans in the stadium, and the whole Bills community watching at home. She prayed that our dancing would fill the hearts of all those present today with love and goodwill. She prayed for all the Jills who came before, and for those who could not be here. She prayed that we would dance as well as we could, in the glory of Jesus's name, amen.

Then we lined up in two parallel columns in the walkway of the Miller High Life VIP area. We waved to the people who had purchased the right to stand in this little concrete thoroughfare and watch us and the football players stream through the tunnel and onto the field. People filmed us on their phones, and we shook our poms at them good-naturedly. Though the hallway was air-conditioned to an arctic chill, pinpricks of sweat began to burst along my bra line. My hands were numb. Handlers and cameramen and people with headsets dashed around us. We held hands and whispered chants at each other, like protective spells, preparing for the yawn of the stadium ahead, the eardrum-bursting roar, the vast expanse of field it was our job to fill with our thirty taut female bodies. Our fear was both immediate and ancient. Even in my second season, I felt like I was being sent to the arena to be mauled by lions. Like my abs and mouth and butt all had to get as hard and tight as possible, lest my guts and vomit spill out all over the place.

The fog machine at the tunnel's exit began to billow, and my stomach tried to escape out through my belly button. Sharrice and I bared our teeth at each other to check for lipstick—MAC Ruby Woo, our signature shade. Then we began to march out on tempo, a steady one-two skip with a pom-pom flick every second beat. We streamed into formation on the fifty-yard line while an incomprehensible voice emerged from deep in the echoing shell of the stadium to introduce us.

A lump formed in my throat, an automatic physiological reaction to the swell of cheers that greeted us. Tens of thousands of people, together, all caring about the same thing. And every set of eyes on us, waiting for us to dance. This was the best you could hope for: an audience of more than seventy thousand people screaming with anticipation. A mass of shifting colors coalescing into a single entity, one heart, one gargantuan cheer droning one note. We were all here, caring our guts out. Who wouldn't want to weep at the sight?

The music began and swallowed me whole. A dull, sweeping roar engulfed the stadium, my body merely obeying the rhythms, submitting joyfully to the punch and drive of each beat. I moved as one with the girls around me; our boots pounded into the turf in unison, we panted to the same tempo, our fists and elbows swung into the air in one motion. This was not the part you skipped. Jeanine would never willingly miss this.

OUTSIDE THE STADIUM after the game, where my phone had reception, I waited for the buzz of a text from Jeanine, or a voicemail alert.

We were supposed to leave the stadium in pairs, as a safety measure, to ward off fans who wanted to follow us to our cars and ask for our number. Jeanine was my parking lot buddy, so I strode toward my car alone, phone aloft to catch a band of service. The sun had started to sink behind the silvery clouds, and the lights of the parking lot flickered on as I walked. Already the late October days were contracting into darkness, the crystal chill of coming winter rolling off the lake, four miles west.

A few strides from my car, I stopped short. There, by the nearest lamppost, stood Ray, waving earnestly in his blue polyester Bills jacket. Everyone on the squad knew Ray. We were always running into him in the grocery store, or while out to dinner, or doing errands, leading some of the girls to fret that he knew our addresses and kept track of our movements. He seemed to like me especially; on my birthday, using the Jills fan mail address, he'd sent me a handwritten note: *Virginia you are EVERYTHING the world spins so you can DANCE you bring everyone JOY and when I see you I feel I could be UNDERSTOOD,* accompanied by a painting of me in my uniform, the paper dented from pencil lines erased over and over until the perfect, stiff outline of my form was achieved, with my breasts depicted considerably larger than they are in real life. When I found him waiting by my car after one Jills practice—it was late, and dark, and I had no idea how he knew which car was mine—I had to tell him, in no uncertain terms, that he was not allowed to do this. He seemed horrified that his actions had upset me, and now waited thirty to fifty feet outside the stadium entrance, which wasn't really better. At the moment, he was far closer to my car than he was supposed to be.

"I didn't see Jeanine enter the stadium today," he said. "Is she sick?"

Even with problem fans like Ray, I was expected to maintain the Jills standard of conduct: be professional, smile, deflect. But I was so distracted and fatigued that out popped the truth.

"Actually, Ray, I don't know where she is."

He blinked. "Now, that's strange. Jeanine has never missed a game. I know the lineup has already changed once this season, after Gabby got a new job and switched to ambassador squad. And Ashlee missed the first two home games thanks to that knee injury. But Jeanine's like you," said Ray. "You're the girls I can count on. You don't go disappearing on me."

Yes, Ray kept meticulous track of our appearances and placement on the field. It was clear from the number of comments he left on the Jills' YouTube and Facebook pages and the *Cheer Blog* on the Jills site that he spent the majority of his time squinting into the glow of the computer screen, looking for pictures and updates about us online. I wondered if he kept a spreadsheet more detailed than Suzanna's of our performances and appearance schedules.

"I like when you're all out there together," said Ray, fitting his palms together as though we were a bouquet of flowers he could hold.

"If one of us misses a game, it's for a very important reason," I said, regaining my composure. "We love to be here, just like you."

"If you need help looking for Jeanine—"

"No one's looking for her. Everything's fine. You know what you could do, Ray? Send out good thoughts for us, like always."

"I only have good thoughts for you. There's no other type of thought," he said happily. I wondered, not for the first time, how old he was. He had a moony face cratered by teenage acne. He could be anywhere between nineteen and forty-five.

"Did you know you were on the jumbo screen today?" he said, as I hurried past him to my car. "I always get the feeling when I catch sight of you that everything's going to be okay."

Ray was harmless, probably, but I didn't love having him behind me in a darkening parking lot. It brought to mind the threat of real stalkers. Last season Mackenzie had one who sent her Barbie dolls with the limbs and heads removed. The police told her they couldn't press charges or file a restraining order until the man actually attacked her, so she spent the year waiting for it to happen. Luckily, he got arrested for beating his girlfriend half to death and was now in jail awaiting his court date.

I DROVE STRAIGHT to Jeanine's apartment. On a Sunday evening the streets were empty, and I was able to park by the entrance of her building. I dug out the key buried in my purse. She'd given it to me so I could watch her cat whenever she ran off with Bobby or visited her mother overnight in Rochester on short notice. On instinct, I stopped in the lobby to empty her mailbox, as I always did when I cat-sat.

She'd be in there, I told myself as I rode up in the elevator, the stack of envelopes from her mailbox clamped under my arm. Bobby had taken her on a surprise weekend trip to Tampa. They'd gotten delayed, they'd had mechanical issues on his rented jet. She was inside, unpacking her skimpy bathing suits, smelling of sunscreen and the metallic scent cocaine left in your pores, laughing. "Does everyone on the squad want to kill me?"

In my apartment, the creak of neighbors' footsteps and the smell of cooking oil wafted through the walls, but the residents of Kinsley Apartments & Lofts suffered no such exposure to other human lives. The building was quiet and only half-occupied, as was often the case in these expensive new buildings. Every five minutes, it seemed, another developer was snatching up a piece of battered real estate downtown to turn into luxury condos. As I padded down the hallway to Jeanine's door, even my footsteps were silent, all evidence of my passage swallowed by the plush carpet.

I swung open the door and there, just beyond the darkened threshold, was her little black cat. It mewed and swiped at my ankles, then went careening inside. I flipped on the light.

"Jeanine?" I called.

Her apartment was ridiculously nice, if a little corporate for my taste. The living room opened to a gleaming kitchen of stainless steel and green faux-marble countertops. The new-building smell of fresh paint hung in the air, mixed with Jeanine's scent—the American Spirits she smoked on and off, her Marc Jacobs perfume. The rent had to be a small fortune, but she found reasons to mention—a little too often, a little too casually—that it cost much less than I probably thought, because Bobby knew the building owner and had gotten her a great deal. I wondered if Bobby helped pay for it, but I never asked.

The cat crept out and followed me across the satiny wood floors as I circled the living room. It meowed at alarmingly regular intervals—"Don't, don't!" it seemed to be yelling, or "Help! Help!" The green velvet sofa was gently rumpled, one of the seat cushions dislodged and propped on the floor, and the chairs of the oval dining room table next to the kitchen were askew. I picked up the fallen cushion to put it back into place and noticed a neat tear in the fabric of the couch, as though it had been intentionally sliced open. I stuck a hand through the slit, and felt only the hollow frame inside. Jeanine had ordered all her furniture online, and though it looked luxurious, the quality was dubious.

The bathroom fixture had been left on, spilling a glowing strip of light into the hallway. "Jeanine?" I called again as I turned on the bedroom switch. The bed was half-made, her jeans and heels scattered on the carpet as though someone had run straight out of them. The dress she'd worn on Friday night, when I last saw her, hung on the edge of her hamper.

I became suddenly convinced there was a presence in the living room. I hurried back out and circled the patterned rug, taking in the total emptiness of the apartment. Though I was nine stories up, the floor-to-ceiling windows left me feeling exposed, like a telescope or camera had trained its eye on me from a distant high-rise. The presence, whatever it was, seemed to be right over my shoulder.

Inside the bathroom, the litter box emitted the ammonia stench of urine. It hadn't been cleaned in at least a couple of days. Her toothbrush was in a cup by the sink. On the mirror, she'd taped a few old photos of her and her ex-boyfriend, Landon, a likable pot dealer whose only ambition was to be in love with Jeanine. In the pictures they grinned wildly or stared into the camera with the intensity of doomed lovers. In one, a teenage Jeanine wore a choker and Landon's hoodie, her heavily made-up eyes closed while Landon kissed her cheek. In another, taken a couple of years later, they sat on the steps in front of a neon-lit bar, beers in their hands and cigarettes balanced between their fingers, looking mournful and ruined and sexy. I'd done my makeup a hundred times in this mirror and never noticed the ominous quality of these pictures. Like death waited for them in the black, grainy backgrounds beyond their overlit faces.

I picked up the cat, slung it over my elbow, and hurried out of the apartment, filled with the sensation that there was someone right behind me.

In the elevator I hit the lobby button and realized that Jeanine's mail was still crushed beneath my elbow. The cat squirmed in my arms, nearly dislodging the envelopes. Back at my car, I tossed the whole mess, cat and crumpled mail, into the backseat and drove.

Chapter 2

WHEN LAURA HAD failed to come home from a party or meet me at the agreed-upon street corner, my onus was always clear: freak out until contact was achieved. Taking a long time to respond was one of Laura's reliable stalling tactics. She dragged out replies, insisting her phone had died or been stolen or was "acting weird," buying time to get high, get sober, or enact whatever scheme she'd come up with.

But Jeanine usually answered right away, unless she was on an airplane, or out of the country, or in the middle of sex—in other words, when she was with Bobby. I sat on the kitchen floor, a plastic container of Caesar salad in my lap, and tossed pieces of chicken at the cat. It had wriggled between the wall and the trash can and stared at me with brainless apprehension. With my free hand, I searched my phone for Bobby's number.

My connection to Bobby Paladino far predated my relationship with Jeanine: Bobby's father, Stanley Paladino, had been my dad's best friend. Before my dad died, my family spent every Thanksgiving at Stanley's house (Laura hiding masticated green beans in Bobby's napkin when he got up for seconds, while I shook uncontrollably with laughter), and we went there for a roast dinner on the first Sunday of every month. These occasions served primarily as an excuse for my dad and Stanley to get drunk on Scotch on the leather couches in Stanley's office, while my mom chatted stiffly in the kitchen with whomever was Stanley's wife at the time. After dinner, Bobby, Laura, and I crowded around our fathers, competing for their attention and laughter, until they shooed us away to watch TV in the living room, while the women in the kitchen stared longingly at the clock.

The Paladinos were an old-fashioned crime family. They started out smuggling booze from Canada during Prohibition, then came to prominence during the steel boom thanks to deep ties with local labor unions, and eventually transitioned into sports betting and underground poker games. My dad had been their accountant. He worked mainly out of the back office at Paladino's Steakhouse, Stanley's classic fine-dining spot on the north edge of Delaware Park, making the numbers look right in the little columns of the business records. Laura and I spent afternoons at the steakhouse after school, bent over homework and coloring books in our favorite booth, drinking Shirley Temples while the waitresses slipped us stuffed olives.

And there, from the primordial slurry of these childhood memories, emerged twelve-year-old Bobby, stalking around his father's restaurant, chucking lime wedges at me and Laura. "I'm the boss here," he'd say. "You have to do what I tell you or I'll fire you and your family will starve." He ordered us to clean the baseboards, dared us to lick the dried wads of gum stuck to the undersides of the tables. Once he came over with a pint glass full of some disgusting concoction—cherries, olives, pickled onions, every soda from the fountain, plus a dash of crème de menthe—and chased me around the restaurant, ordering me to drink it, while eight-year-old Laura screamed her head off at him to leave me alone.

I had a hard time reconciling the Bobby I knew with the man who'd expanded the Paladino business into real estate and whisked Jeanine off in a chartered jet every other weekend.

Bobby and I had spoken only a handful of times in the couple of years since I'd returned to Buffalo. We occasionally crossed paths as he was leaving Jeanine's place, and once I met them for drinks. He'd hung his arm possessively around Jeanine's shoulders and struggled to make small talk with me. Any common ground we'd had as children had eroded; Bobby and Jeanine were their own private island.

The call went to a computer-generated voicemail message: *Please leave a message for: Seven. One. Six . . .*

"Hey, Bobby," I said after the beep. "It's Virginia. I know it's been a while, just wondering . . . if you've seen Jeanine this weekend. Sorry to call kind of late, I'm just—I'm wondering about Jeanine . . . Hey, we three should get together sometime," I added.

I hung up. The cat had inched out of its hiding place and was gobbling down the chicken scraps. I wiped my hands and texted Jeanine: **I have your cat, btw. Did I forget you were traveling this weekend?**

I added, **Can you let me know where you are as soon as you can?**

The cat's name was Ghost. Actually, that was the cat's second name—originally, she had named it Jeanine.

"You named your cat after yourself?" I'd laughed.

"It's funny, right?" she said. "Like, 'Hi, I'm Jeanine. And this is my cat, Jeanine.'" Then she found out the cat was actually a boy, and changed the name to Ghost. "But mostly"—she hugged the cat, baby-talking through pursed lips—"I call him Kitty. Cuz he's my little kitty."

In the bathroom, I set up a makeshift litter box by filling an aluminum roasting pan with potting soil.

I set the cat down in the soil.

"Go here," I said. "This is where you pee. Understand?"

The cat pinned back its ears and stared up at me.

"I know you don't want to be here," I said. "I don't want you here, either."

Then I added, "I'm sorry."

LYING IN BED that night, I reminded myself that though the last time I'd seen Jeanine felt very far away, in truth very little time had passed.

Friday night had been one of our best nights out in a while. We had both made weight on Thursday, which meant we wouldn't have to face the brutality of Suzanna's scale for another six days. Plus we had money for drinks, thanks to the $130 we'd earned dancing at a WBEN radio event. We had only to stumble, dizzyingly high on possibilities, into the night to see what we would do. What we did was get raucously drunk on white wine in Jeanine's apartment and then stay out until three in the morning.

Our last stop of the night was a thumping, black-walled nightspot on Chippewa called Club 716. Jeanine and I sat perched on barstools, yelling happily at each other. Jeanine sparkled in a shimmery black dress and mesh stockings, and I wore an icy-blue velvet dress I'd borrowed from her, which I kept having to hike up by the straps, Jeanine's boobs being bigger than mine. Jeanine had a lot of clothes. She tossed strappy tops and slinky dresses at me with abandon, and I slid them on like discarded snakeskins, feeling sly and carnivorous. We made a contrasting pair: Jeanine curvy and compact at five foot four—though her personality made her seem much taller—me, willowy and blond. As a result, we were often placed next to each other for Jills photos and appearances—one brunette and one blonde, one sexy, one cute. That night, we were "undercover," as we called it; we'd tell no one we flirted with that we were Jills, because we did not intend to behave in a manner becoming of a Jill.

We had reached the part of the night when everything the other said sounded genius and poetic. We were talking about clothes, actually—or shouting about them. The thing about growing up poor, Jeanine was explaining, *and* about being a pageant girl, was that you became obsessed with clothes.

"At some point you realize we're all just making shit up about each other based on surfaces. All anyone *actually* sees of you is the surface, and from that they extrapolate all kinds of meaning—but they're literally just guessing based on the tiny bit of data they get." Jeanine had her cocktail straw clamped between her fingers like a cigarette, and she jabbed at the air to emphasize her points. "But once you realize *that*, you realize you can manipulate your surface to steer them to whatever conclusion you want. But to do that, you need money! Or wits, which is what I used, until I could get the money."

"It's like the Jills," I said agreeably.

"But I respect the Jills more because we don't pretend it's not about surfaces. We have a uniform. No one is expected to be original."

I liked it when Jeanine ranted about her pageant days. In her closet was a box of sashes collected from around western New York and Pennsylvania. She'd been crowned the Erie County Fair Queen ("I had to pretend I cared about cows") and Miss Flower City's Outstanding Teen, and won first runner-up at Young Miss Buffalo. Among these more legitimate awards was a jumble of ribbons and statuettes from local pageants held in hotels and recreation centers and church gymnasiums: if there was prize money, she competed. She'd shown me pictures of teenage Jeanine in a red sequined fishtail gown, beaming, her teeth bleached by drugstore whitening strips she'd shoplifted from Walgreens. Her talent was dance; another photo had shown her mid-leap, in a two-piece yellow costume decorated with fringe and rhinestones. It was clear that the crowd didn't scare her, nor did the judgment of the other girls, nor the peering eyes of the judges. *So what?* her smile said. Or *Why not me?*

"The sad thing," Jeanine went on, "was the pageant girls who tried to make the image they were projecting match up with their real selves. I mean, that shit was tragic to watch. The judges don't want your *authentic self.* They don't want some bleeding heart onstage asking to be loved. No one wants to feel they're *yielding* to another person's need! They want a show, to be taken on a ride."

I chewed on the stem left over from my cocktail cherry. "Oh, but—is it bad to want to be loved?"

"The problem isn't wanting to be loved, the problem is confusing the rules of the game! In a pageant, you're not asking for love, you're asking for *money.* People get the two mixed up," she added wisely. "It's like wanting your boss to like you. It's not important that your boss likes you. It's important that your boss *pays* you."

Her eyes went a little dark. She stabbed her straw into the ice at the bottom of her glass.

"Every rich bitch on that stage knew I was Rust Belt white trash in rhinestones," she said. "And I *still won*."

I studied her. There was nothing particularly out of the ordinary in Jeanine's pronouncements, but the *way* she said them—the way she'd been talking all week, really—was a bit . . . well, crazed.

"Jeanine." I dropped the mangled cherry stem back into my glass. "Are you okay?"

She tilted her head back to drain her vodka tonic and peered at me through one narrowed eye.

"Yeah," she said after she swallowed. "Why?"

"You've been pretty . . . *zingy* this week."

She put on a show of squinting as though I wasn't making any sense, but she knew exactly what I was talking about. All week, she'd swung between being distant and unusually clingy. She'd ignore my texts all day, then respond wanting to know what I was doing *right then* and could I come over? When I made motions to leave at the end of the evening, she'd ask, "Where are you going?" with forced brightness, her whole body tense with—not panic, but a prelude to panic.

Jeanine was not the type to sit alone and contemplate her thoughts—nor was I, if I could help it; constant company was fine with me—but I'd never slept over at her place five nights out of seven before. Clearly, she didn't want to sleep alone. She was distracted and talkative, and she checked her phone compulsively. And she had been drinking way more than usual, so much that I had to force myself to stop counting her calories.

With Jeanine you couldn't push or prod, you had to let the great unsaid thing sit there in the air between you until she was ready to bring it up. If I asked the right question, after all these nights of frenetic avoidance, maybe I could get it to come out.

"Like tonight," I went on. "Aren't you supposed to be at work? Did you call out again?" She'd skipped her Wednesday shift at the bar where she worked to have dinner with Bobby.

"I feel I deserve a break from time to time."

"Did you and Bobby get in a fight?"

"We never fight," she said unhappily. "Bobby's fine. I had lunch with him today. Am I being annoying? I've been having a lot of fun."

"I have too!"

"I just want to be around you. When I'm around you, I feel—" She searched for the right word. "You have a very protective quality. Like . . ." She arranged her arms into a semicircle, as if she were holding an exercise ball. "When I'm with you, I'm in the buffer zone. Nothing can touch me."

I felt immensely gratified.

"If someone touches you, they get a stiletto right in the eye," I said, lifting my foot to show off one of the borrowed heels and nearly toppling off the stool. "What do you think?" I said, righting myself. I hitched up the blue dress, which Jeanine called her "ice bitch" dress, and flashed a smile. "Could *I* be a ruthless pageant girl?"

"Oh, V. You would have been completely beloved." She cupped my face in her hands, her eyes bleary. "And you would have been completely broke." She knocked back the last few chips of ice from her glass and grabbed my hand. "I'm getting us another drink. Then let's find some boys to pay attention to you."

The night dissolved into a blue blur. I wasn't planning on going home with anyone that night, thinking Jeanine might want me to stay over with her again. But by the time we made it onto the dance floor, we were instantly folded into a group of four men. We all had a fantastic time shouting at one another, screaming when we recognized the song. I had never done this before Jeanine—talked to strangers, like it was nothing.

The skinny hipster of the group showed an interest in me, and Jeanine took extra care to ask questions that forced us to talk to each other. She was a genius at this, at getting people to do what they already wanted to do but didn't know how. The skinny guy and I began to ignore the rest of the group. He stared at my mouth while I talked, and I knew he could be mine. We danced to a Rihanna song, and by the time it was over we were making out, falling into the wall while we groped each other.

At times, my behavior when I was around Jeanine stunned me. In my early twenties I'd been too busy trying to keep Laura from OD'ing to sleep around the normal amount. I'd been good and had made my life dull and small in the process. When I met Jeanine, two years ago, I wasn't anywhere near breaking double digits. But here I was, on the verge of collecting my twelfth guy.

For a wild moment, my face pressed against his, the smell of beer and sweat in my nose, I was filled with terror that I was flying too close to the sun. What made me think I could be the sort of person who stayed out all night and had a blast with her best friend and slept with whomever she pleased? The song changed and, with a lurch, I staggered off to find Jeanine, convinced she was mad at me or had abandoned me—now it was I who did not want to be alone, dangling from the limb of my own daring. I found her in the hallway that led to the bathrooms and grabbed her by the arms, and we became one of countless pairs of drunk girls across the nation, furiously reassuring each other and proclaiming their love. "You are everything," she said. "That guy should lick your shoes. You can do whatever you want. You are alive."

My friendship with Jeanine wasn't like my relationship with Laura, or like the dance friendships I had in college, which alternated between obsessive closeness and a ruthless assessment of status. It reminded me of my dad's bond with Stanley. Their friendship, though perfectly visible, was private and inaccessible to others, built on trust and secrets, marked by an intimate shorthand that comes from years of breaking rules together. They guarded and balanced each other. In the same way, Jeanine's wily shrewdness rubbed off on me, making me quick-witted and decisive. And I rubbed off on Jeanine, too, providing her a certain grounded assurance. I think we both helped the other feel that she was *real,* that she truly existed.

"Go!" she said, pushing me back to the dance floor. "Go into that good night, bitch!"

Off I went. My terror, which was really guilt mixed with a propensity for self-deprivation, shrank to a point and, *pop,* disappeared. I collected my skinny hipster, and we took a five-minute cab ride to his apartment in Allentown, where we had quick and ferocious sex. His sheets smelled like detergent and men's deodorant and I was happy. It was so much easier than I'd ever thought it could be.

These nights with Jeanine were magic. I was having so much fun I could cry. A door had opened, and I'd been brave enough to walk through it, but the person who'd unlocked it was Jeanine, my friend, the best one I'd ever had. With whom I was the most worthwhile person I'd ever been.

OUR FRIDAY HAD been typical in every way except one.

There'd been another incident, one I'd pointedly avoided thinking about. Jeanine had just finished her rant about pageants and surfaces and was getting us another drink before we careened to the dance floor. I was swaying on my stool, sucking at the ice in the bottom of my glass. Then I caught sight of Jeanine across the circular bar, talking to a guy. The blood drained from my head into my legs, where it pooled in my feet.

It was Jason Morley, leaning close to Jeanine and speaking into her ear, his muscled arm resting on the bar. *No,* I thought. *No, no, no.* Jeanine could not be talking to Jason Morley.

Their cheeks nearly touched, but their bodies were angled away from each other—they looked like a couple that didn't want to be seen together. Jason took a step away, but Jeanine grabbed his arm and pulled him back to say something else. Jason nodded briefly, in apparent agreement. I marched over at top speed.

Jason saw me before Jeanine did.

"Virginia," he said, subdued. "Been a while. You back in town?" Jeanine spun around to face me.

"I moved back two years ago," I said. "I'm a Jill."

"Go fucking figure. Always the cheerleader."

Jason had the body of a former football player, stocky and solid. His face, a little puffy with age, bore the craggy handsomeness that had made him seem much older than everyone else back in high school. He'd been the running back for Kenmore West, and an exceptionally good one, because he hadn't given a shit about anything, especially other people's physical well-being. He started dating Laura during her junior year, while I was a senior, after Laura tore a ligament in her ankle and had to quit the dance team. She was hurt and vulnerable, and Jason Morley pushed his way in. She fell madly in love with him.

We went through the motions of catching up—what are you doing now, all that—our voices heightened by drunkenness and forced smiles. Jason kept shifting, putting an elbow on the bar, then straightening to cross his arms, then letting them hang by his sides. Jeanine had arranged her face to appear amused, but she looked like she'd been stuffed and put on display.

"So, how's Laura?" Jason finally asked.

"Fine," I said. "Apparently."

"Yeah, she texted me back in February that she was going into rehab and changing her number. I said congratulations. I was glad to hear it. Genuinely."

"Uh-huh," I said, nodding and nodding.

It disgusted me that Jason knew even the vaguest details of my little sister's business. He kept looking toward the exit. I wondered if his discomfort came from the fact that we hated each other or that he didn't want to be seen with Jeanine.

"Let's hope that's the last time I ever hear from her," said Jason. "If she starts texting me again, you know she's in trouble." He grinned.

"Well, you could not answer," I said. "If she texts, you don't answer. It's easy. Right?"

He shrugged. "I couldn't reach her if I wanted to. Ball's in her court. What about you? Do you keep in touch with her?"

"Kind of."

"Good. Family's important."

I hadn't inhaled once during this entire exchange. Jeanine handed me her vodka tonic, and I gulped it down, sucking air desperately through my nose. I felt myself panicking that I'd ruined the mood—but why shouldn't I ruin Jason fucking Morley's night? But no, I decided, it was Jeanine making things weird, the way she was standing there like she'd been taxidermied.

"So how do you two—?" I said.

Jason looked to Jeanine and she shrugged.

"We don't really," she said.

"At a party," he said, at the same time.

After Jason left, Jeanine and I fought. That's *Jason,* I yelled, on the verge of tears. That's *the* Jason who fucked up Laura's life, and mine. Didn't she know she should never, ever talk to anyone named Jason?

"I hate him, Jeanine," I spat. "I hate him."

"It's okay," she said. "There's nothing going on."

"He was very bad to Laura. Very. How do you know him? You were talking like you knew each other."

"We literally met for two seconds. I can't even remember the event. Some corporate after-party bullshit Bobby dragged me to."

"What party? A Paladino party? Where?"

"I said I don't remember. You don't have to yell at me. It's not my fault you know everybody in this stupid city. It's not my fault you have trauma with every goddamned person there is to meet."

She covered her face with her hands. I calmed down, and we hugged. "I'm sorry. I'm crazy. I don't know why I'm like this," I said as she wrapped her arms around me. "I see you with Jason and sirens start going off in my head, like *Danger, danger.*"

"I know. You have a fucked-up brain, V. You look sane but you're actually a psycho with a dysfunctional family and that's why I love you. You don't have to be upset. Everything is okay."

A tequila shot later, we were happy again. We both started crying and saying "I love you," then laughing hysterically. Jeanine said, "Let's find you someone, let's get the night going, let's hurry."

We stumbled to the dance floor, where we were absorbed into the swaying lights and the thump of music, and I fell for a while into the arms of number twelve, into the life I'd built since I'd moved back to Buffalo, leaving Laura to fend for herself in Columbus.

I managed to forget the incident for a while, but it bothered me that I had not gotten the answers I wanted. How well *did* Jeanine and Jason know each other, and had there been a spark, some familiarity between them, or had I, in my drunken panic, imagined it?

Replaying the evening in my mind, I couldn't help but feel that Jeanine had wanted to shake me off after that, to send me out into the night with number twelve. The trouble with Jeanine was that it was hard to tell if she was being cagey out of habit, or because she was hiding something.

THE CAT MEWED outside my bedroom. I climbed out of bed and pulled open the door, and it went tearing off down the hallway to hide in the living room.

Jeanine's cat was the perfect conduit for her playful narcissism, the way she smothered it in fierce affection but also felt no real obligation to it, pawning off her responsibility to care for it whenever she wanted to leave town. But wasn't a lack of obligation arguably the purest form of love? A love without debt. Feeling entitled to pleasure, demanding it, instead of glowering at the person you wanted things from, thinking, *You owe me.*

I grabbed my phone from the nightstand. Squinting into the white glow of the screen, I scrolled through my last text message exchange with Jeanine. Our last interaction was at two-thirty in the morning on Saturday, as I was leaving number twelve's apartment. She hadn't picked up when I called, so I'd texted, asking where she was. I could walk from Allentown to Chippewa in fifteen minutes if I took my heels off.

She wrote back, **I'm good tonight, stay with your man!**

I typed, **I already left! I'll come find you! Are you still at 716?**

No I'm good! Need a night alone. Love you, love you.

I didn't make you feel weird??? I wrote back.

No! I love you!

Love you, she wrote again, before I had time to finish typing it myself.

After this exchange I'd spun north, teetering happily, to walk home up Elmwood Ave, past the divey bars and Irish pubs of Allentown, the brick nineteenth-century apartment buildings, the dense rows of brightly painted old two-flats and Victorians, drinking in the cool air of my freedom. The truth was, I was grateful for a night in my own bed, and too drunk and happy to be worried, to even feel the blisters burrowing into my ankles from the heels, which were a size too big for me.

I'd texted her again when I woke up on Saturday morning but got no response. I figured I'd see her for the Bills game the next day anyway, and decided to give her some space. That's what a normal person did: give other people space, even though you knew you were creating an opening into which they could fall and disappear forever.

After rereading our last texts, I tossed my phone aside. I opened Facebook and typed **Jason Morley** into the search bar. He hadn't posted in almost two years. I friended him with the message: **Hey, great to see you after so long. Let's catch up—what have you been up to?**

My tone sounded gratingly false. The chances of him answering were next to none. Jason didn't want to talk to me; we each wished the other were dead.

I studied his blurry profile picture, frowning. These two boys from my past—Bobby and Jason—I'd lost them, and all these years later, Jeanine had found them. In the dark, I imagined I could hear the cat pacing the hallway. I listened to the building creak, the squeak of the pipes in the apartment below. Like how it feels in the woods at night when some creature, some force, is out there beyond the trees.

Chapter 3

"If jeanine doesn't come through those double doors in the next five minutes," said Sharrice, "we should call the police."

It was the midway break at Jills practice. A group of us sat cross-legged in a circle, wolfing down high-protein snacks—turkey slices with cheese, energy bars—the floor in front of our white sneakers littered with wrappers. I hadn't had time to eat dinner before practice, so I speared a lightly dressed spinach salad out of a Tupperware with a plastic fork.

Practice was held in what used to be a Kmart, in a well-maintained strip mall a few minutes east of the stadium in Orchard Park. The floors had been ripped out and replaced with faux wood, and a mirror installed on the back wall, but the flickering fluorescent lights and pocked rectangles on the ceiling remained. Behind us, the rest of the squad milled about, stretching and practicing choreo. We were learning a new third-quarter routine to mark the end of Breast Cancer Awareness Month, which would be performed with pink poms to the chorus of "Firework" by Katy Perry. The routine was needlessly complicated, and nobody was picking it up quickly enough.

"This has never happened before," Sara was saying as she leafed through the binder where she kept her copy of the Jills handbook.

She'd pulled an oversized Canisius College sweatshirt over her practice gear—sports bra, dance shorts, our eternal pantyhose—to keep her muscles warm. Next to her, Sophie sat cross-legged, scraping a cucumber slice through a container of hummus with a miserable look on her face. She'd had a rough time during choreo and was becoming known, regretfully, as our problem rookie. On the Jills you sank or swam, and she was sinking.

"I've been doing this for six seasons and no one has ever just—not shown up," said Sara. She was the most tenured veteran on the squad, and we often looked to her to clarify the rules. "I thought I was going to barf watching the doors before practice, waiting to see if she'd show."

"So what are we supposed to do?" said Ashlee. "I mean, besides redo the lines."

"There's a protocol for absences." Sara flipped the binder shut and rubbed her eyes. "Suzanna will send Jeanine a warning email later tonight, since missing practice is her second major infraction after missing the game. One more infraction and her contract will be subject to termination."

"But what's the protocol for involving the *police*?" said Gina. "It's been more than forty-eight hours since the game, right? Could we fill out a report? Or should her family do that?"

"You don't actually have to wait forty-eight hours to file a report," I said. "And you don't have to be family. But if it's for an adult and there's no sign of violence, the police usually won't do much."

"That's true," said Sharrice, and I could tell she was surprised I knew this. "But we'd at least have it on file that something was wrong."

"Guys, are we sure she's *missing* missing?" interrupted Maria. "Shouldn't someone call her work or her parents first? It would be so embarrassing if we called the police and it turns out she's on vacation with her boyfriend."

Carmen gathered up her napkins and wrappers with exaggerated fastidiousness. "If this is another case of Jeanine getting preferential treatment, I'm going to be so mad. There's no excuse for not showing up. I don't care if she is Suzanna's little rehab project."

"Carmen!" Sara exclaimed.

"What?" Carmen stood, trash gripped in her fist. "The rest of us who work just as hard, and maybe harder, frankly, don't get the same attention or opportunities. I'm not the only one who feels this way. Some of us drive over an hour from Rochester to be here. Brianna commutes from Canada!"

"Like you get extra points for driving from Rochester," Gina muttered under her breath.

Sharrice was shaking her head at Carmen, who often confused badmouthing the other girls with showing "firm leadership." Though Carmen was right that Suzanna and Jeanine had a rapport. Suzanna had her favorites, and they fell into two camps. The first were her watchdogs, like Carmen and Maria, who tattled on girls who danced with ripped tights, or snuck a bite of food at an appearance, or wore the wrong lipstick shade. They also reported more subjective infractions, like if a girl clammed up around a sponsor or wasn't witty enough, so Suzanna could keep them away from high-profile appearances or out of the suites with high rollers.

But then there was her second type of favorite, which was the kind Jeanine was: the underdogs. Girls from working-class backgrounds who scrimped and hustled to be cheerleaders, who glued rhinestones to their hand-sewn audition solo costumes, who sparkled from sheer power of will. The catch to being this type of favorite was that you had to outdo everyone else on the squad. And that's what Jeanine did. She was a secret weapon at fundraisers, a vamp one moment and the girl next door the next. She could talk to rich people, to seniors, to sick people in the hospital, to brick walls. She was not sloppy, she never got her makeup wrong, and she never seemed like she was trying. She and Suzanna would chat one-on-one in Suzanna's office, then exit together, Suzanna's head thrown back with laughter (to make Suzanna laugh: this was the greatest wish of most of the girls on the squad).

"She's one of our best dancers," Sharrice said to Carmen. "People can't help looking at her."

"I don't think her technique is that great," said Carmen. "She's good at mugging."

"Well, stage presence is half the job." Sharrice leveled her gaze at Carmen. "Don't be mad that she has it. We're supposed to support each other."

"*She's* the one who doesn't hang out with *us*," said Maria.

"Drawing people's attention isn't always a good thing?" said Mackenzie from Line 6, who'd been stretching a few feet away, eavesdropping. Mackenzie had a breathy little voice and a small face, reminding me of a doll. "My old sorority sister? She cheers for the Jets? A couple of her teammates were driving home from a night game, and they were followed by these crazy drunk fans from the opposing team? They almost ran them off the road, screaming, 'You feel like dancing now?' and calling them horrible names. You have to watch *out*, you know?"

"Jesus Christ, Kenz," said Gina.

"There are creeps everywhere," said Mackenzie, her hands clasped at her chest like a child praying before bed. "And some of them know our work schedules, and the route we take to go running, and they have nothing better to do."

"See, this is why we need security," said Sharrice, stabbing an index finger into the opposite palm. "Our job carries risks. We need cooperation from the NFL organization to get security involved, if there's a dangerous situation or a girl gets hurt."

"But Jeanine didn't get kidnapped at a Jills appearance," said Maria. "If I stop showing up for work, it's not my employer's job to track me down. The NFL isn't our employer anyway. Can you imagine Terry Fitzsimmons springing for security?"

"This should be investigated," Sharrice insisted. "We have to do more than send warning emails and terminate her contract. Jeanine is one of our own. She's our responsibility."

"Could we hack into her social media?" said Gina. "See if she was getting threatening messages?"

"Are you guys talking about Jeanine?"

Natalie, a third-year veteran on the ambassador squad, had wandered over, eating from a gallon bag of carrot sticks, to stand behind Sharrice.

"Her boyfriend, Paladino?" she said. "He was at the game on Sunday. In the Dugout Suite."

A clump of spinach fell from my fork onto the floor. I wiped at the smear of dressing, wishing desperately that I had been the one to run into Bobby at the game. The ambassador squad was distinct from the dance team; ambassadors attended only one practice a week and didn't dance at games. Instead, they were dispatched into the stadium to mingle with fans or visit the private suites.

"He asked me why Jeanine wasn't on the field," said Natalie, snapping a carrot in half with her teeth. "I said she must have been late, because if you're late you can't dance. I made some joke that if a Jill is late to a game she must be in the hospital or dead, which, obviously, I feel terrible about now. He kept trying to text and call her, then he asked me if *I* would try calling her. He took a lap around the stadium, looking. He seemed confused."

"Can we please refrain from speculating about a Paladino?" said Sara with an imperious flip of her hair, which moved, thanks to the sweat soaked into her hairspray, in a single mass. "Considering the Paladino Restaurant Group is one of our biggest sponsors?"

"I'm not speculating," said Natalie, palms out, carrot stick bag swinging from one hand. "He acted like he expected her to be at the game. Like, he doesn't know where she is, either."

"Okay, so we should be *more* worried," said Sharrice. "Right? I mean—"

"Virginia."

We stiffened at the sound of Suzanna's voice. The other girls turned quickly back to their binders, began to study choreography notes.

Suzanna stood at the open door to her office. She crooked a finger at me.

Sharrice tugged on my shorts. "Tell us if she says anything," she whispered theatrically, "about *Jeanine*."

SUZANNA'S OFFICE WAS cramped but neat: white desk, white shelves, white chair. On the walls she had hung several photos of herself from when she was a Jill in the nineties, including a framed newspaper article that featured a photo of her, all platinum hair and white teeth, under the headline "DESPITE COSTS, JILLS RAISE FUNDS TO VISIT TROOPS." The weigh-in scale glowed in the corner, its screen beaming up a dim blue light from the floorboards.

Suzanna did not sit, but gestured that I should.

"Can you explain to me what I'm hearing out there?" she asked.

I tucked one ankle behind the other, which was how we were required to sit. I folded and unfolded my hands, let them hang at my sides, stacked them on my thigh. Around Suzanna, I forgot what to do with my body.

"Infighting?" said Suzanna. "Criticizing the Bills organization? Snide remarks about Mr. Fitzsimmons? Implying that *Bobby Paladino* should somehow be scrutinized?"

"No one was implying—"

"Even beyond what the Paladinos have done for you, personally, think of what that family has done for this squad. And that's to say nothing of how these rumors reflect back on me. This is a family affair. Of all people, you must understand what I mean."

"I do understand," I said.

Suzanna pressed her fingers into her forehead, as if to dig out the source of a headache. I felt my cheeks, already burning, flush a deeper red. She was right that this was a family matter, or at least as close to family as you could get. Suzanna was Stanley Paladino's girlfriend. He and Suzanna had begun dating while I still lived in Columbus, so I had missed the inception of their relationship. I suspected that she'd overlapped with Stanley's third wife.

Suzanna's partnership with Stanley could, perhaps, be construed as a conflict of interest, considering the amount of money that traveled from his businesses to the Jills in the form of sponsorships, gifts, and appearance fees. But who was going to challenge Suzanna's private romantic inclinations? Certainly not I, nor Terry Fitzsimmons—who, at this year's preseason fundraiser, had called Suzanna "the brains and balls of this whole operation." I worried more that my connection to Stanley influenced Suzanna's expectations of me or had played a role in my getting a place on the squad. I felt I had to work twice as hard to show I deserved what I got, and to tamp down any speculation that I was the beneficiary of nepotism. To what extent we were allowed, now, to trade knowledge about Jeanine's disappearance was also unnervingly unclear.

Suzanna let out a long exhalation, her face softening.

"I don't mean to snap. My mind goes to the worst place. I take what happens to you girls very personally. If I can't keep track of my girls, if I can't protect—"

She trailed off and sat back on her desk, bringing us nominally closer to eye level. I was relieved to see that she looked shaky, though her smart Prada boots and gray cashmere cardigan projected her usual demeanor of tightly controlled calm. She reached for the can of Diet Coke on her desk—she drank them one after another, like water, at room temperature—and popped it open.

"What bothers me most is the implication, which is coming from a girl on *your* line, by the way, that 'no one is doing anything,' " said Suzanna, gesturing to the girls beyond her office window. " 'No one' means *me*. Sometimes I think you all have no idea how much I do behind the scenes. How hard I work to raise money and make the right connections and control your image. How many private dramas and personal crises I negotiate for each of you, how many problems are dumped on my desk."

"We do know."

"I'm on the phone constantly. I check up on everything. Your job is to understand your choreography and your assignments and execute perfectly. I handle everything else so you can focus on that."

She stared at my hands, and I realized I was picking at my manicure. I stopped. I wanted to ask if she'd spoken to Jeanine's mom, or if Jeanine had another emergency contact on file, but doing so seemed tantamount to questioning her efforts.

"Have you talked to Bobby?" I ventured.

"Only over text message." She took a long drink. "He asked me why she wasn't at the game. I asked him when he last saw her—on Friday, for what it's worth. They had lunch."

"I know. That's the last day I saw her, too."

"Ah." She nodded, as if to politely acquiesce to my role as the best friend.

"The girls are asking about calling the police," I said.

"Right." Suzanna fiddled with her Diet Coke tab. "When to make the call? Discretion is key. Jeanine's *privacy* is key. Someone finds out there's a missing person report on a cheerleader, that might go public, very quickly. And Jeanine has connections, you know. It's . . . it's a hard call."

We nodded meaningfully at each other, but otherwise let the implication hang there. We had never established enough intimacy to discuss our relationships with the Paladinos outright, or our knowledge of their business. Occasionally, an opening for such intimacy appeared, but I never brought myself to take it. Now that door hung open and we both ignored it.

"In any case, I'm inclined to give it some more time," said Suzanna. "I'm not sure what the police would do beyond checking her apartment anyway."

"I've already checked it," I said. "She left her cat. Usually, she asks me to watch it if she's leaving town."

"Did everything else look normal? No break-in, no sign of a struggle?"

"Her couch was ripped," I remembered.

"Her couch?"

"Yeah, under the cushions. But for all I know, it came that way."

"Hm." Suzanna shook her head. "That's a relief, I suppose. Yes, that's good. Of course you went to her apartment to check. You would know to do that. You understand what it is to lose people."

I tried to keep my face open as my body stiffened. I didn't know how much Stanley had told her about me, my father, about Laura. Not knowing bothered me. I didn't want to be Stanley's special orphan girl. I didn't want Suzanna to feel sorry for me.

"You know I see a future for you on the squad, long-term," Suzanna said. "You're always calm and professional. The girls go to you for help with choreo, even the girls who aren't on your line. I could see you in a staff role, as choreographer. Who knows, maybe the Jills need to create an assistant director position. If there was ever a time to show me you can step up."

My face flushed as I nodded. I wanted that. The other girls had established careers—we had elementary school teachers, nurses, real estate agents, a radiologist, a tax accountant, a dental hygienist, a pet photographer, a few fitness instructors like me—or they were still in school, studying communications or medicine or nutrition. But I wanted more of this world; I wanted dance. Suzanna had already upped my responsibilities this season by choosing me as a line captain, and I was even being allowed to choreograph and lead conditioning workouts once a month. Beyond the Jills, there was—nothing. There was nowhere I could go to dance like I did here.

"So we keep everyone calm?" she said. "No vigilante detective work?"

"The girls are being very respectful about Jeanine," I said. "I'll make sure it stays that way."

"Good. And if I hear from her, or news from my own sources, I'll let you know immediately."

"I will too," I said.

She straightened briskly, in a way that indicated I should stand, too. "Good. We understand each other."

At the door she stopped, gripped my shoulder.

"And you're okay?" she said.

Actually, I'd been walking around with a lead ball in the pit of my stomach since Sunday, every vibration of my phone sending my heart into palpitations, every second of the day expanding and contracting with the Great Silence, the Silence of Two Unbearable Options: that you were being ignored or that something terrible had happened. In either case the result was the same, you knew nothing and you were powerless.

Of course I could bring none of that to practice with me. Jills were always better than okay.

So for Suzanna, I smiled. I said, "I'm okay."

OUTSIDE HER OFFICE, Suzanna clapped her hands to get the girls' attention. She reminded us that she took unannounced absences extremely seriously, adding that we should notify her immediately if we heard from Jeanine.

"This is not the first time a girl has quit mid-season," she said. "It's rare, but it does happen. If you are feeling overwhelmed or have concerns, do not sit around tit-tittering and gossiping. Who does that help? You come talk to me or your line captain, so we can get you sorted out. The whole point of a team is that we don't suffer alone. We move in unison. We lift each other up. Right? Right?"

We yelled, *"Right!"* back and jumped up, to suffer together.

"Practice resumes in three minutes," Suzanna boomed as we scurried about, gathering backpacks and Ziplocs and binders. "I want this floor cleaned up. I want captains lined up in front. Next run-through of the routine we're doing full out, no holding back, and I want perfect kicks and splits. Two minutes and *thirty seconds*, let's *go*."

Dashing around the Kmart with the other girls, I struggled to convert my unease into adrenaline. My whole life, I'd equated dance practice with safety. Practice was where I got to be with Laura, protected by the noise and warmth of other bodies, surrounded by laughter and touch, the snap of a pulled leotard and the jab of bobby pins reminding me that I was alive, I had a body. Practice gathered everyone up and held them close. And yet it was also the place where you were forced to go on when everyone wasn't safe, and *wasn't* there, because there was a job to do, a show to run, and the show was bigger than any one of us.

As I shoved my oily Tupperware into my duffel, I felt an arm on my elbow. There stood Natalie, twisting her hands.

"Can I ask you something real quick?" She cleared her throat. "I'm not sure who else can help me."

"Of course," I said. "Whatever you need, Nat."

"It's nothing really, it's just . . . Jeanine would hook me up," she said. "With Adderall. I have a prescription, but it's not enough. Do you know . . . I mean, could you . . . do you know where she got it?"

"Oh," I said, drawing back a little. I had never thought of what Jeanine did—passing off a few pills to girls who needed a little pep—as *dealing*. But at this moment, it felt a lot like that. "Sorry, Nat. I can't help you. That was all Jeanine."

OUTSIDE THE KMART, a surprise: Stanley's white 1967 Pontiac Firebird, parked in the handicapped spot. I broke off from the other girls as they milled about under the glaring lights of the entrance, and sprinted to the driver's side.

"Virginia!" He rolled down the window. "You know you made it on TV on Sunday? They put in a nice long shot of you right before the commercial break. I've got it on DVR. Next time you come by I'll play it for you."

Though I had not gotten back in touch with Bobby upon my return to Buffalo, Stanley and I had resumed the monthly Sunday dinners—just the two of us now, nattering away over red wine and the biggest steaks on the menu at Paladino's Steakhouse. He listened with the same attentiveness he'd shown Laura and me as children, sitting with us in our booth, nodding as we complained about our homework or who we were fighting with at school. I gave him a hug through the window, and he gestured toward the passenger seat.

"Out early today?" he said as I slid onto the leather seat. The car was full of the smell of Stanley, vetiver and juniper hair oil and musk. He was wearing a long tan coat, his gray-streaked black hair slicked back from his ears.

"Maybe ten minutes earlier than normal," I said. "But things are kind of off today. We danced like crap."

"I'm not surprised," he said. "I heard about Jeanine. You and Bobby have the same type. Wayward and unavailable. But I suppose you each had a bad influence in me. Can't stand a sane woman."

"Except Suzanna?"

"Except Suzanna," he agreed. "A painfully sane woman. She might whip me into shape."

"You're never too old to change," I joked. "And I don't think she's that wayward. Jeanine, I mean. I know she's got a past, but she doesn't blow people off. She always returns my texts, unless she's out of the country."

"She certainly knows how to keep Bobby on the hook." He raised his gloved hands defensively, which meant he was about to say something he didn't think I was going to like. "I admit," he said, "when I heard he was with the beauty pageant dropout—"

"Stanley . . ." I warned.

Jeanine's pageant career ended when she was eighteen and on the verge of competing at Miss New York Teen, after pageant officials found drugs in her hotel room. ("I got reported by Tiffany Harshbarger, that *bitch*, after she *bought* diet pills from me," Jeanine said.) How Stanley knew this story I had no idea, except to assume he knew the Miss New York pageant organizers. Stanley knew everybody.

"What?" Stanley said. "I hardly know the girl. I can't get Bobby to bring her to family dinner. I have to rely on reports from friends who see them eating lunch together at the golf club."

"It's a modern relationship, Stanley. She doesn't have to play wife. She's a lot like *you*, you know."

He sputtered. "Oh, sure, lecture the old man. In any case, we're obviously not going to let her stay missing. We'll track her down, one way or another."

"I've thought about filling out a missing person report," I admitted.

"Why, so it can go in a drawer somewhere? So crazy people can call in fake tips? No, we'll sort this out before there's any need to fill out a report. Nothing goes on in this city that I don't find out about."

I immediately felt better. My whole childhood, my father had told me not to go to the police. If you had a problem, you went to Stanley. You don't broadcast your problems to the whole world, you don't bring in outsiders to muck up the situation, you deal with it internally, like family. The Columbus police department had validated this approach by proving themselves to be completely useless when dealing with Laura. They tried to put her in a mental institution after finding her lying out on the street near campus one night. I was newly graduated from Ohio State and beginning to learn what being an adult meant; apparently it meant marching down to the police station to fight tooth and nail for your little sister, screaming that she wasn't insane while she went in and out of consciousness in a holding cell, head bobbing atop her rubber neck.

In any case, I was happy Stanley had put himself in charge. I also understood that a police report about a missing Jill might mean a news story, and the news story might include a line about Jeanine being "romantically linked to Bobby Paladino," and this might give the police a convenient pretext to scrutinize the Paladinos.

"Can you tell Bobby I've been trying to call him?" I said.

"Of course. He hardly picks up the phone for his father anymore, the bastard. Mr. Downtown High-Rise Developer."

There was a knock at my window, and I jumped. Suzanna peered in at me, smiling tightly, her silvery hair stained orange by the parking lot lights.

I opened the door. "I was just leaving."

I climbed out of the car, and Suzanna took my place.

"Get some rest tonight," she said. "Don't stay up worrying. Take a sleeping pill. Do you want one of mine?"

She dug into her purse as Stanley leaned over her. "Hang in there, kiddo."

Suzanna pressed a small white pill into my palm and pulled the door shut.

My car was the last one remaining in the lot. I waved at Stanley's receding brake lights and felt some of the tightness in my chest dissolve. After my dad died, it was Stanley who stepped in, who made sure Laura and I got picked up from school and shuttled to practice when our mom refused to leave the house or hadn't gotten out of bed that day. It was thanks to Stanley that we had sparkling recital costumes and endless leotards for practice. It was thanks to Stanley that

I never had to take out student loans to pay the tuition my dance scholarship at OSU didn't cover. And it was Stanley—not my mother—who I'd called in tears when Laura relapsed after eleven months sober, and Stanley who set up my new lease in Buffalo so I could move back. He'd kept an eye on Laura after I left Columbus, calling her every Sunday and paying for her second round of detox. Stanley didn't ask what needed to be done, he just did it.

That the Paladinos made their money through illegal means was a moral conundrum I couldn't afford to consider. He'd made my life livable. He was able to do things other people weren't able to do. There was a lot of illegal activity I'd be willing to overlook if it meant bringing back Jeanine from wherever she was.

Chapter 4

BECAUSE I HAD no early morning clients or classes on Wednesdays, Jeanine and I always went out for a drink after Tuesday practice. A dive bar, since we were sweaty, flaking makeup clouding the skin under our eyes. The sort of bars that didn't appeal to the other girls.

It was only ten-fifteen when Stanley rolled away in his Pontiac, and though I had a half-hour drive back to the city ahead of me, I wasn't tired at all. There was a place I could go if I needed someone to talk to about Jeanine.

I COULD HEAR my dad's voice prattling in my head every time I drove to Black Rock. The neighborhood sat directly north of where I lived but was distinctly more working class than Elmwood Village: the houses older and more lived in, the businesses less centralized beyond the strip of dives and restaurants on Amherst Street.

On days when Laura and I didn't have school and Mom wanted us out of the house, Dad would drive us around while he checked in on Stanley's many businesses. In Black Rock he'd detour, point at the old shuttered factories on Chandler Street, proclaiming, "All this was *used,* first for cattle, then for production, for steel and furniture and hospital beds—we made planes, goddamn it, for war! Forges, foundries, burning night and day, trains and trains coming through." He'd gesture wildly at the narrow metal bridge, stained green with time, that carried the Belt Line over Hertel. "Can't you picture this packed full of cars and buggies and train cars and smoke and people? You've got to use it, cities are for using, for living in!" These industries had fled overseas, and now no one was building anything in the right place, according to him, and it was hurting businesses, shutting down opportunity, screwing the people who'd made this city what it was. "We've got waterfront!" he'd boom. "We've got a skilled labor force! We're the hub connecting the East Coast to Canada to the whole bleeding rest of the United States! Where are the jobs, the jobs!" Laura would pretend to listen while I tapped out the music to our latest jazz competition routine on my thigh, practicing the moves in my head.

If I kept driving up Niagara Street I'd reach Paladino's Neapolitan Gardens, Stanley's famous banquet hall, which overlooked the river on the other side of the 190. (I oriented myself, always, by my proximity to Paladino businesses.) Instead I turned east on Amherst, continued past the Tops supermarket and the smoke shops and dives, until I saw the flickering plastic sign of the Foundry, the low brick building where Landon Maher tended bar.

IF LANDON WASN'T working behind the bar, you could track him down by the pool table in the back, which was where I found him, shooting a stripe into a corner pocket.

"My God," he said, leaning on his pool cue with a grin. "It's the Friend."

When Jeanine introduced us a couple years ago, Landon had said, "Is this the friend?"

"The *friend*?" she'd shrieked. "As in only one? I have tons of friends!"

To me, Landon had said, "She doesn't have friends. She has ex-boyfriends, former roommates, and mortal enemies. You are the first friend." He'd squinted at me. "So what's your damage, Jeanine's friend?"

To be told that I was the first to carry this title, that I was different from the people who'd come before, ignited a little golden glow in my chest. Landon, for his part, accepted me immediately. He liked me because Jeanine did—so liking me could become something *they* shared.

I used to hang out with Landon often, visiting him at the Foundry with Jeanine. Jeanine and Landon had remained friends since she started dating Bobby, maintaining a closeness that Bobby, she acknowledged, wasn't particularly pleased with. Twice she and Landon had slept together, which she felt a little guilty about. But they'd been together on and off since the beginning of high school. They were each other's first loves. She didn't want to give up Landon just because he bothered Bobby.

Then, about six months ago, Landon surprised Jeanine by establishing boundaries, a progression that shocked and amused her. "He'll be back," she promised. But no, Landon had held out. He was tired of waiting around for Jeanine. He'd wasted too much time trapped in holding patterns, spinning in eddies on the outskirts of life; now he was going back to school to finally get a degree. "In LIBRARY SCIENCE!" Jeanine shrieked. "He wants to work in a library!" Apparently, Landon had always liked to read.

We hugged hello, the stubble of his new beard scratching my cheek. He glanced over my shoulder. "Is Jeanine with you?"

I told him to join me for a drink after he finished his game.

There were no windows in the Foundry except the little circular one on the door. The whole place had a lacquered, dirty feel, like it had been laminated decades ago and the plastic was all filmy and greasy now. I ordered a Michelob from the bartender, whose mustache was so long it covered both lips.

Landon didn't make enough to live off bartending, I knew. He supplemented his income by selling weed out of the men's bathroom. Half the time you couldn't track him down to pour you a drink because he was making an exchange in the handicapped stall. He used to deal far worse drugs, Jeanine told me early on in our friendship, when we were out cruising in her maroon Mazda. Just for a few years, she said, during a dark time in both their lives.

Things had gone a little sideways for Jeanine after she was kicked out of Miss New York Teen. No more pageants meant no more prize money, no hope for a scholarship. She was enraged to have been expelled from a world she'd fought so hard to get inside. She and Landon moved in together and enrolled in Erie Community College, though they spent more time doing drugs and making plans than going to class. Jeanine decided she would be a model and started landing local shoots, cobbling together enough cash to give some to her mother in Rochester and blow the rest on booze and weed and Adderall and coke. She considered studying broadcast journalism so she could be on TV, but she couldn't bring herself to apply for a degree. She considered moving to New York City to model for more money, but she didn't like to be more than an hour or so from her mom. She considered a lot of things but didn't do any of them. Landon dealt and supported them both, accompanying her to sketchy shoots and standing near her while she collected payment. They did more drugs.

This routine provided a sort of frenetic stability to their days, which collapsed when the two of them got into heroin. "I wasn't addicted, exactly—it was just something I did," she told me. "We were already druggies, and smack was the next logical step." They only snorted it, never shot up. Landon started selling it, and their lives became dark and complicated. They lived in a basement apartment with Landon's connection, a paranoid who always thought people were stealing from him. They were so sure he was going to kill them in their sleep that they bought a gun to hide under the mattress, and once Landon told Jeanine she should go ahead and use it on him because he was so sick of how shitty everything felt.

Then, like a switch flipped it seemed, Jeanine got fed up with being a beauty pageant dropout with a burgeoning opiate problem. She cleaned up, got in shape, earned a degree in communications from the community college. Pageants were a racket anyway, she said. She still had her face, which drugs had not yet worn out. And she still had her talent: dance. She was only twenty-four years old. She went to a Jills audition workshop with plans to be a star one way or another. She got onto the squad, started dating Bobby Paladino, and then she met me.

Her simple, matter-of-fact recounting of that time in her life had felt like cool water running down my spine. In Jeanine's telling, the darkest events became a story out of which a life could be made, could go on.

I was glad that Landon had followed suit, cleaning up fast on Jeanine's heels, and now dealt only weed. It made it easier for us to be friends. I felt bad that I, too, had underestimated him when he'd told Jeanine he was going to focus on his education. But of course anyone who'd survived what the two of them had lived through could do anything.

Landon joined me at the bar, shaking a handful of bills he'd won in the pool game, demanding Jameson. He sat down and pulled a paperback, worn at the corners and dog-eared, from his back pocket and chucked it on top of the bar—*Angels* by Denis Johnson.

I asked him about his application to the University at Buffalo.

"Already turned in," he said, rubbing his hands together. "I'm on top of my shit. I'm taking care of my gen ed writing requirement at Erie Community this semester. I have an A, thank you very much. I know I sound like an idiot when I talk, but this thing really does work behind the scenes." He tapped a finger to his forehead.

"I don't think you sound like an idiot," I said.

"My teacher writes things like *This is very well thought-out, Landon,* in the margins of my papers, and you can tell she's surprised."

"So keep surprising them," I said, raising one of the shot glasses just deposited in front of us at the bar.

Landon cheers'd me, looking pleased. He downed his shot, jumped up from the stool.

"Want to play darts?" he said. "I want to win something else."

"You forgot your book," I said, pointing to the battered copy on the bar.

"Leave it there, I have another copy. Books are for everyone. Hey." He spun to face me, walking backward in the direction of the dartboard. "Don't get me wrong, I'm glad to see you, but—what are you doing here anyway?"

LANDON FIRED OFF his first round of darts while I explained.

"Nothing since Friday night?" He rubbed his beard, which he'd started to grow out since the last time I saw him. A new post-Jeanine look. "I get it. This would freak me out, too, if I didn't know her. But the truth is, this is old hat for Jeanine. She goes off the radar for a few days. I'm sure it's fine."

"I'm used to her running off every weekend we don't have a Jills appearance," I said. "But this is different."

"How?" He handed me a cluster of darts so I could take my turn. "I don't want to sound like I'm blowing you off—I'm just used to this kind of thing from her. You know the story about Hoboken?"

I shook my head and sent a dart into the wallboard.

"This was back when we were still trying to do college the first time, so Jeanine would've been around twenty. She was planning to be a model then, she'd literally tell people, 'Oh, I'm a model,' even before anyone had professionally taken her picture. But that's what she does: she says what she is and people believe her, and she makes it true. So anyhow, she'd been hired for this shoot for a music video somewhere in New York City, and the shoot got canceled, and she was supposed to be waiting for a ride to Port Authority so she could take the bus back to Buffalo—and a car pulls up. The driver, some older guy, says, 'Cindy?' And Jeanine, I'm guessing without missing a beat, says 'Yeah, that's me.' "

He clearly took pleasure in telling this story, tossing darts now to emphasize important moments, not to score points.

"So this guy took Jeanine to some big warehouse loft in Hoboken, and she stayed with him and this group of hipster artist types for six days—pretending to be Cindy the entire fucking time. Meanwhile, *I'm* freaking out. I heard from the friend who got her the gig that the shoot was canceled, and I had no idea where she was. I'm going absolutely crazy, calling the fucking bus station to see if she was there, begging anyone with a car to drive me to New York City. And she was just off in Hoboken, being Cindy for a bit. Eventually, she hitched a ride back to Buffalo and showed up at our house like, 'What? What'd I do?' "

I waited for him to finish his turn, though we'd both stopped bothering to tally the points. "Landon, that's insane. Weren't you mad?"

"Yeah, I was pissed! But you get used to it. It's a cyclical thing for her," he explained. "I've known her for a long time, remember. She's a schemer. She tries things on, runs them into the ground, then abandons them. Then it's on to the next scheme. It's pretty addictive when you're around it. If you want to know what I really think, I think the cheerleading scheme ran itself out."

"Scheme," I repeated.

"Yeah," he said, apologetically. "I couldn't see Jeanine holding out as a Jill much longer. Sure, she likes you, and she likes that Suzanna lady, and she likes the attention. She likes when the Jills send her to cool places, like when she got to go to Hawaii to perform for the army base her first season. But honestly, it's just not a high enough payout for her. She likes money coming at her in these big, giant clumps. That's why she liked pageants when we were in high school—she wanted a big check with a lot of zeros. It didn't matter that the cost to compete, with the dresses and the makeup and all that shit, nearly outweighed the prize money. It was the hunt she liked. She felt like she was stealing money from rich girls, beating them at their own game. She'd run home and wave her money in her mom's face and the three of us would blow it on steaks and lobster. It was *fun*.

"With the Jills, she doesn't get that. Sure, you get all this proximity to power and wealth. But being that overscheduled, for that kind of money? The math doesn't add up, not for her. I think she bailed out. That's the honest truth. I'm sorry she didn't tell you."

"Okay, so she quit." I had the darts now, but I didn't bother throwing. I felt deflated and left out, even though what Landon had suggested was far better than the many alternatives I'd imagined. "She's allowed to quit. But we're best friends. She still has to text me."

"That part is weird, I admit, about her not contacting you. She's attached to you. I don't know why. No offense—I like you, too. I mean, I don't know what it is in *her* that makes her like you. It's a surprise."

"Why do you say that?"

He thought about it, collected the darts from my hand, and fired one off.

"Because she can't get anything out of you."

LANDON KEPT BUYING us Jameson shots, carting them to the booth where we'd found a seat. Being a Jill, I got bought a lot of drinks at bars, and I knew how to discreetly flick alcohol out of my glass.

I slammed my empty shot glass on the table, pretended to swallow.

"Okay, so you think I should relax," I said. "You think she's off being Cindy again or finding another scheme."

"I'm saying don't freak out yet. Jeanine's a homebody at heart. Wherever she is, she won't be gone for long. She's not going to leave her mom."

"Hey, her mom," I said. "Do you think she's visiting her mom?"

"Want to call and ask?" Landon pulled out his phone, his eyes glassy with whiskey. "Hell, I love to talk to Marianne."

"You've got her number?"

"We talk all the time! I've known her since I was fifteen. Don't worry about the hour, she works nights. She's always up."

Marianne picked up right away with a cheerful "Hi, baby doll."

Landon put the phone on speaker, and I could hear a TV in the background. He explained why we were calling.

"Good!" Marianne barked. "Good for her skipping out on those stingy motherfuckers. Fuck those NFL fat-cat bastards sitting on their blocks of gold. Tell her to skip the rest of the stupid games, too. My genius daughter bopping around half naked in blizzard conditions for half the year while they toss pennies at her? I'm proud of her for blowing them off. I hope that ice queen who runs the Jills shits a brick."

"But Ms. Chanowitz—her cat," I tried to say.

"Who are you again?"

"Virginia. I drove Jeanine to your house that one time. After she got her wisdom teeth out."

"Oh, yeah—the teeth girl. You're sweet to worry. But she's a free spirit, my baby. I raised her that way. She's probably in Bali with that real estate guy. She still has some steam to blow off before she settles down with my Landon here."

"We'll see, Marianne," said Landon.

"Yeah, we'll see. *You'll* see. I know about these things. You've got to let her roam. Heck, maybe *you* should try skipping town, Veronica. Break a couple rules. It could be good for you."

"Virginia," I corrected her.

But she'd hung up. Landon had pulled his T-shirt over his nose to cover his laughter. Marianne had been like this when I'd dropped Jeanine off at her house, too. Talking to her felt like getting clobbered with a Wiffle bat—not exactly painful but bewildering and embarrassing.

"I don't feel better," I said.

"*I* do."

"She's not with Bobby Paladino. I know that for certain."

Landon let his T-shirt fall back into place. He made a face and reached for his next shot.

"Sorry," I said. "Sore subject."

"No, it's not. I don't even care." He took the shot, winced theatrically. "She's only with him for the name. You see that, right? She wants a dangerous guy, she scoops up a Paladino. It's mob tourism, and I judge her for it."

"There are much more dangerous people than the Paladinos," I said, thinking of Jason Morley. The Paladinos' business ventures were unethical, but in terms of damage done in the lives of actual people, their impact was minimal. A person like Jason, who made a game of getting girls high on smack for the first time, did a lot more damage. The Paladinos toyed with systems but took care of people. People were more important than systems.

"They're not the *mob* mob," I clarified. "It's just sports betting, that kind of thing. Who cares?"

"Well, you have to say that. Women in these families, they shrug and go, 'Oh, it's just a little extortion, a few busted kneecaps, but he's a very good businessman, a wonderful father.'"

"Stop using that voice! That's not how it is!"

"I'm not criticizing it. It's a survival mechanism and a good one. I wish *I* had a mob husband. I wouldn't have to work so damn hard."

"I work," I muttered. "I've always worked."

"Virginia, darling, I don't know the details, but I hear shit down here at the ass end of the grapevine. It all trickles down eventually. You know how a whale dies and gets eaten up by those glowing worms and trilobites at the bottom of the ocean—it's like that. We're scuttling around on the bottom, picking up the scraps. But the thing about Jeanine: she's a whale. Bobby Paladino may be a shark, but Jeanine's a fucking whale. She's not going to toe the line and pretend she doesn't know how things work. She's going to run the world."

I thought about this. "If Jeanine's a whale and you're a trilobite, then what am I?" I asked.

"You're one of those nice orange fish with the fancy fins."

He pushed the beer he'd been drinking as a chaser closer to me and I took a sip, frowning. To my mind, Stanley was an "alternative" businessman, a trickster in a Brioni suit. I was pretty positive he'd never gotten into trafficking anything truly dangerous—like guns or drugs. But what did I know about the way Bobby did business? Jeanine once told me she was never on the passenger log for the trips they took on Bobby's rented jet. She said Bobby was always working—he'd leave her by the pool or the beach, and she'd drink and play cards with his driver. "He doesn't pay attention to what things cost," she'd said. "He can do whatever he wants." She probably had more insight into the Paladino business than I did.

"What if Bobby doesn't want to deal with a whale?" I said. "What if Jeanine intimidated him? What if she knows too much about his work? What if the police contacted her to ask questions, and Bobby found out and panicked?"

I hugged my elbows. I didn't say, *What if Bobby knew that Jeanine was out flirting with other men, getting to know people like Jason?*

Landon put a hand on my forearm. "Hey, you gotta chill. You've been in that family your whole life—have you ever felt scared? Been contacted by the police?"

"No."

"Here's my guess," Landon said sagely. "Jeanine's been trying on a new hat with this mob-girlfriend shit. You can't blame her if she's getting bored of it and needs a break. We can judge her, but we can't blame her. I know her. She'll be back, and we'll all laugh about this."

Once, Jeanine told me Landon was the only man she couldn't pretend to be someone else with. It both comforted and bothered her. On the one hand, it was a relief not to have to explain yourself, to have a friend with whom you could use a kind of shorthand because they knew you so well and could fill in the blanks. On the other hand, sometimes you didn't want to have to keep being who you always were.

LANDON WAS A popular man at the Foundry. After our fourth round of shots, a man in a long polo shirt came by our booth. He clapped Landon on the shoulder, saying, "I hate to interrupt, but can I get some help?"

This was the third time this had happened. Landon made a show of bowing to me, saying, "A moment, a mere moment," in a British accent as he stumbled away to the bathroom.

I took a sip from the shot Landon had bought me and poured the rest out on the floor. Even with my alcohol-tossing techniques, I was tipsy by this point, though not nearly as drunk as he was. I felt bad for having a good time, but the truth was, I liked Landon. Like Marianne, I always thought Jeanine should have stuck with him.

"It's so funny you coming here to ask me about Jeanine tonight," said Landon after falling back into the booth across from me, as if he'd read my thoughts. "I wish I could stop thinking about her. We've been through a lot together. Too much. You can't toss that shit out on the curb. There's no collection service to come pick up your memories. I try to move on. I've got school. I've even started seeing this other girl. But I feel bad because so many things—everything, really—reminds me of Jeanine." His eyes slid into focus. "Hey—you took your shot without me."

"Have you been paying for all these drinks?" I said. "Do they even charge you here?"

"I got it, I got it, I'm the fucking gentleman of the Foundry. I'm in good shape."

"Business is booming?"

He straightened. "What do you mean?"

It slithered across my consciousness that Landon was getting his life in order and might not want anyone, even well-meaning friends, running their mouths about the way he made money.

"I was just joking," I said.

He squinted at me, blearily, then seemed to forget what he'd been so concerned about.

"Does she ever talk about me?" he asked. "Never mind, don't tell me. I don't want to know."

"Poor Landon," I said. "Have you ever considered moving at least three hundred miles away? I recommend it."

"You did that for an ex? Wow. Tragic."

I'd meant Laura, but I shrugged without correcting him. "I think she should be better to you."

I saw his eyes go hazy with affection and immediately regretted that I'd said this.

"Would it be bad to try to kiss you right now?" he said.

I peered at him. The prospect was interesting. Jeanine had tossed

Landon aside, which meant he was fair game. Were she in my position, she would almost certainly say "Go for it," and relish the chaos that might ensue. Landon was probably making the same calculations regarding me—maybe he wanted to sleep with me just to see how Jeanine would react when she found out.

Or maybe we both wanted to do it because it might be fun. I took a hurried sip of what was left of his beer to tamp down the thought. I told him this was not the moment.

"Probably not ever the moment," I added.

"I thought so. You just look so sad. And mad. Who are you looking like that for?"

"For her," I said, and I was pretty sure I meant Jeanine. We were quiet for a moment.

"Are you really going to be a librarian?" I said.

Landon drew a long breath, spreading his hands flat on the table. He had a look of great equanimity on his face.

"There was a time," he said, "when Jeanine and I didn't have enough money for gas to drive around, so do you know where we would spend afternoons? The goddamn library. It's the most democratic place in the world. You can sit in there for free. There's stuff to look at. No one kicks you out. Everyone is safe there. Hell yeah, I'm going to be a librarian. I'm going to be on the other side of the desk this time, and I'm going to love everyone who comes in."

I was a little stunned. And touched.

"I told you my brain works," he said. "There's poetry knocking around in there."

"That's beautiful," I said.

"You're goddamn right it's beautiful. I want a beautiful life. I don't care how it sounds. It's up to us to make it beautiful, Virginia."

"It's up to us," I whispered.

He tried to clink my empty shot glass and missed—which I realized was my cue to go.

"Thanks for the drinks," I said as he walked me to the door. "And the talk."

He waved an arm grandly. "Anything for the Friend."

On the stoop, he paused and pointed upward. Above the door, a cluster of brown moths flew again and again into the lone bulb, dusting it with their wings, making soft, assertive pitter-pats as they slammed into the glass. “Do you think that’s what we look like to God?” Landon said.

I stared up at the moths.

“I ought to be tired of doing this,” I said.

He frowned, confused. “You do this a lot?”

Chapter 5

When I stumbled through my door, the cat tried to shoot out past my legs. I barely managed to catch it between my ankles.

"I'm sorry, okay?" I said, dropping it by its empty food bowl in the kitchen, which I'd forgotten to fill that morning. "I have a lot on my mind."

I filled the bowl until it spilled over, then pulled a half-drunk bottle of white wine from the back of my fridge. It was one-thirty in the morning. Sleep was very far away, and I didn't feel like letting it come for me.

My apartment, on the top floor of a sturdy old converted Victorian, was cozy. I didn't have to pay for heat, and the landlord kept the building hot in winter, the way I liked it. I measured one-half cup of white wine—120 calories—poured it into a glass, and settled on the stool at my kitchen counter with my laptop.

You do this a lot? Landon had asked. I hadn't done it in a long time, but I'd retained the muscle memory of certain tried-and-true methods. I opened my laptop and began.

When Laura would go missing, the first thing I would do was call the hospitals. Only once did I actually find her at a hospital: she'd passed out at a party and her idiot friends, thinking she'd OD'd, dropped her off outside the doors of the emergency room. But after you found someone at the hospital one time, it became the first place you looked every time.

Both Buffalo General and the Erie County Medical Center told me they had no patients by the name of Jeanine Chanowitz on file. So she wasn't lying in a hospital bed—not in the city, at least.

Next I would call Laura's work, provided she had a job at the time. If she did have a job, it was because I'd finagled it for her, asking the various gyms I taught at to hire her at the check-in desk or as a lifeguard (she'd worked at a pool during the summers in high school). She was always so grateful to me for getting her the job, and then she always lost it by falling asleep during shifts, or not showing up, or worse. A sickening memory: sitting on a cold metal chair in the back office of the downtown fitness center while the square-headed manager explained that Laura had been caught letting her boyfriend in the back door so he could sell dope (the manager's words) in the men's showers. When I confronted her, Laura insisted her boyfriend had done no such thing, the manager was out to get her, and anyway it didn't matter because she'd been about to quit to enroll in bartending school, bartenders made *great* money, could I loan her $800 to go to bartending school?

So, work. Buffalo Underground, where Jeanine worked as a cocktail waitress, stayed open till two A.M. if there were enough patrons.

The floor manager picked up. He was young and severe and wore overly tight button-up shirts to show off his weight-lifting regimen. Jeanine and I made fun of him behind his back.

"Jeanine's not working tonight," he said. "She's supposed to be in tomorrow. Which is *today* now. Is this her friend? Virginia, right? Tell her if she blows me off one more time she won't have a job to come back to."

"I can't get ahold of her," I said. "She's missing."

"Next time she wants to go missing, she can do it when she's not on the schedule," he said and hung up.

Jeanine pulled down more in tips in a single night than I made for a full day of fitness classes, and she almost never missed a shift. On a scrap of paper I wrote down *hospitals* and *work* and crossed them both out.

Next was boys. If Laura wasn't in the hospital or at work, she was with the boyfriend she'd secured as a means of getting drugs. After Jason, there was a stringy-haired boy that got her through three years of college, and then she found a long-term dealer named Gabe who terrified me. I was always afraid she was with Gabe, or had gotten back together with Gabe, or was pretending to be at work when she was actually with Gabe. He had vacant eyes that were a little too wide, and always looked like he was on the verge of exploding. He owned a gun that Laura had bought for him, because of his record. She was completely devoted to him, except for the periods when she was afraid of him. Gabe would bang on my door looking for Laura, whom he always assumed was hiding out with me when he couldn't find her. Sometimes she was—she'd be shut inside my bedroom while I fended him off at the door, my hand on the chain, praying he wouldn't try to kick it down. Other times, I didn't know where she was, either.

There was no equivalent to Gabe in Jeanine's romantic life. Though she cultivated an air of promiscuity, Jeanine was actually quite loyal sexually. Landon and Bobby were the only two people she'd ever mentioned having sex with. Getting men to pay for things was more interesting to her than sleeping with them. Seeing her with Jason Morley was the first time I'd wondered if she had other relationships with men I didn't know about.

I opened Facebook. No reply from Jason.

I opened a new tab to hunt for him elsewhere online. It took a lot of clicking around, but I eventually put together that he owned an importing company called EUSA that primarily supplied restaurants with fancy international goods, like aged sausages and olive oil. EUSA did not have a website, but it showed up in the online white pages. I tried the number, hoping for voicemail. It rang for a full eight minutes before I gave up.

I scrolled around on Facebook and LinkedIn looking for traces of Bobby or his real estate company, the McKormick Group. The company website featured the tagline "Buffalo's most trusted developer for real estate, construction, and leasing. Let your neighbors build your neighborhood." His work contact info was nowhere to be found.

I added both Jason's and Bobby Paladino's names to the list and circled them each three times.

Next: exes. I wrote down *Landon Maher* and put a check mark next to it to show that we'd talked.

I did the same with Marianne's name. I paused, wondering if there was other family I could put down. Jeanine had been adopted as a newborn by Marianne and her husband, a former marine prone to angry outbursts followed by tears. Jeanine hadn't had contact with her adoptive father for eight years. When I asked her if she'd ever considered reaching out to him, she said, "No biological imperative."

As for her birth parents, she told me she had never searched for them. "I hate that term, 'birth parents.' I don't have birth parents. I emerged fully formed out of Marianne Chanowitz's forehead."

To my list I added *Father?* I didn't even know her adoptive father's name. Just like all the other men whose names I didn't know: men she'd casually flirted with, to whom she'd given fake phone numbers. Or the nameless men, like Ray, who fixated on her picture in the Jills calendar. What was I supposed to write down for that—*MEN* in all caps?

I HAD JUST finished scrolling through the Jills fan sites and Jills-related Facebook groups, scanning for weird comments or posts fawning over Jeanine, when a clatter and a crash tore my gaze from my laptop screen.

I shrieked at the sight of the cat crouched next to the sink, its dirty little paws on my kitchen counter. On the linoleum was a spray of forks and plastic spatulas he'd managed to knock out of my drying rack. I leapt around the counter to chase him off.

Along with the silverware, the cat had knocked over a pile of envelopes. Jeanine's envelopes—the mail I had taken. I set them on the counter one at a time, like tarot cards. I toyed with the bank statement as the cat peered at me from the hallway.

"What do you think?" I asked. "Should I commit a federal crime?"

The cat flattened its ears, and I tore into the bank statement. It was from September and contained nothing particularly interesting. As a cocktail waitress, Jeanine dealt almost exclusively with cash. She'd spent $58 at an H&M on the fifteenth. Over the course of the month, she'd made four cash deposits ranging from $180 to $300. On the twenty-ninth, she'd withdrawn $800—probably for rent? None of this seemed out of the ordinary.

I pushed the junk mail aside to consider the hand-addressed envelope with the Pennsylvania return address. This was the most undeniably personal piece of mail, perhaps the biggest breach of her privacy. I ripped it open quickly, like tearing off a Band-Aid.

Inside was a short, typed letter.

Ms. Chanowitz,

Can you confirm receipt of the forwarded documents from the Calhoun Birth and Wellness Clinic?

This is our third attempt to confirm. Should you need any further information or support at this time, we are happy to assist.

Linda Sulzener

Linda Sulzener's email address was below her signature.

I searched for the Calhoun Birth and Wellness Clinic. The first website in the search results was disabled. The clinic was listed on Yelp but had no ratings or reviews—just a banner saying NOW CLOSED. On Yelp it was described as a "trusted ob-gyn in Dayton, Ohio."

This was curious but not necessarily alarming. Jeanine had moved around a lot while she was growing up, before Marianne divorced her husband and brought Jeanine to western New York. It was possible she'd visited the clinic in the past and was getting her medical records up to date. Recently, she'd mentioned switching to an IUD . . . perhaps the letter was related to that.

Well, what did I have to lose by bothering a stranger from Dayton, Ohio? I wrote Linda Sulzener an email: **I am a concerned friend of Jeanine Chanowitz. I have not heard from her in several days. I know you were trying to get in touch with her, can you please let me know if she has contacted you recently?**

Before I could talk myself out of it, I pressed Send.

Almost immediately, my phone began to ring. An unknown number.

Linda Sulzener? I thought, ridiculously, blinking at the screen, and then: *Jeanine?* I answered it, breath caught in my throat.

"Who'd you drive three hundred miles for?" said the voice on the other end.

"Landon?"

"Yeah, it's me. At the bar, you said you left someone three hundred miles away. Who'd you leave?"

"Oh." My disappointment that it wasn't Jeanine calling faded. Phone tucked under my ear, I migrated to my comfy armchair. "I was talking about my younger sister, Laura."

Landon made a noise of surprise. "That's not what I was picturing."

"You were picturing a boy?" I said. "You know romance isn't everything."

There had never been a boy for whom I'd make myself drive three hundred miles. My longest boyfriend, whom I dated my first year out of college, lasted a year. He worked as a personal trainer at one of the gyms where I taught aerobics, a dark-haired, soft-spoken guy who was studying to become a physical therapist. I'd planned to move in with him, but then Laura got kicked out of the apartment she was sharing with three other girls after they found a baggie and foil in her room, and I didn't feel like explaining to him why Laura needed to crash on my couch, why she wasn't in school anymore, why she couldn't keep a job. It was all too much to explain.

I cleared my throat, trying to swallow the sadness from my voice. "Laura had enough boyfriends for the both of us," I said wryly.

"She had drug problems, Jeanine said. Heroin? She wasn't gossiping about you, just to be clear. She thought it was an important part of who you are."

"I guess it is." I pulled the blanket over my shoulders to keep out the draft from the window. "Jeanine is pretty much the only person I talk to about it."

"She talks to you, too. About her problems. She trusts you."

I'd always wondered what it meant to Jeanine, that she told me about her past. It didn't seem to cost her much to tell me those stories, no matter how difficult the experiences may have been at the time. She didn't seem ashamed of having a screwed-up family, a screwed-up life. More embarrassing to her were the mundane humiliations that came along with being human: that someone had made her feel stupid or that she missed somebody. She'd much rather talk about how she'd done heroin for a couple of years.

It occurred to me that maybe Jeanine trusted me not because she had given me some precious secret of hers, but because *I* had given her a secret of mine—I'd told her about Laura. And what happened between me and Laura was a lot to give; it *did* cause me shame. I'd been taught to keep family business in the family. By letting myself talk about Laura with Jeanine, I'd made her family.

To Landon I said, "We used to be the same person. Laura and I. At least that's how it felt. We were in dance together. I had all these plans for us—I was going to get us both into a college out of state, so I could cheer for a Big Ten school and she could major in dance. But then she got hurt, and things weren't . . . things weren't the same after that."

I paused. This was the moment where Laura's life, along with all my plans for her and me, had splintered and fractured: Laura's injury, in February of her junior year and my senior year, when she landed wrong practicing a jump and tore a ligament in her ankle.

Before the injury, we'd spent nearly every waking moment together. After our dad died, our mom retreated further into herself, staying up late playing hearts online at the desktop computer in what used to be Dad's office, relying on Stanley to pick us up from school because—it was becoming increasingly apparent—she'd begun to fill her mug with vodka as soon as she'd drained it of coffee. I got busy keeping Laura and me out of the house, hitching rides with other dance girls, or asking Stanley to drive us from practice to Paladino's. We spent every day hip to hip, elbow to elbow. Laura, my buddy, my twin, joining forces with me against rival girls, cracking jokes, dancing in that powerhouse, full-hearted way of hers. We didn't need our mom to want us. We were going to get out of this city where the last of the factories were closing. We were a team.

Then came the ankle injury, and Laura was grounded like a plane. All of a sudden, we were separated.

All of a sudden, she was home with our mom all afternoon instead of with me, her foot in its boot propped up on pillows, the two of them on the couch, watching TV.

All of a sudden, she was on her phone constantly, claiming "No one" when I asked her who she was texting.

I'd look up at cheer practice to see her in the bleachers, busted leg extended, laughing coyly with Jason Morley. I'd come home from practice to find her gone—she was getting invited to parties, hobbling out into the night on her crutches, carried off in Jason's SUV.

Now that we weren't attached to each other most hours of the day, I realized my sister was different from me. She was not the dutiful do-gooder I'd assumed us both to be; she was a party girl, the running back's girlfriend, and I was the obedient Girl Scout on the sidelines with my tight ponytail, thinking I would be rewarded with an interesting life at some future date as compensation for my good behavior. Injuring her ankle was how Laura split our lives into two separate tracks, taking us further and further away from each other, until she was nothing more than a blurry and confounding outline of a person I used to know.

"Was that what got her started?" said Landon, snapping me out of my memories. "The doctors put her on oxy? That's how it happens for a lot of people."

"It was a boy," I said firmly, eager to turn the subject from Laura's ankle injury—I didn't want to *think* about her ankle, what it represented, and how it changed everything. It was easier, always, to talk about Jason Morley.

"It was a boy from our high school." I sank deeper into the chair. "After she got hurt, they started dating. He was a pusher. It started with pot, then painkillers, and then, after I left for Ohio, he got her into heroin. It was like a game for him, to get girls high for the first time. He'd get them hooked, get them buying from him, and sleep with them. I had no idea people did stuff like that. I just thought he was the hot running back, you know, kind of edgy and dangerous, and now she got to go to parties I wasn't invited to. I didn't realize until too late that I had to protect her from him. He didn't even use heroin himself. If he'd been doing it, too, then I'd be like, 'Okay, it's his life on the line, too.' I'd still hate him for getting her hooked, but I would—I could understand a little better, I guess. But he didn't use. He just kept giving her shit to see what would happen, like she was a lab rat, and she was so in love with him she kept taking it and taking it."

I managed to inhale.

"I thought once I got her to college with me, they would break up, and she would be safe." I exhaled in a hurry. "But they went on dating off and on, like he was a flu she couldn't kick, with her driving back to Buffalo every school break to be near him, talking to him on the phone all the time. I found out she'd get high because he called her up and told her to, to do it on the phone with him. Can you believe that?"

"I can."

"I couldn't. I was so stupid. And after he got bored of her, she went and found another guy just like him, then another. Turns out guys like that are everywhere, and I didn't know how to keep her away from them. So I guess I screwed that up pretty bad."

"I don't think so," said Landon. "I think you love your sister. I think if she didn't have you, it would have been worse."

"Well, she's in some sobriety support group now, no thanks to me," I said. "She got sober once before and couldn't make it stick, so we'll see how it goes this time. Last I heard, she's getting trained to be some kind of massage therapist, the kind that works with energy fields and chakras or whatever."

"Ah. She's doing the whole higher-power recovery shit."

"What kind of recovery shit are you doing?" I asked.

He snorted. "Spite. I stay alive out of spite."

I laughed.

"Now, that's the kind of higher power I can get behind," I said. "You should go door to door with that. Make pamphlets."

"Maybe I will." I could hear a smile in his voice. "What are you still doing up at four in the morning?"

My laptop screen glowed from where I'd left it on the kitchen counter, filling my dimmed apartment with blue light.

"Making lists," I said.

"You're a good friend, but you gotta relax."

"Go to bed, Landon."

"You, too. Hey, listen: it's gonna be okay."

"Yeah?"

"Yeah. Keep in touch if you hear from our sweet Jean."

He hung up.

I hugged my knees. I felt lighter from having talked to Landon, but also a bit woozy, like I'd just thrown up something that had been making me sick. I didn't want to be trapped in the role I'd always played in my relationship with Laura—alone and humiliated, making flailing attempts to fix things, to hold everything together. I was operating out of sheer habit, or perhaps an impulse even more automatic: the kick of the leg when you hit the knee in the right spot. It frightened me to realize how close that past version of me lived beneath the surface, how ready she was to take over.

Jeanine didn't need me to do this for her, I reminded myself. There was an explanation for her absence, and soon she'd call me and I'd know what it was. And when that happened, I could say: I looked for you, I worried. Loving someone was something you did; you didn't sit around just feeling it. Well, here I was doing it. These were the motions of love.

Chapter 6

I MANAGED FOUR HOURS of sleep before getting up to prepare for my first personal training client, at noon. Wednesdays were for burning calories and earning money, filled with clients and dance aerobics classes I could barely muster the energy for that day. Between classes, I ran to my phone to check for a text or call from Jeanine, receiving nothing.

Then, after my six-thirty Ballet Booty Blast, I picked up my phone to see I had four missed calls and several texts from Sharrice asking me to call her back, all from the last twenty minutes. Adrenaline chased the fatigue from my mind.

Sharrice picked up right away.

"Can you come to Buffalo Underground?" she said. "Me and Gina are here—we were booked for an appearance at the 5K downtown, the multiple sclerosis one, and it ended close to Chippewa. We decided to swing by to talk to Jeanine's coworkers. Can you come join us?"

"Why? What's happening?"

"She was here, with a guy. On Saturday night. That's after you saw her, right?"

"What guy?"

"We don't know! Jennifer Speight saw them together. She didn't get the guy's name, but it definitely wasn't Bobby. Do you want to come talk to her?"

"I'll be there in ten."

I left my mat and equipment on the floor, not caring that the next instructor, a Pilates teacher who pulled her hair into a ponytail so tight it tugged her eyebrows up to the top of her forehead, would complain to the front desk.

Buffalo Underground was loud, as always, with bass and white noise, the blue lights on the tables giving everyone a cold pallor. It stayed open late even on weeknights, attracting ball-capped former frat boys, men in suits entertaining business clients, out-of-towners staying at the new Hampton Inn, and service-industry people from the fine-dining restaurants popping up around the corner on Delaware, looking for a late-night spot after work. I found Sharrice and Gina at a high-top.

"We have updates," shouted Gina, pounding on the table. "Here comes Jennifer. Jennifer—tell her what you told us."

Jennifer Speight appeared behind my shoulder, carting a tray of tall orange drinks, each served in a highball glass with a salt rim. She was Jeanine's coworker, a Jills alumna who retired from the squad five years ago and still came to reunions.

"Hey, babe." She deposited the tray on the table and pulled me into a one-armed hug. She wore the Underground uniform: a vintage cigarette-girl outfit with a tiny skirt, suspenders, and fishnets. "I just got cut. You're all having my shift drink with me. It's on the house. Only a hundred and twenty cals, so don't worry about having a couple."

"Who did you see Jeanine with?" I said.

"I'm an idiot and didn't ask his name," said Jennifer. "We figured you might know. He was medium height, kind of cute in a scruffy way. Had the start of a beard. An old boyfriend, she said."

My glass slipped from my hand and shot a few inches across the table in a smear of condensation. "Landon?"

"That's it," said Gina. "We've got him. That's the bastard."

"Got him for what?" said Sharrice. "All they did was drink together, right?"

"That's all I saw them do," said Jennifer. "She came in to pick up her check, and he was with her. They stayed for a few drinks and got pretty sauced. She was hanging all over him, talking super intensely. Then they left. It was early. Like eight. So maybe they went somewhere else after that?"

"You're sure that's who it was?" I said. "Landon."

"I think she said he was her high school boyfriend," said Jennifer. "Did she have a lot of boyfriends in high school?"

I hid my face in my hands. He was a drug dealer obsessed with his high school girlfriend, and I hadn't had the sense to distrust him? Was a little Jameson and sentimentality all it took?

"How well do you know this guy?" Sharrice asked me. "What's he like? Does he have a record?"

"I don't know—no? He's never been in jail. He's not violent. He's going to be a librarian."

"A what?" said Gina. I turned back to Jennifer.

"Did no one else hear from her after you saw her on Saturday?" I asked. "She didn't call in sick?"

"She wasn't due back until today," said Jennifer. "She's only scheduled Wednesdays, since she cut her hours."

"Cut her hours?"

"Yeah, ages ago. She said she was getting other gigs."

That couldn't be right. Jeanine made a lot in tips, but not enough to cut her hours to one day a week. She hadn't said a word about any new modeling gigs or another side job. I was hot, my armpits clammy with sweat. The racket of the bar filled my ears with a staticky clump of cotton.

"Wait, there's one more thing," Jennifer said, rifling through her clutch. "You are not the first person to come in here asking about Jeanine. A man came in this afternoon asking the staff questions about her. He left me this."

She extracted a business card that read simply, *S. Antweiler, Consulting,* with a phone number underneath.

"Antweiler?" said Gina. "Who the hell is that?"

"He was asking all the same things you've been asking: when she last showed up for work, if she was seen with anyone, et cetera. I thought he might be a creepy fan and told him to leave. She doesn't have a stalker, does she?"

There was some cyclical event taking place in my body, a series of gatherings and surges.

"Can I keep this?" I said.

"Sure. It's weird, right?"

"I'll look him up at work," said Sharrice, typing the name into her phone. She worked as an administrative assistant in the district attorney's office and could look up arrest records. "And Landon, too."

"That can't be right about her hours. She's been busy the same number of nights," I said, though I remembered, with growing apprehension, that she had hardly gone to work last week. "And how can she afford rent?"

"Um." Gina winced. "Bobby pays it?"

"Did she tell you that?" asked Sharrice.

"No, babe, that's context clues." Gina tapped her temple. "I've said for ages her money situation doesn't make any sense. Her apartment? Do you know what units in that building go for? More than a cocktail waitress makes, especially one who only works one day a week. The only thing that makes sense is Bobby. I'm not here to judge, but having your boyfriend pay for all your stuff while you cut off work?"

"It's no different than having family money," said Sharrice, her eyes darting toward me. "Or a trust fund. It doesn't have to be embarrassing."

"Yes, it is different," said Gina. "Of course it is."

"How?"

Gina and Sharrice began arguing about this, but I had flown from the table, with the dizzying sense of having been catapulted toward the ceiling. The way people could lie, and lie, and lie to you. My phone started buzzing in my purse, startling me, and I pawed at it. I should have known better than to trust what was said to me. I should have checked, should have barged into Jeanine's work unannounced to see if she was there—

"Let's focus on the facts," Sharrice was saying. "She cuts her hours, she goes back to an ex-boyfriend. It's bad, but it's not, like, total panic."

"I'm panicking," said Gina.

"She would've told me," I insisted as I dug around in my purse, which vibrated urgently. "She hasn't been any less busy. She was definitely going to work more than once a week."

"Maybe she was going out with this Landon guy, and didn't want to tell you," said Jennifer.

I dumped the contents of my purse out on the table, yanking my phone from the folds of my spare shirt, where it had gotten tangled. When I saw the screen, I froze.

It was Laura.

I looked up from my bright screen to the darkened club. A smudge floated in front of Sharrice's face. The girls had frozen in place, their faces etched with concern. The whole world brought to a halt by a call from Laura. All the blood cells in my veins paused, gathered momentum, and then surged forward.

"Oh my God, is it Jeanine?" said Sharrice.

I PRACTICALLY RAN to the bathrooms, which were all thankfully single occupancy. Laura had sent a text after I didn't pick up: **Hey! Can we talk?**

I sat on the closed toilet lid and stared at the tile floor. Laura and I had not spoken since I left Columbus, other than a stilted, polite phone call after she got out of rehab in April and a brief text exchange on my birthday in July. How much time had I spent over the last two years staring into my phone's screen, struggling to come up with an innocuous reason to text her? I'd stare and think and fail to find a quippy opening line and then notice that an hour had passed. I wondered if Laura did the same thing.

Someone knocked at the bathroom door, then rattled the knob. I opened my mouth to shout that I was in here, but nothing came out.

All that time I lived in Columbus with Laura, I stopped whatever I was doing every time she called or texted. I'd walked out of college classes and gym classes and doctor's appointments, I'd walked away from boyfriends in the middle of a fight.

I put my phone away, flushed the toilet I hadn't used, and left the bathroom, heart pounding. It was her turn to wait.

SHARRICE WAS AT our table, gathering up her and Gina's coats and bags.

"It was just a family thing," I said in response to her concerned frown. "Not important."

"Okay." Sharrice's expression didn't change. "Jennifer is getting another round, but I should really take Gina home. I don't think she realized how strong those drinks were. She's in the bathroom, probably throwing up. She's going to kick herself tomorrow—she barely made weight last time, and she does *not* have the calories to spare."

"I may stay with Jennifer a bit longer," I said.

"You sure you don't want to leave with us? Where are you parked?"

"My car is only two blocks away. I'm okay, really. I'm totally fine."

Jennifer appeared with four more drinks. Sharrice looked torn, glancing toward the bathrooms. She shouldered her purse reluctantly.

"Don't try to contact this Landon guy, okay?" she whispered as she hugged me goodbye. "And don't finish those drinks. I love you. Get home safe."

Chapter 7

AFTER TWO MORE drinks with Jennifer, I left the bar, drunk.

The rest of downtown was dead on weeknights, but this section of Chippewa Street was lightly buzzing. Buffalo met the exact specifications for the old adage: a drinking town with a football problem. You had the Bills and you had the bars. There was always somewhere to drink: the dark clubs on Chippewa or the dives and Irish pubs serving up baskets of fried food and beef on weck four inches high, two beers on tap to choose from, air thick with cooking oil, windows foggy from the cold outside. And more and more you could find nicer bars, with tiled floors and gold fixtures. I headed toward Delaware to find one of these bars. I thought about how I'd sat there like an idiot talking to Landon, bonding with him, sentimental with whiskey, and he'd been lying right to my face. He'd seen Jeanine and he hadn't told me. He'd seen her, and then she was gone. Disappeared. And that meant . . . that meant—

I sat down at a cocktail bar a few doors down and ordered another drink.

I was too dismayed to worry about being caught drinking alone on a Wednesday. A picture of me drunk making its way to Facebook could get me benched or dismissed altogether—and Suzanna took care to monitor all of our social media, checking every photo we were tagged in. I was a Jill every minute of the day. We had to adhere to certain professional standards. We could go to clubs, sip cocktails, flirt tastefully, we could whoop and bop on a dance floor and have discreet one-night stands, but we could not get sloppy, could not attract unwanted attention. I should have let Sharrice keep an eye on me, but I didn't want to be kept an eye on. I wanted to be the way I was when I was with Jeanine.

When I went out with Jeanine I drank enough to stumble, I kissed on the dance floor, and I always felt like I could afford it because she was there, holding me upright, shielding me from embarrassment with her brassy confidence, her chin-jutting defiance. How could I explain what a relief it was to stop self-assessing, second-guessing myself, every second of the day? Before Jeanine, my technique in bars was to look pretty and wait around for a man to pursue me. If he didn't, I figured there was something wrong with me. Any fumbled interaction or shortage of attention, I attributed to my lack of expertise, my failure to be more desirable. Jeanine, after a few nights barhopping with me, expressed her horror. "All you're doing is sitting there, gazing around with your big Bambi eyes. Well, what do you *want*? Because if you keep this up, you're either going to get some creep who preys on clueless-looking girls or a mind reader who can anticipate your every desire. You want to wait around a thousand years for the second guy to show up? The only one who is going to get you laid is you," she said. "These ding-dongs don't know what they want."

Her words shook me out of myself. I could see, in the mirror behind the bar, that I looked exactly as she'd said, passive and frightened. I realized there might be a different way I could look. Maybe I didn't have to be trapped inside my fear of displeasing everyone. Maybe asserting a preference or a desire wasn't a punishable offense. I resolved to be different. And Jeanine helped me, pressing me up against a guy she could tell was interested, taking the first step for me.

I imagined her behind me now, tilting me toward the guy next to me at the bar—and it worked. He asked if I was alone. He asked if he could buy me my next drink, and I said yes. He was the kind of guy Jeanine would have picked out for me rather than herself: a little younger, blond, tattoos peeking out from his long-sleeved shirt. He was a bartender, he said, at a new hotel bar on Franklin, and the martinis here were great, if I wanted a martini. If all went well, he would be my thirteenth—and only five days after the twelfth. That would be a record for me, that kind of turnaround.

Oh God, would I never be able to do this with Jeanine again? Was I on my own, alone in a bar, gripping desperately to the life she'd allowed me to have?

Or was this the real me, which only she'd been able to uncover?

After a bleary vodka martini with the tattooed boy, I blinked to find myself halfway across the bar floor, marching toward the back door. Now was the perfect time, I thought while I unlocked my phone, to call Laura back, while I was thriving and confident. I could handle it. I could handle anything.

"Hi!" she answered after one ring, and there was her voice, so sweet and relieved my heart cracked. My little sister. Oh, God. I loved her so much.

"I got your text," I said. "I didn't mean to make you wait."

"That's okay," she laughed. She sounded so, so pretty when she laughed. "It hasn't been that long."

This was a bad idea. My body had become a column of zinging liquid, water filled with electricity. One note of Laura's laugh and I was slung back in time—to Laura and me in matching gold leotards and black top hats, trying to teach our dad our jazz recital routine, screaming with laughter as he went into a kick line.

Laura and I draping our mom with all her gold jewelry, exclaiming, *You're so beautiful! So glamorous!,* shrieking with pleasure at every smile we eked out of her, every goofy face she flashed at us, these tiny gifts of approval we hoarded and cherished.

Laura was the only one who could make our mom laugh after Dad died. She got the best parts of him, right down to her voice, which was identical to his—husky with laughter waiting to be expelled, crackling with life—a voice that was now saying, apparently, that she wanted to visit Buffalo.

"Wait—what?" I said.

"For Mom's birthday. I thought my present might be to come up to Buffalo."

Good thing the brick wall of the building was there to hold me up.

"I think it's the perfect opportunity," said Laura.

"Opportunity for what?" I said.

"To, like, reconnect."

"How long would you stay?" I said. The shrillness in my voice startled even me. The new boundaries of our lives were, I thought, quite clear: Buffalo was my territory, where I'd chosen to pick up the pieces of *my* life. She got Ohio. Fair was fair.

"Just a few days," said Laura, sounding a little deflated. "I know it's a lot. We haven't had a real conversation in the last two years, but . . . I have some things I'd like to talk about, if you're open, and maybe you do, too. I can stay with Mom, so you wouldn't have to host me or anything."

"Are you sure you want to do this? You know how you get around Mom."

"I know—"

"You can't drink with her. Are you allowed to drink in— Which thing are you doing now? What group?"

"NA," she said. "And I don't intend to drink with Mom. This is a restart. I'm trying to set new patterns. And I miss Buffalo. I think coming back to the place where I first became, you know, *me*—I think coming home will help."

"Help what?"

"Recovery," she said, with forced patience. "In recovery there are some relationships you let go of, and some you keep, and some you have to rebuild. You and Mom are two people I want to rebuild my relationship with. So I'd like to come to Buffalo for her birthday. I'm sure you and Mom want to reconnect with each other, too."

I scoffed. My adult relationship with our mother could be described as a never-ending game of emotional chicken, wherein neither of us picked up the phone and both of us always lost.

"Are you sure there isn't someone else you're coming back for?" I said. "Like Jason?"

The silence on the other end of the call was so cold my stomach dropped.

"Why would you say that?" Her voice fluttered with a laugh meant to convey shock and cover up hurt. "Are you drunk?"

Laura, asking me this! Finally, something funny. A joke—not the kind you told, the kind you found yourself in the middle of, living it. *You* were the joke.

"I just want to make sure you don't have other motivations," I said.

She was quiet, but I could hear her endeavoring to keep her breath even.

"Look, I can't blame you," she said, "for being suspicious. I understand that your reaction comes from a place of pain, and also that it is a habitual response. I think we should hang up and talk when you're sober. Clearly you have things to say to me, and I want to hear them. But I can't have a healthy conversation with you when you're like this."

What was this scripted recovery-speak? "Habitual response," "healthy conversation"? But there was no point in arguing about it now, when the odds of her actually coming were low. Laura was not big on follow-through. And anyway, there was another reason I'd called, a question I needed to ask, rising up my esophagus, fighting its way to the tip of my tongue.

"Laura, I want to ask you . . ." Fuck, what did I want to ask? "Do you have friends?"

She sounded as surprised by the question as I was.

"I cut a lot of people out of my life the past few months," she said. "But I have a community. Or, I'm starting to."

"It's the most important thing in the world to have friends. More important than romance. And definitely more important than family."

"Oh. Okay?"

"Romance doesn't work because of all the baggage." I pushed

myself away from the wall and began to pace, a glass beer bottle tumbling away as I kicked it by accident. "You know, worrying about marriage, and if he's going to cheat, and should you move in together, and the insanity of sexual desire, and all that stupid crap. All that attraction, it's too chemical. You can't make choices, because you're not in control of what's happening inside you. And that's the problem with family—it's entirely chemical! With the shared genes and the emotional imprinting and the nature versus nurture, or whatever. You're a mess of chemical reactions. The only thing that can change you is real connection, and you can only connect with someone when you have a choice in the matter."

I felt a striking sense of clarity, made sharper by the five to six vodka cocktails I'd consumed.

"Laura, that's the thing," I pressed. "We're sisters. Not friends. What we have between us is bigger than *us*. It binds us together, but it keeps us from each other, too. We can't be *ourselves*."

"I'm not going to lie to you, Gin: you sound nuts," said Laura. "We can talk more later. It's a boundaries thing."

"Oh, a boundaries thing!" I said. Did she know how many of *her* rants I'd endured when she was very not sober? How often I'd listened to her when she desperately needed to unload her conscience on me, only to forget about it the next morning?

"I'm hanging up now. I love you."

"I love you, too," I sputtered, trying not to cry.

"I'll call you when I know exact dates."

"Sure. Fine."

I stabbed ineffectually at my phone screen, trying to hang up with gusto, annoyed that my throat was so tight it hurt. My phone dinged in my hands.

I love you and hope you're doing okay. We'll get there eventually. Love you always.

Goddamn Laura and her nice texts. She expected me to suddenly be able to *get there*? Where were we going? Toward reconciliation? I hadn't agreed to that! What would that even look like?

The tattooed guy was still at the bar where I'd left him. He was halfway through another martini and greeted me ecstatically, like I was a friend who'd been away. I pressed into him and willed him to help me forget my best friend was missing, to forget Laura. In my head, Jeanine stood behind me, chanting, *This is your life. You can have whatever you want*. I whispered to him that I had a secret, I was a cheerleader—not sure how it would go over, what with the tattoos and all—but he liked it, he wanted to know how I memorized all those dance moves.

It worked, was the thing. Saying you were a cheerleader.

We cabbed back to his place and rolled around on the couch, then in the bed, and he said "Wow, wow," a lot, and he didn't kill me, and he even looked hurt when I called a cab at four A.M. I felt bad, was the thing, because what he wanted from me—a little sweetness and attention, even for a couple of hours—was so easy for me to give, but I was depriving him of it because I could, or perhaps to prove to him, or to myself, that I could stand to be deprived of it also.

When I got home, I picked up Ghost and carried him, protesting, into bed with me, without brushing my teeth or wiping off my makeup.

I woke up to the sun shining assertively through the curtains. My phone was ringing. I fumbled for it beside me on the bed, eyelashes stuck together from last night's mascara.

"Want to go on a ride?" said Landon.

Chapter 8

Landon didn't drive—he'd racked up too many points on his license over the years and now didn't bother owning a car. He texted me an address where I should pick him up.

First, I had to take a cab to my car, parked overnight on Chippewa, a sixty-dollar ticket stuffed under the wiper. Between the cabs and the ticket and the drinks last night, I'd blown over a hundred and fifty bucks I didn't have.

I followed my phone's GPS to the address Landon had given me, and realized he was sending me to the East Side. I calculated: it was my day off at the gym, but I had Jills practice at seven. If Landon's plan was to drag me to a weird abandoned house and kill me for asking too many questions about Jeanine, my absence would be noticed immediately. I had a can of pepper spray in my jacket pocket and a certification from a self-defense class I'd taken three years ago and mostly remembered. I tried to picture the moves from the class, like how to get out of a headlock or out from under an attacker. Only twice had I been in situations where I thought I might actually have to fight someone off. First, when I'd been hired along with five other Jills to dance at a sponsor's bachelor party. In attendance were only six men, all of whom were, first playfully, and then seriously, insulted when we refused to stay after our "performance," which took place in the cramped space between the coffee table and the big-screen TV in the groom's apartment. It did not escape our notice that there was one of us for each of them; you'd have to be pretty stupid not to guess what they'd been hoping for. The other time was when we danced at a disastrous conference in Niagara called the Buffalo Men's Show, where I'd had beer spilled down my top by a man who owned a chain of tanning salons that sponsored the Jills. I'd complained discreetly about the incident to Suzanna, who hadn't been able to do much about it at the time besides express indignation on my behalf and remove me from future appearances involving the tanning chain. Luckily, during my second season she'd found a tanning salon owned by a woman to sponsor the Jills.

In both of these cases, it had been a matter of charming and wriggling my way out of the situation, with as much of my dignity intact as possible. The guy who poured beer on me had endured countless beatings at my hands in my imagination, most of them involving a baseball bat—but I'd never had to fight anybody in real life.

I picked up the baseball bat in my mind. When I tried to aim it at Landon, the image fell apart.

"I GOT A lead," Landon said as he swung into the passenger seat. "An old friend said he saw Jeanine right before she split."

He'd emerged from a little yellow one-story house a few blocks north of the Kensington Expressway. This particular street was scrappy—lawns patched with dead grass, one car on cement blocks—but quiet in the gray afternoon chill. Through my side window I squinted at the yellow house, saw the curtains flick. A girl about my age, with platinum-dyed hair and thick eyeliner applied in a cat-eye, peered out. This was the new girlfriend, I supposed, the one Landon hoped would fill the Jeanine-shaped hole in his soul.

"That's Brittany," he explained, when he saw me looking. "The girl I'm seeing, who I told you about."

"Oh," I said, hitting the gas pedal. "Did you move in with her? I thought you still lived by the Foundry?"

"I do. I'm just staying with her for a few days."

I was too hungover to decide if this was suspicious or not. Every so often, I'd get a whiff of the scent of the tattooed boy's sheets stuck to my skin. The smell made me feel grimier, tougher. "Where am I driving us?"

"Turn left here, and get on the Thruway going south. You know the Pink Fountain?"

I hit the brakes, squealing to a stop in the middle of the intersection.

"What's at the Pink Fountain?" I said.

"The guy Danny, who runs the place—he said he saw Jeanine there with someone else. Last week."

"Saw her with who?"

"That's what we're going to find out."

"Why can't you just call?"

"He's not the type of person to answer questions in detail over the phone. And to tell you the truth, you can't count on Danny to give you the same story twice. If we go there, we can be totally sure."

"How?"

"You'll see, I promise. Will you pull out of this intersection, please? Another car is coming."

I pressed the gas and we lurched forward. I knew the Pink Fountain by reputation. You could score drugs there, along with a room to take them in. People from our high school would use it as a party spot because it was cheap and discreet. They didn't check your name or your ID, they let you pay in cash, and you could get drugs you might not otherwise know where to buy. When I came home during winter break my freshman year of college, Laura admitted that Jason was taking her to parties at the Pink Fountain. At the time, she'd insisted that she never did any drugs on the premises, and at the time, I still believed what she told me.

"I don't see why we have to go there," I said. "Unless you think Jeanine is literally there now."

"She could be. Hiding out or—hell, maybe she is getting high again. Let's cross it off the list. If we trace her movements before she disappeared, then we might find her. Are you okay?" Landon added. "You're acting really tense."

I was tense, and confused. *Landon* knew her movements before she disappeared. Landon had seen her the night before. Was he just pretending to search for her, to deflect suspicion away from himself?

He told me to take the next exit, and we drove past a long stretch of low brick buildings, their windows clouded and streaked. This was not my Buffalo. I'd grown up in the dense suburban comfort of Kenmore, attending sleepovers with my dance friends, gossiping on the plush carpets of their finished basements, swiping fat-free ice cream from their dieting mothers' stash in the freezer. Occasionally I watched other neighborhoods flicker by the backseat window of Dad's car as he ran errands for Stanley. As an adult, I stuck to the narrow strip between Elmwood Village and downtown, with regular forays south to Orchard Park for practice and games, and north to visit Paladino's Steakhouse on the other side of Delaware Park. Jills appearances took me to shopping malls and hospitals and senior centers, to casinos and corporate events in Niagara, but never to the East Side, or to far-flung suburbs like this.

It occurred to me, as I watched the storefronts change, that Laura had known a different Buffalo than I had. She'd traversed neighborhoods I'd only heard warnings about. This was Laura's Buffalo, and Jeanine's and Landon's Buffalo, and I was still learning it.

A quarter mile later, we pulled into the lot of a two-story motel, the kind where all the rooms were accessed from the outside. The sign read, *Pink Fountain Value Motel* in swirly script. Underneath, plastic letters had been arranged to form the word VACANTS.

"Don't be nervous," Landon said as he pushed open the squeaky glass door. "You'll be fine as long as you're with me. We're doing this for Jeanine, right?"

The lobby was a small, square room with a streaked pink carpet. A TV hung in the corner above the pink Formica counter, the volume muted; on the grainy screen a music video by a hardcore band played, showing a man with thick eyeliner rolling around on the floor. The room smelled like a chemical approximation of lemon, mixed with mold and urine. Disgust rippled up from the soles of my feet toward the top of my head as I thought of Laura standing in this very spot, holding hands with Jason as he checked them in, surrounded by teenage degenerates, breathing the same sickly air.

From a door behind the desk lumbered a bearlike man with a prodigious beard and a black baseball cap. At the sight of Landon, he lifted the cap to palm a bald head.

"Whoa. Did I enter a time warp? Is it 2008?" he said.

They gripped hands, each testing the other's strength, reestablishing status. Danny glanced me up and down, trying to interpret what my presence said about Landon and, therefore, about himself.

"How do you always have girls around that are too pretty for you?" he said to Landon.

"She's a Jill. Jeanine's friend."

"I knew you looked familiar." He pointed at the Jills calendar tacked to the wall behind him. The October girls, Maria and Alicia, smiled from the prow of a boat, the use of which had, coincidentally, been donated by Stanley as a photo shoot location. "You were Miss May, I believe?"

"That's me."

"I always buy a stack of calendars for Jeannie," he said. "It's nice to see someone you knew way back when make something of themselves. That's why I don't like seeing *this* guy hanging around here anymore." He jerked his chin toward Landon. "Aren't you supposed to be in school?"

"Jeanine is the reason we're here, actually," said Landon. "You said she came by?"

Danny's eyes shifted. He blew out a long exhalation.

"Look, dude," he said. "I can't help you, and I didn't say that."

"Dude, you did say." Landon pulled out his phone. "Last Monday, you texted me, 'Shit, it's eight P.M., know where your lady is?' And then you made a little face with a semicolon and a P, like a tongue sticking out." He brandished the phone in Danny's face. "See? She was here."

Danny sighed and scratched his beard.

"It doesn't say that," he repeated.

"Danny, it's cool. You ran your mouth, and now I'm here. All I want to know is where Jeanine's been the past few days. It's no big deal." Landon jabbed a thumb in my direction. "Are you worried about *her*? She's cool. She's helping me look for Jeanine. Do you want her to wait outside?"

"You don't have to worry about me," I said. "I'm not a narc."

"Oh, she's not a *narc*!" said Danny. "Hey, great. I feel a lot better."

"She can wait outside. You might need to go outside," Landon whispered to me, giving my arm a squeeze.

"It doesn't matter either way," said Danny. "I don't know shit. If you want to know where Jeanine's been, talk to her yourself."

"I can't," said Landon. "She's missing."

Danny's eyes fluttered closed. He lifted his hat and rubbed his head again.

"Just tell me what she was doing here," said Landon. "It's simple. She's missing. I'm *asking* you."

I could see now that the cavalier attitude Landon had shown at the Foundry had disappeared. Danny was shaking his head, looking anywhere but at us.

"You looked out for the two of us back in the day," said Landon, "made sure no one messed with us. You care about her."

"That was a long time ago. She's a big girl now, and if she's gotten into some fucked-up shit, I can't help her. I gotta think about me. I gotta keep my house clean. I don't like mess."

"What mess is she getting into?"

"Leave me alone."

"*You* started it with the text, Danny," said Landon.

"Has anyone else come around asking about Jeanine?" I said. "A guy named Antweiler?"

Danny went rigid. He drew in a breath through clenched teeth.

"What the fuck does this girl know about Antweiler?" he asked Landon.

I looked to Landon for help and saw he had gone white as a sheet.

"I don't need you bringing random chicks to my motel trying to start shit," said Danny. "I don't need Antweiler breathing down my neck. I don't need this going on in my house. Everyone thinks they can come to Danny, ask for shit from Danny, push Danny, and I'm just going to take it." Danny waved a hand in my direction.

"At this time," he said, "I'm going to have to ask you both to get the fuck out of my motel."

"FUCK," SAID LANDON once we were out in the parking lot.

I hurried behind him, ducking to shield my face from the burst of cold wind, frightened and annoyed.

"Who's Antweiler?" I demanded.

"Why don't you tell me how *you* know Antweiler?"

"He's some guy who was looking for Jeanine at Buffalo Underground."

"Okay, that bothers me," he said. "That really fucking bothers me. Why didn't you tell me about that? Now Danny won't talk to us. We're so fucked."

"Landon, what does it matter what he tells us?" I said. "There's no sign-in sheet. No one uses their real name. He could say whatever he wants about Jeanine, and we wouldn't know if it was true. You could have called him on the phone."

"He's got footage," said Landon. He pointed over his shoulder, back at the front desk. "Security cameras."

"Where?"

"In the back office, behind the desk. The only reason I know is because once, Jeanine and I got a room here, and somebody busted the door down and robbed us. Danny had this paternal streak toward Jeanine, so the next day he asked me to come back and ID the guy. He showed me the footage, and that's how I know he's got cameras. They're the only record of who comes and goes."

I slowed a little, feet dragging on the potholed pavement.

"We've got to see that footage," I said.

"Yeah, no shit."

I marched back toward the motel. We'd tried negotiation. All the time I'd spent tracking down Laura had taught me that negotiation rarely got you what you wanted. Through the window I could make out Danny, facing the TV behind the desk, his back to the parking lot. I started trying door handles.

"What are you doing?" said Landon. "You're not going to find footage in the *rooms*."

Finally one of the doors popped open. Inside was a grimy room, green carpet, textured wallpaper, ceiling fan. The place was completely trashed: piles of takeout containers on the bed, heaps of soda and beer cans, pizza crusts scattered around, a mountain of dirty laundry in the corner, the air thick with the reek of chemicals and cigarettes. The room was freezing; one of the windows had been left open.

"Virginia, stop," said Landon. "Someone's clearly living here. Are you crazy?"

I cast around, looking for some way to cause a problem. The trash bin between the beds was made of wicker. I tore out the plastic lining and began filling it with the crumpled, crusty napkins scattered around the room. Landon watched me, hands hanging by his sides.

"You got a lighter?" I asked him.

He did. I took it and lit the napkins, and they burned up in seconds, turning black, the flame extinguished. I kicked through a pile of dirty clothes to reach the bathroom. On the sink counter cluttered with cans and cigarette butts was a bottle of nail polish remover. I soaked one of the dirty washcloths wadded up on the back of the toilet with the remover and touched the lighter to it. The washcloth burst into a sustained, leaping flame, and I dropped it into the bin, along with fistfuls of toilet paper and fast-food bags, then placed the whole burning lot onto the bed directly under the smoke detector.

We ran out to my car and climbed inside to watch. Two minutes passed, then five. Nothing happened.

"I guess the fucking smoke detectors don't work," I said.

"It was a good try," said Landon. "You get that from a movie?"

"I tried a similar thing once before," I admitted. "I was trying to get my sister out of her boyfriend's place. She wouldn't return my texts or my calls and I got scared, so I went to his apartment building and knocked on the door. She wouldn't come out, so . . ." I shrugged. "That time, I pulled the fire alarm in the hallway."

"You know that shit's illegal, right?" he said. "Did it work? I mean, did you get her to come out?"

"No," I admitted. "I stood across the street and watched the whole building evacuate except her. I don't know if she was too fucked up to hear it, or if she didn't care if she burned, or what—but she didn't come out."

"Shit," said Landon. "I think the basket lit on fire."

I looked up to see smoke pouring out the open window.

We watched as the smoke thickened and drifted across the parking lot. The office door flew open and Danny came running out with a fire extinguisher. Through the cracked car window I could hear him say, "Goddamn fucking junkies with their fucking stupid shit," before running into the smoke-engulfed room.

Before I could react, Landon sprang out of the car and sprinted toward the lobby.

By the time I caught up to him, he was tearing through Danny's papers and junk on the front desk.

"He moved the key," said Landon. "He used to keep it on top of the doorframe. Help me look."

"What key?" I said.

Landon pointed at the door behind the desk, which led to what I assumed was the back office. I joined him in tossing room receipts and catalogs and car magazines around. My sneaker caught on a loose square of carpet, its edges ragged as though they had been sliced with scissors or a box cutter. I bent over and pried it up.

"Landon!" I said, pointing at the silver glint of a key on the filthy linoleum under the carpet.

He grabbed the key and shoved it into the lock—it fit.

"Watch for Danny," he called as he disappeared through the door.

The muted TV flickered above my head in the sudden silence. I tiptoed over to the window and peered out. From this angle, I could see down the walkway to the rows of motel doors. In a stroke of incredible luck, Danny seemed to have gotten into a fight with the residents of the room I'd lit on fire—a disheveled couple, backpacks hanging off their arms, shouted at him in the parking lot, one of them carrying a pizza box. They were all screaming at one another, Danny brandishing the fire extinguisher, as smoke drifted across the lot. Other guests were opening their doors to watch the scene.

I abandoned my post and followed Landon into the back office. It was a musty little room with a gray carpet, most of the space taken up by a bulky wooden desk. At the desk, Landon was clicking furiously on a desktop computer.

"I told you to keep a lookout," he said.

I leaned over his shoulder. On the screen was a desktop folder containing a list of dozens of files, and a window displaying video footage. The camera was trained on the parking lot in front of the motel, the angle tilted slightly. It appeared to be fixed above the front door, so it captured about six parking spaces, as well as the walkway in front of the motel. The doors were elongated and swerved crazily into the edge of the computer screen.

"I'm almost through Monday," he said. "That's the day Danny texted me."

He scrubbed furiously through the footage. Cars zoomed in and out of the lot, spitting out figures who made their jerky, staccato journeys up and down the walkway to disappear through the motel room doors or the lobby door beneath the camera's gaze. This went on for some time until—

"Wait, slow down," I said. "Something's happening."

In the video, a big red Toyota pickup skidded into the lot, pulling to a stop across two parking spaces. The driver's door flew open and a man jerked his way out, wearing a low baseball cap. The grainy outline of the other figure in the car, barely visible through the front windshield, gesticulated wildly, then kicked open the passenger door. Out spilled a woman, short and dark-haired—

“Stop,” I gasped. “Stop, that’s her. I know the dress.”

Landon paused and there she was, blurred and tinged green, frozen in mid-step as she ran after the man, who was approaching the entrance to the motel. She had on a wrap dress she wore all the time, black, with a tiger leaping down the skirt. That was Jeanine’s tiger dress, Jeanine’s tall black boots. Her face was pixelated, but I could tell by Landon’s rapid breathing that he recognized her, too.

When he pressed Play again, Jeanine resumed her chase on the screen, grabbing the man’s wrist. He jerked his hand away, and the camera caught the face beneath the ball cap. My hands flew to my mouth.

“Oh my God,” I said. “That’s Jason Morley.”

We watched as Jason and Jeanine began screaming at each other, mouths gaping open and closed, the whir of the computer providing the only sound. Jeanine and Jason Morley, having a fight in the Pink Fountain parking lot.

“Hold on—you’re telling me *that’s* Jason Morley?” Landon pointed at the screen. “How the hell do you know Jason Morley?”

“He’s the one I told you about.” My voice was crazed, bouncing around my vocal cords. “He went to my high school. He got my sister into heroin. What—do you know him?”

“Know him?” Now Landon’s voice was zooming, high-pitched. “I know *of* him. I sure as fuck *heard* of him. How did Jeanine meet him? Through you?”

“God, no,” I spat. “I don’t know how they found each other—she wouldn’t give me a straight goddamn answer.”

Landon stared, gaping, at the screen. My heartbeat got louder, until my whole skull reverberated with it. On the screen, one of the motel room doors flew open, and Jeanine and Jason turned to it; someone inside must have been yelling at them, because Jason started yelling back, storming toward the door. Jeanine got ahold of his arm, and he whipped around to face her. She held both his wrists. She looked to be talking to him urgently. For several long moments they held this pose.

"What was she doing here with him?" Landon whispered. "I don't understand it."

Now Jason was holding up his hands, palms out, as if to say, "Okay, okay." She pulled him again toward the car, and this time he followed.

I nearly reached out to touch my fingers to the flickering pixels of her figure as it retreated toward the red pickup, as though I could tap her shoulder, make her turn around so I could see her face—was she high or frightened? I had *seen* Jeanine that night. The time stamp on the bottom corner of the video read 7:45 P.M. on Monday. She had called me later, around ten, claiming she'd been cut early at work and asking if I wanted to spend the night at her place. She was all adrenaline when I came over. She wanted to go out—it being a Monday and the bars quiet, we'd walked all the way down Main Street to Hanover, passing a bottle of vodka back and forth, until we reached the waterfront. She was wearing that same tiger dress, cracking jokes, spinning pirouettes on the big empty, quiet sidewalks of downtown. How could I have known that she had just had a fight in a parking lot? But I felt like I should have.

I watched the screen, breathless, as her figure slid inside the truck, yanking the door shut behind her.

We heard the squeak of the lobby door swing open and shut. I had placed my hand on Landon's shoulder without realizing it, and I felt his muscles tense under my fingers.

We listened as Danny shuffled around at the front desk, which we'd wrecked, muttering, "Who the fuck is fucking with my shit."

"Out the back," Landon whispered, scooting away from the desk.

With difficulty he forced open the window, partially concealed by a metal shelf full of binders.

"Would you hurry?" I said as he struggled to fit himself through the gap.

Landon's legs disappeared as he fell face-first onto the pavement outside the window. As I hoisted myself onto the sill, the door to the back office opened. I had enough time to hear Danny start roaring incoherently behind me as I dropped to the pavement below, and started running.

Chapter 9

Before I'd walked into the Pink Fountain, I had been under the impression that there was not a whole lot left that could surprise me.

Though I'd dreaded the mornings when I woke up to find Laura missing from the couch where she was supposed to be sleeping, or the phone calls from unknown numbers, or the knocks on the door that might have been Gabe, they did not surprise me. I was always, in some capacity, ready for them. In fact, I felt a sense of fruition—not satisfaction, but the relief of a wait being over, so that the next series of tasks could begin.

I had not been surprised when Laura relapsed, either, after eleven months sober. In a way I'd been expecting it, though those eleven months had been some of the happiest and most tender of my life. After detox, Laura had moved into my apartment in Grandview full-time. She was all wonder and rawness, like a child experiencing the world for the first time, free of blunted edges and ecstatic lows. We moved carefully and clumsily around each other in the apartment, like two baby horses learning to walk. We began—as another drug-free month passed, and then another—to talk. We talked like we had in middle school, when we stayed up late whispering under the covers with the lights off, rule followers, as if our mom would bother yelling at us.

We talked about the guilt Laura had labored with after I left for college, the pressure she'd felt to stay in Buffalo and keep Mom happy, the war raging inside her—she wanted to please our mom, and be Jason's girlfriend, and keep partying, but more than that, she wanted to please me, especially after I'd worked so hard filling out her applications, basically writing her personal essay for her. We talked about how she never had an identity in Ohio beyond being a druggie. She hadn't majored in dance, like I'd hoped, but chose accounting, because she'd read that accountants made a lot of money, and she didn't want to end up like Mom, her life withering away while she relied on Stanley's money to get by. We talked about how demoralizing it had been when she couldn't pass the math classes (which, I managed not to remind her, was exactly what I'd told her would happen), and how this had confirmed what she always expected: she had nothing going for her except that she was able to handle a lot of drugs.

We talked about the chance she'd been given now, to figure out who she was. We talked about getting her back into dance. Her ankle still hurt during cold months, she said apprehensively, and she had lingering hip problems she attributed to years of doing splits. Using her body again would make it stronger, I assured her. I told her I'd pay for any class she wanted. I'd sign up for one, too. I found us a modern dance class at a recommended studio and put it on my credit card.

Things were going so well that when the day finally came, the day she showed up to my birthday gathering at my favorite fajitas place blitzed out of her mind—stumbling to the bathroom every five minutes, unable to keep her eyes open, sitting at the wrong tables, drinking out of other people's glasses—my only thought was that this was as good a day as any to get it over with. I had not been surprised; I had been ready.

So, as I pulled the car into a diner in South Cheektowaga, after speeding a few miles west of the Pink Fountain, I endeavored to feel only readiness—to move as quickly as possible to the part where I took action.

Landon requested a booth by the window so he could keep an eye on the parking lot. Cars deposited and collected diner patrons, mostly older couples. He ordered a bacon cheeseburger, and I got an egg white omelet. I wiped my hands and checked the time—two hours until practice. Miraculously, my mind had room to acknowledge, with a lengthening sense of dread, that there was no way I would make weight. I let Landon push a few fries onto my plate, and picked out one to dip in mayonnaise. One fry had twelve calories, which I could burn off in two to three minutes at my next dance aerobics class. Somehow, it was always possible to make these calculations.

"I like that," he said, watching me. "It seems more sophisticated than ketchup."

I pushed the plate away, stopping after four fries—eight to twelve minutes of exercise—and folded my hands on the greasy table.

"I know you saw Jeanine last week, Landon."

His eyes flicked up to mine. Surprisingly, they did not contain anger or fear. Instead, they were wide with regret.

"I wish I'd told you," he said. "I know it looks bad that I didn't. How'd you find out? Did you talk to someone at the Foundry?"

"The Foundry? I'm talking about you drinking with her at Buffalo Underground. On Saturday."

"Oh." His face fell.

"Landon! How many times have you seen her?"

"Just those two times, I swear. She reached out to *me*. I hadn't spoken to her in months prior to that. I'm not proud that I saw her. I told you, I'm trying to move on, I've got this girl, Brittany—"

I put up a hand. "You are officially the last person to see Jeanine before she disappeared. Seeing her act like a lunatic in front of the Pink Fountain with that shithead Jason Morley makes me want to scream my head off. But the fact is, you outpace Jason in terms of suspicious behavior. I don't need to hear how bad you feel about running around on your new girlfriend. I need to know what the hell you did with Jeanine on Saturday."

"Hey—I'm here talking to you," said Landon. "I brought you to the Pink Fountain. I'm helping you look for her. And you're giving me the third degree?"

He flopped around in the booth for a moment, trying to catch his indignation and hang on to it. This was good: information. I needed more information. This was how you kept from being stunned into silence, like a deer hypnotized by headlights, frozen stupidly, as if you couldn't see the car coming straight at you to blow you to bits.

I did it on purpose, Laura had said the night she relapsed. I shook myself to repress the thought.

Landon put his elbows on the table and pressed his face into his hands, rubbing his stubbled cheeks furiously. I waited, forcing myself not to think, to simply take what came. He began to explain, haltingly at first, that it was Jeanine who'd shown up on his turf.

He saw her for the first time on Tuesday of last week, the day after her visit to the Pink Fountain. She was coming from Jills practice (which she'd left in a hurry, I remembered, saying she was spending the night with Bobby). She showed up at the Foundry unannounced, like she used to before he asked her to stop contacting him. She asked if he wanted to catch up. She had no agenda, she claimed.

"Was she high?" I interrupted. "She'd just gone to the Pink Fountain the night before—did you two get fucked up together?"

"No, God no. It was friendly. Kind of businesslike, really. We played pool, we hung out. We didn't have sex," he added.

"I don't care if you had sex," I said impatiently.

"Well, we didn't. It was a big surprise to see her, and of course she'd broken the rules by visiting me. But we had a lot to talk about, and . . . I felt good about the way we left things. Everything seemed okay. The night we went to Buffalo Underground was weirder."

"Weirder how?"

"Well . . . she cried, for one thing."

I straightened, shoving aside another wave of surprise. In our two years of friendship—barhopping and babbling away through the night, endless miles in the car together driving to practice and games and appearances, sharing stories, disclosures—I had never seen Jeanine break down, never seen her cry. I tried not to be offended that she had gone to Landon and not me.

"I have no idea why," he said in response to my look. "It was total emotional chaos. She kept saying what a great guy I am, how much I do for her, how much I mean to her. She'd drunk a bit, but not that much. She said, 'I love you, I love you.' I thought she was having some kind of crisis about her relationship with Bobby. Now I think . . . now I think—"

He trailed off. I piled our napkins onto the plates. How was I supposed to know if he was lying? There was nothing to do but pretend to believe him for now.

"Did you go anywhere else after Buffalo Underground?" I said. "Because Jeanine's coworker said you left early."

"No, she split after we left the bar. That's the last time I saw her." He was clearly still lost in thought. "I think she's in trouble."

"Yeah, Landon, I do, too," I said.

"No, I mean . . . I think Jeanine might have done something bad. She had some weird blowout with Jason Morley? And now Antweiler is out looking for her?"

"*Who* is Antweiler?" I said.

His eyes darted up to mine grimly. "He's a leg-breaker. Works for your friends the Paladinos."

I drew back. It unsettled me, seeing the fear elicited by someone associated with the Paladinos. Then again, Stanley had told me he would look into it. He obviously wasn't hitting the pavement himself. He had people like Antweiler to do these things for him.

"But why would a guy like that be interested in Jeanine?" Landon said. "Because she's Bobby's girlfriend?"

"Well, I told Stanley Paladino I was worried about Jeanine," I admitted. "And he said he'd take care of it. I guess he sent Antweiler."

"No offense, but Stanley Paladino isn't sending out his big guns just because you asked him to check on your friend."

"Okay, so why *would* he send out someone like Antweiler?"

Landon laid his palms flat on the table and stared at his hands. The question seemed to have sent him to a place very deep inside himself.

"You said you think Jeanine did something bad," I said. "What do you mean by 'something bad'? What else happened between you two?"

The waitress dropped the check between us and we fell silent. Before I could make a move for it, Landon slapped thirty bucks on the table.

"Let's get the hell out of here."

LANDON CHECKED THE mirrors as I drove west on Broadway with no idea of where we were going.

I did it on purpose, Laura had chanted the night she relapsed, repeating it over and over as I dragged her to my car, drove her home to my apartment, carried her to the couch. She wouldn't stop saying it. *I did it on purpose.*

I tried to keep Landon talking.

"You said you thought Jeanine was having a crisis with Bobby. Were she and Bobby having a fight?"

"I don't know. She didn't talk about Bobby."

"What have you heard about Jason Morley?" I said.

"I only know his name. Guys like me don't know guys like Jason Morley directly. I can't believe you went to fucking high school with him. He's in imports/exports now. He's a scumbag. You know—you can put it together."

"Imports/exports, like—you mean drugs?"

"Listen, Virginia, I'm sorry to say this, but—I need you to shut up for a second so I can think about what to do."

One hour until practice. I gripped the wheel. I had to get to the Kmart in time to put on full makeup and blow out my hair. These terrors stung at me in turns, like wasps, before I could swat them away. *I did it on purpose.*

"Where should I take you?" I said to Landon, my voice cracking. "I don't have much time, and I don't know where I'm driving."

"Just take the next right," he said. He had me turn onto a side street, circle the block, and get back on Broadway, to check if we were being followed. Before we hit the intersection with Bailey, he directed me south for several blocks, until we pulled up in front of a tavern. It was nothing more than a cube of concrete with a green door and a sign that said, "You don't have to go home, but you CAN stay here."

Landon put his hand on the door handle.

"Listen to me very carefully," he said. "I want you to go home, and not ask any more questions about Jeanine for a while. Leave it alone. And don't try to contact me. Maybe don't mention to anyone that you saw me."

"What's going on?" I said. "You're not telling me everything."

But he was opening the car door.

"Where are you going?" I cried. "Landon, I can't deal with people not telling me things. I can't stand it. Do you know what it will do to me to not know what happened to her? You have to tell me, Landon. I can't take not knowing. I can't take it. I can't."

I did it on purpose. I wanted to slap my own face, knock the phrase out of my head, where it was repeating as relentlessly as Laura had repeated it that night.

What, I'd shouted at her. She'd done what on purpose? Ruined my birthday? What, what, what?

No, she'd cried, collapsing on my couch, her voice snotty with tears.

You don't understand me, she'd shouted. *You never got how much I hated it, how bad I wanted to quit. I rolled it as hard as I could landing that jump. I put my whole weight into it. I just wanted it to stop, to stop.*

"Landon," I called after him. "Tell me what else happened that night. Talk to me."

And when the pain came, Laura said, *I thought, Thank God.*

Landon slammed the door shut, and I began to panic. I was a person who could not be told things, because I could not be trusted to understand them, because all my preparedness merely led me to do the same wrong thing over and over, never getting it, never understanding what was really going on.

Laura had hated everything I had ever done for her. And that was the moment I realized that if I kept trying to save her, I was going to kill us both. I couldn't survive another moment like that again. I'd been ready for everything but that.

Landon watched me wistfully as he walked backward toward the tavern, taking his secrets with him. Then he turned on his boot heel and disappeared inside.

Chapter 10

Vic, sharrice, and I stood in the parking lot next to the Mighty Taco in Williamsville, near the airport, waiting for Sara and the other girls to arrive with the van and equipment. Sharrice was fixing Vic's makeup with products from her own makeup bag.

"You look really good, V," Vic reassured me, her eyes lifted toward the sky so Sharrice could line her bottom lids.

I did not look good. I'd had clients all morning and afternoon and was exhausted. I had not made weight at practice the evening before, after the Pink Fountain. It was my first time being over this season—my first time over *ever*—so I was only on probation. ("Tummy," Suzanna had said as I did the jump test. "We talked about this last season. I want you working on abs all week. I need to see abs.") My appearance was satisfying enough to keep me off the bench, for now, provided I made weight next week.

Vic and Sharrice thought this was the sole source of my anxiety. My heart was a tormented horse inside my ribs, and every so often it leapt and kicked. My mind labored to put the revelations of the last forty-eight hours into a narrative I could understand. Clearly, Jeanine was on a bender. With her humor and charisma, she'd tricked me into thinking she had her life under control, and now she was lying dead somewhere. Jason Morley had gotten her hooked on drugs again, and she'd gone to Landon sobbing because she was planning to kill herself. My fate was apparently to replay this plotline over and over, with Jason Morley robbing me of another person I loved, on a loop, until I was dead. I was fat and hideous, and had to smile at a million strangers at a Mighty Taco.

The wind picked up, ruining our hair. For this event we were wearing our Jills tracksuits, which were thankfully more forgiving than our uniforms. I slid my hand under the zippered fabric to grip a handful of fat on my stomach. I imagined slicing it off with a sharp knife, leaving behind a gleaming swath of perfectly tight skin. In my mind, Jeanine shut herself again inside a truck with Jason Morley.

My phone began to buzz. Stanley calling.

"I'll be right back," I said to Vic and Sharrice. I huddled by the brick side of the building, to hide from the wind, and answered.

"Kiddo," he said. "I need you to confirm something for me. Can you meet me?"

The wind kept blowing my hair into my lipstick, where it stuck.

"I have a Jills appearance. Can I meet you after?"

"Ah. No, this is time-sensitive. I'm going to text you a picture. I would like for you to tell me if you recognize it."

"What's going on?"

"Hang on. Look at the picture, please."

My phone vibrated and I pulled it away from my ear to look at the screen. My hair stuck to my lips and stayed there. Stanley had sent me a slightly blurred picture of a tan suede ankle boot, the side spattered with mud. All the blood rushed into my ears, where it surged and surged.

"That's her shoe," I said. "That's her shoe, Stanley. Where did you find it?"

"Trunk of her car. With the pair."

"Her car?" The pavement bucked, and I bent my knees to stay upright. "Where'd you find her car?"

"I'm looking into it. Don't worry."

"Tell me, please. Maybe I can help."

"Tonawanda Island," he said. "Near the banks of the river. It's been banged up."

"Like she crashed it?"

"Not exactly."

"I'm coming out there. Where is it?"

"No," he said. "Don't do anything silly. Stay calm, and whatever you do, do not call the cops and send in some random schmuck with shit for brains who happens to be patrolling this area. I'm working with the right people, and I don't want anyone else involved. Hang tight until you hear from me. Thank you," he added. "For your assistance with the shoe."

"Stanley—" I began, but he had already hung up.

The pavement was still pitching. Behind me, Vic and Sharrice were calling my name.

"Virginia," Sharrice hollered over the wind as I spun around. "We're about to go in. Are you okay? What's happening?"

I must have been sinking to the pavement because Sharrice was now running toward me at an odd angle, as if she were descending upon me from the gray skies.

"IF ANYONE WANTS to leave," said Sara, "you will obviously not be penalized."

The six of us stood dumbly in the lot outside the Mighty Taco, in our tracksuits. Sharrice paced twenty feet away, phone to her ear, talking to the police. Great swirling surges of anxiety rolled their way up and down my body. I had not meant to blurt out to everyone that Jeanine's car had been found, but my brain was incapable of forming sentences about any other topic. Stanley did not want the police involved, but what on earth could I say? *Don't call the police, Stanley will be mad*? Of course the police had to be called. Her car had been found. Beneath my anxiety was a current of gratitude to Sharrice, for shouldering the burden of exposing Jeanine to the cops, a burden that I, as a person bound to the rules of Paladinos, could not.

"Do we *say* something?" said Sophie. "To the crowd?"

"Good God, no," said Sara. "We go on like normal. But if you're not comfortable performing your duties tonight, you're welcome to go. We'll sort it out with Suzanna later."

This last part was clearly for my benefit, but I was unable to acknowledge that I'd heard it. Sharrice strode back toward us, a hand to her forehead.

"The Buffalo police told me to call the North Tonawanda police, because Tonawanda Island is technically in Niagara County," she said. "But the North Tonawanda police said I needed to file a report in the precinct where she resides. But the car is outside Buffalo police jurisdiction, so they told me to try Niagara again. No one will take the freaking report! I'm going to the precinct in person. We're stupid for letting this much time go by, and I'm not losing more. I'll meet you all after the event."

She gathered up her bag and binder and marched to her car. I envied her certainty. The girls were all looking at me, waiting for me to tell them how we should behave or what I needed from them.

All I knew was that there's no good thing to do in the hours following such news. The morning we found out our dad died, Laura cried because we weren't going to school that day. *I want to go*, she'd screamed, tears streaming. *I have a spelling quiz!*

I didn't want to have to think up another way to survive the evening. I wanted to get through these next two hours—just get through. I walked over to Sara's van and began pulling the long folding tables out of the back. Sara and Ashlee leapt over to help grab the other end. With that, the spell of stillness and uncertainty was broken, and the other girls began going through the motions of preparing for the event.

Inside the Mighty Taco's cramped dining area, we set up a table for signing autographs and a cardboard backdrop featuring the Bills logo to take pictures in front of. We had Bills jerseys to sell, as well as eight-by-tens and Jills calendars at a bargain-bin price. It smelled like limp iceberg lettuce and hot sauce and the halfhearted lemon Pledge that coated the bathrooms. A line had already formed outside the doors.

I thought, *This will always be the thing I did after I learned Jeanine was, in all probability, in every scenario I could imagine, dead.*

Sara put me behind the cashbox because it involved the least amount of posing. We smiled for pictures and hawked calendars. Everyone got half-off coupons for tacos. We were asked approximately eight million times if we could put our numbers under our autographs. We were asked if there was a coupon to take one of *us* home.

All the while my mind reeled. Her car. Her car! What was it doing on Tonawanda Island? Where even was that? In North Tonawanda, Sharrice had said. There was no reason for Jeanine to go there. Had she died in her car? My dad died in his car. He got in the driver's seat in the parking lot of Paladino's Steakhouse, turned on the ignition, and died of heart failure. He was found when the closing bartender peered into his window. Now Jeanine might have died in her car.

I was thinking all this, my jaw aching from smiling, when a preteen kid was pushed by his friends to the front of the line. He stood in front of Vic and me. She greeted him with a big Jills smile.

"I was wondering," said the kid, "is part of your job that you have to, like, do it with the football players?"

The room was loud enough that no one else in line heard, except his two friends behind him. He'd clearly said it on a dare—the other boys suppressed laughs, hands covering their mouths. They had the look of boys who knew they were breaking rules but there would be no consequences. The consequences would happen to *us*—we would be flustered, upset, angry—but nothing would happen to them. They could revel in their own daring, and they actually believed making a crude remark to a cheerleader was *daring,* like it wasn't as typical as you could fucking get. This was the problem with boys: they had no concept of their unrelenting lack of originality. They thought they'd invented cruelty, that they were the first to try it and they should be applauded for their audacity.

The kid who'd said it was doing his best to look defiant and indifferent, but it was taking a lot of effort.

Vic yelled, "Next!" and waved up the woman behind the boys.

"Wait," said the boy who'd spoken. "I wanted an autograph."

"No," said Vic. She kept her eyes bright and fluttery but was otherwise completely unreadable.

"This is messed up. I came to get an autograph. You have to sign my thing." He dug through his pockets and pulled out an old receipt. "Here," he said, handing it to her.

Vic took it and put it in the wastebasket under the table. She continued to wave forward the woman. "It's fine, come on up."

One of the other boys took a turn. "Uptight bitches," he mumbled.

"What if I complain to someone about this?" said the first boy.

"Feel free to write to the Buffalo Jills and explain exactly what happened between us. Our mailing address is on the website." Vic smiled winningly at the woman behind the boys, taking the calendar she had bought to get signed.

The boys stood off to the side, sighing and rolling their eyes. The whole exchange had gone wrong, and they couldn't figure out why. I worried that the first boy would keep practicing, insulting more women until he got it right, until he got the flustered and affronted response he'd anticipated.

"Thank God for you," I whispered to Vic, as the boys made a big show of stealing all the hot sauce packets before they kicked open the door. None of us felt like we'd gained any ground.

"Just pray they don't go straight to the Jills Facebook page and fill it with their stupid little comments," muttered Vic.

WE BROKE DOWN the tables, gathered up the leftover merchandise, and Sara slammed the van shut.

"Everyone's coming to my place," she said.

We were only a short drive from Sara's enormous Tudor in East Amherst (she was one of many girls who drove over forty-five minutes, if there was traffic, to get to practice). Sara had a rich husband and was also independently wealthy. She herded us, like nervous sheep, into the gaping tiled foyer, where her husband greeted us.

"Be scarce, Greg," she said to him.

Greg, shrugging amiably, brought a glass of red wine upstairs to listen to records in the entertainment room while we took over the downstairs.

We sat, silent and lost, on Sara's massive L-shaped couch in the den, while Sara poured us all white wine. Sophie slouched over to the upright piano and—surprising everyone—began playing "These Days," the Jackson Browne version. The doorbell rang, and Sophie's fingers faltered. Sara opened the door to reveal Sharrice.

"The Buffalo police finally took the report," she said, collapsing on the sectional. "It was so annoying. They kept saying they'd do a wellness check, and I had to say, '*No*, we don't want a *wellness check*, I want to fill out a *report*.' Finally the bit about her car being abandoned seemed to concern them enough to take my report. As if they were doing me a favor, as if that isn't their *job*."

"Thank you for doing it," said Sara. "It should have been done earlier. I feel so stupid now."

Sharrice drained her glass in one gulp and stood up again to pace behind the couch. After a moment of silence, Sophie resumed her playing, this time Cat Stevens, "Where Do the Children Play?"

"The last time I saw Jeanine, she made me laugh," said Vic suddenly. "It was last Thursday's practice. I was talking about how hard it is to date while having a kid, and how I didn't think I was ever going to find anyone, and how I shouldn't have dumped that guy Rob I was seeing. And she said, 'Vic, listening to you talk about that guy was like listening to someone talk about a vacation they took somewhere shitty—someplace like *Cleveland*—and you can tell they want you to think they had a good time, so you're nodding and smiling, but the whole time you're thinking, *Girl, go to Atlantic City! Go to Vegas! Stop pretending you like Cleveland!*' And I started laughing so hard, because Rob *is* boring and he does suck and that was exactly what it was like."

"Easy for her to say stuff like that," said Sophie without pausing her playing. "She was beautiful."

"She was tough," said Vic. "Did you notice how no one ever made snide comments to her? Something about her look—they knew she'd reduce them to rubble."

"It doesn't matter how tough or savvy you are," said Ashlee. "If they're bigger than you, and they hate you, then it doesn't matter."

Sophie's fingers stumbled. She lifted her hands to cover her ears. My own ears felt clogged; I could hear each of my shallow breaths rattling loudly in my skull.

"Everyone stop," said Sara. "She's not dead. This is not a memorial. We should stop using past tense."

"It doesn't look good, Sara," Vic whispered. "She doesn't return our calls for five days, and then her car is found, abandoned?"

"We can't give up hope," said Sara. "How will Jeanine feel if she finds out we all gave up on her?"

"Her phone is disconnected," said Sharrice.

We turned to look at her. She was standing behind the couch, phone in her hand. My heart made a dizzying descent down to my feet.

"Can someone else try it?" said Sharrice. "Maybe it's my phone?"

I pressed her number, hands shaking, and lifted my phone to my ear. A woman's voice said, "The number you have dialed has been disconnected or is no longer in service. Please check the number and try again."

"That's not good," said Vic. "Oh, that's not good."

"Could it have been stolen?" said Ashlee. "Or she broke it?"

The woman's voice repeated, again and again, that the number I was dialing was not in service. But it was *her* number. I didn't need to check it. I had countless text messages from this number. It was hers.

"I could use a little of that hope right about now," said Vic.

AT THAT POINT, I was extremely drunk.

Ashlee sat me down on the floor in front of the couch and started brushing the hairspray out of my hair. She spoke in an even, hypnotic voice. She said she was reading a book of female-centered myths and legends from across cultures.

"The last one I read," she said, "was about the Sumerian goddess Inanna, the queen of heaven and the living realm. One day she hears a call to go visit her sister, who is queen of the underworld. Her sister, Ereshkigal, had lost her husband and was in deep mourning. Inanna goes down to visit her, passing through seven doorways on the way. At each one, she's stripped of another protective garment. When she reaches her sister, she's completely laid bare. And her sister fixes a death stare on her and kills her and hangs her corpse on hooks."

"God, Ashlee."

"No, it ends well. Inanna's servant, her handmaiden, sends for help and gets Inanna out. Inanna forgives her sister—she understood she was crazy from grieving her husband's death. You know—the normal stuff people put each other through."

I wasn't sure why we were talking about this, but it seemed terribly important. It was the only thing that had managed to capture my mind's attention and hold it since Stanley's call.

"I think the reason I like those stories," continued Ashlee, pulling my hair back, "is because I like the idea that you can get as far from life as humanly possible and still come back. Some people go through experiences that send them through thresholds not everyone can cross. It happens all the time, in ways we can't see."

Sara, who was quite religious and sitting within earshot, stood up abruptly to go get another bottle of wine.

Ashlee slid off the couch to join me on the floor. She whispered, "Grief is one of the things that will send you through a doorway. It'll send you through doorway after doorway, stripping you down each time, until you feel like you've been hung up on meat hooks. Some people never know what it's like to walk through those rooms. But you've been there."

Been there? Had I been there? When my father died, I was asleep in my childhood bed. I was woken up by the phone ringing. I heard my mom banging around in her bedroom, then clattering down the stairs. I padded down the hall to watch her from the upstairs landing.

"Go back to bed," Mom said. She was yanking on her coat below me in the foyer. "I have to run an errand."

I checked on Laura, who was fast asleep, clutching her stuffed buffalo, then lay in my own bed in the dark, waiting for the sound of my mom returning home. It never came.

When I went downstairs in the morning, I found her sitting on the couch still wearing her trench and pumps, her little gold cross glinting against her collarbone. She was red-eyed and stiff. She looked like her limbs would crack if she tried to move them. I had the impression she'd been sitting like that for half the night. She drew a breath, and her jaw popped. She said, "Your father isn't coming home."

I wasn't sure what she meant, so I waited for her to indicate how I was supposed to react. She seemed to be looking straight through me. The two of us were completely still, me looking at her, her looking through me, until Laura clomped down the stairs and my mother said, "Your father has died." Laura began to scream and the spell broke. Mom jumped up and ran to Laura. Laura cried and wailed. I stood there, waiting to understand. I remembered nothing else from that day—not if we left the house or what I ate, nothing. I wondered what I would remember from this day, the day Jeanine's car was found.

Ashlee put her arms around me.

"But the thing is," she said, "no matter how deep you get, you can't get to where they are and bring them back. You have to come back on your own, to the world of the living."

"Let's do a ceremony for Jeanine," interrupted Vic. "Like, an offering. To Inanna."

"Not in my house!" said Sara, but it was too late. The girls gathered around Ashlee, our resident shaman.

"Let's ask her for help to make the truth come out," said Ashlee. "Peace for Jeanine, and peace for us."

"How do we ask her?" said Sophie.

"We're making this up as we go," Ashlee said. "It's not a science."

"Let's burn something," said Sharrice.

Sara moaned and clutched her hair.

Ashlee agreed that this was a productive way to express ourselves. "It has to be something that matters," she said.

I grabbed my uniform bag, and the girls rose in a collective lunge to tear it out of my hands.

Ashlee took out a hundred-dollar bill—her payment for our appearance at the Mighty Taco. She held it over the lit candle on the glass coffee table and it went up in flames.

All the girls leapt up and started screaming.

Ashlee said, "Give us safe passage through this dark time, give us protection, give us knowledge, give us strength. And whoever brought us all to this terrible place, let them know justice."

In a sort of trance, I reached into my pocket and pulled out my hundred and added it to the flame that had consumed Ashlee's.

Sharrice threw hers in, too. The other girls shrieked and batted at the smoke as the edges of the bills burned neon green, then blue, then burst up in yellow. I stared at the flames, which seemed huge and blinding in the dim room. The smoke alarm went off, and the girls howled even louder.

Greg came tearing downstairs, asking, "What's wrong? What in God's holy name?" and was met with the sight of six girls, crying out, swiping at the ashes on the coffee table, fanning the screaming smoke alarm, so full of fear and shock and anger that we'd gone fully mad from it.

Part 2

Chapter 11

I WOKE TO THE smell of eggs frying in my kitchen.

"We're going full fat today," Sharrice announced, flicking a chunk of butter into the pan.

She tossed me a bottle of Advil. I sat on a stool across the counter and rested my forehead against the Formica. I remembered, vaguely, Sharrice helping me get into a cab. I remembered her pulling my shoes off as she put me into bed. And I remembered crying, crying and crying while she pulled the covers up to my shoulders.

Sharrice set a plate of eggs and toast in front of me.

"I'm sorry I got so drunk," I croaked.

"You weren't the one who started a Satanic ritual in the living room," she assured me. "I can't believe I burned my money. I felt *possessed.*"

She sat on the stool next to me and put a hand on my knee.

"You did everything you could, Virginia. This was not your fault. It was a failure of management. Of the whole system."

The smell of the eggs made my stomach flip with ravenous hunger and nausea. I picked up a triangle of toast and poked at my eggs.

"I meant what I said about us needing security," said Sharrice. "We bring in so much money for the organization, through sponsorships, and the basket auction, and the annual fundraiser—that's thousands of dollars we raise every year that could be spent on us, for training or safety measures. But we don't see any of it—in fact, *we're* paying the squad more money, just to participate. Take the six hundred dollars they charge us for our uniforms—and that's *if* you get the sizing right the first time and don't have to buy another—and add that to what we pay for all the calendars we have to buy, and the money we had to drop on our winter gear this year, *and* the money that's deducted from our pay for infractions. I mean, how much are they making off us per year? I knew what it cost to participate when I signed up, like everyone else, but jeez—I'd still like to know where it *goes*? It's unbelievable what we're supposed to do and figure out on our own with all this cash flying around."

She seemed to realize she'd gone into lawyer mode, and smiled apologetically. Sharrice was studying for the LSAT while she worked for the DA's office. She was businesslike and irrepressible, a steamroller with a beaming smile. I could tell she'd been reciting this argument to herself all morning, refining and sharpening it, and I wished I could summon her outrage. She was going to make a great lawyer.

"I know this must be hard," she said. "Especially after losing your sister. How long has it been?"

"What do you mean?" I said. "How long since what?"

"Since . . . since she died."

"My sister's not dead," I stammered. "She lives in Ohio. We just—we don't talk very much."

Sharrice clapped a hand to her mouth. "Oh my God, I—I thought she died. I'm so sorry. I feel so stupid."

I began to apologize too, and we traded *I'm sorry*s back and forth. I didn't know what I was apologizing for. Perhaps for her discomfort, for misleading her—though I hadn't misled her, not intentionally. I didn't talk about Laura because she was no one else's business. And even if I did, there was nothing anyone could say in response, except *I'm sorry* or *That's so hard*. Like if you were to say, *My friend died*. What happens next? You watch the other person's eyes get that funny glaze as their mind races to say the thing that will make them the good friend who said the good thing. What have you communicated then? Nothing. You haven't said anything. Here was one more thing about which nothing could be said.

"I'm glad I was wrong, at least." Sharrice laughed uncomfortably. "I really am sorry."

"It's okay. It doesn't matter," I said.

Her face showed clearly that she thought it mattered very much.

AFTER BREAKFAST, SHARRICE tried to get me to go out with her—on a walk, to a coffee shop—but I was afraid I'd start crying or screaming or acting crazy. As soon as I closed the door behind her, waving as she blew me a kiss, I wished she were with me again.

There was no word from Stanley. I worried that the police were causing him problems, but there was nothing to be done about that now. I tried the last number Landon had used to call me and got an automated voicemail. I looked for my laptop, which had ended up in the bedroom under my nightstand. I sat at the edge of my bed and opened it, and the screen lit up to reveal my Facebook page, with Facebook Messenger pulled up. It took me a few moments to process what I was seeing: a string of messages I had apparently sent to Jason Morley after blacking out the night before.

What's wrong Jason you don't want to be friends???

Answer me you piece of shit

I know you saw her before she disappeared.

Did you take her to the same places you took Laura? Did you do the same things to her? Is it your fault she's gone? Did you give her too much?

If you hurt her I'll kill you.

I slammed the laptop shut and put it back on the floor, struggling to catch my breath.

There, on the screen, was evidence of my unchecked rage. I remembered the last time I'd spewed that rage at Jason. He had come to visit Laura in Columbus, had slept with her on my couch. Laura had not yet dropped out of OSU, though she was going to class less and less. I spent the weekend stepping and tiptoeing around them as they sprawled out in my living room, ate my food, watched my TV. Then I came home from my job at the gym to find Laura splayed across the couch, nodding out. She tried to lift herself up on her elbows, then fell back into the cushions, laughing. She tried to talk, but it came out as gibberish. She tried to lift herself and fell again. Jason was standing there, beer bottle in hand, contemptuous of my concern. "She's fine," he said. "She just woke up. Will you chill out?"

I had responded by bending to pick up a beer bottle from the pile of empties they'd left all over the floor. I remembered the feel of the bottle's neck in my hand, the sour smell of old beer filling the room. I had hurled the bottle at his head, then another and another, so they smashed and shattered against the mantelpiece on the opposite wall.

Laura had wailed after he'd fled. "Why did you do that? Why? Why can't I have anyone except you?"

The broken glass had taken me a full day to clean up, and for weeks afterward, I kept finding tiny spears of glass embedded in the soles of my feet. The memory left me weak with humiliation. I had screamed and screamed at Jason as though that would save my sister, or me, and now I was screaming at him again, because I was too helpless to do anything else.

I kicked my laptop under the nightstand and leapt up from the bed. The cat, I realized—I hadn't seen the cat all morning. I went banging around the apartment, yanking the fridge from its alcove to check behind it, tearing the pillows off the couch, clawing through the clothes in my closet, terrified that Sharrice, distracted by my messy, drunken state the night before, had let him out. Finally, I found him under the bed, eyes aglow and tail flicking, and almost cried with relief.

"Here, cat," I said, reaching under the bed. "Come here."

He tensed up but didn't fight me as I hooked my hand under his front legs and pulled him across the rug. I held him to my chest, feeling his quivering ribs under my fingers, feeling sorry for myself and for him. His warmth and the rubbery solidity of his bones were sweet and pitiable in my hands, and I was nearly lulled into a state of calm. Then he stiffened and shot out of my hands.

It took me a moment to realize my chest was burning. In the bathroom mirror I saw two long, deep claw marks running from my collarbone to my sternum. The most exposed part of my body, the part of my chest I was supposed to prop up and thrust forward, erupted with pinpricks of blood that swelled to glistening, spilling rivulets.

I stumbled out from the bathroom, a roaring in my ears. I strode through the apartment, chest stinging, and found the cat's tail sticking out from behind the fridge. I grabbed a coffee mug from the sink and hurled it at the tail. It hit the refrigerator door and shattered, ceramic shards spilling across the floor.

The tail disappeared. "Fuck!" I screamed. "Fuck! Fuck, *fuck!*" My lungs burned, ragged with rage. I took another glass and threw it and screamed as it, too, shattered.

I stood there panting, my anger a surging, churning, white-capped river. I cast around inwardly for its object: the cat, then the broken glass, then myself for throwing the glass. I pulled on my hair and paced my hallway, hating myself, repelled by the mess I'd made. I caught sight of myself in the hall mirror: a crazed woman, my eyes dark and red. I must have swiped my hand across the scratches above my breast—my whole chest was smeared with blood.

I PATCHED MYSELF up with Band-Aids and left the apartment.

There were plenty of main arteries I could take north to Tonawanda, but I chose Delaware Ave because it was familiar. This was the route my dad had taken when he drove to check on Stanley's storage units in North Tonawanda. I snaked through the park, passed Paladino's Steakhouse, then shot north through Kenmore, the neighborhood where I grew up, with its perfect grid of clean lawns, its 1950s suburban homes. Just a block over was my high school, if I cared to go look at it, and after that, in the northeast pocket of Kenmore, my childhood home. I pictured all the stages of my life in Buffalo lined up in a row and collapsed, like an accordion, time compressed and compacted. I passed under the Youngmann Expressway, then hopped on Main Street to pass through the city of Tonawanda, with its dense rows of brick businesses peppered with signs that looked preserved in the midcentury. I crossed the creek onto River Road, traversing older, industrial North Tonawanda, and reached the left-hand turn for Tonawanda Island.

I had not even known there was an island here. There was no reason to drive to this little river outpost twenty minutes north of the city. Jeanine would have no business coming here.

Across the bridge was an intersection, and I guessed left.

A short drive down the unlined road brought me to a parking lot, a nautical-themed restaurant, and a slip rental. Along the banks of the river was a row of docks lined with boats. I circled the parking lot before continuing on to the opposite end of the island. Scattered on either side of the potholed pavement were ugly, long warehouses, ragged chain-link fences, sparse gray trees, and gravelly parking lots. There were no residences on the island, just the restaurant and slip rental, and the boat docks, and the outposts of unknown businesses and their storage facilities. The road beneath my wheels turned to gravel, diminishing the farther I drove, until all that remained were two tire ruts fringed by mysterious empty swaths of pavement, then grass.

Up ahead, where the road dead-ended alongside the banks of the river, I saw a tow truck, yellow lights flashing, pulling Jeanine's maroon Mazda out of a dense scrabble of shrubbery along the river.

"Hey!" I slammed on the brakes and threw my car into park. "Stop!"

I jumped out of the car, waving my hands. The tow-truck driver, a dark-haired man of forty or so with a trucker cap over his eyes, turned off the ignition in the truck. He opened the door but did not get out.

"Ma'am?" said the driver.

"I know whose car that is," I said, standing breathless in the grass. "That's my best friend's car."

"You can tell your best friend to call the number right here on the truck." He tapped the door. "They'll tell her where to pick it up."

"The girl whose car this is is missing. This could be a crime scene."

The driver tilted his head and sighed. "Kids mess with cars all the time."

"Kids?"

"I get calls like this all the time. Kids find a car, and they try to light it on fire. That's what kids do," he explained. "If your friend files a report and calls her insurance company, she'll be fine."

"Insurance?" I couldn't believe the words being used. *Kids? Insurance?*

"Take a picture of the number," he encouraged me. "I've got to do my job. Can you get out of the way?"

I backed away and watched as the tow truck hauled the Mazda, in which I'd spent so many hours driving around Buffalo, out of the grip of the dense bushes. The state of the car shocked me into silence. The back end was blackened, clouds of carbon staining the maroon paint. Clearly someone had lit it on fire. The back window was spider-webbed with cracks, the taillights smashed.

The tow truck disappeared, bumping down the gravel road with Jeanine's busted and blackened car behind. I began to kick through the sparse brown grass, as if I might find something Stanley had missed. Rusted steel beams of indeterminate use sat abandoned, leaves sprouting up around them. I forced my way into the brush surrounding the banks of the river. Prickly branches tore at my leggings as I pushed a path to the edge of the water.

The river, bloated from the early fall rain, lapped at the grassy banks. Across the river was Grand Island, the big mass that split the Niagara, and on the other side of that was Canada. Silvery stripes of current broke through the smooth stretches of water. There I squatted, elbows on my knees. The possibilities of what might have happened in Jeanine's car began to separate themselves from the logjam in my mind and unfurl.

She and Landon had gotten into a fight and he had killed her, maybe accidentally, then driven her to this island, shoved her car into the brush, and tossed her body in the river. Jason had driven her out here to get high, and she'd died of an overdose in the driver's seat. Bobby had murdered her in a jealous rage and dumped her car in the only spot he could think of. I imagined Jeanine in her car, a dark male presence beside her, her head bobbing, her mouth filling with foam, before she went limp in the driver's seat. I imagined an attacker lunging at her across the gearshift while she screamed and kicked, scratching his face, sticking her thumbs into his eyes as he tore at her clothes. I imagined the male figure removing the fuel cap and shoving a towel or T-shirt into the filler line and lighting it aflame, to destroy the evidence of what had transpired.

I imagined this in excruciating detail, crushed under the fruitlessness of my imaginings, knowing I could not prevent anything that had already happened, but unable to stop myself until each fantasy concluded. I imagined her dying in as many ways as I could, praying I was protecting her from each fate by enduring it on her behalf.

Then I brushed off my legs, dried my eyes, and straightened up to fight my way back to my car.

MY PHONE BUZZED with a call as I swung back across the bridge exiting Tonawanda Island. Laura. I didn't pick up. I couldn't quite remember how we'd left things when we'd talked on Wednesday night, and I couldn't bring myself to speak to her even had I wanted to.

She texted: **My clinic hours got canceled next week, so it's the perfect time for me to drive up to Buffalo. I'm thinking Monday?**

I pulled into the lot of the Niagara Street Tops.

The last time Laura and I were in a room together was two days after her relapse at my birthday party. I'd told her I needed a break, and I was going to Buffalo for a while, and the Grandview apartment was all hers for the next sixty days, until the end of the lease. "I don't understand—are you *moving*?" she'd kept saying. "Are you not coming back to Columbus?"

"I don't know," I'd said, because I didn't.

She'd watched me pack, looking resigned, like something she'd dreaded was finally coming to pass. I had not confronted her about her admission that she had hurt herself to get out of dance. I wasn't sure she even remembered confessing to me.

"You can keep the couch and the bed and the kitchen table and all the dishware except this set," I said, wrapping the last of my bowls in a T-shirt. I was taking only what I could fit in my duffel, my two suitcases, and a few boxes.

"Okay," she said. "Thank you. Let me know where you're staying in Buffalo and I'll send you rent."

I said, "That'd be great," though we both knew she was never going to send me rent.

She watched me roll my suitcases to the door.

"I can keep it under control," she said, desperation edging into her voice. "I know I slipped up the other night, but it's not going to be like it was before. I have a handle on it."

"Okay, Laura."

"I think going from one extreme to the totally sober extreme was too much. I can be somewhere in the middle. We don't have to be so dogmatic about it." She stood at the door as I arranged my bags in the hallway to carry them down the stairs.

"Is this it?" she said. "This isn't one of those moments, is it? Ginny, you're coming back, right? You don't have to leave. It won't be like last time."

Her voice had grown so frightened and small I nearly turned around and dragged my things back inside. But then I remembered that though Laura might have been scared to lose me, she didn't actually want me. I remembered all the times she had pushed me away and locked me out and disappeared with no message about how to find her, forcing me to imagine a thousand different horrific ends. Even before the drugs, even sober, she didn't want the life I was building for us.

"Laura, please don't contact me," I said, "until you're back in a rehab program."

And I hefted my suitcases and left her there.

In the Tops parking lot, I steeled myself and called Laura back. She sounded cheerful when she answered.

"By 'Monday' you mean the day after tomorrow?" I said. "And what do you mean, 'clinic hours'?"

"I'm training to be a massage therapist. I told you."

"Oh—right."

"Anyway, I have the whole week free. The timing is perfect for Mom's birthday. Are you okay with that? If I come?"

She was asking my permission? "She's your mom, too, Laura. You can come whenever you want."

"I know you're busy with the cheerleading stuff, but I'd like to see you."

Cheerleading stuff. A cheerleader at the bottom of a river—was that cheerleading stuff?

"Ginny, you there?" Laura said. "Is that okay?"

"Yeah, we'll . . . it's fine, we'll figure it out."

"Okay." She sounded disappointed. I could tell there was more she wanted to say, but all she added was "I guess I'll see you when I get there."

I hung up.

My head pounded from my hangover, and also from a terrible pressure building at the base of my skull. I already had a last time I'd seen Laura. I now had a last time I'd seen Jeanine. Laura coming to Buffalo meant I would see her again, thus creating a *new* last time I'd seen Laura. Then if she relapsed or disappeared at some future date, I'd have to once again accept that I would never see her again, and the new last time would hunt and haunt me, like all the others. All the last times.

To Laura's credit, she'd followed my instructions after I left her at the top of the stairs in Columbus. She did not contact me. As I finished decorating my new apartment in Buffalo, I heard from my acquaintance at the barre studio that Laura had stopped showing up for her job at the front desk. As I choreographed and practiced my first Jills audition solo, I heard from my old landlord that I wouldn't be getting my security deposit back because a guy matching Gabe's description had broken one of the windows and spilled beer all over the hardwood floors. As I hustled for work at Buffalo gyms, I got a text from the barista at my old coffee place that Laura had come in looking faded, asking for free water, free coffees, before passing out in the bathroom.

I made myself forget her, and mostly managed to—except for the small moments throughout the day when I woke up, or went to sleep, or sat at a traffic light, or waited in line, and wondered if my sister was dead.

I'd had to go on with life as though she were dead, as if I didn't have a sister at all. I never let myself fantasize about seeing her again. But she was coming, coming toward me across a great expanse. The tenuous distance, this limbo we'd held, it felt so permanent now, it seemed impossible that she would ever get here. I had no idea who we would be when the gap closed.

Chapter 12

Pulling into the parking lot behind Paladino's Steakhouse filled me with the sensation of falling backward in time. Here I'd spilled juice and colored with crayons, begged the bartenders to slip me maraschino cherries, made the hostesses watch my latest jazz competition routine. Here I'd gotten my period for the first time, so one of the waitresses had to dig a tampon out of her purse and explain to me how to use it. (*Waitresses,* I thought with wonder. *Waitresses had been my mother.*) The day after I lost my virginity, I'd sat in a booth squeezing my legs to feel the rawness between them. Simply approaching the doors gave me the jittery tingle of having homework due the next day.

It was an hour before opening, so I knocked at the locked front door. I was surprised when Suzanna opened it, and not the weekend hostess or bartender.

"Stanley should be here in a few minutes. Come on in," she said.

I peeked under the collar of my T-shirt to make sure I wasn't bleeding through the Band-Aids, then followed her inside. I half-expected to find the place redecorated in Suzanna's signature minimalist style—but it was, of course, the same restaurant: a little old-fashioned, crammed with dark wood and white tablecloths and plush maroon carpet and cushioned dining seats. No matter whom Stanley dated or married, this place would outlast us all. The entire city could shift and evolve, revitalize and gentrify, turn into a spaceship and blast off into the atmosphere, and Paladino's Steakhouse would still be here, selling thirty-six-ounce T-bones with baked potatoes and béarnaise.

"What will you have?" the bartender asked as I sat down at my usual stool. His face was covered in silver paint, and a cone-shaped silver hat sat on his head. He wore a shiny metallic vest.

"I'll have a smoothie, I guess," I said. I was disoriented, the bartender's appearance yet another thing I could never hope to understand. Suzanna sat down beside me.

"No mangoes," I added as the bartender retreated toward the back. Too many carbs. "Otherwise, you can blend up whatever you've got back there."

"I'm happy to see you getting healthy again," said Suzanna. She waved at the crepe-paper bats I hadn't noticed hanging from the ceiling and the tiny pumpkins arranged among the bottles behind the bar. "Please ignore the Halloween nonsense. It's the annual costume party."

"Oh. That's right." I'd forgotten the date—it was the Saturday before Halloween.

Among the pumpkins behind the bar was a large black-and-white framed photograph of my father. He was mid-laugh, wearing his wire-rimmed glasses. (Laura got his bad eyesight; I had twenty-twenty.) The photo was placed in such a way that people drinking at the bar might ask about it, and give Stanley an opportunity to launch into stories of Dominic Barton. Sitting here with Suzanna, in the presence of my father's image, I felt self-conscious and singled out.

"I heard," said Suzanna. "About the car. Sara said a missing person report was filed. It was too long coming. I blame myself for not filling one out the day she missed the game. I did so many things wrong, and I may never forgive myself."

The bartender set a pinkish smoothie in front of me. Though I hadn't eaten since the eggs Sharrice made me that morning, the sight of it turned my stomach.

"It's my fault," I said. "She wasn't acting right the week before she . . . she disappeared. I should have said something, or intervened, or told you—"

"Virginia, stop. You cannot help people who don't want to be helped, and I'm convinced Jeanine didn't want help, from you or from me. I tried to crack that shell," said Suzanna, her hands turning to fists on the bartop. "I tried to help her figure out what she wanted, who she could be. Turns out I didn't know anything about her. She slipped through all our fingers."

"Her car was all burned up," I said. "Like someone was trying to cover something up."

"Yes," said Suzanna. "I heard."

"Do you think we're looking for a body?" I said.

"I do," she said quietly.

A sludge of the smoothie I'd just sipped shot up my esophagus. I coughed and swallowed.

"Correction," said Suzanna. "I think the *police* are looking for a body. You're not looking for anything. Your attention belongs with the Jills. You are not the only one who lost a teammate. You're going to show up for them and help them navigate this hellish labyrinth of fear and trauma. The best thing to do in a situation like this is get busy and help others."

I watched dumbly, the back of my throat burning, as Suzanna pulled out her phone. She swiped gracefully at the screen to bring up her calendar, her long nails flashing. "I'll pull Carmen off the ribbon cutting at the hospital next week and put you on. She's been getting a big head, and I'd like to take something away from her. And you've got the Timberland store opening after that."

She considered the schedule, finger hovering above the screen.

"If you want, I'll take you off the Junior Jills fundraiser tomorrow so you have a day to adjust."

"No, I want that one," I said. "You're right about keeping busy, and you know I like to support the Junior Jills. I love doing events with the kids. I want to be there. I can handle it."

Suzanna poked at her phone, chewing on the side of her cheek.

She had devoted her life to the improvement and management of Jills. She'd helped Gina get her real estate license and Ashlee register her homemade soaps business. When Vic left her ex-husband with an eighteen-month-old in her arms, Suzanna got her an apartment. She found girls housing and leads on jobs, she convinced them to ditch their current careers. She'd been encouraging me since my first day on the squad to open my own fitness studio, even offering to help me set up an LLC for myself.

Suzanna loved a project. The girls from wealthy backgrounds, the ones who had it all "together," failed to capture her interest. She offered them obligatory attention and praise, but in her heart, she preferred a girl in a scrap. That was why she liked Jeanine, and why she made a project of my development on the squad. But I already had an ally I could turn to: I had Stanley. If I ceased to turn to him, and looked more to Suzanna instead, then I would belong to him a little less. Belonging to Stanley was another piece of ground I refused to cede.

"All right," said Suzanna. "I know you can handle it. I'll see what else I can dig up for you."

She tapped at her screen, before letting her eyes dart to the photo of my dad behind the bar.

"Stanley says you take after him." She nodded at my father.

"No," I said. "That's Laura. I hardly even look like him."

"I don't mean appearances," said Suzanna.

My heart leapt at the thought that Stanley had told Suzanna my dad and I were alike. I was about to ask what she meant when the door opened behind us, letting in a draft of cold air, announcing Stanley's arrival.

"I was going to call you," Stanley said, wrapping me in a hug before planting a kiss on Suzanna's cheek. The restaurant was beginning to rumble to life. The second bartender had arrived and was having the cocktail menu explained to her. The waitresses stood around the host stand, reviewing plans to circulate appetizers.

"I've been at it all day," Stanley said, "following leads on your friend. I need to ask you a few things."

"Stanley, please. Virginia is tired. People will be arriving in no time. We both need to change."

Stanley looked at his watch, loosening the fingers of his leather driving gloves to remove them. "You go change in the back. I'll be right behind you."

Suzanna exhaled but didn't leave. She moved to stand behind my shoulder, almost protectively.

"Landon Maher," Stanley said. "You know him?"

"Yeah. A little."

"Has he been in contact with you? Sent you messages? Asked you to meet him anywhere?"

"Oh—no. I haven't been able to reach him, he's—well, I haven't talked to him in a few days."

"If he contacts you, call me immediately. Do you promise?"

"What do you want with Landon?"

"Kiddo, there are things I can't tell you, but I can tell you this: this Landon is a bad kid. You got drinks with him the other night, where he works—the Foundry? Is that right?"

I nodded, feeling chastened, like I'd been caught sneaking out at night.

"Don't do that again. You shouldn't be associating with these types of people, Virginia." Stanley pointed a finger at me. "Your father would have a fit. You are supposed to have good friends, good people around you. Jills are supposed to be *good people.*" Stanley's voice rose as he spoke, his forehead glistening. "If you don't have the sense to stay away from lowlifes like that, then I'll keep them away from you myself. Understood?"

My neck and chest flushed. I couldn't remember a time when Stanley had ever spoken to me so forcefully. The cat scratches itched, and I clawed at my T-shirt to avoid scratching.

"If your father were here, he'd be in full agreement," Stanley continued. "He'd tell me to ground you, to lock you in your apartment."

"That's enough, Stanley," said Suzanna. "Virginia is an adult woman. If you tell her this Landon person is a bad kid, she'll stay away from him. She's a smart girl and her best friend is missing. There's no need to talk to her like this."

Stanley looked again at his watch, ran his hands through his hair. The tears gathering in my throat made it difficult to breathe. Stanley never spoke to me harshly, and he never disapproved of me. If he found out I'd gone to the Pink Fountain with Landon, I might dissolve into a million particles and disappear. Suzanna put a hand on my shoulder, which only made me feel more like a child.

"Kiddo," said Stanley, softly now. "I never had a chance to promise your father that I would look after you. I have had to make that promise to him after the fact, every day, with my actions."

"She knows, Stanley. There's no question that this comes from a place of love."

"You are my responsibility now. Mine," said Stanley, and I realized he was choked up, too.

"It's not about me," I said. "It's about her—Jeanine. She's the one who got hurt. If Landon hurt her, I have to know. I have to know what happened. Stanley, her car—I saw it. I saw what they did to it. Are you saying Landon did that?"

Stanley softened. He ran the back of a hand down the length of his face.

"How did you know to look for her car on Tonawanda Island?" I begged. "Did she go there with Landon?"

"Okay, kiddo, okay. Here's what I can tell you. I asked my contacts to send me any information about a maroon Mazda or a girl matching Jeanine's description. Thankfully, I have friends in North Tonawanda. One of the officers on duty last night gave me a heads-up about a car fire that was called in, and said I might want to take a look at it. There were no weapons and no blood at the scene. From the police's perspective, the only crime that has taken place is arson. Though with this missing person report, that could get more complicated—there's some argument between the Buffalo police and the North Tonawanda police about who the case belongs to, and it's causing trouble. Anyway, I've got a bird's-eye perspective that the police lack. I'm working to figure out how her car got onto the island and who lit the fire and why. That's where we're at, okay? I'm going to get it sorted out."

"But where does Landon come in?"

"There's a party starting in twenty minutes, and I have to turn into Catwoman," Suzanna said. "You need to go home and rest, Virginia. You're exhausted, and you look it. If you don't get a full eight hours, I don't think I can let you work the fundraiser tomorrow."

"You know I love you," said Stanley. "Let me do what I do. This is my city, and I keep track of what happens in it. I'll handle this Landon kid, I promise."

Suzanna waited while Stanley wrapped me in another hug. I was comforted by the extra squeeze he gave me, an apology for the way he'd spoken. I had a hundred more questions, about what made Landon a bad kid and what Stanley knew that I didn't, but behind his shoulder a butcher-block table was wheeled out from the kitchen, with a heat lamp for the prime rib, and the kitchen staff were unloading stacks of metal trays for the buffet. Suzanna walked me to the door.

Before exiting, I asked, "Is Bobby going to be here tonight?"

"No," said Suzanna. "Go home."

OUTSIDE, I SAW Maria, Lana, and Natalie getting out of Lana's Subaru.

They were wearing their official Jills jackets over skimpy black tops with denim short shorts, a vague attempt at a Halloween costume atop their heads: Natalie wore a witch's hat, Maria wore bunny ears, and Lana had on a policeman's cap.

Lana gasped when she saw me. "Wait—you're not booked for this? Don't tell me you have an appearance today."

"Booked?" I said.

"It's not a Paladino party without Jills," said Maria, her bunny ears trembling above her head. "Have you never done a gig here?

They're a riot. You get to meet, like, city officials. I think the owner of the Sabres is supposed to be here tonight."

"More importantly," Natalie said, lifting a pinkie and tipping her hand in front of her mouth, "Suzanna tends to look the other way if you hit the open bar."

I shouldn't have been surprised to see them. Hundreds of parties had passed through the steakhouse over the years: holiday parties, Super Bowl parties, parties to commemorate the 1993 comeback game against the Oilers, Bobby's sixteenth-birthday party. Growing up, I saw Jills at almost every single one of them. I would yank on my dad's hand, begging him to take me over to talk to them. But in this context—while Jeanine was missing, the busted shell of her car recently dragged out of the underbrush—the thought of Suzanna and Stanley picking out which girls would be most fun at a Halloween party felt . . . gross.

"I haven't had a chance to say sorry yet," Natalie said, reaching for my arm. "I heard about Jeanine's car. God, what a nightmare."

"Yeah, I'm so confused," said Maria. "I don't get it, like, who found the car and what was it doing on Tonawanda Island, like, where even is that? Like, Virginia—can you explain to us what's going on?"

Chapter 13

SHARRICE CALLED ME while I was in front of the mirror in my bedroom, trying desperately to camouflage my cat scratches, which were exposed by my uniform's plunging neckline. I was supposed to have left for the Junior Jills fundraiser twenty minutes ago.

"I know I'm late, I'm sorry," I said, pinning the phone between my shoulder and my ear. "I'm almost out the door."

"It's okay, it's not that. Are you driving? Sitting down?"

"I'm running around like a maniac," I said, darting into the bathroom to rinse the foundation off my hands.

"Well, slow down for a second. I stopped by the DA's office this morning to see if I could scrounge up any files that reference Landon Maher. I didn't find anything, so I called my friend at the county clerk, to ask her to check her files on Monday. And she was like, 'Oh my God, I just filed a warrant for that name this weekend. The judge was called at home and everything.' "

"A *warrant*?"

"A search warrant, to search his home. It has to do with a murder. A man's body was found a week ago, last Saturday."

The phone tumbled to the bath mat. I grabbed at it and pinned it against my ear. Sharrice was saying, "—I don't have the police report, so I don't know the details, but it looks drug related. The murder, I mean."

"Murder? Are you really saying the word *murder*? Is he a suspect?"

"I don't know for sure. If they got a warrant, they either think he did it or he knows something about it. For drug-related stuff, they go after little fish to get intel on bigger fish. He hasn't been charged with anything, and even if he was, he's innocent till proven guilty. But, Virginia . . ." She lowered her voice. "*If* he killed this guy, what else is he capable of?"

I sat down on the toilet lid.

"I hate that I'm telling you this right before an appearance," said Sharrice. "But I couldn't watch you dance and smile all afternoon while I knew this *thing*, you know? Do you want me to help find someone to cover for you?"

"No, I'm okay. I'll be there. What else am I going to do? Sit around my apartment?"

"I know. I feel the same way. But I also feel insane doing a fundraiser."

"Someone tried to light her car on fire, Sharrice. It was all burnt up."

"God, this is horrible." She drew a sharp breath. "Just get here as soon as you can."

I hung up. I was now a half hour late, but I couldn't move. The only thought I could form was that the person in charge of paperwork at the county clerk's office must have made a terrible mistake. If the police, or the Paladinos, or anyone, wanted to question Landon, it ought to be about *Jeanine,* not the murder of a strange man. Maybe the county clerk had mixed up Landon's file with someone else's, and they were now investigating him for the wrong crime.

There was a rushing sound in my head that I was afraid was a panic attack making its way toward me. Then I realized I'd left the sink running. I reached over and turned off the tap.

VIC'S FACE FELL when she saw me. "What on earth—were you mauled?"

My scratches throbbed, like shards of glass had been stuck into my skin.

"Shit, can you see it?" I said.

"See it? You're bleeding!"

I must have sweated the foundation off when sprinting across the parking lot. I'd sped up the 190 like a madman, already in my uniform, which we were absolutely forbidden to wear while driving, and managed to make it to Paladino's Neapolitan Gardens in twelve minutes. Even after all that speeding, I was not early, which meant I was not on time.

"Thank God you're already dressed. We're all set up," Vic said as she led me to the staff closet behind the bar. "We've got the photo backdrop by the bar and all the marketing materials on the tables. The stage looks sturdy. Doors open in twenty. Put your coat and purse here."

I pulled on my boots as she dug a bottle of liquid foundation out of her bag. As she shook it, I saw her nervously appraise my appearance. I had spent so much time trying to cover the scratches I'd failed to fix my busted French manicure or finish curling my hair.

"I'm paler than you, but it'll have to do," said Vic as she got to work on my chest. "Sorry, does that hurt? God Almighty, don't let me get blood on your uniform."

"It's Jeanine's cat," I said weakly.

"Well, keep it away from your boobs from now on!" She bit her lip and assessed her work. "Are you going to be all right? You look like you're going to cry."

"I'm fine," I said. I pulled my face into a smile, cheeks aching. "Do I look okay? I'm fine."

I followed Vic toward the area where we would be performing. I knew the layout of this space by heart. I'd performed here as a Jill for bar mitzvahs and corporate retreats. My senior prom was held in this very room—though I'd spent half the night in the bathroom comforting Laura, who was crying because Jason hadn't shown up like he'd promised. It was spacious and airy, designed to be rented for special events. The creamy textured walls and light wood fixtures evoked a more Mediterranean feel than Paladino's Steakhouse. A wall of floor-to-ceiling windows looked out at the Niagara River, so that guests could admire Canada on the other side, and on the opposite wall, a gleaming black marble bar corralled the vested bartenders. There was a small stage where live music could be played and upon which we would be dancing with four Junior Jills who had learned our routine for the occasion. The tables had been set up with donation envelopes and brochures featuring photos of little girls waving poms, alongside quotes extolling the many ways the Junior Jills changed the lives of young women.

On a normal day, a day when I had not just learned there was a search warrant tying Landon to a drug-related murder, I would have enjoyed an appearance like this. The Junior Jills program was one of my favorite outreach initiatives. I'd been a Junior Jill myself from ages seven to thirteen. It was just a weeklong day camp when I was a kid, but Suzanna had expanded the program enormously during her tenure, to include scholarships and funding for local squads. I knew all four of the girls who were performing with us today, since I helped run the summer camp as a Junior Jills leadership ambassador. My favorite was Olivia, an eleven-year-old with plucky confidence, who was counting steps authoritatively for the other girls.

Suzanna was helping Sharrice and Carmen set up easels with posters of smiling Junior Jills, posing in mid-jump. She looked frazzled. Sharrice caught my eye and started to wave, but then her eyes dipped down to my chest and her face blanched.

Suzanna clapped her hands as Vic and I came even with the stage.

"All right, ladies." She pointed to the girls. "Junior Jills—I want you practicing your high kicks. The rest of you, gather round."

Suzanna began passing out little wicker baskets she'd decorated with Bills colors, which we'd use to accept pledges as the guests came in. Seeing Sharrice, I felt a bit dazed. A man's body had been found—

I struggled to remember exactly what she'd said—had been found last Saturday. Jennifer Speight had seen Landon with Jeanine in the evening on that same Saturday, at Buffalo Underground. It seemed impossible that the two events had anything to do with each other. How could Landon have drunk with me at the Foundry on Tuesday while knowing a man was lying dead?

Suzanna handed me a basket, and her eyes went dark. She scanned me up and down.

"No," she said, taking the basket back.

The other Jills looked at me, then down at their baskets or at the stage.

"Virginia, step to the side, would you please? Junior Jills, huddle up," Suzanna called to the girls.

The Junior Jills hurried into a circle around Suzanna. I took a step back, bumping into the chairs of the nearest table, the scratches on my chest prickling.

"Change of plans," Suzanna said to the girls. "We'll do the same routine, but I want an equal four in front and back. Olivia, you'll come to the front because you're shorter, to make it look even, and Sharrice to the back. Same dance, slightly different positions. We Jills have to make last-minute adjustments like this all the time. Are you ready to step up?"

The Junior Jills agreed bravely, and collected a high five from Suzanna. It was clear that I was the source of the problem, and they stared at me as Suzanna escorted me away.

"Good God, what happened to you?" she said. "Are you hurting yourself?"

"What— No!" I exclaimed. "It's a cat scratch. I can put on more makeup. I've got foundation in my bag."

"I'm not letting you anywhere near that stage in the state you're in. You cannot be seen like this in uniform. It's disrespectful to the *uniform,* Virginia. You want there to be photos out there, of you literally bleeding from the chest?" She brought me to the staff closet to collect my coat and purse. "I'm not trying to embarrass you. I don't want to punish you for grieving. I don't bench girls for losing family members or friends. I'm trying to work with you. If you need time off—"

"No!" I said. "Can I just try—"

"Stop." She put my purse in my hands. "Your only job today is to recuperate. Put antibiotic cream on your chest. Go to the gym. Eat some fruit. Get yourself together while I think about what to do with you." She handed me my coat. "And I'm not even going to mention your goal weight. I'm sure it's on the forefront of your mind."

She directed me to a side door, which deposited me outside the venue far from the main entrance, where the guests would be arriving imminently. I stood a few feet from the dumpsters and loading dock, coat clutched in my hands. I could faintly smell the river to my right on the far end of the lot, slow and wide, chilling the air.

I felt so stupid for wanting to cry. I felt even stupider for having shown up in the first place. But where else was I supposed to go? This was my life. Taking time off meant you couldn't hack it. Vic had been back on the Jills less than a year after giving birth to her kid. Kelsi from Line 1 missed only one week of practice after her mother died. Last year Lana danced with a knee injury until the end of the season, and only then did she get the surgery she needed. You knew how much it took when you signed on. You signed a paper saying you could handle it.

I checked my phone, saw that I had no calls from Stanley or anyone else. I brushed my chest with my fingertips, and they came away streaked with blood and foundation. I wiped them on the inside of my coat pocket and tried to think of what I could do to not be alone, where I could go that wasn't my empty apartment.

And then, because things in life often happen either not at all or in great overwhelming clusters, I heard a voice calling my name.

"Is that Ginny? Ginny Barton?"

I spun around. There, stalking toward me from the staff parking lot, was Bobby Paladino.

"Holy shit," I said. "BJ?"

He came to a halt and stared at me, his brow furrowed in a mix of concern and dismay. At first I thought he was angry that I'd used his childhood nickname—Bobby had been named after his grandfather, so for years he'd gone by BJ to differentiate him from the elder Paladino. Around age thirteen, he announced that he would no longer respond to the nickname, a proclamation Laura and I answered with a chorus of "What's that, BJ? Can't hear you, BJ! BJ, speak up, would you?" until he turned red and stormed off to the kitchen.

Adult Bobby pointed at my chest. I waited for an accusation or a statement of judgment. But what he said was "Did you know you're bleeding all over the place?"

Chapter 14

"I CAN'T GO BACK in there," I said as Bobby steered me toward the venue.

"Suzanna's not sending you away if you're talking to a major Junior Jills donor," he said, pulling open a side door. "Come on, have a drink with me."

Inside, we slunk down a narrow hallway to look out over the banquet room. From this vantage, I could see the stage, partially obscured by a large column, where Suzanna was making her welcome speech to a room now full of seated guests.

I glanced over at Bobby, who was leaning against the wall, watching. Every time I encountered him, I was surprised to see a man and not the doofy kid I once knew. In truth, he'd grown into a good-looking guy, if a little wide-eyed and jumpy. He had his dad's penchant for a well-tailored suit and a sharp haircut, though not the same charisma.

Bobby noticed me studying him, and grinned. This was the first time, I realized, we'd been in each other's presence for more than a moment without Jeanine. His face still held the palimpsest of his teen features, and they leapt forward when he smiled.

"So, Mary," he teased, using the nickname he'd monikered for me around age twelve—first shortening Virginia to Virgin, which then became Virgin Mary, then just Mary. "You look like shit. Is that why you got sent out to sit by the dumpsters?"

"Yeah," I admitted. "I'm not doing so great, to tell you the truth."

"Me neither," he said. "Jeanine?"

The music started, too loud, startling us. The Jills and Junior Jills streamed onto the stage, clapping to the beat of a Black Eyed Peas song, one of the many routine songs that haunted me in my sleep.

Bobby dipped close to my ear. "Let's go to the office. We could use a talk."

He led me down the hallway, past the bathrooms, to a door that said STAFF ONLY. He held it open for me, revealing a small office with white walls, a water cooler, and several filing cabinets, a little jumbled with stacks of paper. By the big wooden desk was a metal folding chair and a wheeled desk chair. Bobby gallantly rolled out the cushioned seat for me. From the bottom drawer of the filing cabinet, he pulled a bottle of gin and a few browned limes.

"Is this your office?" I said.

"Nah, but I know where the manager keeps his stash," he said proudly, arranging the metal chair so we could sit facing each other.

He poured gin into a couple of plastic cups from the water dispenser and handed me one. The muffled music thumped through the closed door, and the tempo told me they'd switched to the second song, our famous "Shout" routine. I swiveled in the desk chair, holding my gin. I felt a bit like I was on a date.

"So—big Junior Jills donor?" I said. "You grew up to be a hero for junior cheerleaders?"

"Every business needs a philanthropic arm."

"Ah, of course. And if you're going to benefit any organization, why not make it your future stepmom's nonprofit?"

"Don't say it," he groaned. "I can't attend any more of my dad's weddings."

"This one might stick, right? Where's your sense of romance?"

"Oh, yeah. Fourth time's the charm."

Bobby's mother lived in New Jersey, I believed, and did not call. The second wife died of breast cancer; the third, who'd lasted only about a year, came along while I was in college, busy with Laura. I did not know what happened to her.

"I remember you being a little Junior Jill back in the day," he said, cutting into a lime with his pocketknife. "Did you get one of those cheer scholarships?"

"No, they weren't doing all that yet. Junior Jills was just a summer cheer camp when I was a kid. Suzanna's the one who expanded it to include all the scholarships and the cheer funding program. I got my dance scholarship on my own."

"And my dad covered the rest."

He dropped a slice of lime in my cup. I shrugged.

"Sorry, that sounded accusatory. I don't resent it. Anymore." He grinned. "You and your sister got to go to a Big Ten school while I barely hacked it at UB."

"It didn't matter where you went. You were going to be successful either way."

"How do you know?"

"Because—you're ruthless," I said.

This was true enough—I had always seen Bobby, striding around Paladino's Steakhouse with his boyish scowl, as a more humorless and ironfisted version of his father. That was why it was fun to tease him: he took it hard. Bobby looked at me wonderingly, then wolfishly, and I realized that calling him ruthless could easily be misconstrued as flirting, especially if you were the sort of man eager to be seen as a killer.

The music stopped, and there was a murmur of applause from beyond the closed door. I took a gulp from my plastic cup.

"I've been trying to reach you, you know," I said.

"Ah, I know. Sorry." His face tightened as he drained his cup. "I'm a busy guy. Can't reply to every little thing. If I'd known how fucked up this whole situation was about to get . . ."

He trailed off and the room grew smaller with sorrow. He'd retreated into that scowling childhood version of himself.

"So, what do you know about this Landon Maher guy?" he said with sudden force. "Did you know Jeanine was stepping out with him?"

"I had no idea, Bobby. I wish I had."

"Right. Cuz you look at some low-life shithead like Maher, and then you look at me. I mean, who would you pick?"

"I don't know what she was doing with Landon. She wasn't talking to me about it." I fiddled with my cup with both hands, unsure what else I should say. What came out was, "I guess he might've killed somebody?"

Bobby looked at me with surprise. "How'd you hear that?"

"My friend works at the DA's office," I admitted.

"Wow." He regarded me with newfound appreciation. "I guess Stanley taught both of us the value of good connections. Okay, yeah—looks like he might've. I'm looking into that, too. I've got my fucking eyes on Maher, all right."

"Do you know the person who died?"

"I'm interested in any murder that goes down in my city, on my turf. Especially if it's committed by some creep hanging around *my* girl."

He drank quickly, emptying his cup. The darkness descended again. I swallowed nervously.

"Bobby, listen, I'm really, really sorry—"

He grabbed the gin bottle, face screwed up in a wince.

"Look, I don't want to get all depressed. I've got this thing covered. And anyway, there's no reason to be sorry, because Jeanine's definitely not dead."

He tipped the gin bottle a little aggressively while refilling my cup. It sloshed over the sides, spattering his shoes.

"It doesn't look good though?" I said, surprised, while he wiped at his shoes with a crumpled napkin he'd fished from the jumble of papers on the desk.

"How could she be dead? There's no body. This Maher's no criminal mastermind. He can't hide a body so good we can't find it—case in point with the body that *did* get found. There was no blood or anything in her car. It wasn't even hid that well. A bunch of teenagers found it."

"Teenagers?" I said, remembering my exchange with the tow-truck driver—kids, he'd said, lit cars on fire all the time. "How do you know that?"

"Security footage from the slip rental on the island. It shows teenagers doing doughnuts in the parking lot, then heading in that direction. The timing lines up. Now," said Bobby, "is it possible these kids were hired, to destroy evidence? Maybe so. Again, these are not masterminds we're working with."

"But what was her car doing on the island in the first place?"

"I'm trying to figure that out. The security footage only goes back forty-eight hours. But I'll sort it out. Some little shit tried to take something away from me, and he's going to get crushed for it. End of story. You want to party?" he said suddenly.

"Huh?" I gripped my cup and gin dribbled over the sides.

"I seriously can't talk about this Landon guy. I get so mad I freak out. Do you want to party? I don't even know what you're into these days. Jills party, don't they? The fun ones. Want to have fun?"

Just like that, he grew animated, and the room brightened again. The swing surprised me; he could fill a room much larger than this one, it was clear, with the force of his moods.

"I . . . guess," I said as he pulled a little baggie of white powder and a short soda straw from his inside jacket pocket.

Bobby, excited now, scanned the wooden desk for a usable surface, then selected a framed photograph of a blond woman hugging two little boys. He tapped out a line of white powder on the glass and snorted it in one fluid motion.

When he raised his head, he had a dopey look on his face.

"I'm really glad to see you," he said.

His eyes watered as if he might cry, whether from the coke or Jeanine or both.

"It's good to see you, too," I said, surprised again by the switch in emotion. I reached over and gave his hand a squeeze of acknowledgment.

He grinned dumbly at me.

"After all this time, I finally got your attention," he said.

"My attention?"

"Yeah. All those pranks I used to pull? You know that was me trying to get your attention."

This was so patently ridiculous I laughed.

"Come on, you were like the first girl I ever noticed!" he said. "The original girl. I remember going away to sleepaway camp for a week and when I came back—*bam*. You had tits. It's the kind of thing a kid notices. And of course you were too good to talk to me, you were in your own little club with your sister. I always felt like I *could* talk to you, if you would let me. Because you understand my world. You know what it's like to have a father who—well, you get it." He tapped out another line on the glass of the picture frame. "After your dad died, I really didn't know what to say to you. I feel bad about that."

I was at a loss as to how to respond to this. He straightened out the line and presented it to me.

"Is it just coke?" I said.

"Don't you trust me? I wouldn't give you less than the best."

I took the straw and leaned over.

"You sure you trust me?" he said. "I'm kidding. It really is just coke. It's great coke."

It burned in my sinuses, though not unpleasantly—it did in fact seem to be high-quality. My heart began to race and I held on to the edge of the desk. I could handle one line of coke. It would fade in no time. And—God, it *was* good. It seemed extremely funny, all of a sudden, that I was doing drugs with BJ Paladino.

He was watching me eagerly. "These events—you have to get fucked up to get through them, right? Do you ever party with Jeanine?"

"Sometimes," I said, wondering if he meant Jills events, or life events.

"Does she talk about me?"

A flash of a memory: Jeanine and me, sitting on the floor of her apartment draining a bottle of pinot grigio, Jeanine rolling her eyes, saying, "He just wants someone to step on his balls." I rubbed my nose furiously, as though to erase the image and any chance of me describing it out loud.

"She's very private about certain things," I said.

"But she must talk to you, right? You two are best friends. You go on trips together. Like, you'll do Atlantic City or whatever."

I laughed as a means to expend the incredible energy radiating out from my collarbone. "I have never been to Atlantic City with Jeanine."

"What? Oh. Maybe you didn't go on that trip? No, you must have. It was for your birthday. Over the summer. Right?"

"She wasn't in town for my birthday," I said. "We celebrated it the weekend after. In Buffalo."

"What about Vegas? You went a couple of months ago with a group of Jills, right? Am I crazy?"

He leaned over to take another line. I pressed the heels of my hands into my closed lids to help me think. A small group of Jills *did* go to Vegas in September, during a bye week, but it was a cliquey group of ambassadors, girls Jeanine and I barely spoke to except to exchange pleasantries at practice. Then I remembered something.

"We didn't go to Vegas," I said. "That weekend of the Vegas trip—she told me she was with you. In Miami. I remember."

Bobby straightened, his brow furrowed in concentration. Then he stood up, the picture frame, dusty with powder, gripped in his hand. I realized what I was implying: that Jeanine had lied to Bobby, had pretended to be in Vegas with the Jills to avoid him. But then—if she'd lied to Bobby, she'd lied to *me*. I'd thought she was with *him*.

Bobby was turning in circles in the little office, nostrils flaring. I looked for somewhere safe to rest my gaze, but everything it landed on—the pattern on the carpet, the mess of papers on the desk, the lime wedges that had ended up on the floor—contained too much information. The coke was *really* strong. I either had too much oxygen in my body or too little. No matter how much air I sucked in, there didn't seem to be enough.

"She was lying?" he said. "Where was she going? To see that shithead? Landon?"

"Do you have some water?" I said.

"Is there something wrong with me? What else do I have to do? You have absolutely no idea how much I've done for this girl. I talk to her, I depend on her. And she goes and lies to me, and sneaks off? What did I do wrong? Wait—did *you* talk to her about me?"

"What would I tell her?" I said.

"Did you, like, make fun of me?"

"I didn't make fun of you," I said, panicky. "I had no comment on the whole situation. Honestly, it was too weird for me to think about you and her together."

His manner shifted again. "Really? Why?" He was excited.

"Because you're—you," I said.

"And you're you," he said. He knelt in front of me. There was powder on the tip of his nose. "You think that's why Jeanine didn't want us all to get together? Because she could sense something would have happened?"

"Um . . ."

"Can I be honest with you?"

"I don't know," I said blearily.

"I'm a bad motherfucker, Virginia."

I had to turn a laugh into a cough.

"For real," said Bobby. "I'm a bigger deal than my dad at this point. People shouldn't underestimate me. They underestimate me, and they regret it."

"I can see that," I stammered.

"I'm, like, losing my mind. I am so fucked up that this girl is missing. I don't like losing things that I care about. I'm not a loser. But this *guy* tried to take something from me, and I don't know what to do. I don't know what to do!"

He started laughing, a high-pitched trill that sounded exactly like his laugh as a twelve-year-old. It was either the sheer adrenaline from the coke or the dissonance of that sound coming out of a grown man's mouth—I couldn't help it, I started laughing, too. It felt so good—my arms, which I'd been afraid were going to float off my body, began to feel normal again. The relief made me laugh harder.

"I don't know what we're doing here!" I said.

"You don't?" he said. "You really don't?"

Then his face was on mine. We were kissing. Bobby, the boy who'd chucked olives at me while I tried to do my homework, was kissing me. My disgust dropped down through my torso and into my hips, turning my pelvis into rubber. It felt almost like desire.

He pulled back, staring into my face to see if I'd liked being kissed. I wasn't sure that I had—but I also hadn't not liked it. My heart was still pounding, and it felt a little like excitement. He looked so hopeful I felt generous, and leaned forward to kiss him back. In a whirl, he hoisted me out of the chair by my hips and pushed me up against the desk.

We were kissing ravenously now, his tongue in my mouth. The escalation startled me. He gripped the crotch of my skirt's built-in liner with two fingers and I gasped—I couldn't wear panties under my Jills uniform, because of lines, and his knuckles pressed against the thin barrier of my tights. I was practically naked in my uniform, and the skin of my cleavage, still smarting from the cat scratches, brushed against his button-down shirt—that did turn me on a little, the feeling of my bare skin pressed against his fully clothed body. I'd never had sex with a man Jeanine had had sex with before. What would it feel like? Would it bring me closer to her? The only thing I felt certain of was that I was wanted, badly, by someone from my youth, who'd felt like he couldn't have me before. I was dizzy with the grope of his hands on my hips and stomach, with his hot breath against my neck.

Quite abruptly, Bobby pulled away.

"Hang on," he said, hand down his pants. "I need a sec."

"Oh—" I stared openly, the coke funneling all my attention toward his hand working away under the fabric of his dress pants. "Yeah, no problem."

"You looking at me is kind of intense, can you, like, turn around?"

"Um—sure."

"Maybe shimmy your skirt down. If you don't mind. And maybe you could, like—slap me? In the balls?"

"Well—do you want me to turn around, or to—"

"Forget it, forget it. Turn around. Like that. Yeah."

Facing the desk, I tugged at my skirt. My eyes were wide and dry, and no amount of blinking relaxed them. "Yeah, come on. There we go," Bobby said behind me. I leaned over the desk, praying no one would walk in, suddenly very eager for this experience to be over. What was I doing in a—frigid, I was now noticing—office, leaning over a desk, my skirt pulled down, while Bobby, Bobby *Junior,* tried to get a hard-on? I kept my eyes on the papers splayed on the desk beneath me, trying to block out Bobby's grunting and self-encouragement. If we kept going, he'd be number fourteen, and that would be—good? My eyes hurt. My scratches hurt.

Then, from among the mess of papers, a name jumped out at me in bold letterhead emblazoned across the top of an invoice: EUSA.

The sound of Bobby behind me disappeared. EUSA was Jason Morley's company. I pushed the surrounding papers out of the way so I could read the invoice: it detailed several orders shipped from Italy—olive oil by the gallon, prosciutto, fancy olives in buckets. The final line item read simply, "Labor & services." The total was $8,000.

I straightened and spun around, and collided with Bobby, who had closed the gap between us, his pants pooled at his feet. There, gripped in his hand, was his eager, straining pink cock. I thought: *There is nothing I want touching me less in the entire fucking world.*

With his free hand he grabbed the back of my neck, pulling me in for another kiss, but I appeared to be screaming.

"No!" I said. "No, no, no!"

He stumbled backward—I'd pushed him—still holding his cock in his hand. I tripped on the metal chair and caught my balance on the filing cabinet.

"What the fuck?" he said, his hair flattened, face screwed up in dismay. He looked offended, like a boy. Like a small boy. "What's wrong? Why are you acting like this?"

"I can't do that, I can't do that," I chanted as I yanked my skirt up, stumbling past him toward the door. "I cannot do that with you."

I caught the knob and spilled out into the hallway, shaking. My boots clicked on the hardwood floor as I careened toward the banquet room, now loud with voices and the clatter of silverware. At the end of the hallway I was met by a wave of noise and color—the guests were seated, their plated lunches half-eaten, Jills circling the tables for photos. I turned and fled back down the hallway.

Before I could reach the side door to exit the building, I heard Bobby's footsteps behind me.

"Hey," he said, catching my arm. "Come back. What's wrong?"

"Jeanine!" I said.

I must have shouted it, because he shushed me.

"Hey, everything's chill. It's all good. Here, sit down."

I slid down the wall to a crouch on the floor. My heart was pounding like crazy. Oh God, I was mortified, my eyes stinging.

But Bobby was patting my hair, my shoulders, saying, "You don't party that often, do you? Don't worry, I've got you. It's all chill. It's okay."

He crouched down and wrapped his arms around me. What was happening?

"Being with Jeanine made me forget," he said into my ear, "that most cheerleaders are good girls. Hold on." He jumped up. My lipstick was all over his face. "I'll get you water. Just sit there. Don't go. I don't want you to leave yet."

In a flash he was gone, his expensive shoes clopping down the hallway toward the dining area. I didn't trust myself to move until my heart rate slowed down. I gripped my knees and waited. She had been lying. She'd lied about where she was going. She had used me to cover for Bobby, and vice versa. She'd secretly met up with her ex-boyfriend, and she'd visited a seedy motel with Jason Morley, who apparently supplied the Paladinos with imported goods. If I thought about it hard enough, if I could focus and not be distracted, it would start to add up.

I lifted my head. My artificially speeding heartbeat seemed to have dismantled my internal clock; I had no idea if five minutes or thirty had passed. I got gingerly to my feet and clicked down the hall to peek around the corner and take stock of the event. The lunch service was wrapping up, waitstaff darting around to bus tables.

Guests stood in clusters, networking, and some were beginning to line up in front of the photo backdrop. I scanned the room and saw Bobby standing at the bar, about ten feet away, staring up at the sleek flat-screen TV installed above the rows of liquor bottles, his mouth hanging open.

The TV was muted. A newscaster in a red coat stood in front of the wide glass windows of a downtown apartment building. Then the screen cut to a picture of Jeanine, her headshot from the Jills website. The heading at the bottom of the screen read: "JILLS CHEERLEADER DECLARED MISSING."

I joined Bobby at the bar, not caring who saw me. We stood, rumpled and smeared, side by side.

"Shit," he said. "This is not what I wanted."

A clatter beneath the TV; Suzanna had rushed behind the bar and was gesturing to the flummoxed bartender, pointing at the screen, swiping a flattened palm across her collarbone, begging him to turn it off.

Chapter 15

My commands during my dance aerobics classes the next day were loud and desperate. In the mirror, we looked like we were wrestling with invisible assailants. "Reach up—and pound down! Reach up! And slam it down!" I shouted at them. The pop music drenching the room sounded menacingly upbeat. We lay on the floor and kicked our legs into the air. "If you have nothing left, get mad!" I yelled. "Get pissed off!" Afterward, my regular attendees lingered to ask me about Jeanine. "Do you have updates on that poor girl who disappeared? Was she targeted because she's a cheerleader? You all must be so scared. Are you scared?" They thought I had privileged information, and they wanted it.

After my last class, I lay down on my mat until my endorphins drained and left my body an empty shell. I stayed there on the floor, feeling grimy and ill, and watched the ceiling fan spin. Jeanine's disappearance had made the *Buffalo News* site that morning, under the headline "BILLS CHEERLEADER MISSING." Suzanna had sent an email out to all the Jills with a boilerplate response we were instructed to use if we were approached by the press. It read: "We draw strength and hope from our community. We are grateful to the Bills fans and the Buffalo community for their support and love, and thankful for the incredible hard work of our uniformed officers."

The message was so short it hardly seemed worth typing up and sending out. Jeanine's name wasn't even mentioned.

My phone vibrated next to me and I groaned. If it wasn't the Jills sending another spate of heart emojis, it was probably Bobby. He had been texting me nonstop since the night before, wanting to know what I was doing, what I was up to today, what I was thinking, saying things like, **Hey, I don't want you to feel weird about anything going on between us.**

And **Jeanine's not here and I need someone around me who understands.**

And **We got a little rowdy in that office, didn't we? Wish we could've done that way back in high school ;)**

I indulged him with **Thank you**, and **Oh, wow**, and **That's sweet**, wanting to keep the line of communication open. I remembered Jeanine dashing off texts to him unthinkingly, tossing her phone to the side. Had he texted her this often? Had he been this needy, this desperate for attention?

I wiped the sweat off my palms, steeled myself, and grabbed my phone.

So I'll probably get in around 4 today. Dinner and cake with mom?

Laura. It was Monday, and though I'd nearly convinced myself it wasn't going to happen, she was coming. I typed, backspaced, typed. I was so tired of coming up with things to say. I forced myself to tap out, **Sounds good!** Then I turned off my phone, to give myself an excuse not to text back anyone else today.

The next instructor came in and flicked on the lights.

"Uh," she said, standing over me. "Are you okay?"

FIRST I SWUNG by the Foundry, which was populated only by committed alcoholics at that hour of the day. Landon was, unsurprisingly, not among them.

Next I drove out to the little yellow house where I'd picked him up the day we went to the Pink Fountain. I slowed to a stop in front of the house and saw the platinum blonde who'd peered through the curtains that day crossing the lawn, a full garbage bag in hand. I located her name in my memory: Brittany, Landon had said.

Our eyes met as she dropped the bag inside one of the blue bins on the curb. She stopped short at the sight of me.

I got out of the car, waved uncertainly. "Are you Brittany?"

She eyed me up and down. "Where do I know you from?"

"You may have seen me with Landon? I came and picked him up this past Thursday."

Brittany let the lid of the bin fall shut. She sported heavy makeup and a Monroe piercing near her red lips. Under her coat she was wearing a shiny black halter top that exposed her midriff and black pants that appeared to have been vacuum-sealed to her legs.

"You're friends with Landon then?" She propped her fists on her hips. "So do you know what the hell is going on?"

"Maybe we can talk inside?"

Brittany's house smelled like weed and bong water and incense. In her living room was a coffee table scattered with stems and seeds, a wooden-framed futon, and a massive beanbag chair. Purple leopard-print and skull-and-crossbones patterns featured prominently. She pulled a couple of bottles from the fridge and nudged a nonalcoholic beer into my hand.

"Hope this is okay," she said. "I can't drink the real stuff anymore."

She turned on the lava lamp and collapsed onto the futon, O'Doul's in hand. I perched on the edge of the coffee table, unwilling to face the indignities of the beanbag chair. She lit an elegant pipe with movable parts, and on the inhalation asked, "So are you and Landon fucking?"

I laughed nervously, shaking my head.

"Oh God, no. He's way too obsessed with Jeanine."

She gazed out at me from under her eyelids, her lips tightened in sympathy. I'd hoped to imply that she and I were united in our frustrations—rejected and treated irresponsibly by the hopelessly Jeanine-addled Landon—and form a tenuous sort of unity between us.

"Well, he's not here, obviously," she said. "You may have noticed his ex-girlfriend is in the paper?"

"I know. I shouldn't even want to talk to him, really. He's got this messed-up relationship with Jeanine, and now she's missing, and I don't know what I'm supposed to think. But . . . I'm worried about him, and I want to know how he is. It's a problem of mine," I added. "Getting led on by guys whose interests are clearly elsewhere."

She nodded sagely and handed me the pipe. I tried to mimic the process she'd used to take a hit.

"Landon and I keep it open," she said. "We've been friends for a couple years. I did two tattoos for him. So I know the score with him and Jeanine. As long as she's in the picture, he can't make up his mind about what he wants. Guys will endlessly put off making a commitment, because they don't actually want to decide anything. They act like kids, so then we act like their mom, which is what they want, but they don't want to admit that it's what they want, so they hate us to avoid hating themselves." She shrugged. "You can't win. So it's better not to get attached."

I coughed as I exhaled, saying, "You're so fucking right." I was exaggerating how impressed I was by this speech, but not by all that much.

"But whatever the fuck happened between him and Jeanine is too complicated for me. I'm not taking care of his shit. He can go crawling to someone else."

She said this forcefully, as though trying to convince herself. She put a hand out for the pipe, and I gave it back to her.

"You know that afternoon you drove off with Landon is the last time I saw him?" she said. "He never came home after that."

"And you haven't heard from him since?"

"Nope." She exhaled, jutted her chin toward me. "What about you?"

"Not a word."

She nodded for a while, staring into the center of the coffee table. Then she gulped the last of her O'Doul's and stood up. "I'm going to take a bath," she said. "You can stay."

I HEARD THE splash of the tub turning on as I walked uncertainly from the kitchen to the living room, peeking into the closets and pantry.

I chugged the rest of my fake beer and sat on the futon. The light through the windows dimmed as the sun sank below the tree line. Brittany's street didn't particularly concern me in the daylight, but the local truism was to stay away from any neighborhood east of Main after dark. There were a string of maxims about what streets you were supposed to avoid, and I tried to remember them as the weed took effect, pulling me slowly downward through a hole at the base of my brain, like an elevator going underground. No streets named after states, or after fruits, and no numbered streets. Brittany's street didn't meet any of the latter criteria. I worried briefly about my car parked on the curb outside, and the weed chased the worry away.

I thought of all the rundown houses that Laura had passed through, like the one she shared with two other girls in Columbus her junior year, the drywall reeking of years of smoke, couch cushions gritty with dropped leaves or powder, fridge empty except for beer and tipped mustard containers. And the peeling stuccoed one-story off Cleveland Ave where her dealer boyfriend Gabe had lived, which I'd never been inside but would drive past whenever she dodged my calls, to see if her car was there. I thought about how I'd known from the first time Laura mentioned him that Gabe was going to take over her life, but I'd had no such instinct about Landon. *You could never be sure if a house was safe or not,* I thought dully. Nobody was ever worried about the right thing.

The water shut off and Brittany called out, "Come keep me company. Bring me another near beer."

I sat on the closed toilet seat and handed her a bottle. She'd arranged the purple shower curtain so it obscured her lower half, though she was mostly concealed under a layer of bubbles. Her hair was pulled up in a bandanna to keep it dry. She'd kept her makeup on and it had started to run, turning her into a smudged and beautiful doll. As she reached for the bottle I saw she'd been wearing a vicious push-up bra, the red marks under her breasts inflamed by the heat of the water. The pipe was sitting on the edge of the tub—I guessed she never went anywhere without it.

"I was coloring a huge chest piece today," she said. "Leaning over people for hours will kill your spine." She blew smoke out of the corner of her mouth, then handed me the pipe. "Do you work in an office? You could be one of those 1960s secretaries. Or a flight attendant."

"I'm a fitness instructor." I opened my fleece to reveal my gym clothes from my morning classes.

"Oh God," she said. "Are you another cheerleader? Landon is so fucking predictable."

"I started on the Jills the year after Jeanine."

"No offense, because it's totally fine. But you're kind of basic for Landon. Kind of straight."

"Well, I agree," I said.

"But you're hot. Like you were made in a factory. They just put in the code for hot girl."

There was no point in assuring Brittany that she was hot. It was like saying "Good try" to the kid who keeps missing the Wiffle ball. This was doubly annoying because Brittany was very obviously hot. How *did* Landon find himself dating so many attractive girls?

"At the end of the day, maybe the movies are right," she sighed. "They all want to fuck a cheerleader."

"I always thought they wanted a sexy pinup girl," I said, raising my eyebrows at her pointedly.

"Whatever they want, Landon is getting more than his fair share."

"We didn't hook up that day. When I picked him up," I said.

"All right." She folded her hands atop her breasts and waited for me to tell her what did happen.

I told her an abridged version of our visit to the Pink Fountain, leaving out Danny's and Jason's names. Brittany knew the motel's reputation, and that Landon used to go there.

"Hm." She made little mountains out of the bubbles, frowning. She'd been chewing her nails while I spoke, leaving a chip of purple nail polish on her chapped lips, the lipstick worn off. "That sorta makes sense."

"What does?"

"Jeanine at the Pink Fountain."

"Why does that makes sense?"

She kept her eyes focused downward, on the water. There was a silence, made comfortable by the buzz of weed and the steaminess of the room. I began peeling the label off my O'Doul's, leaving space for her to decide to keep talking.

"I think she and Landon, like, bought drugs together," she said.

A wet, transparent piece of peeled label hung between the bottle and my fingers like lace. I had an image of Brittany as a large rock I was pushing slowly up a hill, taking care not to move too quickly, lest it fall backward on me.

"No shit?"

"Yeah," she said, pushing the bubbles around on the top of the water. A little time slid past us. Thanks to the weed I wasn't sure how long.

"So . . . what drugs?" I said.

She abandoned her work with the bubbles. "You didn't come here to shake me down, did you?"

"Who, me?" I said. "I'm just a cheerleader."

She gave me a smile under her half-closed eyes. The bath and the weed had melted her.

"And I'm just the girlfriend," she said. "The cheerleader and the girlfriend. A couple of dumb blondes."

She pulled the plug on the drain.

BRITTANY HANDED ME the pipe while she padded around the living room in her bathrobe, lighting incense. I took a shallow hit and waited for it to kick in. Already I felt like I had been encased inside a pillar of slightly hardened air. Six inches away from my skin was another boundary, my aura maybe. Maybe Laura was on to something with this energy business, I thought.

Brittany took the pipe back while we sat together on the futon. She had become pliant and energized in the bath. Her bare feet stuck out below the robe, toes painted black.

"Are you, like, a customer?" she asked.

It took me a second to understand what she was asking.

"No," I said.

"Oh, so you're just with him for his personality?"

She grinned hugely, like this was a hilarious joke. I smiled back, relieved.

"I had to ask," she said. "I wouldn't peg you for a junkie, but you can't always tell. Nice kids do it. You know Landon used to do it, right?"

"You mean heroin?" I said. She winced at my directness, and bopped a shoulder in a vague motion of assent. "But he hasn't sold that for years. He swore it off, both him and Jeanine."

"Well." She let her gaze go slack and jiggled her foot up and down. "You can make a lot of money."

Anxiety spiked in my chest, then spread in a prickling river down my arms. That Landon had survived his years of dealing and using heroin and come out the other side clean was at the core of my affection for him. I had looked straight in his eyes at the Foundry and seen a person I liked.

"Landon is not all that ambitious," said Brittany. "But like everyone else, he has dreams of a big break. Like how I dream of getting my work featured on a documentary, or on *LA Ink*. You probably have dreams, too. Maybe dancing for real? Like on tour for Madonna?"

I squeezed my eyes shut. "Sure," I said. "I have dreams."

"I wanted Landon to get a big break, too. But you have to be careful what you wish for. It comes with risks. I try not to know about it. It's better not to know."

The room tunneled and expanded. I regretted the third hit, though without it, I doubted we would have gotten to where we were now.

"He got a big break?" I said.

She let her head bob slowly up and down.

"He got a break," I repeated, opting for statements, like I already knew. Like it was no big deal to talk about it with me. She kept bobbing her head.

"He said it was going to turn things around for us," she said. "He told me it was good shit. I said, I guess you know what you're doing. I'm not too worried about him using it anymore, I guess. I was more worried that he'd have trouble getting rid of it. Or that he'd be stepping on somebody's toes. I told you, I try not to know too much about it. For a couple days it seemed like everything was fine, but then he started acting nervous, staying over here every night, I think to avoid being found at home. Then he goes off with you and never comes back. And all of a sudden I have people knocking on my door, asking about him."

"Who?"

She raised the pipe to her lips, then went cross-eyed as she watched the lighter flare up.

"A big, tall guy," she said, throat tight. "Scary as shit."

A name rose up, almost unbidden, from the depths of my recent memory.

"Antweiler?" I said.

She coughed, smoke pouring out of her mouth. "How'd you know?"

I couldn't believe I'd gotten the name right. For a moment I thought that by smoking from the same device, Brittany and I had become inextricably linked, and we would be forced to think the same thoughts for all eternity.

"Landon mentioned him," I stammered as I dispelled this line of thought. "He said to watch out for a guy named Antweiler."

"Whoever the fuck he was, he was standing right here in my living room. He could've killed me if he wanted to."

"Sounds scary," I whispered. I did not like thinking of a man employed by Stanley scaring a girl alone in her house. Perhaps Antweiler had gone rogue, I thought with muddled hope.

"You can fucking bet it was. Because . . . Okay, listen. I shouldn't say, but—well, someone should know."

She stood up and retreated into the kitchen. There was a wooden creak of a cabinet door opening, and she came back in unzipping a black camera bag. Inside was a thick roll of bills, held together with a rubber band.

"I gave this Antweiler guy six grand of what Landon earned from the stash he came home with. There's two grand in here I managed to squirrel away, and another thousand Landon already spent. But this guy, he was talking like there was a lot more. He kept saying, 'Where's the rest, where's the rest.' Finally I told him Landon took it with him when he left, to get him off my back. But there *wasn't* more. This guy was convinced there was a lot more money, but there wasn't."

We leaned close together and stared down at the rolled bundle of bills, crammed in the bag like a porn stash. I was surprised by the overwhelming urge to remove it and slip it inside my purse.

"The point is, Landon's not stupid about this stuff," said Brittany. "He's not dumb enough to sell product he's not supposed to, in places he's not supposed to. But *she* might be."

She stopped, red eyes boring into me like, *Get it?*

"Maybe she fucked up and got him in trouble," she said. "*She's* the one going to the Pink Fountain, right? Maybe she got sloppy. Got greedy and sold to the wrong person, or to a rival. You know what I mean?"

She zipped up the camera bag and went back to the kitchen to store it, while I sat there weighing a million pounds on her futon, trying to make sense of what she was implying. I thought of Antweiler taking six grand of this girl's money, regardless of where it came from, and felt a little sick.

As Brittany arranged herself back on the futon, I blurted out, "Someone is dead."

I couldn't find my way toward a less blunt phrasing. But she nodded, unfazed.

"Someone kind of high up, I think," she murmured. "A distributor. That's what I gather from rumors around town, at least. I think that's why everyone's making such a big deal about the money. A bigger deal than it should be."

Hearing her link these two unlinkable events—the death of a stranger and the disappearance of Jeanine—stunned me a little.

"My theory?" Brittany went on. "Jeanine and Landon got their hands on these drugs, and she did something stupid with them. Then this distributor went after them—someone higher up on the food chain who was pissed. It was their lives or his. It was self-defense. And now the whole thing is blown out of proportion, and Landon had to go on the run."

Brittany sank back into the futon beside me. She packed the pipe again. Time was continually renewing itself. We were in a new universe at each moment.

"But you don't know for sure that they bought drugs together," I said.

"All I know is suddenly he had a big-ass block of heroin, and it showed up the day after he was out all night with her."

She passed the pipe to me, and I sat there with it dumbly. Taking a hit was an impossible task.

"I wonder where he's hiding," she said softly. "I'd like to know how he's doing. He must be so scared."

There was a question I wanted to ask her, but it was far away. It took me a while to reach it. "You don't sound . . . the way you talk, it doesn't sound like you think Landon killed Jeanine."

"Do I think he did it . . . or do I think he *could*?" She paused, staring down at the table, as if stumped by her own question. The red in her eyes made it impossible to gauge her emotional state. "If he got pissed because she'd put him in a bad situation, if it was between his life and hers . . . then maybe he could do it. But it would only be because he was scared. Not out of malice. And I think if he did hurt her, it would fuck him up forever."

THERE WAS NO way I could drive in the state I was in. Brittany put a frozen pizza in the oven. We ate it and streamed *Survivor* on her laptop. I scraped off the cheese and ate it, leaving the empty carbs in a pile on my plate. Brittany squinted at my crust carcasses and rolled her eyes.

"What a life," she mumbled.

While the tinny music of the reality show played from the speakers, I tried to make sense of what I'd just been told. The facts drifted around in wisps before settling into a sort of order. Jeanine and Landon had spent the night hanging out at the Foundry on a Tuesday. The drugs, I gathered, probably showed up sometime between that Tuesday and Saturday, when they were seen together at Buffalo Underground, and the dead man's body was found. Had Jeanine and Landon been making plans to cover up their connection to the death? But Jeanine had no connection to the death, other than Brittany's speculation. Had Landon murdered Jeanine because she knew he'd killed the man? And at what point was her car driven to Tonawanda Island? I pictured Jeanine forced to drive out to the dead end of the gravel road, cornered by Landon—Landon desperate, Landon afraid, Landon made crazy by the chance to make money.

Brittany kept glancing over at me. The cartoonish soundtrack of the reality show swelled, deepening the quiet of the house. I wondered dimly if I'd be high forever. I wondered if there would be a knock at the door.

When Brittany leaned forward to start the next episode, I gasped.

"Shit," she said. "You scared me, weirdo."

I leapt up from the couch, trying to locate my position in time, on that long thread of minutes strung between morning and when my sister was scheduled to arrive in Buffalo. I checked my phone. I was due at my mother's house for dinner. I was already ten minutes late.

"Hey," Brittany called as I ran out the door. "You'll keep your mouth shut, right?"

Chapter 16

ON THE DRIVE to Mom's, fearing cops, I vacillated between staring too long at the rearview mirror and tracking the needle on the speedometer, before a surge of panic would send my eyes leaping back to the road. To get to my mom's, I took almost the same route I used to drive to Jills practice several times a week. She lived in a condo in West Seneca, about twenty minutes south, her exit just a few miles north of Orchard Park. According to the clock on the dashboard, it took me about that long to get there, but it might have taken an hour for all I could tell. I felt like I was passing through a tunnel, leaving Brittany's little yellow house a million miles away, in another universe.

I parked on the street outside the condo and started down the walkway toward the door, praying that by the time I reached it, I'd miraculously be done with being high.

The condo was townhouse-style, stacked vertically among the other identical little condos with their white siding and black shutters. She'd found this place soon after Laura left for college, saying she couldn't stand being left alone in our childhood home. West Seneca was nondescript, and affordable enough—it wasn't tony like Clarence or East Aurora—but I sometimes wondered how much it cost to live here, and what Mom's finances were like now, and if I was supposed to be concerned about them.

The air smelled like burnt leaves. On the front door, which I appeared to have reached, was an orange-and-black wreath for Halloween. It was almost November. Time was passing. Every day took me further and further away from . . . took me further from—I felt very panicky all of a sudden. Had I rung the doorbell yet? I couldn't remember, so I pressed it again.

Laura answered. She answered the door and there she was.

My first thought was that she was pretty, so pretty, standing there under the porch light with her sweet round face and the beautiful blue lanterns she had for eyes. She had them rimmed with heavy eyeliner, and she also wore a nose ring, on the nose she got from our dad. My sister—there was my sister, alive and whole, in our mother's condo in Buffalo.

"Hi, Gin," she said.

Her smile was helpless and uncluttered. My face was . . . I didn't know what. Its muscles had turned into pillows. Who knew what it was doing.

"I didn't bring anything," I said. "I'm not prepared."

"Okay," she said uncertainly. Then she met my eyes, which were dry as rocks in their sockets, and her face split with shock and delight. She clapped her hand over her mouth.

"What?" Mom appeared. "What's funny?"

"Nothing!" said Laura.

Mom leaned in to give me a kiss. She was pretty, thin, angular. Growing up, everyone said Laura took after our father. She had Dad's assertive nose and square jaw, an almost masculine face she'd never been comfortable with growing up but today might earn her the description of "striking." I, however, was a mini version of our mom. I had her small upturned nose and large eyes (features that kept me forever in the realm of "cute"), and also her personality—a worrier, uptight, swinging wildly from bossy and invasive to wounded and withdrawn.

Mom said, "Honey, you're an hour— Well, it doesn't matter. You're here. Doesn't Laura look well? She looks so good."

"I had to come from the gym," I explained. Dear God, my mouth was dry.

"You work too much. She works too much," Mom said to Laura. "The Jills have her running around to every corner of the city twelve months of the year. Look—" She pointed into her office, to the left of the front door. She'd hung up the Jills calendar, turned to the month of May. "I keep it turned to your picture. I don't really need to see the other girls posing. You don't mind that I keep it out of the way. People might think they've walked into a garage."

What people? I wanted to ask. Mom didn't have visitors. But she'd already retreated to the kitchen, while Laura moseyed over to inspect my picture.

"Nice boobs," she said.

"It's makeup." I exhaled. "You can make them look bigger with makeup." How long had I been here? Was it time to go yet?

"Well, you did a bang-up job."

Laura saw I was suffering and smiled pityingly.

"Hey. We'll get through this. It's just dinner. You know"—she pinched her thumb and index finger together and brought them to her lips—"you might've brought some to share."

I didn't appreciate this joke, but Laura was on her way to the dining room before I could address it. The table was set; they'd been waiting. I tamped down a surge of guilt before it could twist into panic. I flashed back to Christmas break my freshman year of college, coming home to find Laura still dropped out of dance, letting Mom pour splashes of vodka into her soda, wiling away the afternoon before Jason Morley picked her up for yet another party. All the work I'd done to keep Laura busy and out of the house, undone. It was the two of them against me.

I slowly sat down at the table. All I had to do was keep my consciousness gathered in a normal, calm pocket of my brain long enough for the weed to leave my system, and everything would be fine. There were things I had to remember. Like how Landon had gotten a bunch of heroin, maybe with Jeanine. This fact floated around and I grasped at it, as though it were possible for me to forget. I'd have to find a way to talk to him, before Bobby, or Stanley, or this Antweiler person did. I was the one who needed to know. I was the one who loved her best.

"Did you want to eat, sweetheart?" said Mom.

I looked down. Beef stew! This I could work with; avoid the potatoes. Laura and Mom were talking, pleasantly it seemed, while I focused on the incredible texture of the carrots.

"Honey, did you hear me?" said Mom. "Laura asked about your cheerleading."

"Where do I start?" I said through my cotton mouth. For some reason this struck me as an incredibly funny response. I bit my lip to keep from laughing. "Laura doesn't want to hear about my cheerleading."

"That's not true," said Laura.

"You should see what they make her wear," said Mom, tipping Ketel One from the bottle into her glass. "I never really understood the whole dancing thing you girls did, with the ribbons and the sparkles, but I at least appreciated the athletic elements. The NFL takes all that stuff out."

"It's very athletic," I said. I was watching her glass: Mom's technique was to fill a bulbous wine glass to the top with ice, then pour in vodka until it hit the rim. The ice made it so she could fit in only a shot's worth of vodka, she claimed. This was not how space and physics worked, but there was no point in arguing. She'd keep refilling with vodka, letting the ice melt as she went, leaving room for more and more vodka with each pour. Once all the ice was gone, she'd again fill it with ice to the brim, and start the process over. Her glass was still mostly ice, which I hoped meant she was on her first round of the cycle.

"You should come see what we do," I said. "I get comped tickets every home game. All the other girls' families come."

Laura lowered her spoon in surprise. "Have you never been to a game?" she asked Mom. "The stadium's what? Ten minutes from here?"

"I don't like to be around all the rowdy fans, yelling who knows what. Your father took you to them, not me. I don't need to see—" She waved her glass, seeming to search for what it was that she did not need to see, then gave up.

"Come on, Mom, go to a game," said Laura as she got up for seconds. "What the hell?"

"I know what they do at the games," Mom muttered. "I don't need to look at it."

She drank deeply while I used the back of my spoon to mash the potatoes in my bowl. Once the swinging door to the kitchen closed behind Laura, Mom leaned forward and whispered, "Ginny, this is our opening. We need to get her back in Buffalo. Help me talk to her. She listens to you. She does what you say."

"No, she doesn't."

"She can live with me till she finds a job. Tell her I said that. It's because of you that she moved away in the first place. You can get her to move back."

I went right on mashing the potatoes. It was perfectly clear that my mother blamed me for taking Laura away from her, to Ohio, where she completely lost control of her life. She certainly didn't blame herself, for letting Laura get hooked on painkillers and snort heroin with Jason Morley right under her goddamn nose, or for failing to notice when Laura lost weight and her grades dropped. As far as Mom was concerned, I'd taken Laura away and then had the gall to return to Buffalo without her, and I couldn't even claim that it had all been worth it because all I'd become upon moving back home was a cheerleader. An image arose, unbidden, of me picking up my fork and stabbing it into my own forearm, and for a heart-stopping moment I was afraid I would do it.

"I caught up with Stanley the other day," I said loudly.

I stopped Mom dead with that one, which was what I'd intended, but I immediately felt bad about it.

"What's new with Stanley?" said Laura as she sat back down with a refilled bowl. "I miss that guy. He still calls me every Sunday, and he always sends me birthday money."

"Well, he's dating the Jills director now."

I'd intended to divert the conversation from cheerleading, but this was the only update I could think of. Mom let out a "Ha!" that sounded like a bark as she poured more Ketel One. "Of course he is. What's her name? Christy? Kelly? Bunny? You'll notice I took care not to give you girls cheerleader names. No *y* or *ie* at the end. I wanted my daughters to have real names."

"Her name is Suzanna. It's a normal name."

Mom set down the bottle. "Not Suzanna Spencer?"

"Yeah. You know Suzanna?"

Mom stood up. Her vodka sloshed. She left the room.

I sat there, stunned. Laura winced theatrically and poked at her stew.

"Yikes," she said. "What was that about?"

"I don't know. I have no idea how Mom even knows Suzanna's name."

"Did she cheer for the Jills?"

"In the nineties. For, like, eight years."

"Ah." Laura arched her eyebrows.

"What?"

"I don't know, exactly. Mom has said a few things to me over the years implying . . . well, I think it's possible Dad might have had an affair."

The room tunneled.

"An affair, you mean—Suzanna and *Dad*?"

"I don't know who he had it with. It's possible there was more than one. But—" Laura waved in the direction of the kitchen. "Well, look how she reacted. I think we can safely bet there was a cheerleader involved."

"When did Mom say this to you?" I gasped.

"Oh God, ages ago, when I was still home after you left for college. It seems plausible, when you think about it. I mean, Stanley and Dad's lifestyle was pretty wild when we were kids. He was never home."

"He was home," I said, though in truth, most of my memories of Dad were set at Paladino's Steakhouse or in the car.

"It bothered Mom, all those women around Dad, at the games and Paladino's parties. She said she didn't want to see you in the same position."

"What *position*?"

Laura shrugged, a retreat. We sat in silence for a moment, Laura shifting the remnants of her stew with her spoon. Finally she said, "I'll go check on her."

Left alone at the table, I heard the murmur of them whispering in the kitchen. Talking about *our father,* apparently, and *my* cheerleading, and secret fears and suspicions Mom harbored but didn't trust me with. All at once I was eight years old, at a party at Paladino's or in the Dugout Suite, Jills towering over me, with their beautiful white boots and their legs a mile long, their hair big and backlit by the sun, white teeth smiling, smiling, smiling, the most beautiful women in the world. They were sexless, they were perfect, they were untouchable. I would have met Suzanna at one of these occasions, as a little girl. Suzanna and I had discussed this—she remembered meeting me, perhaps signing an autograph for me, but I could not distinguish her in my memory from the other treelike blondes I'd gaped at, openmouthed. And there was Dad, laughing in the background. Dad in the Dugout Suite, Dad in the back office of the restaurant, surrounded by women, and among these women, a young Suzanna. Suzanna at a Paladino's party, Suzanna sent up to the stadium box, where men were waiting.

Time expanded and flattened. My mind struggled to eradicate images of Suzanna cozied up to my father. Finally its attention landed on Laura's glass. I picked it up and sniffed, then sipped. Just water.

LAURA EMERGED FROM the kitchen, her face aglow from the lit candles on the cake in her hands. Mom followed behind, a freshly iced glass in her hand.

"Cake!" said Mom with forced cheer. "Is it time for cake?"

All the wild emotions of the day were sucked down into a single point of guilt and terror in my navel. I'd forgotten my mother's birthday. That's why we were here. It was the whole point of Laura coming to Buffalo. The cake was from the bakery we'd always ordered from when we were children: chocolate with hazelnut icing, twelve candles pressed into the silky top. "No need to be precise about the number," Mom said. Laura turned out the lights, and the hollows of our faces darkened and danced in the candlelight. Mom conducted with her index fingers while we sang "Happy Birthday."

"Mom," I said once the candles were out. "I didn't bring a gift. I'm so sorry. I had to come straight from work."

Laura started pulling the candles out of the cake, eyebrows raised.

"Don't you think on it for one more second," Mom said, reaching over to grip my forearm. "All I want for my birthday is both my girls home. Both my girls in Buffalo. That's what I want."

"Well, we're right here," Laura said.

"You could look into jobs while you're home. To explore."

"Mom, I told you," said Laura as she deposited a slice of cake on Mom's plate. "I have a great community in Columbus. I have a support system with NA. I'm not ready to disrupt my life."

"You could stay with me while you get on your feet. Buffalo's changing. They're putting all kinds of money into the city. Even Ginny's decided it's good enough for her after she rejected it for school."

"That's not why—" I said.

"I'm not here because I want to move back," Laura interrupted firmly. "I'm here to acknowledge the impact my addiction has had on my family and the early experiences that made me who I am."

There it was again, that mode of speech that sounded like recitation. It didn't sound at all like Laura.

"I thought you were here for Mom's birthday," I said.

"Obviously, there's a lot we three don't talk about," said Laura. "We don't talk about Dad dying, and we don't talk about him being in the mob, and we don't talk about how those experiences affected us. We haven't even talked about me being sober. I know me not drinking with you is not what you're used to, Mom. We could talk about that."

"What's there to say? I don't care whether you drink. You can do what you want," Mom said.

"But can we at least acknowledge how you lean on me to lighten the mood for you? And that that probably influences how you feel about me living in another state?"

"I don't lean on you," said Mom. "Alcohol has never been a problem. Why are we talking about alcohol?"

"Laura," I said. I was exhausted, and still fighting off the image of Suzanna striding across the Dugout Suite, toward my father. "Cut it out. We didn't agree to be part of your steps."

"Is this the steps?" asked Mom.

"Things need to change for all three of us to have a relationship," Laura insisted. "We need to speak the truth to each other. Like, how Dad died. Dropping dead from a heart attack at his age—that's not normal. You said yourself, Mom, he was out constantly. He had problems, his own demons. That stuff gets passed down. It's called generational trauma. Drug abuse runs in families."

"Dad wasn't doing drugs! What drugs do you think Dad was doing?" I said.

"Are you kidding?" said Laura.

"It was the stress of that job," Mom said. "His fingerprints all over the money, the money."

"It wasn't just stress." Laura was getting upset. "He was forty-eight years old. He shouldn't have died that young. I want to talk honestly about who he was and the choices he made, so I can understand where I come from. I want to engage with reality. That's the only way to experience real healing."

The person who would rather try to *break her own ankle* than tell me the truth about how she felt now wanted to engage with reality? Who'd lied about school, about whether she was passing classes, about the jobs she had and the training programs she was in and the boys she absolutely wasn't seeing, and the drugs that—for *real* this time!—she definitely wasn't doing: *now* she was ready to engage with reality, and we were expected to fall in line? We had to talk about reality on her terms? What about my terms? What about my life?

"You don't get to change how Dad died to suit your stupid recovery narrative, Laura," I said. "I have the same dad. Why aren't I on drugs?"

"Ginny, don't yell at her," Mom protested.

"I'm not yelling," I said. All the air particles around us seemed to have stopped moving, forming a hard shell around us, trapping us inside. "This is bullshit. If you want to make up bogus stories about our family to impress your little NA club so they'll all gather around and clap for you, do it in Ohio. I'm not playing along. Forget it."

Laura put her fork down.

"It would be great if we didn't stomp all over the thing that saved my life," she said.

"You're always too hard on her," Mom said to me. "You push and push, and you never let her relax. She was so stressed out in high school trying to keep up with you."

"Okay, so *I* gave Laura generational trauma. Perfect. There's another excuse you can give your NA friends."

"Is there another way you'd prefer for me to stay sober?" Laura said. "I want to be sure I'm doing it in a way you would approve of."

"We're just so glad you're better," said Mom. "Virginia. Isn't it wonderful that Laura is better?"

LAURA AND I stood awkwardly in the carpeted finished basement, where Mom had shooed us after the cake. We were aware that we had been banished here to make up. Mom had set up a sofa bed down there for Laura's visit, placing a patterned bedspread on the pullout and a vinyl tree in the corner in an attempt to brighten things up. We could hear her upstairs washing dishes in the kitchen, full of enough vodka to sing Carole King loudly out of tune.

Laura sat on the edge of the sofa bed, playing with the threads of the afghan blanket.

"What do you get," she said, "when you put a cheerleader, a junkie, and an alcoholic agoraphobe together in a room?"

She gave me a smile that begged for a smile in return. I tried to give her one.

"Tough night to be high," she offered.

"It was sort of an accident," I said.

"You don't have to explain to me about smoking weed to cope with Mom. Frankly, I like it. It's a refreshing change of pace."

She went on playing with the blanket, looking hopefully at me. I didn't know what to say. There was nowhere to sit except next to her on the sofa bed, so I gripped my elbows and remained standing.

"I didn't mean for the conversation to go that way," said Laura. "I have to remember I'm not in a meeting, where everyone is ready to lay their trauma on the table. I'm sorry I upset you about Dad."

"It's my fault," I said, which was what I always said when Laura was worried I was upset, to keep her from being upset about me being upset, so no one would be upset.

"No, it's okay. I pushed too hard, and it wasn't cool." She buried her fingers in the afghan. "Mom really gets to me. The denial, the delusion. I knew it would be hard to try to talk to her sober, but I didn't know how hard."

"You should ask Stanley if you want to hear stories about Dad. He tells them all the time."

"I already know Stanley's stories about Dad. I know his version." She crossed her arms. "Dad would come home late, when we were little, remember? He'd come home late, and he'd stumble around. He and Mom would argue. It was noisy. You'd pretend to be asleep, but I know you weren't. You heard it, too."

"Lots of people's dads work late."

"No one's ever told us a straight story about how he died."

"We know how he died. It was a heart attack. He got in the car, leaving work, and his heart gave out."

I didn't want to argue. I understood that Laura was on some "journey," probably devised by her NA group, to explain why she wanted to spend every minute of her life obliterated out of her mind.

But I resented her using our family, our *father,* as an out. Dad had loved a party and a table full of wine bottles at dinner. It wasn't the same thing.

Laura was looking at me, bereft.

"You look really miserable. And tired. Is it because I'm here? Is being around me just, like, too painful for you?"

"No! No, Laura, no. I'm sorry."

"I can go back to Columbus earlier, if this is too hard. Maybe we're not ready for this."

I rubbed my eyes, tired of explaining myself. I sat on the bed next to her. "I'm not acting like this because of you."

"Then what's wrong? Please. We can talk about it."

She waited, cross-legged on the sofa bed, desperate for me to speak. How could I speak one word to her about my friendship with Jeanine, about Jason Morley and the Pink Fountain, about blocks of heroin, about a missing girl?

"Go ahead," she said. "You can say it."

But who else could I talk to, who could I trust?

"My best friend bought a bunch of heroin and then went missing," I said, the words coming out in a rush.

Laura's face went blank with shock. Our mom flicked the lights at the top of the stairs, startling us.

"Oh," she said. "I just love seeing the two of you together."

Chapter 17

"Did you see anyone outside?" said Suzanna when I arrived in her office thirty minutes before practice. "Any press trucks? Reporters? Ray?"

"No," I said. "All empty."

Suzanna stood from behind her desk and peeked out the window that looked over the practice space, to check that no one had followed me inside.

"Ray knows he's not allowed at practice," I said.

"He seems to have forgotten, because he tried to intercept me as I walked to the door. You didn't see his car in the lot?"

"I don't think so."

"That's one less thing at least. Anyway, have a seat."

I sat across from her desk. Suzanna had requested I arrive at practice a half hour earlier than usual. To redeem myself for my appearance at the Junior Jills fundraiser, I'd spent the whole afternoon putting myself back together: more than $300 went on my credit card to fix my nails, hair, and eyebrows and get a spray tan. I wore a halter top to cover my cat scratches.

The problem was that I couldn't look at Suzanna without thinking about her with my father. Half of me wanted to believe that my mom had simply been mistaken, that she'd been unfairly paranoid about my dad gently flirting with cheerleaders he had no real interest in. The other half wondered, fitfully, what kinds of events Suzanna had been hired to do during her days as a Jill, and if my dad or Stanley had arranged these appearances unofficially, under the table. What did Suzanna know of the Paladinos that I, as a daughter, niece, or whatever I was to Stanley, didn't? What, for that matter, did Jeanine know?

The phone on Suzanna's desk rang. She stacked her hands on the desk and let her forehead fall briefly onto them, in a show of exhaustion.

"Reporters. They keep calling. I can't pick up because I don't want them to figure out our practice hours and start showing up to ambush my girls. It's giving me heartburn."

She stared at the screeching phone, as if willing it into silence.

"It's not a bad thing, maybe, if they get the story out," I suggested, over the shrill, incessant ringing. "Maybe we should do a news segment. Spread the word."

"It's not our place to interfere with investigations, or attract the attention of the press for activities not involving the Bills or our sponsors. We are meant to be neutral, supportive, and uplifting. The police are working as quickly as they can. They don't need us sticking our noses in it."

The ringing fell silent. Suzanna watched the phone guardedly, waiting for it to erupt again. Satisfied that it had stopped ringing, she turned her attention to me.

"You look better today," she said gently. "I can see you've been taking care of yourself. But there's one problem." She pointed at her eyes. "When I look at you here, I can tell: you're not better."

I nodded, focusing on the wall behind her shoulder, littered with its framed photographs of Suzanna as a young cheerleader.

"You have shown commitment to the Jills to the point of compromising your health," she went on. "Now, you made poor judgments this weekend. But you clearly care deeply about this team and will do whatever it takes to fulfill your obligations. I have the same drive myself. So I want to help you."

She opened a desk drawer and produced an envelope. She set it in front of me. Inside was a check. I looked at the memo line: *Appearance Fee, Junior Jills.*

My hand flew to my mouth. I had expected to be reprimanded, benched at the next game, pulled from my remaining appearances—not given money.

"Suzanna, I didn't—I didn't perform. And even if I had . . . *no* one else got paid for this event."

"It's all right," she said. "It's all taken care of. I appreciate the work you put into the Junior Jills camp over the summer, Virginia. I see your devotion to this squad, and its future. We start planning Junior Jills programming in January, and leading up till then, I'd love to hear your ideas for expanding the summer camp. We'll call it consulting."

"I don't think I can let you do that," I stammered.

"Why?" She looked at me pointedly. "Are you implying I don't know how to handle the finances of my own squad?"

I didn't doubt Suzanna's financial prowess. She'd once said to Sara, loud enough so anyone standing nearby could hear, "I drained my ex-husband so dry he has to drag his dead husk from door to door begging for loose change to stay afloat." Whatever small fortune she'd gotten out of her divorce, she'd leveraged it into an enormous house in East Aurora, a closet full of understated designer clothes, and a sleek gray Lexus that purred around the parking lot. She certainly understood money better than I did.

"Why are you doing this for me?" I said, the check dangling from my fingers as though it were hot to the touch.

"Because you need it, clearly! Virginia, not to be callous, but it's quite clear at this point what happened to Jeanine. Once they find this Landon and put him away, this will all be over. Until then, I'm trying to help each and every one of my girls to get through this time, and you are proving to need more help than anyone. I want your focus back on the Jills, back on your responsibilities. Will you let me help you?"

There was a muffled clang; I twisted in my chair to see, through the small window of the office, Carmen and Maria opening the doors of the Kmart, the first to arrive for practice.

"It's all settled," said Suzanna, standing up. "Oh, and next practice—I'm coordinating a grief activity for the entire team. Mandatory. The girls should arrive one hour early. Waterproof makeup is a must. Make sure Sharrice hears this, please? If she tries to schedule one more meeting with me to 'discuss best practices,' I will just—"

Suzanna shook her head, flicking her bangs back as she came around the desk. She seemed satisfied by our exchange, as though the check had eliminated a problem she was proud to have solved so efficiently. I floated from my seat, nodding mechanically.

She held the door open so I could join the girls trickling in to begin stretches and warm-ups. I paused, check clutched in both hands.

"I saw my mom yesterday," I said.

Suzanna let the door fall partway closed, her hand still on the knob. "Yes, and?" she said.

"Did you ever know her? Lisa Barton?"

"How would I know your mother? She doesn't participate in Jills activities."

"I mean, before. When I was a kid. At a Paladino's event. I wondered if you met her."

"I know twelve hundred dollars a month goes into her bank account to pay for that condo of hers."

I drew back. I was aware that Stanley supplemented my mom's income, though I hadn't known to what extent. It embarrassed me that my mom still took money from Stanley, like it embarrassed me that he'd paid for Laura's two stints in rehab. I wanted to explain: I didn't take Stanley's money for granted, and I didn't treat him like a cash register. This was why, I supposed, he remained eager to help me financially even when I was well into adulthood. I logged each of his checks in my finances notebook, the way my dad taught me. My rule was to never use Stanley's money for rent or living expenses—Stanley helped with extras only. It was not income. My dad had been careful to explain to me the difference between gifts and income.

"Don't get audited," he would say, and though I didn't know the meaning of the word, I nodded gravely in agreement.

But to Suzanna, clearly, my entire family was a charity case, just as I was a charity case, so seemingly desperate for money that she wanted to pay me for work I wasn't even doing.

"I was just asking—" I stuttered. "I didn't mean—"

"Sorry," said Suzanna.

I couldn't remember ever having heard Suzanna utter the word *sorry.* She put a hand on my shoulder. I thought again of my father, the sepia-toned photograph version of him that lived in my head, the version of him that had long replaced any real memory I had of his face, and I imagined him smiling at Suzanna.

"Sometimes this city feels a little too small," she said. "Everything feels so close. Do you ever feel it, too?"

TOWARD THE END of practice, Sharrice, in a Wonder Woman costume, sidled up to me.

We were all standing around, waiting to get into formation for our Halloween photo. My line had chosen superheroes as our costume theme, and I'd changed into a blue leotard paired with a red cape in an approximation of Supergirl. The leotard was low-cut, exposing my cat scratches, so I kept my hand pressed to my chest to hide them.

"Hey." Sharrice squeezed my arm. "How you holding up?"

All practice I'd had a knot in my stomach. I had to tell someone about the check. And Sharrice, certainly, would know if this was a legal issue or merely an ethical one.

I motioned for her to follow me to my duffel. I unzipped the outer pocket and flashed her the check.

"Oh," she said while I stuffed it away. "Oh yeah. Suzanna's done that before."

"Excuse me?" I said, straightening.

"I mean if one of the girls needs help with money, she'll . . ."

Sharrice glanced over her shoulder to make sure we were out of earshot. “Well, she finds a way. Like two seasons ago, when Vic walked out on her kid’s dad? Suzanna put Vic in the system as camp director so she could pay her enough money for a security deposit on a new place.”

My jaw dropped.

“Wait a minute—*director*?” I said, struggling to keep my voice down. “There’s no camp director—*I* practically ran that camp last summer, for free!”

“I know,” she whispered. “But, Virginia, it’s not real. It was for the paperwork, to make Vic look like ‘staff.’ And I know Suzanna did the same thing for Alyssa last season, when she had to move her dad into assisted living. She does it for girls who are really in trouble.”

I was shocked. Suzanna’s habit was to insert herself into the lives of her favorite girls and make herself the solution to all their problems, but I had never heard of her supplying Jills with actual money.

We both watched Suzanna and Sara on the other side of the room, furiously discussing the photo setup and how to get us all into frame.

“Maybe you can consider this back pay,” said Sharrice wryly, glancing toward my bag.

“There’s no way it’s free money,” I said. “What’s the catch?”

“I feel gossipy.” Sharrice fiddled with her gold bracelets. “Okay, I’m just gonna say it. Vic said Suzanna brought her to this special event where there were prospective sponsors. Vic’s job was to sort of butter them up, make them feel special. She said Suzanna supervised the whole thing, and she felt totally safe. But it was clear Vic was there to help seal the deal.”

“Oh my God.”

“I wouldn’t worry,” said Sharrice. “You’re, you know—sort of exempt from that kind of thing. Because of the family connection.”

I stared at her. “Exempt?”

Sharrice’s face screwed up with embarrassment. “Oh God, I hope that didn’t sound, like, accusatory. You work so hard for the Jills. I shouldn’t have said it like that.”

“No, it’s okay—”

"I just mean, you know." She gestured weakly. "We're not all treated the same."

Before I could respond, Suzanna started shouting, waving us all closer.

"Ladies—squeeze in!" she said.

Sara began calling out instructions for who was to kneel, sit, or stand, while Suzanna held up her iPhone like a mother at Disney.

I knelt next to the girls on my line, feeling deeply conflicted. I had known, when I auditioned for the first time two years ago, what it would take to be on the Jills. I knew it would be hard, and occasionally humiliating—but after half a lifetime of squeezing into jazz recital costumes and being singled out in front of everyone for bad form, after years of comparing the width of our thigh gaps with my fellow dancers and seething when another girl was chosen to solo instead of me, I felt I understood humiliation. I knew its costs, and I knew its deep satisfactions. And I knew the payoff: if I got onto the squad, I reasoned, then no one would know I was not a serious person, that I did not have health insurance or a savings account or a real family. No one would know I'd abandoned my sister back in Columbus because I couldn't deal with her failing me, or me failing her, anymore. And in return I would get what I desperately wanted, which was structure and friendship and intimacy that was not based on saving someone from drugs, or from themselves. I would get a team of people who would look out for me and make me laugh. God, I wanted to laugh again.

Kneeling amid all these chosen girls, everyone smiling and fidgeting with their costumes, sucking in their stomachs, I became aware of a terrible sense of loss. It was the loss of Jeanine, of course, but of something else, too. A façade, slipping. The ability to maintain the façade was the yardstick we used to measure our success. And thank God for the yardstick, because otherwise how would you know where you stood or if you were okay? You could be broke and tired, estranged from your family, terrified of your husband, distracted by hunger, crazed with grief, but here it didn't matter. Here you were fun, and sexy, and sociable, and good at parties. You were okay. Even if everyone who was supposed to be in the photo wasn't there. Even if you had to pretend to enjoy things you didn't enjoy or be places you didn't want to be. Even if, apparently, your director had to write you a check under the table so you could keep up the act.

"Can someone get in front of Virginia?" Suzanna shouted. "So it doesn't look like we have a knife-fight victim on the squad?"

IN THE PARKING lot, I dug my phone from my bag while waiting for my car to warm up. It finally felt like real winter, with the sky spitting out a horrible combination of ice and snow. As my phone flickered to life, it buzzed with an incoming text from Bobby. I opened it, and there, on the glaring brightness of my screen, was a dick.

This is what I look like when I think about what we could've done in that office :)

My whole body went rigid. My fingers shook as I tapped and swiped at the photo, trying to delete it.

Send me a pic back? he'd added.

Please?

Just one.

Make my day.

I threw the phone facedown on the passenger seat. How had I gotten myself into this position? This was the sort of situation Jeanine knew how to handle. She would contextualize it, make it funny, turn it into a story.

I sat listening to the prickling sound of ice falling on the roof of my car, my heart breaking as I grasped for her voice in my head, the voice that could help me decide how I should feel about Bobby, and Suzanna finding me pathetic enough to give me money, and my whole stupid life—when there was a knock at my window.

I jumped. Ray crouched there, waving both hands at me in the darkness of the parking lot. He wore his usual Bills jacket, his hands and face white from the cold.

"Virginia!" he said, his breath frosting the glass of my window, eyes tearing up in the wind. "Can I speak with you?"

There were three cars left in the parking lot. Suzanna and the few remaining Jills were shut in her office, discussing social media strategies, I believed. I was, for all purposes, alone in the parking lot.

I rolled down my window an inch. Ray leaned in to speak through the gap.

"I know I'm not supposed to come to practice," he said. "I wouldn't be here if it wasn't important. I have relevant information I hope to pass on to the correct person."

I shifted the car into drive but kept my foot on the brake. "What would you like to tell me, Ray?"

"I've been thinking about the news article about Jeanine, about her car being found, and I was just wondering . . . did Jeanine have a second car?"

"No. Why?"

"Because I saw her driving another car. A white Hyundai."

My foot slipped off the brake pedal and my car lurched forward.

"Sorry," I said, as Ray jumped back and I put the car back into park. "Sorry—say again?"

"A white Hyundai," he repeated. "A sedan. I've seen her driving it on two occasions. The first was exactly nine days before the Bills game she missed. It was a Friday. I was on my way to judo. She was at a gas station on River Road. I remember thinking that was strange, because it doesn't match her commute to work or to Jills practice. Then I saw her driving it on one other occasion, about seven months ago, when we had that late freeze in March. She got on the 190 going south."

I pushed aside my alarm—Ray clearly *did* know our schedules, and did follow us on our commutes—to focus on the revelation at hand. A white Hyundai? Did one of the other Jills drive a white Hyundai, which Jeanine could have borrowed?

"I assumed she borrowed it," said Ray, clearly thinking the same thing, "since on all other occasions, she always drives her Mazda. Maybe it was a boyfriend's car?"

"No, that doesn't make sense," I said. Landon didn't have a car, and Bobby, being a Paladino, almost certainly drove something more high-end. "Maybe a rental? But how would she get the same rental car twice?"

"I obviously did not want to bother Jeanine to ask her about it. I have learned not to approach you girls while you are out in public. You're always kind to me, but I realize it is a bit disruptive. I know I get excited. But to me, we're not strangers. When I run into one of you, it's like seeing a very close friend—"

"Have you told the police?" I interrupted.

"I wasn't sure if I should make a fuss about it until I spoke to one of you girls."

The cold air seeping in from the window stung the back of my throat. Ray was shivering, his long eyelashes coated with droplets.

"I guess you should call them," I said. "The police can look up car records, at least. I don't know how else we'd figure out where it came from."

"Right," he said slowly.

"You know the hotline number? It's on the *Buffalo News* site."

He nodded earnestly, but I didn't trust him to know what to do. I had the number memorized, and I wrote it on the back of a receipt I dug out of the cupholder. I poked the scrap of paper through the open slit of my window, and he held it with great reverence, in both hands. I resisted the urge to snatch it back; the receipt was from the coffee shop near my gym, and I worried he'd start frequenting it in the hopes of running into me.

"Thanks for telling me this, Ray," I said, and his eyes glistened with pride. "I appreciate it. You should head home. It's really cold."

He nodded but did not move.

"Ray," I said. "Don't wait for them to come out."

My phone buzzed and tore my attention away from his wide face gazing earnestly at me through the window. It was a text from Laura.

It said: **Come to thirsty buffalo I have Jason.**

Chapter 18

THE PROSPECT OF seeing Laura with Jason Morley had the combined effect of quickening my heart rate and slowing down my blood flow with sluggish dread.

I sped recklessly, trying to cut the thirty-minute drive in half. I had told Laura the story of my search for Jeanine as best I could, given the complexity of the situation. But there were two topics I'd left out on purpose: first, that I'd almost had sex in a restaurant office with BJ Paladino, and second, that I had spewed a series of accusatory messages to Jason Morley on Facebook. It was only to protect Laura's safety that I was racing through the slick dark to sit in a bar with Jason Morley. He wasn't going to tell me what transpired between him and Jeanine in the Pink Fountain parking lot, no matter how much I asked or screamed or begged. Not with the history between us.

The roads were getting slippery by the time I spun onto Elmwood Ave. As I pulled up alongside Thirsty Buffalo on its unassuming corner of the Strip, I caught sight of a disheveled figure running along the sidewalk beside me, arms waving.

It was Laura. I jerked to a stop, the car behind me honking in protest.

"You're just in time," she said as she spilled into the passenger seat. "He *just* left. That's his car, up ahead. Go, go, follow him!"

Spurred by her excitement, I hit the gas. Laura pointed out a red Tacoma about four cars ahead of us—the same truck I had seen in the footage at the Pink Fountain. She wore a loose shirt and a long duster over her leggings, and her hands and head were bare, as if she didn't notice the wet and cold.

"I'm so stupid—I let it slip that I'd texted you," she said, arranging the bulky canvas bag she carried as a purse on her lap. "Of course he found an excuse to leave right away. I guess I'm not surprised, since the last time the three of us were in a room together you threw beer bottles at his head."

My throat closed. I pulled to a stop in response to a red light several cars ahead, on the corner of Elmwood and Summer. The icy sleet had halted for now, leaving a fuzzy haze behind, and the streetlights swam in the humidity. Jason was still four cars in front of us, stopped for the same light.

"Thank God I saw you," said Laura. "My car's parked like two blocks over. I never would have reached it in time to follow him."

"What were you two doing?" I croaked.

"Talking." She winced and massaged her left shin just above the ankle. "God, this leg still gets so fucked up when I run in the cold."

"Talking about what?"

"I was trying to get intel on his, you know, less than legal business dealings these days. Jason meets with your friend at the Pink Fountain right before a bunch of heroin drops from the sky and he has nothing to do with it? That's far-fetched even if you believe in coincidences. I got him talking about his importing business and the Paladinos a bit. He was pretty evasive otherwise. He wanted to talk about *you*."

The light turned green as my stomach dropped.

"Me?"

"Yeah, our relationship, like, how I feel being back in touch with you and whether we're best friends again or what. He's easy to talk to, is the problem. So easy to talk to, still."

"What did he say about Jeanine?"

"Nothing! All he would say was that they met at a party, and he never saw her again after that. I couldn't get him to open up at all. I used all my resources. All day long I've been with Jason. And we mostly talked about you! Because that's the one thing I can talk and talk about!"

This last bit she exclaimed with an exasperated laugh. I followed Jason onto the entrance to the 190 while she fussed with the heat vents on the dashboard, then rolled the window down to let in cold air. Was she talking a little too loud, her gestures a little too animated? I couldn't make out her face in the occasional sweep of orange streetlights, or see her eyes. The urge to ask her whether she'd had a drink with Jason at the bar swelled up from my sternum, filling my head with pressure, but before I could formulate the question, Laura said, "You know, back in high school, he said things about you to get to me."

"What do you mean?"

"Like, when he was mad at me or sick of me, he'd say stuff to imply he preferred you. Like, 'If only your sister would put out, if only she wasn't such a prude.' "

With Laura's window down, the windshield had started fogging up. I fumbled to turn on the defroster as the wipers smeared muggy streaks across the glass. "That's terrible," I said. "That's awful."

"And later when you were openly hostile toward him he'd be like, 'Me and your sister should hate-fuck and get it over with.' "

What was wrong with men? Why did they talk about me, about Laura, about all of us like that? Like they owned us, but they didn't even want us? Jason had hooked up with almost the whole cheerleading squad—some even while he was dating Laura—except for me. If he had thrown pebbles at *my* bedroom window to lure me out for a drive at night or written me a note saying to meet him by the bleachers at lunch, I would have followed him anywhere, stunned and drunk on his attention. I would have felt chosen. But he didn't go after me, he chose Laura. I wasn't usable to him. All he had to do was look at me to know he'd never get out of me what he got out of Laura. In a way, he'd known her better than I had.

"He shouldn't have talked to you like that," I said. "He was being an asshole."

She shrugged. "He probably did feel a little rejected by you. I think a lot of boys did. You had a bit of a rejecting energy."

The lining of my stomach clawed at the one protein bar I'd eaten all evening.

"It's not a bad thing!" Laura insisted. "It's like asshole repellent. I wish I had rejecting energy. I would have gotten in a lot less trouble."

Now she was being patronizing. Laura attracted things and I repelled them. We both knew which was more appealing. Girls like Jeanine turned on like a bright, hot light that men could warm themselves under, and girls like Laura welcomed them in like a soft, sweet bed to lie on. The two of them were easy to access and easy to want. I was not easy to want. I was a hard shell covered in spikes, which shot out at every provocation or hint of tenderness.

"I guess no one loves to be told they have a rejecting energy," I said.

"Now we're all turned around, and you're insulted," said Laura. "I'm sorry I said anything."

"Maybe make up your mind if you're criticizing or praising me before you start going on about how little I know about boys and attracting them and what's a good or bad way to be."

Laura groaned behind her hands. The red Tacoma, two cars ahead, put on its right blinker. I told Laura to be quiet while I focused on staying what I hoped was a good distance behind. Jason merged right onto 290. My heart quickened when he took exit 1.

"This is the route to Tonawanda Island," I said. "Where Jeanine's car was found."

"Oh shit," said Laura, our argument forgotten. She pounded the dashboard. "*Shit*. Here we go. I told you!"

Her certainty was contagious. My hands tightened on the wheel as I struggled not to accelerate. What if he went to the site where her car had been left—what would it mean, what would that say?

Then about a quarter mile up the road, where Military turned into Main, he slowed abruptly.

"Oh my God," Laura sputtered, ducking down as we zoomed past him in the left-hand lane. I watched in the rearview as he pulled into a parking lot in front of a small group of white storefronts.

I pulled into the next parking lot, a Jiffy Lube, and parked by the entrance. Laura sank lower in her seat, her feet up on the dashboard. She had her hands clamped over her mouth to hide her scared laughter. My heart was in my ears. The car was facing away from Jason, but I could see him in my rearview mirror. He sat in his truck, facing forward, running a hand along his jawline before opening the door and getting out.

"What's he doing?" whispered Laura into her knees.

He propped an elbow on his open door and directed his gaze toward the lot of the Jiffy Lube, where we were parked. He was about thirty feet away, but in the rearview mirror, I could see he was looking right at us. I grabbed the gearshift, then wondered if peeling off would be too suspicious. I shifted from park to reverse and back several times, frozen with indecision. "What are you doing!" shrieked Laura.

When I looked at the rearview mirror again, Jason was walking toward us across the scraggly grass that separated the two parking lots. We were caught.

He knocked on the passenger window, and I rolled it down.

"Hi," said Laura cheerfully.

"What's going on?" he said.

The streetlights lit Jason from above, casting dark shadows beneath his eyes and nose. He was a chameleon, I realized: when Jeanine and I ran into him at Club 716, he was dressed sharply, like a finance guy. To see Laura, he'd put on a faded gray jacket and black pants. His hair was mussed up and his eyes ringed with red.

"We're following you," said Laura. "Isn't that obvious?"

"Why?"

"Because I'm not done having fun. I wanted to keep hanging out."

"This isn't fun," said Jason. "I see what you're doing."

"What are we doing?" Laura propped her elbow on the edge of the window, her fist under her chin.

He had one arm on the hood of my car, so he seemed to tower over Laura. He jutted his chin at her, but he spoke to me.

"I know we all have history. That's no fucking excuse to send your little sister out to fuck with me."

"How was I—" said Laura.

"You don't see me blaming other people for the way my life turned out. You don't see me antagonizing and stalking and harassing anyone. I don't want to have a problem with you. If you don't keep my name the fuck out of your mouth, we're going to have a problem."

"We just want to catch up," Laura said. "Why don't you want to talk to us?"

Jason was already stalking away. "I can't look," said Laura, pulling up the hood of her coat while I watched his dark form return to his car. The headlights of his Tacoma burst to light, temporarily blinding me. When I opened my eyes again, he was pulling back out onto Main, heading south now, away from Tonawanda Island, which may or may not have been his destination. I would now never know.

LAURA LAUGHED HELPLESSLY in the passenger seat as we drove south, back toward the city. Beneath my terror burned a familiar shame—a sense that I'd screwed up, but I'd screwed up by responding badly to *Laura's* screwing up, but I was still responsible, but it didn't seem *fair* that I was responsible, and— What the hell was she laughing about?

"Laura, Jesus—did you take something?"

She pressed her lips together in an attempt at seriousness. It lasted about three seconds before she snorted and collapsed back into laughter.

"What? What did you take?"

"I didn't! Not in the way you're thinking."

"Then in what way? In what way did you take something?"

"It's really stupid. I'm embarrassed! We did a little nitrous oxide. That's all."

"You huffed nitrous oxide? What, are you twelve?"

"It was supposed to be funny." She covered her mouth with her hands and tried not to laugh. "And then Jason gave me a little codeine cough syrup."

I pulled into a gas station lot.

"Fuck him," I gasped. "Oh, fuck him, *fuck him*—"

"Virginia, it's fine! It's all fine! It's low-key stuff. I don't do that anymore. God, can't I have fun for ten minutes? Can't I laugh about it? You came to Mom's birthday high. Right?"

"So this is my fault? I smoke pot so you get to relapse? Is that it?"

I got out of the car and marched to the other end of the parking lot. I snatched at the scarf around my neck, bundled it up against my mouth, and screamed.

My reaction wasn't even emotional, it was physical. Like a hurricane raging inside me, it would pass in a second and leave wreckage, detritus I would bump into, a mess to be cleaned, a horrible change in pressure that rendered me depressed and gloomy—

"Ginny!" Laura called.

I walked back to the car. She had gotten out and was watching me, hands folded on top of the roof.

"You're supposed to be sober," I said carefully. "You said you were."

"I am. It's cough syrup."

"That's the start, and you know it, and if you had any fucking sense or desire to be alive you would be terrified right now. You'd be calling the, the NA people or whoever, you'd be on your fucking *knees* right now—"

"Maybe I would be if I wasn't so busy standing in a parking lot screaming at you!"

I covered my face with the scarf. It was warm and damp from my breath, still holding my scream. Laura had gotten high with Jason to get him to talk. She had done it for me. My fault. I never should have told her about Jeanine. I never should have given her the excuse.

I lowered the scarf to see that Laura was biting her thumb.

"It's bad, okay?" she said. "I know it's bad. I shouldn't have done it. Fucking Jason."

"It's not Jason. It's me. Apparently you only get better when I'm not around. I leave Columbus, and two seconds later you're sober. You're around me again, and all of a sudden you're high."

"Cut it out. I didn't get sober for you. And I didn't suck on a can of Reddi-wip today for you. I don't do it for you. I do it because of me." She crossed her arms. "And I was fucked up for over a year after you left. You're exaggerating on purpose."

Laura's coat was so thin it made me cold. I gripped my shoulders. She smiled at me sadly.

"Can you take me back to my car? I'll go to Mom's, where I can't get into trouble, and call my sponsor."

We drove silently. I blasted the heater to warm her up. The orange streetlights dragged across the windshield, stuck to the condensation on the glass. She had a sponsor to call now, instead of me. A relief, right? Yes, apparently. Yes. But still.

Chapter 19

LAURA SHUT HERSELF in my bedroom while she called her sponsor.

I couldn't say for sure why I'd insisted she come to my place after I brought her to her car (which was a well-maintained Honda Civic, I was pleased to see). It was late, and I didn't want her driving on wet roads in the dark, and I didn't want to imagine her shut all night in our mom's basement with her shame. So instead, I'd asked if she wanted to see my apartment.

I tossed a wadded-up piece of tinfoil around for the cat to chase and tried to pretend I wasn't listening to her conversation through the door. I caught a few sentences that made my insides lurch, like "Maybe it's not rock bottom but it is square one."

And "This feels like a test, and I'm not passing."

After a while she went silent. I knocked and found her lying on my bed with a pillow over her face.

"I'm so stupid," she moaned. "I can't even blame Jason for how I act around him. I know exactly how he's going to make me feel, and still I seek him out. And we fall right back into our old roles."

I pulled at the pillow, but she gripped it over her face.

"If you don't want to blame Jason, then I will," I said. "I don't mind."

"I thought I had the tools to cope with him now that I'm sober, but it turns out I'm exactly the same. I still just want to show some stupid boy that I can handle whatever he throws at me, and in the moment, I'm dumb enough to think that's power."

I wasn't used to hearing Laura admit that she was in the wrong. This was the most candid remark I'd ever heard her make about herself and Jason.

Seeing her in my bedroom opened up a kaleidoscope of memories: Laura running into my childhood room, collapsing on my bed to gossip after practice, her hair wet from the shower. Laura, a pillow over her face, spiraling because she couldn't get the steps right for dance team, she was failing math, she didn't want me to leave for college, Jason wasn't texting her back, she couldn't get an alternative date for prom. Me, trying to tug the pillow away, reassuring, strategizing, offering solutions, endless solutions. I always had the solution.

"Hey," I said. "I know I blew up at you, but I don't think cough syrup is the end of the world. Any day you're not doing heroin is a good day, right?"

"Now you sound like a twelve-stepper." She peeked at me from under the pillow. "Your apartment is so nice. I knew you'd have a nice place. When did you get a cat?"

I followed her gaze to see the cat perched on my windowsill, peeking through the curtains.

"He's Jeanine's," I said.

She made a small noise in the back of her throat, and we were shy for a moment.

"Can I tell you something?" she said. "The way you acted about me taking the codeine syrup, I could handle. I could handle it because I knew you were right, and it made sense. I felt worse about you getting upset when we were talking about Jason in high school. About how he had this weird crush on you. I knew it would push your buttons, but I said it anyway, because I can't figure out why it makes you so mad to talk about sex."

"I'm not mad," I said. "I wasn't mad."

"Yes, you were. Are you kidding?"

I wasn't mad. I was whatever else I got when I compared sexual notes with other people, which was sort of anxious and crazed, and afterward, racked with guilt. It was toward Laura, I realized, that I'd first begun to act this way: during her sophomore and my junior year, after she admitted that she'd gone all the way with a boy from her math class in the backseat of his car.

A year earlier, she'd confessed to giving her ninth-grade boyfriend a blow job, a fact I'd dealt with by placing it in a category other than sex. A blow job was *pre*-sex. But this new development had been undeniable. My baby sister, who'd arrived here on earth sixteen months after me, was having full-on sex, while I was alone in my bedroom studying for bio. This flew in the face of the laws of nature. How could she have pulled ahead? How did she even know what to do—wasn't she relying on me for guidance, taking *my* lead? This, in my irrational teenage mind, felt like the worst betrayal of all: that Laura could obtain something I wanted so badly, and with such apparent effortlessness. She had clearly seen the distress on my face, because she'd tried to backtrack, saying, "It's not a big deal."

And I, unforgivably, had said, "You know who treats sex like it's not a big deal? Skanks. Slutty girls."

I hadn't asked her if it had gone all right, or if she was happy about it. We didn't talk about sex again until I finally lost my virginity about six months later, at junior prom. After that, I wanted to discuss it endlessly, in crass detail. Looking back, it was obvious that Laura made an effort to never one-up me or bring up positions or experiences until I mentioned them first. I'd taught her to treat every sexual act and partner as a set of points to be tallied and compared and collected toward—what end? What grand equation? Could I answer that even now?

"I know it makes me act weird," I conceded.

"Yeah, but why is it such a sensitive point?" she said. "Don't tell me you don't know you're pretty."

"It's not about me being pretty."

"Then what is it?"

"I don't know!"

She waited for me to explain further, but I didn't want to talk about sex.

"Did Jason say anything," I asked, "about those Facebook messages I sent him?"

Laura sat up. "Ginny," she said, voice low in warning. "What did you do?"

"THIS IS JUST like you," Laura lectured. She paced while I sat holding my laptop on the bed, incriminating messages on full display. "You walk around avoiding conflict, maintaining the appearance of self-control, and then you *blow* up in the most irrational way possible." She pointed at the laptop. "You cannot send messages like that to people like Jason. Do you know how much danger you put me in?"

"I didn't know you were going to *text* him!"

I'd been ashamed of my messages until Laura started lecturing me; now I felt like defending myself. In sobriety, it seemed, she had taken on an air of adult condescension that looked ridiculous on her. Laura telling *me* how to act?

"I'm not scared of Jason," I insisted. "Fuck Jason. I'll say whatever I want to him."

"I know you only think of Jason in terms of how he treated me, but that's a drop in the bucket. He's not the running back getting schoolgirls high anymore. He's a big-time player. Do you understand what he does with his importing business? Jason deals in *volume*. He gets stuff in by the truckful, Ginny. Antagonizing guys like that can get you killed."

My indignation deflated. I was taken aback by the image of trucks, full of—stuff.

"By 'stuff' you mean what?" I said. "Heroin?"

"He moves heroin, and some coke, I think."

"How do you know this?"

"Ginny—" Laura's anger gave way to exasperation. "This was the world, the men I sought out. Like Gabe—you remember Gabe?"

"Do I remember Gabe?" I said. "The one who got you fired from the gym by selling heroin in the locker room? The one who made you buy a gun for him because he wasn't allowed to own one? Which I then found hidden in my *couch cushions* because you were 'keeping it safe while he worked some stuff out'? The one who called me a bitch psycho when I wouldn't let him into my apartment while you were hiding from him in my bedroom?"

"Yes, Gabe," said Laura impatiently. "You're proving my point here. Jason and Gabe—they're career dealers. I always went after dealers. I didn't want to buy off the street, I didn't want to get stuck in crack dens. Dating guys like that meant I could keep getting high, and it would be quality, and it would be clean, and I wouldn't have to pay for it. And you can bet I made myself useful. If I saw a potential client, I got them hooked up with Gabe. I was *the* girlfriend. I fought for my place. I know now that my position was so precarious, that I was so, so close to being homeless, or beaten up, or pimped out—but I was smart enough to stay alive. I know how this world works, is what I'm saying. I was part of it on purpose. Of course I went after men like that. Look at Dad, at the work he was attracted to. It's probably the same reason you like people like Jeanine."

"What do you mean 'like Jeanine'?" I demanded.

At the heart of Laura's addiction was a paradox I did not like to consider: that she was not in control of herself, she was at the mercy of men and urges far stronger than herself; and, at the same time, she was calculating and decisive and intensely purposeful.

Another thing I didn't like to think about was that Laura's hunger for destructiveness might bear any resemblance to my own capacities, or our father's.

Laura raised her eyebrows as if to say, *Come on*. She sighed and sat on the bed next to me.

"Well, look at the position she's in. She's touching every rung of the ladder—she's dating a mob guy, she's got a secret friendship with a major supplier, and her ex-boyfriend is a street dealer. That's a lot of access. It's impressive, but it's also kind of dangerous. You don't *want* to know people too far up the chain, or too far below you. So, what are all these relationships for? Does she use her boyfriends to get high?"

My stomach dropped.

"She and Landon . . . they had drug problems years ago. But the worst thing she does now is drink too much vodka sometimes."

"Okay." Laura tilted her head. "Let's assume, for the sake of argument, that's true. If she's not getting high, what is it? What is she up to?"

I couldn't answer. I stared at the messages to Jason on my laptop screen, the evidence of my fruitless rage. Laura looked at me sympathetically. We had each taken a turn being in the wrong, and now we were back on even footing.

She gestured for me to hand her my laptop. "I forgot to tell you," she said, typing. "Before I texted Jason, I typed his name, along with 'Tonawanda Island,' into Google. Look at this."

She turned the screen so it was facing me. She scrolled down to the sixth search result, an obituary for Greg Morley, Jason's father. Laura opened the article and waved the cursor around the line: *Morley was the founder and CEO of PanAtlantic Imports, an import/export company based in Tonawanda.*

"PanAtlantic is defunct—it doesn't have a website," she said. "Jason inherited it, but he's renamed and rebranded completely. But if you search the name—" Laura clicked on the other open browser tab. "It shows up on Google Maps."

A red pin for the business appeared. It was located on Tonawanda Island.

I studied the pin. I'd driven past the spot when I visited the site where Jeanine's car was found. What did this tell me? At the very least, that Jason had three points of proximity to her: Club 716 two nights before she disappeared, the Pink Fountain a few days before that, and his father's old business right next to the spot where she'd vanished.

Laura picked up the cat, who'd wandered over to sniff at her foot hanging off the bed, and set him in her lap.

"It's weird, right?" she said, raking her fingers over the cat's back. "Why would her car end up near Jason Morley's dad's old business headquarters, unless Jason had something to do with it?"

"So *this* means," I said, pointing at the laptop screen, "that Jason should be the prime suspect, not Landon. Right? Does he still have access to that warehouse?"

"I don't know, Gin," she said thoughtfully. She buried her hands in the cat's fur. "There could still be another person entirely involved. Somebody might have shook your friend down knowing she had access to Landon, or Jason, or even Bobby. People would try to use me to get to my boyfriend all the time. There are so many instances where I should have gotten way more hurt than I did, when I should have died, even."

The cat, sensing Laura's fear, bolted off the bed. We watched him skitter out the door, into the hallway.

"These are the kinds of questions people get beat up for asking," said Laura. "People get guns pointed at them over this stuff. You're in over your head. Those Facebook messages—that is not the behavior of a person who knows what they're doing. Let the police handle this. You said Stanley is looking into it. Let them figure all this out."

"But what if they can't?"

"If they can't?" Laura looked at me helplessly. "If they can't, Ginny, then what the hell makes you think you can?"

WHEN LAURA AND I were growing up, we had a nightly ritual in our house in which I would tuck everyone in. First I would help my parents tuck in Laura and read her a picture book. After turning off Laura's light, I herded my parents into their bedroom and ordered them under the covers. I took off Dad's slippers, cleaned his glasses for him, and attempted to read aloud one paragraph of whatever book was on his nightstand (*The Firm* or some James Lee Burke he wasn't really reading). Mom, I kissed on the cheek.

Then, having settled everyone in their proper places, I crept into my own room and put myself to bed. I slept the deep sleep of a person who has completed all their tasks to satisfaction, while my parents let themselves out of bed and continued on with their night.

As a five-, seven-, and then nine-year-old, I didn't ever stop to think that Dad might be drunk or anything else when I tucked him in. There were subtle changes to his constitution, I suppose—the smell of his neck and armpits changed ("the sugar smell," I called it privately) or he'd laugh harder or get annoyed more easily. Perhaps I did hear Mom and Dad fighting in whispers more often, but I didn't listen at the door like Laura did, preferring to put on my headphones and practice the songs we were learning for our jazz recital.

After I turned ten, Dad stopped coming home as often to be tucked in. At first, Laura and I would beg to stay up till he got home, until our mom shouted, *"Please!"* and covered her face with her hands, after which we got meekly under the covers. After a while, we got used to him not coming home, and the tucking-in ritual became a special occasion.

The night Dad died, I hadn't tucked him in because he hadn't come home. I'd felt a crushing sense of, not guilt exactly, but of having been robbed. If I'd tucked him in, he would have been safe. I felt I'd been denied an opportunity that I was owed, and the unfairness of this filled me with an anger that did not eliminate the sadness but provided some relief from it.

When Laura would stay the night in my apartment in Grandview, she would hold her arms out and say, "Tuck me in?" She might say it smiling, if we'd had one of our good days. She might say it high out of her mind, loopy and demanding affection, oblivious to my annoyance. Or she might say it apologetically, if we'd been fighting. Whatever the case, I complied every time, not for her sake but for mine. When I arranged the covers over her, I would think, *At least tonight, she won't die.* And though I knew that the world didn't really work that way, in my deepest soul I felt it was true.

That night in Buffalo, after our run-in with Jason, I offered Laura the bed, but she insisted on the couch. "Just like old times," she said, "but fully drug-free this time." I brought her sheets and extra pillows and a glass of water, asked her if she needed a book or magazine to read.

"I'm fine," she said, smoothing the blanket over her legs. She held out her arms.

"Tuck me in?" she said.

Chapter 20

At eight the next morning, I snuck past Laura to cover a nine A.M. aerobics class for another instructor at my gym. A vestigial wave of relief washed over me at the sight of her sleeping on my couch, a pillow gripped to her chest, her hand in a fist by her cheek, just as she'd slept in my apartment in Grandview.

All through my morning workouts I nursed a dim, warm glow in my chest, the glow of Laura in my apartment, on my couch, talking to me. Laura being there when I got home. The feeling elated and frightened me. It was the most terrifying type of love I knew, the kind made of equal parts hope and panic, and Laura could fill me with it quicker than anyone else.

As my students streamed out of Pilates Dance Fusion, the short, square kid who worked the front desk knocked on the doorframe of the studio.

"There's a call for you," he said.

"For me—where?"

He shrugged. "At the front desk."

I followed him to the circular check-in desk at the entrance to the gym. He handed me the phone, and I sat at the computer chair next to him.

"Hey, girl," said a hoarse, soft voice I immediately recognized. "It's Brittany, from the other night. I googled you and saw you worked at this gym. How are you doing?"

"Is everything okay?"

"Yeah! Yeah, totally. I wanted to ask you a question. Guess who called me?"

The desk attendant was poking at the keyboard, but I could tell he was eavesdropping. I twisted in the chair so I was facing away from him.

"Not Landon?" I whispered.

"Yeah Landon. No shit, he called me on the phone. Not from his own number—I think he borrowed someone's phone. I searched the number on Google, but it didn't match anything. But guess what? It was a Rochester area code. What do you think of that?"

"Rochester?" I fumbled for a pen on the desk. "Can you give me the number?"

She recited it and I carefully took it down on a Post-it.

"He was totally drunk," she went on. "I could tell from the background that he was at a bar. I heard a woman's voice say his name right before he hung up. Maybe he found someone to hide out with? Anyway, I wanted to ask you, since you know him in a different capacity—do you know if he has friends in Rochester?"

I did know of a friend Landon might have in Rochester, but to Brittany I said, "No. No idea."

"Okay, well if you think of anything, let me know. He was drunk so it was hard to tell how he was. He kept saying my name, and how sorry he was. I kept saying, 'Sorry for what?' He was all, 'I'm glad you're okay, you don't deserve this,' all thc stuff guys say. Some things don't change, even when you're suspected of murder. But hey: at least we know he's alive, right?"

I COULD HAVE called the number to confirm who it belonged to. Instead, I canceled my afternoon clients and classes so I could show up unannounced. It was a bad idea, financially, but I didn't have time for it all.

I knew where Marianne Chanowitz lived from the time I dropped off Jeanine at her house, after Jeanine had her wisdom teeth out. While Jeanine was in high school, she and her mother had lived in a series of small rentals around the Buffalo area. Now Marianne owned a sixties ranch-style one-story off a county road about thirty minutes outside Rochester. If you threw a rock hard enough from her porch, you could hit a neighbor's house, but the thick trees made it feel more like the middle of nowhere than it was. The drive, through a boring sprawl of farmland and winding suburbs, took an hour flat.

As I creaked up the porch stairs, a dog leapt up and started barking, pulled to a stop by a leash tied to an iron chair. I had forgotten about the dog—he'd barked at me the last time I came, along with another one, a scraggly terrier that I didn't see on the porch. This one was a collie mix, thigh-high, big enough to be intimidating.

The screen door clattered behind him.

"Shut *up,* Donny. Oh!" There was Marianne, squinting at me. She had the craggy, lived-in appearance of a much older woman, a woman who'd had to grit her teeth through life but was determined to laugh anyway. She kept her dyed chestnut hair pulled back into a clip and wore a gray Grateful Dead T-shirt. Her eyes were ringed with eyeliner, the lids drooping with age. "I know you. The girl from the teeth. What are you doing here, honey?"

"I was hoping we could talk."

"You tried to tell me before, on the phone. About Jeanine. You were worried before anyone else."

"I was, yes. Yeah."

"What's your name again? Veronica?"

"Virginia."

"What a grandma's name." She considered me a moment longer. The dog whined and wagged its bushy tail, which had dead leaves tangled in it.

"Can I talk to Landon?" I ventured.

SHE LED ME inside. On the squishy plaid couch sat Landon.

"Marianne!" he groaned. "What are you doing? I told you, if anyone asks, I'm *not* here!"

"She knew something was wrong," said Marianne. "This one. She knew it first. She's a friend, isn't she?"

"Oh, she's a friend. She's *the* friend. She still can't know I'm here. No one can know."

"She knew you were here before she walked in the door, so what's the harm. You might as well talk to her. How about a margarita, honey? I think we could all use a margarita."

She disappeared into the kitchen and began clattering around. I sat in the recliner across from Landon, who was shaking his head furiously, at me, at Marianne, at the whole situation. My gym sneakers sank into the thick shag carpet. The living room was cluttered and the narrow windows let in little natural light, but Marianne had brightened the place up with a couple of neon beer signs and string Christmas lights.

The dog dragged a doggy bed from the corner and began to hump it furiously in the middle of the room, as if for our benefit.

"Get out of here, Donny," Landon said, throwing a pillow at him.

"Where's the other one? Marie?" I asked.

"Died a few months ago. How'd you find me?"

I shrugged. Landon watched me from the couch, his face softening. He was gaunt beneath what was now a proper beard, days of fear etched into his usually cheerful face. I couldn't help it: I felt for him, cooped up in Marianne's house.

"I am kind of glad to see you," Landon admitted. "I feel bad about the way I ran out on you after the Pink Fountain. How are you doing? You okay?"

"I've been better. I guess you have, too."

"I guess I have."

He pulled another pillow onto his lap. Donny's face was printed on the fabric.

"Landon, what are you doing here?" I said.

His eyes darted toward the door. "Um. Things seemed a little messy out there."

"On account of that big block of heroin you brought home the week before Jeanine disappeared?"

Landon clutched the pillow and pitched forward on the couch, craning his neck toward the kitchen. Marianne continued banging around in there.

"Will you keep it down?" he whispered.

"Where did it come from?"

"Where did it *come* from?" He let out an incredulous laugh that was mostly air. "I don't know, Virginia, probably from Mexico. Where did it come from? What are you going to do, march up to El Chapo, in your white sneakers? Don't worry about where it came from!"

"You know what I mean," I hissed. "I thought you gave all that up? What about being a librarian? I'm not trying to lecture you on morality, okay—I know you know that shit can ruin your life. I'm trying to figure out how you and Jeanine got wrapped up in something this batshit insanely dangerous. I won't stop asking," I said as he pressed the Donny pillow to his face and moaned. "I'll go back to the Pink Fountain and ask your friend Danny. I'll talk to fucking El Chapo in my white sneakers. You think I won't?"

"I took it to help Jeanine, okay?" He dropped the pillow to his lap. "It was only to help her."

"Jeanine asked you for help with a bunch of heroin?"

The blender shrieked to life in the kitchen, making us both jump. The dog had dragged the doggy bed back into the corner and was now shaking it, as if to kill it.

"Yes, okay?" said Landon "It was a one-time deal, she said. She needed some help moving it. Obviously I didn't *want* it. I told her I didn't know the right people anymore. But what was I supposed to say? 'No, deal with it yourself'? While she's looking right at me, asking me for help? So fine, I took as much as I thought I could handle, which was way more than I wanted and less than she was trying to get rid of. I let my judgment get clouded. I *knew* something was off about it, and I was right, because whoever gave her that shit, it was compromised. Somebody had some garbage shit that wasn't supposed to be had, and they pawned it off on her because she was too ambitious, and she loved quick cash, and she didn't believe anything bad could ever happen to her."

His voice broke and he gripped the pillow harder.

"And now," he said, "I've got the fucking Paladinos after me. And I'll bet you, Virginia, I bet my life on it—it was the Paladinos who killed her."

I was overwhelmed by the smell of dog and the roar of the blender, over which I could barely hear Landon. I couldn't think in these conditions.

"That doesn't make any sense," I said. "Why would the Paladinos kill her, or anyone, over drugs? That's not their business."

"Oh my God." He appealed to the ceiling. "Virginia, this is beyond your capacity."

"The Paladinos are after you because they think you know where *she* is," I argued.

"They already know where she is, because they're the ones who took her out. And now they're going down the line to knock off every single person who ever touched the stuff."

The blender cut out abruptly, and the silence in the room seemed much louder than before. The dog stopped mauling the doggy bed and panted, staring at us expectantly.

"That night at Buffalo Underground," Landon said, "she was trying to tell me something was wrong. It's so glaringly obvious—I thought she was upset about her fucking love life, because I'm an idiot. She wanted to warn me, and she couldn't figure out how. She knew her life was in danger. She was saying goodbye."

"But, Landon—"

Marianne entered, carrying a pint glass filled with frozen margarita, thick as ice cream. I stood up from the recliner, pointlessly, powered by pure adrenaline. Marianne had put on a beautiful robe, shimmery and red, with gold patterns on it, over her Grateful Dead T-shirt.

"Here's yours, honey," said Marianne as she handed the pint glass to Landon. "I got out the stem glasses for us girls. You're not leaving, are you? I just made a killer batch. Come sit out on the back porch, it gets all the sun."

She retreated to the kitchen, humming. Landon stood, pint glass in his hand. Marianne had filled it past the brim, like a snow cone, and globs of frozen margarita dripped down the sides, coating his fingers.

"Listen, I'm sorry," he said. "I know that shit's hard to hear. But if you're going to keep running around town asking questions, you may as well hear it from me. I know what I did was stupid, but it wasn't evil. I don't want you to think badly of Jeanine. I don't want you to get hurt. All I have now are things I don't want." He touched my arm. "What are you thinking?"

"I don't know," I said. "I guess I want a margarita."

"Okay." He started for the back door, then stopped. "Hey—please don't say what I said about Jeanine being dead to Marianne. It'll kill her."

MARIANNE HAD A three-season back porch off the kitchen, enclosed by windows that drew in and held the heat from the afternoon sun. It was bright and warm. She had a stylish patio furniture set, out of place in her comfortable, frumpy house. We sat at the teak table, complete with modular chairs sporting teal cushions.

Marianne handed me a pink plastic wine glass overflowing with frozen margarita, thick and neon green.

"It's nice back here, right?" she said. "The furniture's a present from Jeannie. She got me a new bedroom set, too. And this, she got me a few weeks ago." Marianne motioned to her shimmering red robe. "It's silk. And this—" She held up a wrist, from which a gold bracelet sparkled. "I don't know where she thinks I'm going to wear *this*—at the biker bar up the street? You're gonna get me robbed, Jeannie! That's what I tell her. It's pretty, though, isn't it?" She admired her wrist. "I do put it on at home."

"She can't help herself," said Landon.

His smile was tender, a little pained. Money, I was thinking—like Gina had said a lifetime ago in Buffalo Underground, Jeanine's money situation had never made sense.

"She's very generous with her mother," said Marianne. "She's always been like this. She did those pageants growing up for *us*. We had fun when she won, didn't we?"

"We did," Landon agreed.

" 'I'm gonna take care of us, Mom,' she would say. A fourteen-year-old, saying that! And she does take care of me. She paid for that surgery I needed for my foot last year, and for my medications before that—I had to get hep C treatments, and those are no joke. And she got my teeth fixed. My whole life I thought no one would give me a break because of my teeth, and now I've got *Good Morning America* teeth."

Marianne pulled a deck of cards from her robe pocket and began to shuffle. I was smiling in spite of myself. Marianne had Jeanine's talent (or perhaps Jeanine had Marianne's) to turn even the most depressing situation into a good time. I noticed her teeth now, white and straight behind a slash of red lipstick.

"She wants me to quit my call-center job, but I told her, 'Baby, I have to work.' I've always worked. And she can't keep paying for me forever. She says she can, but how can she? Unless she marries that Bobby guy and *he* pays for us both. But I'd rather her marry Landon."

She was an expert shuffler, the cards liquid in her hands.

"You all know rummy?" she said.

"I'm not sure I want to play," said Landon.

"Drink your margarita and cheer up. I don't know why he's here, and I don't ask," Marianne said to me, jutting her chin toward Landon. "You need a time-out, you come to Marianne. I'll take care of you. This boy is golden. You know he's going to be a librarian?"

"I heard," I said.

"You need people in life. The best way to stave off Alzheimer's is to keep talking to people. Before you showed up today, no one had come around for days except Landon. The only other people who've wanted to talk to me are the police. They asked me to come to the station to give a sample of my DNA, to help test for DNA in Jeannie's car. I had to explain how she was adopted. They've got hairs from her apartment, I think. They said it can take weeks to test hairs."

Marianne flicked her hands in a dance around the table until we each had seven cards, facedown. Her cheerful tone hadn't changed, but the mention of the police had betrayed what was really on her mind. I took a sip of my margarita, which was so strong it tasted of turpentine, and so full of ice I had to chew rather than drink it.

"What did the police say?" I asked her, picking up my cards. "When they asked for the DNA?"

She scoffed. "They asked me a bunch of stupid questions. What do they think *I* know? The head detective had all the charisma of a bowl of Wheaties. They're hardly even trying."

"I'm sure they want the case solved, too," I said, noncommittally.

Landon stared wistfully into the bottom of his now-empty margarita glass. We held our cards but didn't play.

"Marianne," I said. "Could I ask you a few stupid questions about Jeanine?"

"You can ask me whatever you want, honey. You knew to be worried. That's why you called me from the very beginning. They should put you in charge of the investigation. Women know."

"When's the last time you saw her?"

"She came for lunch like usual, about two and a half weeks ago. The weekend before all this started."

"Did she ever talk to you about Jason Morley?" I asked.

"Who? Another man?" She hooted, sucked at her drink. "She likes to keep every avenue open."

"Did she ever talk about how she was cutting her hours at work?" I asked.

"She said she had a ton of work. Lots of tips and cheerleader events. She was doing great with money. That real estate guy was paying for things, her trips, her dinners. I think that's how she's funding this little excursion of hers. I think things were going too well for her and she had to go have a little nervous breakdown. A rich boyfriend, this stuck-up Jills business—it was too shiny and clean, and she had to go and screw it up. Like with Landon—as soon as it's good, she runs."

"Did she talk about buying a new car? Did you ever see her drive a white Hyundai?"

"No. I never heard her talk about a car."

I cast around for other details I could confirm, not wanting to waste this moment with Marianne and Landon. I thought back to the list I'd made, of all the things I had to check: boys, work, her mail—

"She got mail," I said. "From—a Linda Sulzener? The Calhoun Clinic?"

Marianne froze in mid-sip, her eyes sharpened.

"Linda Sulzener? What is *Linda Sulzener* sending my baby in the mail?"

"Who?" said Landon.

I said, "Is that, um . . . is that Jeanine's doctor? Or did you—was the Calhoun Clinic where—"

Though I'd just been reminded of Jeanine's adoption, I nearly asked Marianne if she'd given birth to Jeanine at the clinic. Luckily, she interrupted me.

"That's where I got her."

"Got her?" I said.

"I picked her up two days before Christmas. She was ten days old. She was my Christmas present."

"Wait—I never heard the whole story behind this," said Landon. "Is it like an adoption agency?"

Marianne put down her cards. "Do you know what it can cost to go through an adoption agency in this country? No, this was affordable and discreet. You put your name on the list and they called you when there was a baby. Pay with cash, no muss or fuss. It took ten, eleven months of waiting, and then I got the call. It's better for everyone, without the paperwork and bureaucracy. That's exactly why this Linda Sulzener business bothers me—the whole point was that it was anonymous, and now she's going around trying to make a big reunion out of it, putting everyone in touch with each other."

I couldn't have pictured the conversation going in this direction in a million years. I'd never thought Marianne, of all people, would know who the hell Linda Sulzener was, and I'd never expected *this* would be the reason Linda was contacting Jeanine.

"So has Linda Sulzener been in contact with you, too?" I asked.

"I first started hearing from her about a year and a half ago. She said the clinic was closing, and she was part of this group that was distributing files and documents and everything that had been stored in the clinic, so people could trace their birth story or find the baby they gave up. Which is exactly what anyone who used the clinic *didn't* want. I told her to stay away from Jeanine, and I figured she had. Jeanine never mentioned this woman's name to me, once. Are you going to drink yours?" said Marianne.

"Huh?" I looked at my still-full cup and pushed it toward her. "You can finish it."

Marianne gulped from my glass. "I don't like that. I don't like this woman sending things to my Jeannie in the mail. Do you think—*that's* why she ran away?" She lowered the plastic cup shakily. "She made some horrible discovery about her birth parents?"

"Who are the birth parents?" said Landon.

"I don't know! They didn't leave their names. They gave her up. Why should I want to know their names? She's mine. I gave her the best life I could. Maybe I set her up with a shit father, but I saved up for months to buy her a prom dress. I sewed those pageant gowns for her so she could compete. I got her those ballet classes and helped her film audition tapes and told her she could be anybody she wanted to be. I'm her mother."

Her voice was tight with tears.

"Jeanine loves you so fucking much, Marianne," said Landon. "I don't think this birth clinic has anything to do with why she's gone. I'm just saying."

"She's good enough for any life she wants. When she comes back, I'm going to tell her that."

"We all know that, Marianne," I said.

"That's right, you do. She's better than anyone. And that's how I know," Marianne said, snapping her cards on the table to straighten them, "that she's going to come out of this whole strange business laughing."

I BEGGED OFF after one round of rummy, saying I had to get back home before it got dark. Landon walked me out onto the front porch, leaving Marianne to mix another lethal batch of margaritas in the kitchen.

I stomped my foot. "Did she ever talk to you about that Calhoun stuff? I never heard about any of that."

"You can drive yourself crazy chasing every little detail, but it all comes to the same thing. She's gone, Virginia."

"I don't know. I'm not so sure."

The dog, Donny, whined from behind the screen door, scratching at the frame. I had one more question to ask.

"Landon, did you know the police have a warrant to search your apartment?"

He blanched. "Because of Jeanine?"

"No. Because of a body that was found."

"A body? What body? Not Jeanine's?"

"No. A man's."

"What?" He ran his hands through his hair, which needed a trim. "What the fuck is happening? What does everyone think I did?"

His distress was so bald-faced I had to believe he really didn't know what I was talking about.

"I don't have anything to do with a dead body. God, I hope no one else died because of that shit I took from Jeanine—that cursed shit.

This is a nightmare that won't end. I gotta get out of here. I can't be around Marianne with all this on my head. I can't be around anybody."

He began to well up, his voice tight with despair.

"You really can't be caught having visited me here. Between the police and the Paladinos—you can't be here. I thought Jeanine was the crazy one and you were even-keeled. But you might actually be psychotic. You're going to get yourself killed asking all these questions."

"I'm going to figure out what happened to her," I said.

"Virginia, please go home and stop. Go back to your life, your nice life."

He wiped his nose on his sleeve, his hand shaking.

"Landon," I said. "I swear to God, if I come out of this finding out that you did something to her—"

I couldn't finish the sentence. We both struggled to meet the other's eye.

"This story doesn't end with me hurting her," he said. "But I guarantee you, it ends someplace you don't wanna go."

Chapter 21

ON THE WAY home, I pulled over on the side of the Thruway.

I was struck by a memory so strong it felt like being possessed. Jeanine and I, sitting on the floor of her apartment, high above downtown, an empty bottle of white wine between us, the two of us weak with laughter. This scene had happened hundreds of times over the course of our friendship. On this occasion, Jeanine had received a text from Bobby that made her collapse onto the rug, shaking uncontrollably. *What, what,* I'd shouted, until she gathered the strength to show me her phone. The text read: **I want to fondle your blobs.** We had had enough wine to make this the most magnificent typo we had ever seen. "My blobs," Jeanine shrieked, tears streaming down her face. "My blobs!" Every time we got ourselves under control Jeanine would hold out the screen and we would lose it again. For months afterward, she would send me a screenshot of the text out of the blue, especially if she knew I had something important to do—a radio spot for the Jills or a new personal training client. One peek at my phone, and I would have to excuse myself to go to the bathroom to crack up, or sit there with tears welling behind my eyes, trying to keep myself under control.

Blobs, I thought now, in the car, and began to laugh, my diaphragm shaking. The laughter felt the same as crying, and soon I was crying. I cried for Landon's aloneness, and my own, and Jeanine's. I cried that I might never be sent that screenshot again. This search was breaking my heart, again and again, each new crack another delusion shattered. Alongside all the lies, the fake trips, and the secret meetings, was another omission: that she'd been purchased illegally at a clinic in Ohio. And she'd endured the weight of this discovery on her own. As if she had no one—as if I were no one.

I would have helped her. If she needed money, I could have figured out how to get her some. If she was distressed by some revelation from her past, I would have listened. That's what hurt, more than her lying to me and going to Landon and Jason behind my back: that she hadn't thought of me as someone who could help her.

But I would show her, I thought, drawing a clean breath and wiping my eyes. I put the car in drive. I'd show her—I would help her.

WHEN I SWUNG open the door to my apartment, I heard a little "Eep!" from behind the door to my bedroom.

"Don't get mad!" Laura's voice floated out.

"It's fine," I called. I didn't have the energy to be annoyed that she'd gone into my bedroom—I would certainly have done the same if I were left alone in her apartment. And I was immensely relieved to have someone to talk to, to have Laura.

"I couldn't resist," she said as I pushed open the door.

It took me a moment to realize what she was talking about. My uniform bag lay open, slung across the bed like the skin of a gutted alligator. And Laura—Laura was wearing my uniform.

My sadness fled, replaced by horror.

"I wanted to see what it felt like," she said. "This is so much worse than what we wore for dance team growing up. Look at the cut of this thing." She stuck out her butt to study it in the mirror. The booty shorts under the skirt cut deep ridges into her pale, dimpled skin. "It's like a shame suit constructed to destroy confidence."

"Take it off, Laura."

"Oh, but the uniform isn't even the worst part. Ginny." She held up my Jills binder so that the pages fell open, a handful of my notes flapping to the floor. "What the fuck is this binder?"

"It's our full-season calendar. Be careful, please. Everything I need is in there. Appearance dates, and notes on the choreography, and what routine to do—"

"I mean the handbook. What is this?" She flipped to a page and read aloud: " 'Jills must limit themselves to one slice of bread at seated dinner events'? It says when you should go to the *bathroom*. There's a note on how often to change your tampon!"

I rubbed my eyes, feeling hopelessly persecuted.

"Those aren't *real* rules," I stammered. "They're in there because one time a girl did eat a crazy amount of bread at an event, and another time a girl *did* bleed through her uniform. You know how when one person screws up, everyone has to hear about it."

"You're brainwashed. It's so patronizing I can't even believe it." She squinted at the page. "You're not allowed to talk to the players?"

"Oh, *God* no."

"Why the fuck not? What do they think is going to happen?"

The reasoning seemed to have something to do with protection, though who was being protected from whom was unclear. (The players from our wiles? Us from their rampant masculinity?) Frankly, I was relieved to be prevented from talking to them; I wouldn't know what to say anyway.

"It's so everyone stays professional," I said. "Laura, take it off. *Please.*"

She tossed the binder onto my bed and started shimmying out of the skirt.

"I had a hard time believing that all this shit you do for the Bills could be worse than what we went through growing up, but clearly I was wrong. This kind of pressure can really hurt a person. It hurt me, and I think it hurts you more than you realize. Don't you ever wonder why you feel like you have to do this?"

The back of my neck began to prickle with rage.

"I don't feel like I *have to do* it," I said.

"It's forced compliance, Ginny," she said, struggling with the skirt. "Treating women like show dogs or ponies, jerking them around, telling them how to stand and talk, selling them off to the highest bidder."

"Nobody gets *sold*." I watched in agony as Laura yanked off the skirt, praying I couldn't hear threads popping.

"They do, for God's sake, we grew up with it: women, cheerleaders, everywhere, constantly. I love Stanley, but come on. He collected and traded women like baseball cards. Mom always said it. She said, 'If anyone wanted a Jill, Stanley got them one.' She said, 'What was your dad going to do, say no?' And we admired these women! That's how we wanted to *be*! Can't you see how fucked up that messaging was?"

If Mom and Laura kept talking about cheerleaders without my input, I was going to scream. Everyone thought we were so dumb. Why—because we were pretty? We were bouncy? That was our job, to be bouncy. To get pummeled nonstop with attention and questions and stares and critiques and still bounce back, and bounce back and bounce back. People like Laura and Mom jeered from the sidelines, but what they didn't realize—what no one realized—was that all that bouncing made us the toughest fucking people in the room.

"I'm not some mindless robot," I said, snatching the skirt and holding it to my chest. "You think the handbook's patronizing? You calling me stupid is patronizing. You saying I'm *nobody* is patronizing."

Laura wiggled the top over her shoulders, scowling. "I didn't say you were stupid."

"You don't get to take this away from me because you hated it," I said. "I love it. I'm a person. I love to dance. I get to dance with seventy thousand people watching me. Do you know how many people get to perform in front of a real audience like that? Almost *no one*. How do you know Mom is telling the truth about Dad? She's paranoid. She's scared of other women. She hates Stanley."

"Of course you're a person. You're my sister. *My* sister!" Laura wrenched off the top and threw it on the bed next to the binder. "I'll kill anyone who tries to tell you what to do. I hate them for making you wear that. It's too small, Ginny!"

She picked up her own leggings but was too flustered to put them on. She bundled them up and threw them to the ground.

"Too small!"

She stormed out to the living room in her bra and underwear. I stood clutching my skirt, bewildered, rage draining from my body. In all the years since Laura quit dance, I had never considered that her criticisms of me—of my diet or my exercise regime—could have any motivation beyond trying to make me feel stupid. I had never considered that she was trying, even in her clumsy, judgmental way, to be on my side.

I took a deep breath and counted to ten. Laura was not supposed to come to my defense. I didn't need taking care of. I knew why I did the things I did. I followed her to the living room.

"Laura, wait," I said. "Can we forget the handbook? I have something to tell you."

"IT DOESN'T MAKE sense any way you look at it," Laura said.

She was back in her own clothes, pouring tea in the kitchen while I sat at the counter. The sight of her in my apartment, using my things, made me feel tender and exposed. I was grateful we could retreat to the subject of Jeanine every time we veered into topics too dangerous for conversation—namely, our feelings about each other.

The revelation about Jeanine's adoption made me feel left out and ashamed, so I hadn't lingered long on it when recounting my visit at Marianne's. Instead, I focused on Landon's confirmation that the block of heroin did in fact exist and had, apparently, been supplied to him by Jeanine.

"How would Jeanine have gotten her hands on that much stuff?" Laura said. "Who would sell it to her? I can tell you've got a soft spot for this guy, but I think he's lying. If she was involved, maybe, *maybe* it was as a liaison. She's got everyone's number in her Rolodex. But why would she go through the trouble of coordinating something that risky? And why do the Paladinos care? Are they pissed about the drugs?"

"The Paladinos aren't involved in heroin."

"We don't really know what Stanley does, and we definitely don't know what Bobby is into."

"I think she got coerced into being involved," I said. "Most likely by Jason. You said yourself, it's too big a coincidence that she and Jason were seen at the Pink Fountain right around the time this mysterious block of heroin appears. *He's* the one everyone should be after."

"Maybe," Laura conceded. She tugged the string of the tea bag. "I wish you had talked to me before you went to confront Landon. That wasn't smart. I don't care whose mom was there. I'm not prepared to believe he took on a bunch of heroin because he's a nice guy. He's in a desperate situation, and desperate people do crazy things."

"All I'm doing is talking to people," I said.

"Yeah, to people in *hiding*. You shouldn't even know where this guy is, Gin. Someone is going to think you're more involved than you are. They might come kicking down *your* door to see what you know."

The words had hardly left her mouth when there was a knock at the door.

We went still, staring down the length of the hallway, at the end of which stood my door, my flimsy door. The silence after the knock was so quiet I thought I could hear the steam rising off Laura's tea. I could think of absolutely nobody I wanted knocking at this hour. I thought, nonsensically, *They've finally come to collect.*

"Ginny," whispered Laura as I pushed back from the counter.

"I'll go see who it is," I said.

I started padding down the hallway, glancing back to see that Laura had grabbed one of my kitchen knives. She hovered a few feet behind me, knife raised, breathing fast through her nose.

I pulled open the door a crack, peeked out from behind the chain.

It was Sharrice.

"Uh, hello?" Sharrice said. "What gives?"

The panic dropped out through a trapdoor in the bottom of my stomach as I undid the chain. Sharrice, it was Sharrice! Last practice—yes, I remembered—I'd promised to help her write thank-you cards for the Junior Jills fundraiser contributors.

"What's going on?" she said, hovering uncertainly on the threshold. I realized Laura was standing behind me, kitchen knife in hand.

Laura looked down at the knife. "Oh, I'll—I guess I'll go put this away."

I mumbled introductions as Sharrice bustled her way inside. "Wait," she gasped. "You're *Laura* Laura?" She followed Laura down the hall to the living room. "Yes! Wow! Here you are! Here she is!" she said to me. "In Buffalo!"

"You're a Jill?" Laura surmised.

"Oh, yeah, we're pretty easy to pick out." Sharrice swept her hair over her shoulder proudly.

Sharrice insisted she could leave if Laura and I wanted more time together, but Laura said she should be getting back to our mom. "I already ditched her for one night," she said. "She'll flip if I don't have dinner with her."

I gathered up Laura's coat and socks, which she'd bunched into a corner of the couch, while Sharrice peppered her with a million questions about her life in Ohio. They chatted about Laura's massage therapist training, and how she was getting her yoga instructor license ("Oh my God, *so* good for your core," said Sharrice), and the improvisational dance group she was putting together.

"You dance?" said Sharrice, as I shoved Laura's socks into her bag. This was the first I'd heard of Laura starting a dance group.

"Not like you guys do," said Laura. "I used to dance like that, till I tore up my ankle in high school and quit." She tapped her left thigh. "This whole leg is messed up. The hip pops, and my ankle still hurts sometimes."

"Oh, my hips sound like bubble wrap from doing the jump splits for the Jills," said Sharrice, rotating one leg so it cracked.

"I'd like to find another way to dance, one that isn't about hurting yourself, you know? Like, dance as a form of recovery, reclaiming your body after you've treated it like a garbage can. My goal is to work with other women who are also in recovery, to help them heal their relationship with their bodies."

Sharrice nodded with growing understanding. I avoided her glance, zipping up Laura's bag.

"I get it," said Sharrice earnestly. "Restorative methods. That's amazing."

"Here's your stuff," I said to Laura.

"Wait," said Sharrice. She put her hands on Laura's shoulders and stared into her eyes. "You're Virginia's family," she said soberly. "And that means you're my family, too."

Laura stammered as Sharrice pulled her into a hug. I wanted to sink through the floorboards. These were Jills sentiments: family, support, sisterhood, being the best you could be. If you believed in them, they might save your life. If you didn't, they sounded like platitudes on a Walmart wall hanging. It embarrassed me for Laura to hear Sharrice say these things, because then she would know that I believed them too, and if I believed in them, then that meant I needed them.

"Oh—okay," Laura said, her face unreadable as Sharrice released her. Was she amused? Touched? "Um . . . you too?"

Sharrice waved cheerfully as Laura made her way down the hallway, until the door swung shut behind her. Then she turned to me, bouncing her shoulders happily.

"She's cute!" she said.

Chapter 22

THE BUSINESSLIKE MANNER with which Sharrice set about tidying up my coffee table, ordering takeout for dinner, and setting up supplies for the thank-you cards confirmed that I'd developed a helpless and distracted air that begged for intervention.

She handed me the script she'd drafted for the cards, which we would handwrite, with Sharrice crafting special notes for major donors.

"Do you want to leave a note for the Paladinos?" she said, her purple pen flying. She sat on the floor, working at the coffee table, while I wrote on the couch. "We've got to do one for the Paladino Restaurant Group, and one for the McKormick Group. They are *big* donors, for every campaign."

I got an uncomfortable mental image of Stanley seeding the Junior Jills program with money, to ensure the growth and harvest of future Jills to attend parties at his various establishments.

"No, you do it. I don't need to."

She put her pen down and turned to face me. "You okay?"

"I don't like having to explain to people why I do this," I burst out, gesturing at the cards. "I don't like having to defend my choices.

Even when you spell out as clearly as you can all the things you *get* out of it, no one believes you. They think you're stupid or a victim."

"By 'they,' you mean your sister?" Sharrice smiled knowingly. "I get it. My brothers are the same way."

"How do I stand up for myself, and the Jills, when Jeanine is *still missing* and we're writing these cute little cards, with the hearts and exclamation points? And—oh God, the check from Suzanna." I put my hands over my face. "It's so embarrassing. How do I explain that to Laura? I can't even explain it to myself!"

"Virginia, you don't have to explain. You can love something and commit your whole heart to it and also want to change it. Wanting to change it can be a *sign* you love it. For instance, it's no secret I've got a lot of problems with our funding situation and the lack of transparency. That's why I'm gunning for a captain position next season. I'd like to argue for some changes. I think I could make things better. I'm not dumb. I know there are issues. I love the *Jills*. I'm in it for the girls. No one can understand that who's not a part of it."

"I guess I'm tired," I said, "of trying so hard to make sense."

Sharrice tucked her legs under herself and propped an elbow on the couch cushions.

"Is it weird," she said, "having Laura here? I didn't know she was in recovery."

"She hasn't been sober that long," I said. "Just since February. Last time she made it eleven months before she relapsed, so . . . we'll see." I fiddled with my gel pen. "I'm not saying it's not amazing that she's sober again, I'm just . . . I have to manage expectations."

"You're protecting yourself."

"Don't make me sound terrible!"

Sharrice was taken aback. "Am I?"

"Well, to need protection from your own sister, when she's the one—*she's* the one with the problem, the one who needs to be protected."

"By you?"

"Not anymore," I mumbled.

"So who protects you?"

"Oh, Sharrice." I pulled up the hood of my sweatshirt, embarrassed by the question. "I don't know. Who protects *you*?"

"My mom," she began, counting off on her fingers. "My aunt and godmom. My Line 4 girls. And that includes you. You'd jump to my defense if I needed it."

"Of course I would. You'd jump to mine, right?"

She smiled at me, and I yanked my hood over my face. I pretended to scroll through the donor list on my laptop. Sharrice and I had always been pretty close, but we'd never talked about it. It felt a little like she and I were on a date.

"I would, Virginia."

"I know!"

"I would. I'd like to."

"Well, you are. Okay? Right now. Duh."

"Good," she said happily. "Well, there's a lot more where that came from."

She put a hand on my foot and gave it a squeeze. Her gaze fell on the cards scattered across the coffee table, and her face darkened.

"I know I'm not going to be a captain. I'm not one of Suzanna's favorites. I'm organized and I volunteer for extra responsibilities, and none of it seems to matter. I can feel in the way she looks at me that she's not going to give me a leadership role."

"Don't you know you're not supposed to ask Suzanna any questions," I joked, poking her arm with my pen. "You're supposed to just say thank you."

"I can't help it!" she laughed. "I'm nosy. I work around a bunch of freaking prosecutors. We want to know what's going on."

"I'd like my sister to look you in the eye and call you brainwashed," I said.

"We're all brainwashed," said Sharrice, with a gravity that surprised me. "We're all subjected to the same BS, right? The way it affects you varies, obviously, depending on your background, and your advantages and everything, but it's the same relentless, repetitive messaging. Who's exempt from that? No one. There's no control group. If there's anything I can't stand," she said, signing her name with a flourish on the nearest card, "it's people who think they're so evolved or educated that they're above being brainwashed. Those are the ones you have to watch out for—they care more about maintaining their position of superiority and contempt for other people than they do about making life better for everyone."

Before I could think of a reply, Sharrice's phone dinged.

"Ooh—our takeout!" she said cheerfully.

WE SETTLED ON the first movie we found on TNT—*Clear and Present Danger*—and let it play in the background as we ate Greek salads and filled out stacks and stacks of cards.

After *Clear and Present Danger* finished, *The Hunt for Red October* came on. Sharrice capped her pen, popped open the wine she'd brought, and made herself comfortable under the afghan on my couch. The cat made his first appearance of the night as he hopped up to settle between her ankles.

Sharrice nodded off during the last twenty minutes of the movie. The candle on the table puffed out, eliminating the last light besides the jerky glow of the muted TV. It was warm in the apartment, and the steam from the radiator had frosted the windows with condensation. I felt like we'd been gently encased inside an egg, suspended two stories above the ground, fragile and protected. I reached out to trace Jeanine's name into the silvery frost on the window. I put a question mark after the last letter and gazed at it for a while, before wiping it away with the pinkie side of my fist.

In the clear oval I'd left behind appeared the dark form of a man crossing the street toward my building. I scrubbed out a larger clear spot on the glass. The man continued onto the sidewalk in front of my building. *Keep walking*, I willed him. *Go down the sidewalk and keep walking.* The force of my thoughts was not enough; the man padded across the front lawn before disappearing beneath the windowsill, where I could no longer see him.

I ran to my apartment door to check the locks and pressed my ear to the frame. I heard the echoey squeal of the front door to the building opening below, the creak of footsteps ascending the stairs. My knees weakened, and I bent down into a squat and tried to catch my breath.

The footsteps grew louder as the man reached my floor. I raced back into the living room to Sharrice's sleeping form.

Before I could shake her awake, there was an explosion of knocks at my door. I clamped my hand over my mouth, and Sharrice woke with a sharp intake of breath and sat up. The knocking persisted, dull and heavy on the wood.

"Hello?" A man's voice. "Hello?"

We sat frozen, eyes fixed on the dim outline of my apartment door. The shadow of the man's feet swayed beneath the doorframe.

The knocking stopped, followed by a scraping sound, like the man was fiddling around close to the floor. Sharrice grabbed her purse and yanked out a bundled sweatshirt. She tossed the sweatshirt aside, and I had to blink several times before I recognized what was in her hand: a tiny gun.

I doubled over into a crouched position on the floor, my abdomen clenched in protest, as though to keep the gun from blowing my own body apart.

"Who is that!" Sharrice called out, voice shaking. "Who is it? I've got a gun?"

"Sharrice, please!" I moaned from the floor.

"Go open the door," she said to me. "Let's get to the bottom of this."

"Hello?" said the man.

"No, no, no, no," I repeated, shaking my head.

"Virginia!" growled Sharrice.

I straightened and, through a sludge of molasses dread, approached the door. I gripped the knob and pulled it open, sandwiching myself between the door and the wall. I waited for a gunshot, for the molecules making up my apartment and my skin and the air around me to explode and fly apart.

Through the slot between the door and the jamb, I could see the shape of a crouched figure on my doormat. The figure's hands shot up.

"Please, don't shoot!"

Tears were leaking from Sharrice's eyes, but her arms were straight as toothpicks. "I'm not afraid to use this!" she shouted. She released the gun with one hand to wipe the tears and snot off her face but kept it pointed firmly at the man with the other. "You stay there on the floor! Stay like that or I'll shoot!"

"Everyone please be calm," said the figure, voice muffled from underneath his arms. "Please, please, I beg you."

"No one's going to shoot," I said. "No one move. I'm turning on the light."

I batted at the wall until I found the light switch.

It was Ray crouched on the floor, in his usual Bills jacket, an orange knitted cap on his head. Clutched in his hand was a crumpled piece of paper, which I realized he'd been trying to shove underneath the door.

"Ray," I gasped. "Put that thing away, Sharrice! God, my neighbors— Ray, get in here."

"I didn't mean to frighten you." He straightened slowly, staring at the gun, still in Sharrice's hand. "I couldn't tell if anyone was home. I wasn't trying to come inside."

"What the hell were you doing then?" asked Sharrice.

"Sharrice, would you mind," he said. "Please put down the gun. Is it necessary?"

"Necessary?" Sharrice said. "Some of us have stalkers, Ray! Do you ever think about that? Do you ever think about how it feels for some guy to have your address and show up at your apartment? No, Ray, you don't, you just think, *Oh I'll come to practice, oh I'll send them flowers, oh I'll knock on their door at night, they won't mind, they'll like it*. Has it ever crossed your mind that we might not like it? Clueless! Men are clueless, with their big stupid bubbles they walk around in, knocking into everything, thinking everyone wants them around, never worrying about getting attacked by psychos—"

"Sharrice," I begged. "Stop yelling. You're going to get me evicted."

I ushered them both into the living room. Sharrice set the gun down on the coffee table before collapsing on the couch, hands over her eyes, breathing heavily. Ray stood, shifting from foot to foot, clutching his paper.

"What are you doing here, Ray?" I said. "What's in your hand?"

"Well." He drew himself up, patting the edges of the crumpled paper to straighten it out. "I have the registration information for the car that Jeanine was driving."

"The what?" said Sharrice.

"I did some research and found the car owner," said Ray. "I have the name and address right here."

"Ray . . ." I breathed. He handed me the paper.

"Can someone explain what's happening?" Sharrice said.

I whispered that Ray had seen Jeanine driving a different car a couple of times before she disappeared. Sharrice snatched the paper from my hands before I could read it.

"How did you get this information?" she demanded, shaking the paper at Ray.

"I used the license plate number. I had it memorized. I have a good head for numbers and letters. I know yours, too."

He rattled off a plate number. Sharrice shook her head furiously and groaned.

"My father works in car insurance," Ray went on. "I called the DMV pretending to be him. Said I was researching a hit-and-run. You can put in a records request at the DMV to try to learn the car owner's identity yourself, but it can take a long time, and sometimes they won't release the information. You can get it much quicker if you're an insurance agent."

I could tell by Sharrice's face that this was illegal. I took the paper back from her hands and smoothed it out.

"I can be quite convincing on the phone," said Ray. "It wasn't difficult. And now we have the name. Do you recognize it?"

I looked at the paper. The car was registered to someone named Olena Rossi. Ray had written out the name and address in his cramped, jagged penmanship.

I shook my head. "I've never heard of this woman."

"Now, here's what's really interesting," said Ray. "The address—that's not a residential address. That's the street address of the post office."

"Oh," I said, not understanding.

Sharrice said, "You're not allowed to register your car to a PO box. So if a person doesn't want to reveal their address, or if they don't have a street address, they might do this."

"Right," said Ray. "It's odd, is all."

"Olena Rossi," said Sharrice. "Who is that? Why is that name familiar?"

"Ray, it's very . . . nice of you to do this," I said. "I don't know how to thank you."

"But we're not done yet," said Ray. "Without a real address, this is of minimal use to us. We have to keep going."

A bubble of panic rose in my chest. This would probably lead us nowhere. We couldn't even knock on this person's door. All these disparate clues formed an ocean that swallowed Jeanine every time I came close to grabbing her. How much longer would I have to keep watching her disappear, over and over, as soon as I got close?

"I'm serious about this name," said Sharrice. She brought her laptop over to the coffee table. "I swear I'm not crazy. I recognize it from somewhere."

"There are other searches we can try," said Ray. "Court records and property records and business registrations. With a name this unique, we can probably find some document with a residential address on it. If we work *together*—"

"Ray," I said, annoyed by his use of the pronoun *we*. "That would take so long. And how would we know we've found the person attached to this particular car?"

"We'll knock on every door of every address tied to an Olena Rossi until we find the right one!"

"Yes!" Sharrice interrupted. "I told you. Right there."

She pushed the screen toward me. She'd pulled up her spreadsheet. There, on her computer, was the name Olena Rossi: major donor to the Junior Jills.

RAY VERY MUCH did not want to leave. "I truly would do anything—" he said as I shut the door in his face.

I felt bad kicking him out after all the trouble he'd gone through, but I was desperate to be alone with Sharrice.

We sat cross-legged on the sofa, the laptop between us on the cushions. Olena Rossi's name occupied row 81 of the donor spreadsheet. Latest donation amount: $12,550.

"For the Junior Jills," said Sharrice, shaking her head. "You'd think with all that, we could spring for a few more scholarships?"

The mailing address listed on the spreadsheet was a PO box in Columbus, Ohio. A Google search of the name along with "Ohio" brought up only one result: Olena Rossi worked as a receptionist for an ear, nose, and throat doctor in Springfield, Ohio. She was right there on the employee directory page.

"Why would she have a car registered in New York if she works at a doctor's office in Ohio?" I said.

"The better question is: How can a secretary afford a twelve-thousand-dollar donation to the Jills?" Sharrice zoomed in on the woman's picture. Olena Rossi was blond and slightly overweight, probably in her early fifties. She looked like a hundred receptionists. "Maybe she lives in Ohio but has a business in Buffalo, or vice versa? And she commutes between the two?"

"She's clearly a Junior Jills supporter," I said. "She and Jeanine could have met at an event, and Olena Rossi let her borrow her car? Jeanine can get people to do stuff like that for her. Usually not women, but you never know."

Sharrice sighed. "It's not *nothing*, but . . . All we know is that this woman has the same name as someone who has the same type of car that Ray might have once seen Jeanine driving for one second."

She clicked through the Google street view of the downtown strip of Springfield, as if we might catch a glimpse of Olena Rossi captured there. Then we used the license plate number to search for unpaid parking tickets in New York and Ohio but found nothing.

"We know where she works, at least," I said.

"Virginia, I don't have the strength to talk you out of stalking this woman. I've already pointed a gun at someone today. I'm tired."

The gun lay on the coffee table, under Sharrice's sweatshirt, which I'd thrown over it to cover it up. The cat jumped onto the table to sniff at it. It was past midnight at this point. Sharrice watched me study the "No results" page on the Ohio BMV site.

"I don't even want to ask what you're going to do next."

Chapter 23

All I did next was think. I taught my fitness classes. I had lunch with Mom and Laura at a Panera in West Seneca, a relatively peaceful ordeal during which none of us argued and not much got said. I went to my appearances—a ribbon-cutting for the hospital and an opening for a Bills merchandise store at the airport—and smiled for pictures. I went to Jills practice afterward, arriving an hour early for Suzanna's grief mediation activity.

Suzanna had the lights dimmed and was directing the girls, as they entered, to sit in a circle on the floor of the Kmart.

I took a seat next to Sharrice. Suzanna watched us with impassive grace until we were all seated.

"There is a wound here," she intoned. "We all feel it. We have been bravely continuing on in spite of the wound. We have been dancing and practicing and giving it our all, pushing through the pain. I take responsibility for that pain. I have thought, every day since Jeanine first failed to show up, that we would hear from her. Even when her name appeared in the news, I thought, *The police will bring her home, and we'll take her in our arms, and we'll have her back.* That day still may come. But the waiting . . ." She closed her eyes with a grimace of pain. "There is so much waiting, and the wound is still there. So even though we know so little, and we still have hope, we have to take steps, as a team and a community, to heal and let go."

She held up a copy of *The Buffalo News* with the story about Jeanine's car being found. "We're going to pass this around. When you hold the paper, I would like you to share how Jeanine going missing has impacted you."

My whole body went stiff. Suzanna passed the paper to Sara, to begin.

"I feel," said Sara, clutching the newspaper, "a little more scared, but also a lot more grateful. Like, I realize how precious each and every one of you is to me. And I realize what an enormous role you all play in my life. And I hope that Jeanine is safe, and that she knows how much we love her, and that we're not angry she's gone. We just want her back."

She began to cry, and passed the paper to Natalie.

"I feel more exposed at appearances and stuff," said Natalie. "Like, something bad could happen at any time. So . . . a little less safe, I guess."

"I feel," said Sophie, clutching the paper, "like there's a hole in the squad now and I'm not beautiful or talented enough to fill it, and I wish Jeanine was here because she was such a great dancer and I felt so inspired watching her and like *I* could be better and I just hope I can be good enough for you all."

There was a chorus of "You *are* good enough" and "We love you, Sophie" as she passed the paper to Lana.

The girls' tearful words, their shy testimonies—it all sounded like someone clanging a hammer into a cast iron pan. This was the stupidest thing I'd ever had to sit through. Were we all supposed to have a good cry and feel better afterward like we'd done something? This wasn't doing something! This was nothing!

The paper reached me. I held it. The girls smiled at me encouragingly, waiting for me to make a moving statement. I was Jeanine's best friend. They probably thought I needed this most of all.

"I can't say," I said.

"Try," said Suzanna.

I passed the paper to Sharrice, stonily silent. Sharrice held it uncertainly.

"I feel, um . . . guilty, I guess? That . . . there's not more I can do?" she said.

Around the paper went, drawing confessions and allusions to lost grandparents, friends who'd passed away. Ashlee broke down and had to lean on the girls on either side of her for support. I resented the invitation to experience such structured, tidy catharsis. I wasn't interested in feeling better.

After the paper made its inane trip around the circle, Suzanna had us stand and link hands.

"You girls spread joy," Suzanna said. "You bring light wherever you go. We need to give a little of that joy and light to ourselves sometimes."

She told us to close our eyes and envision an orb of light at the center of our circle. I kept my eyes open, watching the girls as they wept and then relaxed into a state of peace and acceptance. The Kmart filled with the sounds of sniffling and gentle laughing. I was pulled into several hugs with girls whispering platitudes into my hair. "Thank you, Suzanna," they said. "We needed that," they said.

"Now let's dance our goddamn hearts out," said Suzanna, to a burst of applause.

While the girls rushed into their positions, Suzanna pulled me aside.

"I know this is hard," she whispered, as I grabbed my duffel bag. She handed me the paper. "Do you want to try again? No audience. Just you and me. Whatever you need."

I held the paper and shook. Whatever I needed? How could I even begin to describe what I needed?

"Virginia—" Suzanna called out. But I was already out the door.

"IT WAS A fucking funeral," I exclaimed as soon as Laura showed up at my door.

I'd invited her over so I wouldn't be alone. Even Sharrice I didn't want to be around.

"Everyone is giving up," I said before Laura could even say hello. "We have so much power, and we sit around pretending to be helpless? Suzanna has gone to bat for so many girls. Why is she so complacent about Jeanine? Is it because she's bad press? A good cheerleader would never put herself in a bad position? Would never go missing? Where's the cat?"

Laura made tea while I turned the living room upside down, searching for the cat. She wore her hair in two buns on the top of her head.

"Maybe it's a little unreasonable to expect a cheerleading organization to get involved in a police investigation," said Laura. "Do you think you might be upset seeing people express grief you're not ready to process yourself?"

"I never make tea," I said. "I don't even know why I buy it. And you come in and finally someone is using my tea bags."

"You should try it." She held up the chamomile. "Stick with calming flowers. Peppermint and cinnamon are activating. You're activated enough."

"We could be going to the press, for God's sake. Fundraising to hire a private detective. Instead everyone's content to be *useless*."

I kicked at my afghan and couch pillows, which in my search had ended up on the floor. So what if Laura saw me throw a tantrum? She'd seen me act much worse. She was the only person, in fact, whom I could stand to watch me ranting and raving, which was probably why I'd invited her over. Not even Jeanine had seen me at my worst. Only Laura.

"Oh my God," she said.

"What?"

Laura's hands held *The Buffalo News,* which I'd accidentally taken with me when I'd walked out of practice. I'd left it lying open on my kitchen counter.

"I know this girl," Laura said, jabbing a finger at Jeanine's headshot.

"No, you don't," I said. "You couldn't."

"Yes, I do." She picked up the paper. "I met her in Columbus. Her name is Olena."

My ears went cottony, like when I did too much intense cardio on too few calories.

"What's she doing in the Buffalo paper?" said Laura. "Ginny?"

I barely registered the sight of Laura springing to my side to grip my elbow and lower me into a kitchen chair.

"IT'S BEEN MONTHS since I last saw her," said Laura. She fanned at me while I slumped in the chair. "Ages. Before I got clean in February."

I hadn't been able to move or speak for several minutes. Jeanine and Laura were not supposed to know each other. Not in any universe should this have been possible.

"I'm telling you," said Laura, "she used the name Olena. I had no idea she was connected to you. She said nothing about you at all."

"I don't understand," I said loudly. "Who is *this*?" I snapped open my laptop and the screen lit up, displaying the donor spreadsheet with Olena Rossi's name already pulled up. "Why was Jeanine using this woman's name? Who is writing twelve-thousand-dollar checks? Where the hell did you meet her?" I demanded.

"At a party Gabe and I threw, at the last apartment we shared," said Laura, annoyingly calm. "It was almost a year ago, so it's hard to remember all the details. She said she was new to the city and wanted to know where to have fun, and the next day we were texting somehow. So I invited her to another party the day after that. I saw her a few times, over three or four months. She was checking out the scene."

"What do you mean, 'checking out the scene'?"

"She wanted me to show her around. She wanted to know where people got fucked up."

"Why does she need to know where people get fucked up in Columbus? She can get fucked up here!"

"Reconnaissance, maybe? For that crapload of heroin she had

coming down the pipeline. She was buttering me up so I'd introduce her to *Gabe*. I think she wanted access to him, and the people he bought from."

This thought was so horrifying I couldn't address it directly.

"That heroin only showed up a couple weeks ago," I said. "Why would she be scoping out Columbus a *year* ago?"

"Maybe she started smaller. Maybe—" She stood up and pointed at the screen, excited now. "Maybe the Olena who made that donation *is* the same woman who works for a doctor in Springfield. She could be Jeanine's hookup. For pills. Or blank prescription pads. They could be a team. It totally fits: Jeanine wants to sell somewhere outside of Buffalo, maybe to avoid pissing off the wrong people here. She reaches out to me, to ingratiate herself with the people who can distribute, move product. And the whole thing starts getting bigger and bigger, and somewhere along the line this doomed heroin shows up."

"The heroin was a one-time deal," I said, quoting Landon. "A quick way to make money. It was just the one time."

"I don't see how that could possibly be the case, Gin."

"So I have to go to Ohio," I said.

"Well—" Laura screwed up her face.

I left her standing in my kitchen before she could protest. In my bedroom, I threw clothes into a spare gym bag. Packing was the only task that made sense. If I kept moving, I wouldn't have to think about the fact that Jeanine knew the names of Laura's boyfriends and friends because I'd told them to her; she'd known how to manipulate Laura because I had told her what kind of person Laura was. Jeanine had intentionally found my sister and used her. I had cracked open the shell of privacy keeping me and Laura safe.

Something in Jeanine's life must have gone terribly wrong. She'd been put in a bad situation by Bobby, or Landon, or—most likely—Jason. She owed someone money. She'd done what she thought she had to do.

Laura lingered in the doorway.

"Don't worry. I'm going to sort everything out," I said, keeping my eyes on my packing, so I wouldn't have to see her expression while she watched me.

I ASKED SHARRICE to watch the cat. She listened patiently while I showed her where I kept the cat food and the litter, under the sink. He wasn't very sociable, I explained. But if she wanted to come by and watch TV, he might like the company. He might even sit on her lap. He didn't have toys, but he enjoyed chasing the plastic ring you pulled off the top of a new half gallon of milk.

"I'll take good care of him," she said.

She walked me to my car and watched me get inside. Sheets of glowing, whipping snowflakes danced around us. A thin sugar dusting coated the roads.

I rolled down the window, and she set her elbows on the edge of the glass.

"You got a replacement for your Saturday appearance at the Timberland store, right?" she said. "And don't forget we've got an additional practice on Saturday at four to cover blocking for the new routine. It's a field practice. This trip won't count as an approved absence."

"I know," I said, squeezing her wrist.

Sharrice put her hand on top of mine and pressed her lips together in resignation. I was aware that to Sharrice, me going to Columbus didn't make sense. I had not told her about Jeanine finding Laura there, about her using the name Olena. I was beyond explaining myself.

"One more thing." Sharrice reached into her bag and handed me a bundled-up towel. "Handle that carefully."

The shape of the object in the towel was self-explanatory, even to someone who'd never held such a thing before. Still, I gasped as I saw what lay in its folds.

"Sharrice, are you crazy? I don't know how to use a gun."

"I'll give you a quick tutorial." She pulled the gun out of the towel. It looked obscene next to her long pale pink nails. "Here's the trigger lock. Here's the safety. Here's where the bullets go in. You can take them out if you want. My brother got this one for me. It's unregistered, which means you shouldn't think twice before using it."

"I don't want this," I said.

"Put it in your glove compartment. You should have one for long car trips. Women have to be smart about these things."

I shoved it into the glove compartment, and Sharrice nodded, satisfied. She hugged me through the open window, wetting my face with the snowflakes nestled in the fur of her hood.

I started the car and watched her grow smaller in my rearview mirror. I felt light, like I'd shed armor or skin. It was an unpleasant lightness, as if I could float away, or dissolve, or break into pieces.

Laura had left for Ohio from our mother's condo; I would catch up to her. I'd emailed all my clients and the scheduling coordinator at the gym that I'd be out sick all weekend. There was no telling what the next few days would bring. The snow was falling heavier and heavier, the flakes reflected in the beams of my headlights, limiting my sight in a way that was actually pleasant, grounding. I didn't want to see too far ahead.

Driving south carried with it the sensation of going down, falling back through time. When I'd driven north, over two years ago, it had felt like I was clawing my way out of a sandy pit, into my future. Now I would go back to the place I'd left behind to see what was there.

Part 3

Chapter 24

I WAS ABOUT AN hour outside Buffalo when Bobby called me.

The call came during an empty stretch of the drive, the same interminable strip of gray highway under my headlights. At that moment, I was no longer waiting for a call from Jeanine. But as I dug my phone from the cupholder I had the brief, ecstatic thought that because I had stopped waiting for the call, now it would finally come. When I saw it was Bobby, my heart sank again.

"It's been a few days," he said when I picked up, sounding hurt. "I always text you first. I wanted to see if you would reach out to me this time."

"I'm sorry," I said. "I've been busy."

"You never responded to my picture."

"Yeah, I . . . I guess I felt a little overwhelmed by it."

"Overwhelmed?"

"Yeah, or a bit guilty, maybe. You being Jeanine's boyfriend and all."

"Hm."

There was an uncomfortable pause. There weren't many cars on the road, only a few massive trucks, which caused my Corolla to shudder as they passed.

"I can see that," said Bobby finally. "Though it's not like Jeanine was an angel. Just like I'm not an angel, and you're not, either. Right?"

"I guess," I said.

I heard him sigh and the rustle of fabric. I pictured him stretching out in bed or on the couch, and I hoped he wasn't unbuttoning his pants.

"This whole Landon thing has kind of disrupted my grieving process, to tell you the truth," he went on, with a long sigh. "I just want to, like—nail the motherfucker who took her away from me, you know? I can't afford to be mad at her, because she's gone. So all my rage just funnels, like, directly to the source."

"That's understandable."

"Can you help me nail him?"

"Who?"

"Landon. You and him, you went to the Pink Fountain together."

My hands jumped on the wheel and I swerved, briefly, into the next lane. I had told no one, except Laura, that I'd visited the Pink Fountain with Landon. The snow zoomed crazily in my headlights.

"So what'd you do at the Pink Fountain?" His voice was entirely calm, almost theatrically so.

"To tell you the truth, we were looking for Jeanine."

"You were *looking* for Jeanine? With the guy she was last seen with? Huh. That's a weird approach." He inhaled, added languidly, "Stanley's pretty agitated about it."

"How did he find out?"

"You should know by now," Bobby snorted, "we find out everything."

A wave of panic rolled through my stomach.

"If you're close with this Landon guy, you could help us get him, you know," said Bobby.

"I'm not close with him."

"You're close enough to go to a motel with him." He waited, but I couldn't think of a response. "Is there a reason you want to protect this guy? Did he threaten you? Force you to go to the Pink Fountain with him?"

"No." I wondered immediately if I should have said yes.

"You sure? Because I can protect you. I'm about a thousand times more dangerous than this guy is. You should be more scared of me than him. I mean, I'm the one you want on your side."

I nodded and nodded, in the dark of my car. I had to pee. Finally I managed to say the only phrase I could get to come out, the least antagonizing response I could think of: "Thank you."

He paused thoughtfully. The urge to pee grew stronger. A truck surged past me, pulling me into its tailwind.

"Are you driving?" he said.

"No."

"Oh." He waited. "Want to do something, then?"

"I'm not sure I want to right now."

"Why? Are you busy?"

"No . . ."

"So let's do something. You're my friend, right? We've been having a good time. You came on to me, at the fundraiser. So why shouldn't we do something? Send me a picture."

Tears were building in my throat. "I can't."

"You can't? See, this isn't fun. You're not supposed to be out creeping around. You and Jeanine, creeping around with Landon—I don't like that. I don't like you sneaking into motels with the guy who tried to kill her, after she disappeared. That doesn't look good. Do you know what happened to Jeanine, Virginia?"

"No."

"Great. So let's do something! Come on. Tell me what you did in the Pink Fountain with Landon. I want to know all the details."

My grip on my bladder wobbled, and I nearly lost control of it.

"I have to go," I said. "Sorry."

The phone fell from my hand. I pulled over onto the shoulder of the highway, fought my way over to the passenger side, and stumbled out to pee in the scraggly grass on the side of the road, my jeans around my knees, another truck careening by.

I wiped with the napkins I had stored in the glove compartment, under Sharrice's gun. If I was being followed—by Antweiler or

Bobby himself—surely they'd have driven by while I was peeing. They'd have to pull over and wait for me, up ahead, and I'd see them.

I watched the rearview carefully as I merged back onto the highway. My car floated atop the strip of road illuminated by my headlights. For long stretches of time, I was alone, my back window dark. No one behind me, no one ahead.

I MADE IT to Laura's brick apartment building on the south end of Clintonville around three in the morning. She let me in, rubbing her eyes.

Her apartment was nice, with herringbone floors and big windows. There were no end tables, no pictures on the walls, but she had set up a yoga mat surrounded by candles in the corner and strung fairy lights around the mantel of the nonfunctioning fireplace. The emptiness indicated a life stripped down to small comforts, rather than lack. The smell of burnt leaves and patchouli, earthy and pleasant, hung in the air. She'd made up the couch for me, wrapping a fitted sheet around the cushions. It was the first time, I realized, that I'd ever been Laura's guest.

"Not quite far enough from the undergrads for me," she said. "But it's a start."

"It's better than a start," I said. "It's great."

She struggled to keep her lips closed over a huge smile. Her hands hovered around her neck, arms crossed across her chest, as though to protect herself from me being proud of her. She'd taken out her contact lenses and wore glasses, with new frames I'd never seen on her before. Here I was, at the site on which the new Laura was being built. I'd circled her block three times before I'd parked, checking for cars the whole time.

"So," she said. "Where do we start?"

Chapter 25

By ten a.m., the line at the methadone clinic had snaked all the way around the corner of the faux-brick Community Medical Services building off Dublin Road.

I watched as Laura strode across the parking lot toward the line. A couple of people she knew picked up their dose at this clinic, she said. Maybe one of them had run into Jeanine.

I sat in the passenger seat of Laura's car and gnawed on my cuticles, destroying my recently repaired French manicure. Across the lot, Laura was showing Jeanine's picture to a girl. It was warmer in Columbus than in Buffalo, in the low forties, but I worried about Laura in her leather jacket. Her ears were bright red above her cowl-neck knit scarf. The people standing in line—a tall man in Converse sneakers, a forty-something woman in a bomber jacket—formed a little circle around her, chatting and nodding, full of knowing, fluent in a language I couldn't speak. All around me were other cars, with people like me sitting inside them, waiting for their friend or family member to get their dose. In the car next to me, a middle-aged woman rested her head against the window, eyes closed. A few spots away, a kid of about ten hunched over a video game in the backseat, his little sibling asleep in the car seat beside him. We lived in the realm of the waiting. We were moons orbiting the planet of addiction, drawn in by its overwhelming mass, not part of the same world but bound to it, kept at an irrevocable distance. Everything we did and thought was about them. Their problems were so much bigger than ours that we'd lost the right to have problems of our own; their problems became our problems.

I unbuckled my seatbelt, then buckled it again. I checked my phone, which I continually worried would reveal another call from Bobby. I did not like waiting.

Laura was giving the girl she'd approached a hug, before hugging the two other people she'd met in line. Everyone was best friends with Laura, apparently. She broke away and jogged back to the car.

"Got a lead," she said as she dropped into her seat. "That girl didn't recognize her picture, but she'd heard the name Olena. She thinks a guy who sells south of here, across the river, might know her."

She pulled onto Dublin Road. With the leaves gone, we could see the Scioto River on our right. I kept an eye on the sideview mirror.

The silence bothered me, so I asked, "Did you ever try methadone?"

"No. It works really well for a lot of people. But I didn't want to go from being on one thing to being on another, you know?"

"Right," I said. I wished I hadn't asked. I looked in the mirror again.

"NA is the only thing that's made me feel like I belonged to myself again. Like I was a human who could make choices, who didn't have to hate herself for getting better. Because that was the hardest part for me. Feeling like I deserved to get better."

Why it had taken her so long to discover that she "deserved" to get better, whatever that meant, I could not understand. My face was doing some terrible, wide-eyed nodding thing while I chanted, "Oh, good. Good for you." I was both puppet and puppeteer, trying to pantomime the correct responses, making myself grotesque and doll-like in the process.

"I'm sorry I'm talking to you like this," I said.

"Like what?"

"I don't know!"

She sighed. We had come to a red light, and she leaned forward to get a look at my face. "Are you okay? You're jumpy. Don't worry about cops. They're not going to mess with two nice girls like us."

"I just have this feeling like somebody's following us."

Laura wrinkled her nose. "Who would be following us?"

"I don't know. Some guy named Antweiler?"

"Antweiler?" She laughed. "Like Scott Antweiler? Dad's old friend?"

"*Dad's* friend?"

"Yeah, you remember. Scott. He'd drink whiskey with Dad in the office. He came to Thanksgiving with a gun one time."

"Huh?"

"He came to Thanksgiving, and Mom realized he was carrying, and she flipped. Mom *hated* him. Dad said he was always carrying, don't worry about it, he had a license, but he wasn't invited back. Antweiler," she repeated. "Big guy. Broad. At least that's how I remember him."

Yes, there'd been a tall guy, obscured behind the door of Dad's office at home, a fight at Thanksgiving.

"Mom said he broke people's legs, went after people's families. That could be her exaggerating, though. You should talk more to Mom, you know. I know she's difficult, but she can put parts of our childhood in perspective. She's the one who had to manage all those nights alone, and the fear of Dad getting arrested, and our whole family getting thrown into chaos. You know that part of what Stanley gets out of taking care of her, and us, is our silence. Right?" She glanced at me. "Are you okay? What made you mention Antweiler?"

"I don't know, I just—remembered him."

"But why?"

"Because I'm freaked out about being followed!"

Laura raised her eyebrows and looked back at the road ahead.

"When we get to Franklinton," she said, "just stay in the car, okay?"

I WATCHED LAURA disappear into the cemetery by the homeless shelter in Franklinton, where the girl from the methadone clinic had instructed us to go. After a long twenty minutes, she ran back to the car, pulling her jacket tight, shaking her head.

There were other spots we could try, she said, if we wanted to ask more sellers. Even though she used *we*, we both knew she'd be the one to get out of the car.

I took over driving, and Laura directed me from the passenger seat. I parked in residential alleys and abandoned business lots while she approached boys sitting inside nondescript Hondas and Kias. They were always boys: young Latino or Hispanic boys wearing button-down shirts tucked into Levi's under their jackets, skinny white boys who might've been high schoolers, boys in Vans and Misfits shirts. Laura showed them the picture of Jeanine. They shook their heads and refused to look, or they told Laura to get the fuck away from them, or they squinted at the photo, polite and helpful, asking, *Which girl?* But none of them responded that they had seen Jeanine.

It was boring and tedious and also terrifying. Our noses ran, and we had no tissues. By the time we reached our fifth stop, an empty parking lot a block away from the I-70 overpass, it was late afternoon. The sky was cloudy and dark. I'd forgotten how overcast Ohio could be. The sun sometimes hid for weeks at a time.

"I think that's enough for today," said Laura when she emerged from around the ivy-coated fence at the edge of the parking lot.

I drove us onto the interstate. I was fairly certain we weren't being followed, given the circuitous nature of our route, but I kept checking the rearview just in case. Laura wiped her nose on the back of her hand and tried gamely for optimism.

"Just because no one said they recognized her doesn't mean they didn't. If she *did* supply any of those people with pills or drugs, they're not going to go blabbing her name around town."

"Is there anyone else who might have been in contact with her since you went to rehab?" I said. "A friend, roommate, from your old life?"

"Possibly Gabe," Laura said. "Jeanine talked to him a lot at his parties."

"That's not an option, obviously," I said.

I waited for her to confirm or deny this, but she didn't answer, as though she'd rather not have heard it.

"So what do we do?" I said finally.

Laura blew out a long breath. "I guess we go home."

I'd gotten on 315 going north to get back to Laura's apartment, but I couldn't imagine giving up for the night. Obeying a sudden instinct, I took the King Ave exit for Grandview. Laura glanced over at me but didn't speak. I drove us west along a stretch of road that could be anywhere in America: grimy little office parks, consignment shops, and banks. I took King all the way to Grandview Ave and turned south. I saw the salon where I used to get my hair cut flash by, then our Indian takeout place. We reached my old favorite intersection, Grandview and Second, a bustling little corner of bars and restaurants. There was Jeni's ice cream shop and the nice Italian restaurant. I turned on First and pulled up in front of my old apartment building.

"Wow," said Laura, staring at the familiar green awning. "I haven't been back here in a long time. Do you think we left, like, an aura or an energy field?"

"Of pain and suffering? Maybe."

"We had good nights in there, too. But even those I feel bad about, because I wasn't sober for all of them, so they weren't true."

When I'd arrived yesterday, cloaked in night, I could ignore how much of me was still flung about the city. I had the dramatic—but not, I felt, emotionally inaccurate—image of having been hit by a car here long ago, my blood still splattered on the buildings I'd frequented, the bathrooms I'd cried in, the sidewalks I'd paced. This apartment building—where I'd sheltered Laura, fought with her, pleaded with her, hidden her from her boyfriend, and, ultimately, walked out on her—was the most spattered and bloody of them all.

"You still haven't asked me," Laura said, "if Jeanine and I did drugs together."

Before I could decide whether I wanted to ask this question, she began answering it.

"This is what I remember. The first party I invited her to, she drank vodka and did a couple lines of coke. I invited her to another party a couple weeks after that, and she did the same. At some point she wanted to know where to buy oxy, and I hooked her up with a guy. Then she wanted to know where to buy smack, as a present for me. For being so nice to her. I told her Gabe hooked me up, and she said she wanted to buy from Gabe. She said she'd buy a bunch, enough to share with me, if I wanted some, too. Of course I wanted some. I thought I'd found a new best friend. But you get used to thinking any random person who wants to get high with you is your next best friend."

I had to swallow a few times before I could ask, "Did you see her do heroin?"

Laura shook her head. "She bought it, but I never saw her do it. Just vodka and coke."

"That's Jeanine," I whispered.

"I really liked her. She was funny."

If I checked my texts, I could probably pinpoint the exact lies Jeanine had told me on each date, to cover for the weekends she was going to Ohio. How could she have smiled at me, dragging me from bar to bar, laughing, after getting high with my sister? And what had she thought when I'd told her, in early March, that Laura was in detox? Had she been disappointed? Worried? She kept lying about her location long after Laura went to rehab. Had she continued coming to Ohio? Had she gotten everything she needed out of Laura at that point?

"Laura," I said. "I want you to give me Gabe's number."

Laura sighed heavily.

“We can’t keep doing *this,*” I pressed. “Let me talk to Gabe one time, and it’s over.”

“You don’t talk to Gabe ever, Ginny. I couldn’t give you his number if I wanted to. I deleted all my old contacts when I went to rehab. There’s no way he has the same number, anyway.”

“Do you think you could find him if you tried?”

She stared at our old apartment building for a long time.

“Ginny, I’m starving,” she said. “Will you please take me home?”

Chapter 26

Back at the apartment, we ate some kind of tofu stir-fry Laura made, both of us meek and apologetic with each other. After we'd washed the dishes, Laura checked the time on her phone, then started pulling on her jacket.

"What are you doing," I said, alarmed.

"I'll be back in a few hours. Don't worry." She slid on one boot, then the other.

"I'll go with you. Don't go alone."

Laura pulled me into a hug, which only made me feel more like I was sending her to her death.

"It's okay," she said firmly into my ear. "You need to know what happened. I said I would help you. You're my sister."

She released me, and struggled to say more before simply repeating, "You're my sister." And she left.

Laura didn't have a TV, and I had not brought my laptop. I leafed through her books: a handbook on chakras, another on acupuncture points. I lay on the couch. I refreshed the *Buffalo News* site on my phone. I counted the cars on the street outside Laura's house, then checked them again.

I was a stranger in this city, I realized. After graduation, as I'd grown more and more immersed in Laura's troubles, I'd fallen out of touch with my college friends. Either I stopped texting them or they stopped reaching out to me. At that time, Laura's situation was the only thing I thought about, and yet it was the one subject I couldn't bring myself to speak of. I spaced out at coffee dates and ignored my gym friends at parties, checking my phone for word from Laura, failing to give a straight answer when they asked what was wrong or if I was okay. Finally, people stopped asking. And now I had no friends in Ohio. No friends from an entire era of my life. Just one sister, who was probably in a crack den right now, relapsing, all for my sake, to help me find a girl I couldn't admit was dead.

Around one in the morning, the scrape of the key in the lock. The door swung open. I sat up but couldn't make out Laura's expression in the dark. She strode past me, down the hallway to the bathroom. I listened, heart pounding. After a brief pause, I heard the flush of the toilet. She returned to the living room and dropped into the armchair next to the couch.

"What happened?" I said.

"Well." She began unlacing her boots. "I went to the old apartment I shared with Gabe, but someone else is living there now. So I went to this bar north of Morse Road where he used to hang out, and he wasn't there, either. Then I went to another bar he used to go to. The bartender there knows me from before and thought I wanted to buy. So he sent me to some guy's apartment complex off 161, which was so dirty I might burn these clothes. But *that* guy, at least, knew Gabe's new address and gave it to me." She pulled off her boots and collapsed back into the chair. "Boy, was Gabe surprised to see me."

"You went to his *house*?" I said.

"We talked on the porch," she said. "I told him I was looking for Jeanine—or Olena, as he knows her. He kept giving me the runaround, saying, 'Why do you want to see her, you can go through me, I'll hook you up, why are you pretending you're not here to see me,' blah blah. God, it took forever, and he was so fucking *gleeful*." She kicked her boots away with sudden rage. "He loved that I wanted something from him. He was like, 'Smoke with me and I'll tell you if she's around, come inside and I'll tell you.' Fucking stupid idiot."

I felt momentarily dizzy.

"You didn't go inside, though?" I said.

Laura rubbed her eyes, her burst of rage faded to exhaustion. "No, God no. I just stayed out on the porch, freezing, repeating myself, while he blew smoke in my face. Anyway." She pulled a piece of paper from her jacket pocket and tossed it onto the coffee table. "He said he's met her before at this address."

I snatched at the piece of paper, the ripped end of a receipt. I didn't recognize the street name scrawled on it in Laura's handwriting.

"When's the last time he saw her?" I gasped. "Did he say if she was at this house recently?"

"I don't know, Gin, I didn't want to stick around and get his current life story. He was talking about her in the present tense, but that doesn't necessarily mean anything. He said he didn't think she was in town, but I could check. He said, 'Go see if she's there, bring her over and we'll party together.'" She shook her head at the paper in my hands. "I'm like ninety percent sure that address is bullshit, or some random drug house. But we can check it out tomorrow if you want. We can try."

"Laura—"

"Do not say thank you to me. I want this to be over. Whatever you have to do to be done with this and get on with your life." She cleared her throat. "Also. I'm going to need you to help me with cash. I had to buy some. At the first apartment I went to."

"Buy some—" My eyes darted over her layers of sweaters, her chapped lips.

"I don't need much," she said. "It's gotten even cheaper in the last year, if you can believe it."

"Where is it?"

"I just flushed it."

I was on my feet almost before I realized what I was doing. I fished through the pockets of the jacket she'd thrown over the kitchen chair, then marched down the hallway to her bedroom.

"What are you doing?" she called after me. "Ginny! What's wrong with you?"

Her room was so sparse there was nowhere really to look. I ran my hands under her mattress, pulled the cases off the pillows.

"Do you think I *kept* it?" she said from the doorway. "How would I even use it? You think I still have needles? You think I'm going to shoot up with you down the hallway on my couch?"

"Why not? You've done it before with me down the hallway."

"I wouldn't *have* heroin if it weren't for you," she said. "I wouldn't be within twenty feet of these people. I didn't want to buy, I didn't want to talk to Gabe—I did it all for you, for God's sake, for you, for you!"

I pushed past her to the bathroom and stared into the toilet bowl. I flushed it again, then again and again.

"Why are we doing this?" said Laura from the hallway, her hands in her hair. "This is so fucked up."

Chapter 27

"*PROMISE* ME YOU won't go to that house until I get back," said Laura the next morning as she packed up her backpack.

She'd swapped her frustration from the night before for a tired resignation. She made me coffee on the stove and offered toast and two types of jam. She had an NA meeting today, she said, as well as a three-hour clinic to go toward her yoga teacher training, but after that—we could go to the house.

Even as I recognized Laura's right to be angry with me, I was immensely relieved that she wanted to appease me again. She didn't look too much worse for wear from the night before. Her eyes were clear, and she had no marks or scars.

"Keep in mind," she said, "whoever lives there has no reason to talk to us about Jeanine, and they might be dangerous. The last thing I need is my sister confronting some crazed tweaker by herself."

I didn't want that either, I assured her. Once the door swung shut behind her, I waited ten minutes. Then I grabbed my car keys and headed out.

The house was on Como Ave in Clintonville, about a mile and a half north of Laura's building. It was a narrow, neat little two-story with a small concrete porch, white siding, a square patch of lawn, and a detached garage—almost definitely not a crack house. It could only be described as a pretty nice house on a pretty nice street.

Nobody answered when I knocked on the door. I peeked in the house's mailbox by the street—empty—and then settled back into my car to wait. I played a game of waiting as long as I could bear before letting my eyes dart to the clock to check the time. No matter how long I forced myself to wait, I couldn't make more than two consecutive minutes pass. I refreshed *The Buffalo News* on my phone, but there were no updates. In the comments section, posters raged at the police for not having identified any leads. They wrote, **Dang these are the only hot girls in buffalo and one of them has to get murdered.** They wrote, **This happens all the time to women who put themselves out there like that. It's not right but it's the way it is.**

I texted Sharrice that I was doing fine, then stared at the texts Bobby had sent me. I held my finger over the button to call Stanley but chickened out. Forty minutes passed in this manner, in two-minute increments.

I was trying to decide if I should go back to the apartment to wait for Laura when I saw I had a new missed call from Suzanna.

I decided to get it over with and call her back. While the phone rang, I caught sight of a woman about a block away, making her way toward me from the direction of High Street. She was only the second pedestrian I'd seen all morning, besides a young mother with a stroller twenty minutes before. Atop her dry, frizzy mess of blond hair, she wore a comically fluffy pair of black earmuffs. A pair of oversized sunglasses covered her eyes.

Suzanna picked up.

"Thank God," she said. "Do not dodge my messages like that. What is the matter with you? Have you lost your mind?"

I began to reassure Suzanna that she had no reason to worry, but she barreled over me.

"Sharrice tells me you're in Ohio. There's no reason on God's green earth for you to be in Ohio. You're supposed to be at the opening of the Timberland store at the mall today. We have a mandatory rehearsal this afternoon. The new routine. You have to dance."

My stomach dipped. I had forgotten about the additional rehearsal.

"The store opening is covered," I said, weakly. This was the one thing I'd done right. "Natalie's filling in for me."

"Virginia, get in the car and come home. Drive straight to the stadium. If you miss this rehearsal, I swear to God. Send me a picture showing your car windshield pointed the right direction on the interstate within the next twenty minutes, or I will come down there and drag you back home myself. You are not acting rationally. You are a danger to yourself and the people who love you."

I was taken aback. I had heard Suzanna snap at girls plenty of times before, but this was the most crazed she'd ever sounded. My mind raced as I tried to think of what to say—how to stall. The woman on the sidewalk was half a block away. She wore a puffy coat and carried two paper grocery bags in her arms. What I would do, once I got off the phone, was start knocking on doors. Everyone noticed gregarious Jeanine, with her loud laugh and big, wavy hair. If she'd ever been on this street, a neighbor would have seen her. I would knock until I ran out of doors.

"Okay," I said to Suzanna. "But I have to say goodbye to my sister. I'll start driving back in an hour."

"Not in an hour. Now."

The woman neared the walkway of the neat little house across the street and removed her sunglasses. Suzanna's voice cut out as the phone fell out of my hand.

The whole street curved and dimmed like a tunnel.

It was Jeanine. The woman I was looking at was Jeanine.

Suzanna's voice droned thinly from the phone on my lap. I think I said, "I have to call you back," as I hung up on her.

Jeanine. She'd dyed her hair a terrible pale yellow, but it was her. I slid down in the seat, ears ringing. There was Jeanine holding grocery bags, Jeanine pulling keys out of her jeans pocket. No fear, no desperation on her face. Jeanine, walking home from the bodega, down a street she knew well. As though she weren't missing at all.

I sank lower in the seat as she turned up the walkway. She struggled with her bags, nearly dropping one, before getting the door open and disappearing inside.

My eyes felt very dry. I blinked, both hands gripping the wheel.

Jeanine.

Jeanine!

Alive. Alive, alive.

Rockets of emotion tore across my body as I flipped through my imagined scenes of Jeanine reunions—I'd pictured running into a police station to find her battered and dazed on a chair, or creeping into a hospital room where she lay, sleeping. I'd rehearsed a thousand hypothetical phone calls, some featuring her shaky voice at the other end, asking me to come pick her up, others the police, saying triumphantly, "We've found her, miss, she asked for you to bring her home." Always, she reached out to me with her voice or her arms, asking me to come toward her, so the true work of our friendship could recommence: helping her recover, piece her life together, make sense of what had happened to her.

How to impose this fantasy on the bustling figure I'd just seen? Nothing I'd imagined helped me picture what I was meant to do next. *Now this,* I kept thinking, *now this.*

But what was this?

Chapter 28

ACCORDING TO THE clock, fifteen minutes had passed since Jeanine had entered the house. I was beginning to wonder if I'd hallucinated her when the door swung open and Jeanine exited.

She'd brushed her hair and put on a maroon polo shirt with gold stripes on the collar. She rushed across the lawn to the garage, which she opened with a keypad. The door rolled up to reveal a white Hyundai.

She drove toward High Street and turned south. I followed her, trying to keep one car between us, past the university, through Italian Village, into the Short North. This was the trendiest part of town, I thought hopefully. No drug dens, no abandoned lots, no trash-can fires, no parking under an overpass. The white Hyundai pulled into the parking garage of a hotel, newly built. I went careening past and by some miracle found a metered spot on the next side street. I left my car there without paying and sprinted down the block to gaze into the mouth of the parking garage where she'd disappeared.

I paced around the first floor of the garage, panicking. There were at least five floors; it would take forever to find the Hyundai, and, like an idiot, I hadn't even memorized the license plate.

I rushed back outside, trying to outpace my panic, which scampered along behind me. Then I saw, outside the hotel, a bellhop wearing a maroon shirt with gold stripes on the collar.

IT WAS A new corporate hotel, very sleek inside: lobby fountains, right angles, neon lights in the wood paneling.

"Excuse me," I said to the man behind the concierge desk. "Does a woman named Olena Rossi work here?"

The man's smile grew strained. "Concierge services are reserved for guests. What is your room number, please?"

"Room one twenty-three," I said—my assigned weight, the first number to pop into my head.

I could tell immediately that I'd chosen a room number that didn't exist. The man's face collapsed into a look of derision, a false smile devoid of customer service.

"I have to ask you to leave the hotel, please," he said.

"I just need to talk to her for a minute. I'll be out of your way."

"I can't have people who aren't guests visiting her at the desk all the time. I'm sorry. This is a workplace."

I apologized to the man, summoning my best Jills smile, and went to find a spot on the angular, stiff furniture in the lobby to wait. He followed me.

"If you don't have a room here, you have to leave. I will call security."

"I'll book a room, then."

"We are fully booked. You need to leave immediately."

"I haven't done anything wrong," I said. "I'll go to the desk and book a room. I'm a paying customer like anyone else."

My Jills tone of voice was breaking, but I was spared from arguing further when Jeanine emerged from a door behind the concierge desk.

The whole room seemed to fall silent. The concierge pulled a radio from his belt, but I couldn't hear a word he said into it. There was Jeanine. She strode to the touchscreen computer and tapped at it, looking both harried and bored. She pulled at her polo shirt collar, patted her hair, let her eyes roam around the lobby, where they fell on me.

Her face, as her eyes met mine, went blank. She saw me, and there I was. I had made it.

"Jeanine—" I said.

In a flash she was out from behind the desk. The molecules in the air shifted and parted to make way for her to come and grip my arm (yes, those were her real fingers pressing on my arm, with their bones and muscles), to pull me away from the concierge, who was shouting after us. She yanked me down the carpeted hallway past the elevators, pulled open a door that said STAFF, and pushed me inside.

"You cannot be here," she said. "You cannot be here."

We were in a storage closet, crammed against wire shelves holding paper towels, toilet paper, printer paper. Her hand dug into my arm as she pulled sharp intakes of breath, gulping air. I could do nothing except stare at her. Her face looked green under her bleached hair and too-dark concealer. But it was not the hair that made her look so strange. It was the way she was standing, her shoulders hunched, the redness of her eyes, her gasping mouth. I'd never seen Jeanine scared before. I reached out to touch her shoulder, but she pulled away, releasing her grip on me, bumping into the shelf behind her.

"Let me think," she said. "Let me think."

"Jeanine, it's okay," I stammered.

"It's not okay." She gripped her stomach. "Ow. Fuck. I'm going to throw up."

My head was spinning with guilt. Of course she would be afraid: here she was using a false name, working a fake job, like she'd joined some slipshod witness protection program. I wanted to reassure her, make her less afraid, make her happy to see me.

She straightened, regaining a measure of control over her breathing.

"Are you alone?" she said.

"Yes," I said eagerly. "No one knows I'm here."

"Yeah, right," she said, incredulously. She burped and said, "Fuck," holding her stomach.

"Jeanine, I'm not here to scare you. Tell me how to help you and I will. Tell me what you need."

"What I need?" She gripped a fistful of her terrible hair, and pulled. "What I need. Okay. Here's what I need. You go— Actually, you wait here. Wait here, and I'll talk to my boss and beg off work. Okay? Then we can talk."

"Yes," I said. "We can talk." She was looking everywhere but at me.

"Give me ten minutes to get my stuff. Hide here so they don't call security on you. Meet me outside the doors in ten."

"Yes," I said.

She pushed open the door to the storage closet and looked back at me. My breath caught in my throat as her eyes finally met mine. The fear on her face had loosened slightly, and settled into an expression of determination, the look of a woman with a plan, which I was now a part of. I could hardly breathe from relief.

"Ten minutes," she said again—and this was a gift to me, to reassure me, this looking back. Then she let the door swing shut behind her.

AFTER TEN MINUTES, I snuck through the lobby to wait outside the doors on the chilly sidewalk. Minutes ticked past, and there was no sign of Jeanine. I returned to the concierge desk.

"I'm just asking if Jeanine has left yet," I said. "I mean Olena. I'm not staying."

"Go look somewhere else," the concierge said. "She just walked out on me."

Chapter 29

So JEANINE DIDN'T want to talk to me.

Well, I knew where she lived, didn't I?

I drove back to the house on Como and walked right up to the door. I knocked, hit the doorbell, and knocked again.

"Hello?" I shouted. The Hyundai was parked in the driveway. I pushed through the bushes in front of the house to look in the windows.

"Jeanine!" I shouted. I banged on the windows with my palms flat. "Jeanine, I know you're in there! Jeanine!"

Through the narrow gap in the blinds, I thought I saw movement.

"I'll stay out here all day! You have to talk to me!"

Nothing.

I struggled out of the bushes. I grabbed a rock and threw it at the side of the house. It hit the wooden frame of one of the windows with a loud crack. The door flew open.

"For fuck's sake!" she yelled. "Stop that! Get inside. Now!"

She yanked me into the foyer and slammed the door shut behind me. She'd taken off her work polo and now wore a white T-shirt. Her chest rose and fell with panting breaths.

"Jeanine," I said.

I took stock, dazedly, of the space we were in. The front door opened to a staircase, the banister of which I grabbed to steady myself. To my right was a living room with a battered blue couch and milk crates for end tables, and straight ahead, alongside the staircase, was a hallway that led to the kitchen. No pictures on the walls, barely any furniture. It looked like a halfway house outfitted with the bare essentials. By Jeanine's socked feet were the paper grocery bags I'd seen her carrying earlier. One had tipped over and spilled its contents: two bottles of prosecco, Lean Cuisines she'd forgotten to put away, and over-the-counter pill bottles of Allegra, NyQuil, antacids, vitamin C tablets. Jeanine took pills thoughtlessly; she used them to maintain her body's normal processes as though it couldn't be trusted to do so on its own. I was always telling her to try eating well and getting some actual sleep, and she'd say, *What's the fun in that?* while she downed vodka mixed with Airborne. The simple normalcy of these items stunned me. The house could have belonged to anyone, but these purchases could only have been made by Jeanine.

"How do you know where I live?" she said. "Did you *follow* me? How do I make you go away? What do you want?"

"Maybe we could sit down—"

"I can't sit. I have to get out of here. But now *you're* here. What do I do with you? I can't leave you—but how will I—?"

She sank to the floor, her face in her hands. I grabbed at the pile of groceries that had tipped over, unsheathed a bottle of prosecco from its brown paper bag, and handed the bag to her so she could breathe into it. She slapped it out of my hands.

"I'll get you water," I said.

Ignoring her protests, I ran down the hallway that led to the kitchen. I stopped short at the threshold. The kitchen was clean and bright, with gray Formica counters and white linoleum. The ceiling was drop-down, made of the corklike material usually found in office buildings. One of the panels had been pushed aside. On the floor underneath the hole in the ceiling was a chair, and next to the chair was a black suitcase upright on its wheels.

I looked over my shoulder. Jeanine was pulling herself to her feet, using the front door's handle for purchase. She charged toward me and I bolted, grabbing the handle of the suitcase, the top flap of which was partially unzipped. Before Jeanine could stop me, the suitcase swung open, and out onto the linoleum tumbled a wave of thick, rubber-banded blocks of cash.

Jeanine groaned. She kicked at the suitcase.

"Oh, hell," she said. "Want to have a drink?"

JEANINE POURED US each a mug of prosecco. We sat at the little round table in the bright, white kitchen. The suitcase, with its obscene contents, lay on the floor next to us, hovering at the edge of my vision. I tilted my chair so as not to look directly at it.

Jeanine was tearing the plastic wrap off a new bottle of Pepto-Bismol. Her dry, brittle hair floated in tufts away from her head, as if trying to escape her scalp. She took a long chug from the pink bottle.

"I keep thinking I'm going to throw up, but nothing comes out." She knocked a fist against her sternum and let out a small laugh. "I didn't mean to leave you standing there in the hotel. But you've got to understand—that was really scary, you walking in on me like that."

"Are you . . . packing?" I said, pointing at the suitcase without looking at it.

Jeanine drank again from the Pepto-Bismol and winced. She hadn't met my eyes the entire time we'd been sitting there. Instead, she addressed my collarbone or the wall over my left shoulder.

"I don't know. Yeah? I thought I'd get a motel," she said. "Provided nobody else kicks down my door and shoots me in the head while I'm sitting here talking to you."

"Who would want to shoot you in the head?"

She laughed bitterly. "Where do I start?"

Her hands shook as she reached for her mug. I focused all my attention on her fear. The fear was the reason I was here. It made everything clear and focused. I had to find the root of the fear, and solve it.

"Can we talk about the cash?" I said, gesturing toward the suitcase with my foot, while Jeanine drained her mug in one long gulp. "And how you got it? And who you might owe money to?"

"No," she said, swallowing. "We can't talk about it. I need *you* to talk. I need you to tell me how you found me, so I can figure out where exactly I fucked up and how long I have before someone else tracks me down and blows up what's left of my life."

"I went through a lot to get here, Jeanine," I said, my voice growing shrill. "I came all this way. I thought you were *dead*. The least you can do is talk to me."

"For Christ's sake, what do you want me to say?" Jeanine snatched at the bottle and poured more prosecco, the neck cracking against her mug. "Clearly, things haven't turned out so great for me, considering I'm in fucking hiding, with a bunch of cash stashed in the ceiling. I don't need to be lectured or punished. Surely the situation I'm in is punishment enough."

"What situation?"

Jeanine righted the bottle and set it heavily on the table. She clutched her hair and groaned.

"I already know," I said. "Jeanine, I already know. I know you took something you weren't supposed to."

"Oh, God." Jeanine shook her head back and forth, hands still in her hair.

"It's all right," I said. "I know you established some kind of operation here. I know you transport drugs from Buffalo, every two or three weeks, since that's when you seem to disappear for a few days at a time. I know you're selling through Gabe. I know he expects you regularly, and he knows he can find you at this house."

"Oh, Christ," she said. "Fuck, that's worse than I thought."

"I know you touched some drugs that—either belonged to the Paladinos, or you went around the Paladinos, or whatever it was. I'm not thrilled about that part, obviously. I guess it was a little idealistic of me to think the Paladinos never . . . well, it's just *Bobby*, really, who does that part of the business. Right?"

"But, V, what I did wasn't that *bad*," she burst out. "The Paladinos still make obscene amounts of money. It's not like I *hurt* them. I didn't hurt anybody! From any normal person's perspective, it's not some terrible crime, what I did. I was just—rerouting some things."

"Rerouting?"

"You know how in retail they have what's called shrink?" She gripped the scattered wrappers on the table from the prosecco and Pepto-Bismol and waved them around, as though to illustrate what she was explaining. "It's the merch you expect to lose. You know—boxes fall off the back of the truck. Shipments damaged by rain. You budget for it. So I just—" She grabbed the cork, which had tumbled from her hands, and brandished it. "I took the shrink. See? That's it. It's a victimless crime. I collected money that was expected to be lost."

The prosecco gurgled in my stomach as I struggled to understand what I was hearing. I squeezed my eyes shut, and little lights exploded behind my lids.

"You've been taking the Paladinos' shrink?" I said.

"It's just shrink," she insisted, waving her hands. "It's out there. I took it. Who cares?"

"But how did you—?" I struggled for purchase; the ceiling lights made everything seem flat and white. "How did you *get* it? Was it—Jason? You were working with Jason Morley?"

She drew back. "Who said anything about Jason Morley?"

"The shrink has to fall off someone's truck, right? Jason's the guy with the trucks. Do *not* lie to me and pretend you don't know him that well," I said, as she opened her mouth to argue. "You know him well enough to get in a blowout fight with him at the Pink Fountain."

Jeanine looked ill. She crossed her arms across her stomach and leaned forward.

"Oh God," she said. "How do you know about that? If you know, then everyone must know. Oh God, I'm so *fucked*."

"Jeanine, it's okay," I said, though of course it wasn't okay. I wanted answers, real answers—Jeanine's side of the story. I was waiting for her to say that Jason had blackmailed her into helping him steal from the Paladinos, or that Landon had forced her to act as a liaison between him and Jason, or that Bobby had concocted the whole plan as a way to expand his personal wealth at Jeanine's expense.

I was waiting, I realized, for Jeanine to say something that would help me erase what she'd done to Laura, or would make it someone else's fault. Maybe Laura didn't remember it right. She said herself her memory of that time was fuzzy. Maybe Jeanine had been more frightened or desperate than she'd seemed. Maybe she'd been as afraid then as she was now.

Jeanine put her head between her knees, and I tried to get her talking again.

"Just tell me what you and Jason were doing at the Pink Fountain," I said. "Why'd he bring you there? How'd he get you involved in this?"

"Get me involved?" Jeanine righted herself, her face contorted in a terrible laugh. "That guy hasn't had an original fucking idea in his whole life. *I* took all the risk. I did all the work. He didn't do shit for me except make things worse."

"Please, take a breath," I said. "Tell me how it started."

She let out a long sigh and wiped her eyes with her shirt, leaving a smear of eyeliner on the collar. I handed her what was left in my mug of prosecco, and she finished it.

"I met him while he and Bobby were working on a contract for the Neapolitan," she said. "And we got along. He realized I could be useful to him, being Bobby's girlfriend, privy to pretty much every goddamn thought that runs through his head. And I thought Jason might be useful to me at some point. You get a feel for people. We started meeting up every so often to talk, and—you know. You get ideas. Like, how to make a kilo disappear, make a quick twenty grand apiece. Then that goes well, and you think . . . maybe we do it again? After a while we were taking enough that we knew we'd draw attention if we sold it all in Buffalo. Columbus is a good town for heroin. It's not mobbed up. And Jason knew, from . . ."

She paused, and poked at the detritus on the table, twisting the Pepto-Bismol wrapper in her hands. "He knew from visiting Columbus a few years ago that it might be worth looking into."

She trailed off, cleared her throat, looked toward the kitchen window.

We had reached the part where Laura came in. Laura and Jeanine. Jeanine had found Laura. And no one had made her do it. No one had threatened her, put a gun to her head. What she was describing was not an act of desperation, it was a strategy. Calculated, planned. A balloon expanded behind my sternum, filled with tears, or maybe a scream.

"Well, next thing you know," said Jeanine into the silence, "I'm driving to Ohio every few weeks, and here we are. Trust me, if I could do things differently, I would not rely on Jason Morley to be my business partner. But he's what I had to work with. I needed supply, and he had it. And we were turning over a lot of money, V. Like, a lot of money."

"You bought her heroin," I said.

I could barely speak around the balloon. Jeanine's face fell. She let her forehead rest for a moment in her hands.

"*Fuck,*" she sighed. "Oh, goddamn it. I never wanted you to find out about that."

"You bought her heroin," I said, and for a moment I was terrified that the balloon had forced out every other word, every other thought, and I would spend the rest of my life repeating this one phrase, this one horrible fact, trying to make it make sense.

"Look, V, before you freak out, just let me say this. I only hung out with Laura a few times, and each time I took really good care of her. I kept an eye on her, I checked how much she was doing and how she conducted herself. If I'd thought for even a second that she was going to do something stupid and kill herself, I'd have found a way to stop it. I did absolutely nothing to put her in danger or mess with her life. I just wanted to make friends, so I could meet her boyfriend. I was on her side the whole time."

The balloon snapped.

"On her side?" I said. "You getting her high is being on her side?" I snatched up the wrappers on the table and threw them at her.

Jeanine ducked as I shouted, "She could have *died*. What if she'd OD'd on that shit you gave her? Huh? You could have killed her!"

"Okay, well—not to argue, but she could get it for free. Look, I know you like to think of Laura as some wounded puppy that bad guys kick around in the gutter, but that girl was a shark. She had no one looking out for her but herself, and she knew it. Her boyfriend was—*is*—a fucking psycho. You'd left her. She had no one. But she was smart and she was ruthless. She clocked me as a good customer the second she met me. She knew I'd buy and I'd be a good hookup for Gabe. On the drugs front, it was one businesswoman to another."

" 'Businesswoman'?" I sputtered. "She's an *addict*. She was nose-diving. I woke up every day desperate to know if she was safe, or even alive, and *you* were seeing her! You weren't *supposed* to see her! *I* was supposed to see her!"

"You could have driven down here to see your sister anytime you wanted. You didn't. You were too afraid to face her. That's what this is about, ultimately."

I gripped the sides of my head. How was this conversation going this way? But Jeanine had an answer to everything, and the answer was always that people could do whatever they wanted, that *I* should be doing whatever I wanted, and if I wasn't, that was my own fault. But she didn't get to do drugs with Laura just because she wanted to or because she could get something out of it. There had to be limits to what a person could do. With Jeanine, I lost track of what they were.

Jeanine seemed to realize she was pushing it too far. She reached for my hand, and I yanked it away.

"V, please. What went on between me and Laura had nothing to do with you. It's not your world, and you don't understand it. There's you and me," she said, cupping her hands on the table as though cradling a bowl of soup. "Then there's me and Laura"—she shifted her hands—"and then there's Laura and you. They're all separate. You do the same thing. Like with your family drama and your sister and the Jills, and *me*—you keep it all separate."

"It's not the same thing," I said. "You don't get to separate Laura from me. You don't get to say that what happens to her has nothing to do with me. It has everything to do with me."

"V, I'm sorry," she said. "Please look at me. I'm *sorry.* There's only a few people in my life who I actually care about not hurting, and you're one of them. I did use Laura. I admit that, and I understand why it upsets you. But I used her very carefully and considerately, and only as a means to get to someone else, who I don't give a fuck about. But I do give a fuck about you, and I gave a fuck about her, I promise."

I kicked at the suitcase so it tipped over sideways. "My sister for a suitcase of heroin money."

"I can't pay rent with virtue, Virginia. I've never had a legitimate job. I don't have a résumé. Nobody cares that I won pageants in high school. What am I supposed to do, if not this?"

"You could do literally anything else."

"For two bucks an hour plus tips? Great. How about a hundred bucks to stand around some trade show for eight hours so I can call myself a model? Or I can spend ten hours in Ralph Wilson Stadium in exchange for a parking pass? I can't do that shit anymore. I can't be like you, living off of Stanley Paladino's handouts. Who, by the way, is also making money off heroin, through Bobby. You get that, right? This is your money, too."

Looking at the bundles of cash scattered on the floor, I thought this could not possibly be my money, too. But then I thought: my college tuition. If you converted my college tuition into stacks of cash, even after my scholarship, it would be . . . how tall? And how about all the dance classes growing up, and the leotards and costumes? And the discount Stanley negotiated for me for my apartment in Buffalo, the waived security deposit?

She reached for my hand again, and this time I was too confused and mixed up to pull it away.

"Everybody uses each other," she said. "You used Laura, too, you know. You became totally obsessed with controlling her life so you wouldn't go crazy after your dad died. Am I wrong? You use Stanley for money, and he uses you to feel like a stand-up guy, a good dad. You use me, to make yourself braver, to stay one step ahead of the grief and guilt before it can swallow you whole. So what? I do it, too. We have to use each other, to stay alive. The least we can do is try to use each other honestly and responsibly."

"That can't be it," I whispered. "That can't be how the world works."

"I don't think you and I are going to solve the mystery of how the world works at this table," she said.

She released my hand, and it was as if some spell had been broken—or, perhaps, had completed being cast.

Jeanine had a way of knocking the legs out from under me, and usually the effect was freeing—I would feel, without legs, that I could float. At the moment the ground seemed very far away, and I wasn't sure if I was floating or falling. I wasn't even sure what I had come here to do anymore, or if I had gotten the answers I needed, or if there was any answer she could give me that would satisfy me or help me understand why we were here . . . why *were* we here?

"What's going on, Jeanine?" I said. "Why are you here?"

She sighed. "I told you. Columbus was the best option, given—"

"No, no. I mean, why are you here *now*? Why are you hiding? Something must have happened. There was that block of heroin, the one you got with Landon? Right before you left?"

She grew very still.

"I don't know what you're talking about," she said. "Landon was never involved."

"That's not true. He got his hands on a bunch of heroin. And now the police have connected him to some man who—some man who died."

The color completely drained out of her face. It was worse than seeing her go pale with shock at the hotel. She looked gray, the bags under her eyes darkened to purple, turning her eye sockets into caverns. I straightened in alarm.

"Did you know that guy?" I said. "The guy who got killed?"

She got up to stand by the sink. She rinsed her mug and grabbed another one, and filled that one with prosecco. She drained it in one gulp, rinsed that cup, then got a new mug out of the cabinet. She was breathing heavily.

"It's okay," I said. I stood up and reached for her. "Hey—it's okay."

"All right, just—please don't touch me."

I pulled my hand away from her shoulder.

"Was Landon helping you sell the stolen shrink?" I asked gently. "And that man, he found out? And Landon had to kill him?"

She grabbed the half-empty bottle of prosecco by the neck and walked away. I stood at the threshold of the kitchen as she opened the door to the hall closet, got inside, and pulled it closed.

I stepped gingerly down the hallway and stood outside the door.

"Are you okay?" I said.

"I don't want to look at you while we talk about this part," she said.

LANDON DIDN'T KILL the man who died, Jeanine said. Landon didn't kill anyone.

I sat on the floor outside the closet, my back leaning against the wall. Jeanine's voice floated from the narrow gap between the door and the frame.

The man who died was a Paladino guy, one of Bobby's men. The first and only time she encountered the dead man—whose name, she said in a faint peep, was Frank Vicente—was ten days before her disappearance. Jason called her, saying he needed help at a stash house where he'd made one of his usual stops after a shipment came in. Jeanine entered the house to find Jason standing over the body of a man who had been shot in the head.

"Frank was a middleman between Jason and the lower-level dealers, like Danny at the Pink Fountain. I guess he figured out what we were doing with these 'excess' drugs," Jeanine said. "He didn't like being cut out of a chunk of the market. So he made a threat to Jason, or they got in a fight, or—I don't know, I wasn't *there*. I just showed up and he was—*exploded* all over the living room of this house."

"Oh, Jeanine," I breathed.

"I knew Jason was a hothead, but I couldn't believe—I mean, it was the worst thing he could have done. It was horrible. And I had to clean it up, had to— Jason drove away with the body, and I had to clean everything up. We tried to make it look like a robbery, like Frank had run off with the cash and the stash house drugs and disappeared. It was never supposed to have happened."

For the next couple of days she had tried to act normal and get on with life, she said. But everything got so complicated. Her Buffalo clients started getting skittish as rumors spread about the emptied stash house. Jason was acting like a maniac, flying off the handle at the first provocation, assuming anyone even peripherally aware of Frank's disappearance was a liability. And Jeanine and Jason apparently hadn't cleaned well enough: at dinner a few nights later, Bobby let fly a comment about how one of his guys had been "popped," so she knew the situation was being investigated as a murder. In the days that followed, her stomach was a wreck, and sometimes her heart pounded so hard she thought she was going to die.

"*You* saw how I was that week," she said. "I was so paranoid Bobby was on to me that I didn't want to sleep at his place. I kept dragging you around to bars all week, trying to stay in public places. I made you sleep over, so I wouldn't be alone. I was losing my mind. I just wanted everything to be normal so bad. I wanted it all to go away."

"But what happened to make you run away?" I said. "It just got to be too much?"

There was a pause. Her voice was muffled when she spoke.

"The police found the guy," she said, so quietly I had to lean forward to hear. "They found it, the—the body. Jason saw it on the Buffalo police blotter. I couldn't take it. The police *and* the Paladinos. I knew it was only a matter of time. I already had a car I used for my trips down to Columbus, so I packed it up with all the cash I had stashed at my place and just drove. I didn't know what else to do. I threw up twice on the way down here."

She sniffed.

"Everything was going so well for so long," she said in a tiny voice. "I wasn't supposed to be a missing person. I wasn't supposed to be a news story. No one was supposed to die."

I crept to the gap in the closet door and gently pulled it open. The closet, like the rest of the house, was mostly empty, with only a pair of snow boots on the floor next to the prosecco bottle. She was sitting with her knees drawn to her chest.

"Are you going to give me up?" she whispered.

Her hair was limp on either side of her face, her cheeks pale, eyes red, and I saw then the side of Jeanine I'd always known existed deep down. Beneath all her brass and brashness, beneath her makeshift Rust Belt pageant-queen grin, she was a scared girl playing dress-up, praying through clenched teeth that she was getting away with the act, that she wouldn't have to craft yet another new disguise to sneak her way through the gates. She was a girl on the outside trying to get in, using every trick, every ounce of grit she had.

"I would never give you up," I said.

"What about what I did to that man?"

"You didn't kill anyone, Jeanine. Jason did."

Her face collapsed. She hugged her knees closer and buried her head in her arms.

"We're going to fix it," I said.

"I don't think you can protect me, V," she said. "You don't get it. I fucked up too bad. I did too many things wrong."

I said, "Try me."

Chapter 30

I WENT AHEAD AND helped her pack. I didn't know what else to do.

"We should be packing to bring you back to *Buffalo,*" I said as we sat on the carpeted floor in front of her upstairs bedroom closet. "Where else are you going to go?"

"I don't know. I'll figure it out as I pack."

The bedroom was as meagerly furnished as the rest of the house, a fuzzy pink blanket on the twin-size bed the only homey detail. Scattered on the floor around us were the clothes Jeanine had fled with, a hastily gathered assortment of dresses and strappy tops and leggings. She had torn them from their hangers so she could reach the back wall of the closet, which had a panel that could be popped out. From the cavity behind the panel she now extracted an armful of rubber-banded bundles of cash.

"I say we go straight to Stanley and beg for his protection," I said as I watched her dump the bundles—a mix of ten- and twenty-dollar bills—into a black duffel bag. "We can pin everything on Jason. Say he put a gun to your head and forced you to help him with the shrink. He's the one who actually killed someone. He *actually* let drugs 'fall off the truck.' You were, what? A connector? Surely that's forgivable. Especially if you were coerced into it."

"Sorry, V, but it's totally unrealistic," said Jeanine. She had grown animated, unburdened perhaps by her confession and the first bottle of prosecco, which she'd drunk most of. Her ability to rally reminded me of Marianne on the day we played rummy, mixing margaritas and feigning good cheer while agonizing internally over her daughter's disappearance.

"I know you think Stanley Paladino is, like, some Mafia dad Santa Claus figure, but he will literally kill me on sight," she said. "I messed with his son's business, and his business. He's not going to let anyone get away with that. Not even his favorite girl's best friend. Sorry."

"Okay, so what's the plan? You go to a motel and then what? Stay there forever?"

"I don't *know,*" she said. "When I ran away from Buffalo, I was just trying to stay alive, and out of jail. My only priorities were to find a temporary job that could explain some of my cash, and to lay low until I could figure out my next move before fucking Gabe comes looking for another shipment. Now Buffalo is burned, and Columbus is maybe burned, and all I know is I need to get out of this house. You can't plan everything." She shoved a bundle—this one made up of fifty-dollar bills, I noted—decisively into the duffel. "Sometimes you have to take things as they come. No, hiding in this house is not what I wanted. No, I'm not having any fun. But there's always another option. I just have to think of it."

Fun? I thought.

"I hate to keep harping on this—" I said.

"Oh, V, you love to harp." Jeanine grinned over her shoulder at me as she reached into the closet for another batch of bundles.

"Well, I'll say it again: if you'd told me you were in trouble from the start, I could have helped you," I said. "We talked and talked and we never talked about your life. I mean your real life. *This.*"

"For what it's worth, I thought about telling you," said Jeanine. "I can't tell you how many times I thought about cutting you in."

"Cutting me—in?"

Jeanine pulled the last roll from the back of the closet and dropped it into the duffel, now heavy with cash.

"Are you kidding?" she said, turning her attention to opening the second bottle of prosecco, which she'd brought upstairs with us. "You're a fitness instructor and personal trainer. You're perfect. You could fold in extra cash, another business, *easy.* A legitimate business to wash the money through. Even pay taxes on it. And you could have used it to build a real business, like opening your own studio with a bunch of super-rich clients who want the NFL cheerleader fitness regimen. It would have been so fucking fun," she burst out. "We could have made so much money. I'm always picturing big things for you, way bigger than you can picture for yourself."

She ripped off the aluminum wrapping around the cork. The image shocked me: *me,* running a business, helping Jeanine launder money, or whatever it was she wanted me to do for her. And under the surprise, a nagging sense of loss. If I'd been a little bit different, a little more like the person she imagined I could be, more daring, more ambitious, then we would have shared all of this. I would have been a true friend for her, a partner.

"I wasn't sure how you'd react if I told you," said Jeanine, pushing at the prosecco cork with her thumbs. "Because of Laura. And, well—you're a Paladino girl. More specifically, you're *Stanley's* girl. He's way more discerning than Bobby. He'd flip a lid if he found out I'd gotten you involved. No, you were too close to Stanley and you were too risky. That's just what it comes to at the end of the day. I had to hide it from you."

The cork popped off with a bang, sending a spray of foam leaping from the neck of the bottle, soaking Jeanine's leg and the carpet.

"Shit!" she said, yanking the duffel bag away from the foamy puddle of liquid spreading into the fibers of the carpet.

I watched her sop up the prosecco with a wadded towel. She was deranged, and reckless, and probably had PTSD from the awful fallout of Frank's murder. The best thing for me to do would be to say *You're on your own* and walk out the front door. So why couldn't I do it? I was not in the habit of giving up on people or measuring their goodness by normal standards. Stanley was a criminal, and I loved him. Laura had been a criminal, and I loved her. And then there were people like Landon, who were pulled in and out of criminal activity. And what about my dad? Should I wash my hands clean of all of them? Cut them all out and recommit my life to the Jills, and community service, and maintaining a morally upright existence? Be the good girl?

Jeanine had almost, almost seen something else in me besides the good girl. I had almost been the sort of person who could share that part of her life—someone she could use.

"Jeanine," I said. "What do you use me for?"

"Huh?" she asked as she rifled inside the duffel to make sure the cash hadn't gotten wet.

"You said everybody uses each other. But what do you use me for?"

She dropped the duffel and sat back on her heels, face screwed up in thought.

"I don't know," she said. She looked startled.

"You used me to get to Laura."

"That wasn't planned. I didn't, like, come after you to get to Laura. It arose organically." She poured prosecco into my mug, which I'd brought upstairs, and handed it to me. "I guess I just like being around you."

"But why?"

"You always made me feel safe."

My neck prickled as my face flushed. This was all I wanted: to be the source of safety, to be the longed-for presence.

"Sometimes," she said, "I imagine an alternate version of me who's still living in Buffalo. I try to picture exactly what she's doing at any given moment, and most of the time, she's with you: drinking wine, stealing your earrings for a date, making fun of your cute new boyfriend you finally let yourself have, scrambling eggs, hungover and happy. She's like a little video game I play in my head, my avatar I send out to do nice things. It's very relaxing."

I fidgeted under her gaze, which held a mix of wonder and affection. Stubbornly, I had refused to concede that Jeanine was dead until I had real proof, but even so, I had not let myself believe she was alive, either; I had not believed in a future with Jeanine in it. Jeanine had done terrible things, maybe irredeemable things. Maybe I'd never come to terms with what she'd done to Laura. But if there was any chance at a future on the other side of this, for all of us, I wanted to know what it was. A more honest future with Jeanine. If I could make her want that future badly enough.

"You can do that for real," I said. "With the right story. You want to use me for something? Use me for my connection to Stanley. Use me to figure out a solution. Use me to back up your story."

"I can't believe," she said, "that after all the shit you've found out about me, after everything I've done, you're sitting here on my bedroom floor, trying to figure out how to bring me back to Buffalo."

"We can make things right. You have people back home who need you. What about your mom? Are you never going to see your mom again?"

"I know I have to figure out my mom. Do you think it's easy for me not being able to talk to her? It's killing me. This is for her, you know." She pulled at the straps of the duffel. "All this is for her."

It was so painfully obvious that none of it was for Marianne. All the objects cluttering Marianne's life—the red robe, the new teeth, the patio furniture—all those things were obviously, obviously for Jeanine. But arguing about this would take us away from the essential point, which was to get Jeanine home.

"Okay, so let's get you back to your mom. And Landon—" A zap went up my spine. I reached out to grab her knee. "God, Landon. Jeanine, he is the biggest reason you need to come back. I don't think you realize how much trouble he's in. The police think he's involved with this dead body, and the Paladinos do, too. You have to give them the real story, so they'll stop hunting him."

I was expecting her to be alarmed, but she winced and withdrew, and took a slug from the bottle.

"They're literally investigating him for murder," I said, hoping to impress upon her the urgency of the situation. "I know he was selling for you. You got him set up with some of that shrink. You met with him at least twice before you ran away."

Jeanine stood up. "You keep using words like *murder* and *dead body,* and I wish you'd stop. Like, stop talking about it. You weren't there. Please."

"Sorry," I said.

"Can you help me pack up my clothes? I've got another suitcase."

She bustled around, yanking a wheeled carry-on out from under the bed. I could understand her having a major stress response every time I brought up the death of Frank, but I couldn't let her get away with ignoring Landon's predicament.

"We have to help him," I said. "He's a good guy, Jeanine. He cares about you. He deserves to have his life back."

She dropped the suitcase in front of me.

"What's going on between you and Landon? Are you two fucking?"

"Jeanine!" I nearly spilled my prosecco. "God, why do people keep *saying* that!"

"What? Is it totally outside the realm of possibility? I'm not mad if you are. You can add him to your little tally."

"What tally? Why does everyone think I'm sleeping with Landon?"

"Who else thinks that?"

"Oh, I don't know. Landon's new girlfriend, and Bobby, and who knows who else."

"Well," she said. "It does sound like you're spending a lot of time together."

"It— Never mind. I'm not sleeping with Landon. That doesn't mean I'm okay with him being arrested for a crime he didn't commit."

"I didn't say I was okay with it, either. I obviously don't want to hurt Landon."

"Okay, so let's clear his name. Say he found the drugs you and Jason were stealing on the side of the road. Bobby will buy it. He's crazy about you. He wants to be the hero, take somebody out on your behalf. Let him take out Jason."

Jeanine knelt to gather her scattered clothes into a pile. I watched her shove a dress still on its hanger into the bag.

"Right?" I said. "It would work. You save Landon. You get rid of Jason. You get your mom back. Take as much of this money as you can justify having and burn the rest. You'll make new money."

She pushed a hand through her bleached hair. She looked like she was considering it.

"I don't know," she said. "Maybe. Look, where are you staying? I guess you and Laura are talking again, obviously. Does she know you're here?"

"She has no idea," I said. It was a reflex, hiding Laura like this. "She doesn't even know I'm in town."

"Okay, so come to a motel with me. There's no way I can sleep alone here after the scare you gave me. We'll talk and figure out—if there's a way. Maybe there's a way."

"Yes," I said, thinking I could text Laura the next time I was in the bathroom. "We'll think of a story. We'll go through all the details. Tie up all the loose ends. Like— Oh, I have one." I shifted so I was sitting on my ankles. "Who's Olena Rossi?"

Jeanine looked at me for what felt like a long time, her face eerily blank.

"It's the name you gave Laura and Gabe," I said. "Right? But she's also a real person. She owns that car you drive, the Hyundai. She works for a doctor in Springfield?"

Jeanine plucked a dress from the floor and folded it, lost in thought.

"Um," she said after a minute. "I don't know that woman. I was just using the name."

"Did you steal her identity?" I said. "Because that could be a problem. If you're using her Social Security number or something."

"No. I'm not doing that."

"Okay, but—did you meet her through the Jills? She's a donor. Are you working together? Does she help with—like, prescriptions? Or is she paying for stuff to help you stay under the radar?"

"I've never met her," said Jeanine. "That woman is separate. I have nothing to do with her. You don't have to worry about that."

"But—"

She tossed the dress aside and stood, shouldering the duffel filled with cash. "I'm going to put this downstairs with the other one. And then I need a shower. I totally reek of stress sweat. Will you finish packing my clothes?"

"Are you okay?"

"Yeah. I just need to shower and clear my head. And then we'll go to the motel."

She paused at the doorway and looked back at me.

"Thank you," she said. "For the help. Really. I love you."

With that, she padded out of the bedroom and down the carpeted upstairs hallway.

I stood at the top of the stairs until I heard the squeak and spray of the shower turning on in the downstairs bathroom. Then I returned to the bedroom to deal with the packing. I could tell I'd upset her with the mention of Olena in Springfield. There was more she wasn't saying, and I'd have to get it out of her.

I folded the flimsy dress she'd tossed to the floor, which I recognized from our nights out in Buffalo, into the suitcase. Her socks I stuffed into her boots to save space. I fished a few scarves and hats, which looked newly purchased, from the wire shelves in the closet, allowing myself the fleeting thought that she'd need them for the Buffalo winter.

My stomach was bubbling from hunger and prosecco, but also from a growing sense of unease. In the silence, a thought presented itself. It was a thought I didn't want to think, and yet, avoiding the thought was simply another way of thinking it. Like a bell that had been rung and couldn't be unrung, the thought: that big block of heroin, which came seemingly out of nowhere, appeared soon after Jason murdered Frank. He and Jeanine emptied his stash house, Jeanine said, to create the impression of a robbery. Then they realized they needed to cover for a murder. They gave Landon the drugs from the scene of the crime.

The thought wedged itself into my throat behind my collarbone and stuck there. She'd set Landon up with drugs from the stash house. To make it seem as if he had taken them, as if he had killed someone for them. I zipped the carry-on and carefully righted it. I stepped out of the bedroom to stand again at the top of the stairs.

From the landing I could look down at the front door, the door to the outside world. I forced myself to breathe. Thinking a thought did not make it true. The important thing was to get her back to Buffalo. That was the first step in fixing everything, including Landon's situation.

I listened to the splash of the shower, waiting for it to turn off, and for whatever else was going to happen between me and Jeanine to begin. I stared at the front door, standing imperiously down below, and wondered again if I should walk out of it. Then it knocked.

A column of fear rose up from the floor and encased me. I gripped the banister and prayed, nonsensically, that the knock had somehow been produced from within the door itself, and not by a person standing on the other side.

The knocking resumed, louder. I crept down the stairs, wincing at each creak in the wood. When I reached the bottom I dropped to my knees to crawl to the kitchen, hopefully out of sight of anyone peering through windows.

After all this, I might have led them right to her. Antweiler. The police. I crawled through the kitchen, on my hands and knees, and pushed open the bathroom door.

"Jeanine?" I whispered through the steam and white noise of the shower. "Jeanine?"

I stood. I tugged open a small gap in the shower curtain, then yanked it aside. The shower was empty.

I stumbled back into the kitchen and turned in a circle, heart pounding in my throat. The suitcase was gone.

"Hello?" shouted a voice through the front door. "Virginia, are you in there?"

I knew that voice. I opened the door to find Laura, fists clenched, eyes wide with rage, demanding to be let inside.

Chapter 31

"You said you would wait," said Laura, stomping behind me as I searched the downstairs—behind the couch, in the hallway closet. "You said we would go together. You should never have come here alone. Don't you dare use my meetings like that. It makes me feel like I can't go to them."

I was so livid my hands were shaking. I kicked open the back door, calling Jeanine's name across the backyard.

I stood in the grass and stared at the shabby wooden fence. An opportunity had been ripped from me. I wanted to at least finish what I'd started. I wanted to have a say in what happened next to Jeanine. After all this, shouldn't I get a say?

Laura watched from the doorway, arms crossed across her chest. "Come on," she said finally, reaching for my hand. "Let's get out of here."

She followed me out the front door, onto the porch, saying, "You get in your car first. You won't be offended if I follow behind. To make sure you go where you say you're going."

I walked ahead, not wanting to be anywhere near her, or the house, or myself. I was too angry, too sad to speak. Halfway across the street I pulled to a stop. The spot where I had parked my car was empty.

"Oh my God," I said, feeling in my pockets.

"What?" said Laura.

"My keys, I set them down. I left them on the . . ."

On the—counter.

"Oh," I said. "Jeanine stole my car."

WE NEEDED TO go to the police, Laura insisted as she drove us back to her apartment. We needed to report my car as stolen, and get Jeanine into custody so she could get treatment or whatever she needed, and then I needed to go to Stanley, explain every detail of every part of my search, so he could advise and protect me, and then I needed to lock myself in my apartment in Buffalo and not come out.

"You can't seriously be considering covering for this person," said Laura. "You busted in on a drug operation. Do you not understand that? She's not going to let you walk away, not with everything you know. There's too much at stake."

"I didn't say I was covering for her. I didn't say what I'm going to do next. I need to *think*."

"There's nothing to think about." We'd made it to Laura's street. She parallel parked, swinging the wheel violently. "You have to ask yourself, what more are you willing to do for this woman? What exactly do you think your obligation is? At some point, it's time to forfeit personal responsibility for another person. I'm saying that as someone who has put people in a position where they had to do that to me."

"I know that, Laura," I said. "I'm the one who had to do it, remember?"

"Yeah, and instead of dealing with your own issues, and your codependency, and your control-freak bullshit, you went and replaced me with another mess to clean up. You don't know how to form a relationship with me as an adult, independent person, capable of taking responsibility for her own mistakes. You don't want to go through the muck and the work of it, and you don't want forgiveness, and you don't want change. You just want someone to need you the way I needed you, because otherwise, you feel like you don't exist."

She killed the ignition. I was so angry I could hardly speak.

"Are you seriously making this about you?" I managed to sputter. "This is not about you. This isn't the Laura show all over again. I know being an addict means you get to be the center of the universe—"

"Oh, please."

"You and Jeanine are nothing alike," I shouted. "She's not even using. You don't get to be the center of attention. You're not the only one who exists."

"You think I don't know you exist? I think about you constantly, Ginny. When I was in detox, we had to write these life history accounts in our journals every day, and do you know what I wrote about? You. Every little thing I'd done to betray you and make you cry, I accounted for in excruciating detail. And then in group, I would only talk about you, the sister who did everything for me. I went on and on about you, until my sponsor finally had to step in and say, 'Laura, this meeting why don't you try talking a little bit about yourself?' "

"What do you want me to say to that? 'Sorry you felt bad in rehab'?"

"I'm saying I have no concept of myself without you! I'm trying to have a concept of myself, but even now, look at me: I'm letting you call the shots, like I always did growing up. I always did whatever you said. You *taught* me that I couldn't trust my own mind and ideas, you taught me *compliance,* to do what other people want me to do in exchange for love and approval. And *still* I can't go against you, because of all the sacrificing you did for me. I feel like I have to apologize for getting sober without you! Like me surviving on my own is some horrible betrayal of you, just one more fucking way I let you down."

I yanked at the door handle, so I wouldn't hit her across the face, but Laura had the stupid child lock on.

"All I wanted was for you to live," I screamed, pulling at the handle. "I would have given up my whole life so you could live."

"Well, I did live. Now what? Who are we going to be now?"

"Open the fucking door, Laura!"

She hit the button, and I stumbled out onto the street. She called after me, but I didn't hear what she said. I would have given anything for another door to slam, but in her building's foyer, I had to stand there waiting for her to come let me in.

ALL EVENING I lay on Laura's couch, comatose, gripping my phone.

I had about ten missed calls from Sharrice, accompanied by a dozen texts:

Are you back in town yet? We are REALLY worried.

You missed field practice . . .

Everything ok?

Please tell me where you are! No one is mad, just worried.

I registered, on a barely conscious level, that I'd skipped practice. I'd failed to text Suzanna the picture she had demanded, of me on the road back to Buffalo. I didn't know how I'd get back home, seeing as Jeanine had my car. The Bills played tomorrow night. Laura would have to drive me. She had not emerged from her bedroom in several hours, having gathered up her yoga mat and spiral notebook and candles, the trappings of her new life, and locked herself in there. Neither of us had spoken or eaten. Every time I heard the creak of her movements down the hallway, my heart dipped with fear. I was not ready to be honest with Laura, just as I wasn't ready for her to be honest with me. We had not been honest with each other in a long, long time.

I had always told myself it was Jason Morley who drove a wedge of dishonesty between me and my sister, by getting her hooked on heroin when I wasn't there to look out for her. Laura had shattered this illusion the night she relapsed, when she revealed that she'd been hiding herself from me long before she'd started using. But when had this begun, the hiding? It wasn't when our dad died—we'd been united in our sadness, sharing a bed some nights, still baking cakes on his birthday. The onset of puberty couldn't separate us: we got our periods within months of each other, pored over issues of *Seventeen* for advice on how to shave our legs and put on makeup, while Mom slept off the vodka in her bedroom. We'd remained one person, one united front, through eras that divided other sisters.

It was when Laura started having sex. That was when she started lying to me, when she realized I would flip out at the implication that she was more desired than I was, more worthy of attention, more wanted. That was the moment our identities bifurcated: Laura had a part of her life she couldn't speak to me about. She couldn't tell me if she was scared or mad, if she didn't want to go to practice, if her body hurt, if she felt lost or alone, because I interpreted everything she did as a reflection on me. I took any discrepancies between her desires or experiences and mine as a personal affront. She realized the only way to individuate and take her body back from me was to literally break it. I was the one who turned Laura into a liar before Jason ever got his hands on her.

Outside the apartment windows the sky was dark, stained brown by the streetlights. It could have been seven P.M. or ten, or past midnight for all I knew. I didn't bother to check the time on my phone; the numbers meant nothing. I began to sink into a dark, frightening void adjacent to sleep, a place that held zinging nightmares and the terror of falling into my own body, being alone in my own mind. I was spared the full drop into this terrible place when my phone leapt to life, vibrating in my hands.

I jerked awake, dropped my phone, then fished it out from where it had fallen under the couch. The call was from an Ohio area code.

Down the hallway, the creak of Laura's bedroom door swinging open. Her footsteps, padding from the bedroom to the bathroom.

The sound of the bathroom faucet. I hesitated, my finger hovering over the button to answer the call.

Laura appeared in the living room, her face pink from being rinsed in the sink.

"How long," she said, "do you want to wait around for your car to reappear?"

My phone buzzed again. A text from the number that had just called. It said: **hey. pick up.**

"Who's texting you?" said Laura. "Is that her?"

I looked from Laura back down to my phone. It started to ring again.

Laura held out her hand. "Give me the phone."

I bolted down the hall into Laura's bedroom and locked the door. Laura pounded on it. I went into the closet, shut myself inside, and answered the phone.

"Oh, good," said Jeanine's voice. "Don't hang up."

"Jeanine, thank God." My body exploded with dopamine. It was pitch-dark in the closet, except for the thin beam of light emanating from the bottom of the door. I sat on Laura's shoes, her clothes on their hangers tickling my face, surrounded by the smell of leather and plastic and the patchouli scent that clung to Laura's clothing.

"Where are you right now?" said Jeanine.

"Laura's place. She's not home," I hastened to add, cupping my hand around my mouth, to block out the faint sound of Laura pounding on the bedroom door outside.

"You know what's funny?" said Jeanine. "First rule when you disappear is that you can't have contact with your old life. I got rid of everyone's number. I threw out my phone and made my peace with it. But your number, I have memorized. Yours, and Landon's, and my mom's. When I first left, I worried I'd get drunk and call one of you."

"You can always call me," I said. "Where are you?"

"Don't worry about where I am. I'm sorry about your car. I didn't want you following me again. I left it parked in front of your apartment building. In Buffalo."

"You're back in Buffalo?" I gasped.

"Don't get excited. I'm not staying. I've already left. Listen, I appreciate what you tried to do for me. Of all the people I thought I had to worry about, I had no idea you'd be the one to cause me the most problems, but—well, now I'm thinking you showing up at my door was a sign. I've got to keep moving forward. I can't be worried about you or anyone else. I need a clean break."

"Don't make any decisions yet. Just hold tight. I'll get a ride to Buffalo, and we can figure out your next move. You can stay at my place. I'll call my landlord to let you in—"

"Virginia, stop," she said. "You've got to let go of this fantasy that I can reemerge into society. It's not going to work. The Paladinos have cops on payroll, lawyers who crawled out of some pit. You don't know that family the way you think you do."

"But—"

"I just called to say bye. And sorry about your car. Sorry for everything. Hey, V? Have a really, really good life," she said.

"Don't hang up," I said. "Don't you dare."

But what good was it to say that to Jeanine? She always dared. She hung up.

After several long minutes in Laura's closet, I emerged and unlocked the bedroom door. In the hallway, Laura's eyes were dark, her sweatshirt sleeves hanging past her wrists.

"I think she's really gone this time," I said.

Laura watched me sway in her doorway, looking exhausted.

"Can I get a ride home?" I said.

Chapter 32

The temperature had risen back into the forties in Buffalo, the streets wet with melted slush. My Corolla was parked across the street from my building, as Jeanine had promised.

Laura had pushed eighty the entire drive, so we'd made good time: it was eleven in the morning. She stood uncertainly in the street, unsure whether to follow me upstairs.

"Come up and take a nap," I said. "We've been awake since five A.M., and we hardly slept last night. You can't get on the road like this."

She made a show of dragging her feet. We tracked wet footprints up the stairs to my apartment. The cat cried out beseechingly as I fumbled my key into the door, then fled as soon as we stepped inside. Sharrice had kept my place tidy, the cat box clean.

"You can take the bed," I said. I felt a profound urge to make myself uncomfortable, as though this would make up for everything.

By way of reply, Laura fished through my dresser for a clean T-shirt and closed herself in the bathroom. I could hear her gargle mouthwash. I sat on the edge of my bed, unable to make my way to the couch. Laura climbed into bed and threw a washcloth over her face to block out the soft light from the windows. Though she held her body stiffly, facing the wall, she did not protest when I slid under the comforter next to her.

"You know it's over now, right?" said Laura, still facing the wall. "There's literally nothing else to do. You found her. That's got to be enough."

The words hung there in the dim silence of the bedroom. A frantic part of my mind was still churning, grinding, searching for the grist of a plan, a next step. Maybe I could use her new number to track her, maybe I could lure her out of hiding with the right text, maybe, with the right move, I could stave off another goodbye, another sad ending. By now I ought to have accepted the truth about endings, which was that they weren't peaceful or cathartic. They were stunted and abrupt and stupid. It was always impossible to accept that you were driving away, that you'd closed the door for the last time. Or that someone you loved was closing the door, driving away, and not coming back. After that, you could only wait for the mourning to come—and it was coming, and it wouldn't feel grand or dignified, and it would clobber you. And it would take a long time before you'd be able to stagger back to your feet.

I was running out of things to throw between me and the mourning. And what came on the other side of the mourning, which was, impossibly, more life. Because you had to go on living; the other option was to die with them, which at times seemed like the only sensible thing to do. I stood at the brink of these options: to kill myself holding on to her or to move on.

Didn't you ever get a third option?

Laura's breathing began to slow. I became certain that this was the last time she was ever going to speak to me, that if we fell asleep we would be lost to each other forever.

"Laura," I whispered. "Laura?"

"What?" she snapped.

"Did I make you hurt yourself?"

She rolled over and pulled the washcloth off her eyes, frowning. I looked into her face and begged her to understand what I meant.

"Was that the only choice you had, being my sister?" I said "To hurt yourself?"

"Oh." Her face softened with understanding. "Oh, Gin. You mean my ankle."

Once she said it, I couldn't face her. I squeezed my eyes shut. I felt her hand on my cheek, which, I realized, was wet with tears.

"You were all I had," she said. "I didn't know any other way to communicate. If I could go back, I would tell my sixteen-year-old self that her big sister loved her, and would do anything for her. I'd tell her that it was okay."

"But I'll never get the chance to do it right," I said. "To go back, and give you what you needed."

"Ginny, you were just a kid." Her voice deepened with concern. "We have to forgive ourselves. We have to tell our younger selves that it's okay, and we did our best."

Our best. My best. My best was nothing. It solved nothing.

"Will you be here when I wake up?" I said, eyes still squeezed closed.

"It's not a question," she said, straightening the blanket on my shoulders as I dropped toward sleep. "I'm not going anywhere until I'm sure you're okay."

THREE HOURS LATER I sat up like a shot.

"The *Bills*?" said Laura, after she'd stumbled out of bed behind me. She rubbed her eyes, which were puffy from too little sleep, and watched me curling my hair in the bathroom.

I was supposed to be at the stadium *now,* I explained. It was faster to style my hair at home than to fight for an outlet at the Ralph. I would have to do my makeup when I got there.

"Don't go," said Laura. "You have enough going on. You don't have to go."

"I can't not go."

"But Ginny—"

I gathered up my protein bars and makeup bag and uniform bag. I would do my primer and foundation in the car, while I sat in the game-day traffic, which was going to make me even later. Under Laura's baffled gaze, I felt like a child gathering toys: a basket full of plastic fruit, a bag of fake lipsticks and mascara, props for an elaborate pretend, a puerile mimicry of a woman's life.

"You said you wouldn't leave," I pleaded with her, my arms full of little bags.

"Virginia . . ." said Laura.

"You'll be here?" I said as I backed down the hallway to the door, bumping into the walls along the way. "When I get home? Please?"

On the interminable drive to the Ralph, the highway clogged with traffic, my sense of unease grew. Every so often, I would catch the faint smell of Jeanine's shampoo on the headrest, before it disappeared. I peeked into the backseat to see my empty water bottle on the floor, my extra pair of sneakers. My emergency makeup bag was stuffed in the passenger seat flap, where I always kept it. Everything was in its place. But still I had a funny feeling, like she'd messed with the car. Left a note, perhaps. A sign, a clue as to how to contact her.

By the time I got to my parking spot, one hour before kickoff, I had the presence of mind to check the most obvious place in a car for a person to leave a note. I hit the button for the glove compartment, and it fell open. Inside was my registration, a plastic-wrapped bundle of tissues, and nothing else. Sharrice's gun was gone.

AT FIRST, NONE of the girls noticed me entering the locker room. They were gathered in their sideline groups, starting their pregame rituals—handshakes, choreography checks, call-and-response chants.

I pushed my way into the room and stood in the bustle of chaos. I couldn't remember what to do first. I sat down at my assigned mirror and began pulling on my white boots, thoughtlessly, lulled by the dull hum of the room.

Who was she going to use that gun on? If I tallied up all the people who represented the biggest threat to her, the person at the top of the list was me. But if Jeanine wanted to shoot me in the head, she could have waited for me at my apartment. Unless she'd suspected I'd be with Laura, in which case, she might be waiting to get me alone. Waiting for me where?

"Virginia?"

I started. Above me stood Suzanna, her white-blond head eclipsing the ceiling lights like a great moon. She looked as stunned to see me as I was to be there.

"You're here?" she said.

It was a question I didn't know how to answer.

"I didn't expect you." She held the big white binder in her hands, and she opened it, then closed it, flustered. "Okay. It's good. It's good."

"Good?" My head swam with relief and terror.

I'd expected rage, the rage I deserved to be pummeled with. Instead, Suzanna was scribbling in the binder, eyes wide with pregame nerves, telling me she'd take Maddy off my line and put her on ambassador duties.

"Maddy?" I saw Maddy with Sharrice, Gina, Alicia, and Sophie in my line's usual corner—yes, of course, Suzanna had redone the lines again, arranged for another girl to dance in my place. "Maybe . . . maybe she should—?"

"No. No, you stay. I don't want you out there, wandering around, doing—I don't know *what* you're doing, and I can't keep an eye on you today because my eyes are on the field. So that's where I'm putting you, on the field, where I can watch you, and you can't go anywhere or cause any more trouble." She snapped the binder shut. "You have about thirty seconds to get into uniform and finish makeup. We're in standard uniform first half, then pink poms for the third-quarter break."

She put out an index finger, as if I were a dog being trained to stay. "Don't go anywhere. Stay here, where you belong. You're dancing. Do it."

In a whirl, she was gone. Girls were noticing me; I saw Carmen and Maria openly discussing me from the bench where they sat, and Lana giving me a confused wave from her position by the wall outlet, curling iron buried in her hair. I put on my uniform facing the wall so I wouldn't have to see the look on Maddy's face.

"Hey." Sharrice was at my elbow, pulling gently on my arm. "Sit here. I'll help with makeup."

I closed my eyes and submitted to her soft, nimble touch, the puff of her breath, smelling of cinnamon gum, on my eyelids. The gun was gone. The gun.

"Did anyone try to grab you on your way into the stadium?" she whispered.

I opened my eyes, mouth dry.

"There was a guy," Sharrice said, "outside the entrance, asking all the girls who came in if they know you. Not Ray—it was some man, with, like . . . a hat? I tried to reach you, but there's no reception here." She drew a breath. "What happened in Ohio? What is going on?"

I gazed wearily over at the locker room door, which I no longer felt safe exiting.

"Virginia?" said Sharrice.

"Ladies!" called Suzanna. "It's showtime!"

The room filled with whoops and cheers. Over Sharrice's shoulder, the locker room was a sea of craned necks and darting glances. The girls were looking at me. It was ridiculous that I should dance. I should be benched for the remainder of the season. An outrageous exception was being made.

"I can't do this," I said.

Sharrice gripped my shoulders in her perfect clawed hands. She was so beautiful, with her eyes framed by wings of false eyelashes, her cheeks glinting with highlighter, while I was puffy and ugly and banished.

"As long as you're on that field," she said, "you have seventy thousand eyes watching you and no one can touch you. You're with us, and you're safe."

"Yes," I said, thinking, *Yes, take this from me, take my life from me.*

"We'll get security to walk you out at the end of the game. I'll drive home with you. You can tell me what happened in Ohio. Until then"—her fingernails dug into my skin—"you're a Jill. You just have to dance."

Chapter 33

ON THE FIELD the music seemed to fight its way out of the speakers to my ears in slow motion. I hit the moves in the opening routine mechanically. I finished a turn a beat behind everyone else. My leg flew up in the kickline a little early. I flapped my limbs on the sideline like a doll. My brain pulled the steps from the muck of my subconscious. With every move I thought: *I don't have to be here. I shouldn't have come.*

At the end of our last sideline dance of the second quarter, I swayed, poms in the air. I was dehydrated. What force had propelled me to this point? What more did I have to give?

In the tunnel, I kept my eyes on my boots as I marched, with the rest of the girls, back inside the stadium to change for halftime. Fewer fans crowded the area by this point, though some, mostly men, stood in clusters to watch us and the players stream off the field. People with lanyards ran back and forth to complete the various mysterious tasks demanded by the stadium. Out of the echoing drone of noise came the sound of a man's voice, calling my name.

I stopped. I was not used to hearing my name from a crowd, instead of the usual calls of "Hello, ladies" or "Hi, beautiful." My whole name, Virginia Barton, from the mouth of a man leaning over the railing marking the edge of the thoroughfare leading into the locker rooms. He wore no Bills colors, just gray: gray pants, gray jacket, gray hat with a little brim. Ashlee bumped into me from behind.

"Autograph?" called the man. "Can I get an autograph?"

"Do you know that guy?" whispered Ashlee.

"I don't know," I said. "Is he a sponsor?"

"I don't recognize him." Ashlee pulled gently at my elbow.

"It's for Stanley," the man called.

"Just a sec," I said, shaking off Ashlee's arm.

I approached the man, who stood there behind the railing looking familiar.

"I don't have a pen," I said.

"That's okay, honey," he said.

He ducked under the railing, revealing, as he straightened, his true size. He was huge, his well-fitted wool jacket tailored to his massive height. With an outstretched arm, he herded me toward a quiet corner. He handed me a little slip of paper. On it was written, in black pen, *Come quietly.*

And suddenly, I knew I had seen this man before. In the foyer of my childhood home, boots dripping on the mat, towering over me, saying, *Who's this little beauty queen?* And in Paladino's, striding purposefully across the floor to the back office where my father worked, at the bar joking with the waitstaff, eating a steak-tips sandwich.

I glanced over my shoulder to find the hallway empty of Jills, who had charted their busy course back to the locker room, where I was supposed to be. My hands were shaking, gripping the piece of paper. Yes, I knew him. He'd been introduced to me as Uncle Scott, a term I'd recoiled from due to its forced intimacy; my father had no brothers. *Say hello,* my father had said, *to Uncle Scott.*

"Antweiler, is it?" I said.

"Let's go somewhere we can talk."

"I can't. I'm working."

"Honey." He looked at me from under his bushy eyebrows. "You're not working. You are in a lot of trouble."

"Maybe we can talk after the game."

"We know you've been visiting Landon Maher. We talked to Marianne Chanowitz."

"Who?" I lied.

"You've been visiting Landon Maher an awful lot lately, haven't you? How is it that you know where he is before anyone else seems to?"

The thoroughfare was so loud, and so busy, and yet I was so alone, so alone with this man. I made to step around him, but he adjusted his stance to block me.

"And you disappeared this weekend," he said, eyebrows furrowed, as if in concern for a child. "Went on a little trip? Out of town?"

"I have to change," I said. "We have a uniform change for the second half."

"Virginia, I don't want to hurt you," he said. "I don't want to upset you, even. You're family. To me, your father was like blood. I'm here to help you. You're going to come with me. We're going to have a talk."

"I'm working," I said as Antweiler stepped closer. "I have to change."

"Excuse me, sir?"

Now another surprise: Sharrice's voice, followed by the smart clip of her heels, which punctured through the dull noise of the hallway. She walked toward us with purpose, her hair bouncing, poms still gripped in her hands.

"I'm so sorry," Sharrice said with a smile, "but I have to steal Virginia from you. We're working."

"It's fine, sweetheart," said Antweiler. "We know each other."

"I want to be sure you get the game-day experience you deserve," said Sharrice. "And that means we need to be allowed to do our job."

"I said it's fine," Antweiler repeated. "Why don't you let us finish our conversation, please?"

"Hey, man." Behind Sharrice, a fan in a jersey swayed. "Leave the girls alone. The girls are working."

"I'm not talking to you," said Antweiler.

"The Jills are for everyone," jersey guy said. "You don't get to boss them around."

"Thank you, sir," said Sharrice. "I'm handling this."

"Stop walking over here," said Antweiler to the jersey guy. "Stop walking. I'm telling you."

"This guy's harassing cheerleaders," called the jersey guy.

A man in a security uniform appeared, as if from nowhere. I wanted to sink into the floor and disappear.

"Are you ladies all right?" the guard said. He wore a stadium-issued yellow vest over his black jacket. He was a freckled redhead and not at all intimidating, though he spoke in a deepened voice in an attempt to convey authority.

"There's no problem here, sir," Antweiler said. "Just a little mix-up."

"The Jills must be allowed to work unmolested," said the guard.

"Hell, yeah," said jersey guy.

"We're standing around talking," said Antweiler. "It's not illegal. Honey," he added, turning to me. "Tell everyone to calm down, please. So we can finish our conversation. You want to finish this conversation."

I felt his hand close on my forearm. My whole body rebelled at the touch, and I yanked my arm out of his grasp with such force that the back of my hand collided with his face.

I didn't hit him very hard, but he stumbled backward in surprise, his palm on his cheek, eyes darkened with rage. "I got him!" yelled jersey guy, lurching toward Antweiler with his arms up, darting right and left like a drunken basketball player playing defense, knocking into Sharrice, who careened into the security guard, who clawed at the walkie-talkie pinned to his shoulder, yelping that he needed backup near the Miller High Life VIP area.

I INSISTED THAT I did not want to speak with the official stadium security arriving at the scene. I begged the redheaded guard to walk me to my car. No, I did not want to give a statement. No, I did not want to wait for the police to arrive. Sharrice could give a statement. I retrieved my duffel from the locker room without speaking or looking at any of the girls, who were already lining up to return to the field, and met the redheaded guard by the door.

"You can still file a report if you change your mind," the guard said. He tugged on the waistband of his pants, which were a little loose. "It's a privilege to protect you girls, I hope you know that."

The white lights in the parking lot seemed to pierce straight through my eyes and bounce off the back of my sinuses. Suzanna would be furious that I was leaving at halftime after she'd given me a chance to perform, but there was no universe where I remained in the stadium with Antweiler there. Shrieks of tailgaters drifted across the lot, like the calls of wild animals. Although my duffel had my purse and change of shoes inside, I'd accidentally left my coat in the locker room. I had on only my uniform, but my adrenaline kept the chill away, as if a casing of heat surrounded my body.

"Seeing people disrespect the Jills really gets to me," said the guard. "Every game, I'm *looking* for guys trying to mess with you."

"I bet," I said.

"I mean, I am waiting for it. I can't believe it finally happened tonight."

A shout leapt from the darkness of the lot. Over my shoulder I saw a dark figure behind us, walking quickly. Even in my fear, I had room to be annoyed that the presence of the figure sent me swerving closer to the redheaded security guard, for protection I needed but did not want.

The headlights of a nearby car flickered on, illuminating the approaching figure. It was only Ray, calling out my name.

The redheaded guard craned his neck as I sped up.

"Bad ex-boyfriend?" he said. He reached for my hand, and I pulled it out of his grasp.

"Sure," I said. Behind us, Ray slowed to a stop, and I could see that his face had fallen, his arms hanging at his sides.

"This is me," I said as the guard and I reached my car. I stood by the driver's door and waited for him to go. I looked for Ray but saw no other figures nearby.

"Hold on a second," said the guard.

He looked concerned. How much more would I be subjected to? I could not take one more question. I could not take any more flirting.

But the guard simply removed his jacket, sliding off the yellow vest.

"It's getting cold," he said, with a beseeching smile. "Do you want this?"

Chapter 34

I RAN UP THE steps of my building two at a time. Certainly, Antweiler knew where I lived, and once he extracted himself from stadium security, he would be here. I would not be held hostage by some goon, even if he had known my father. Laura would have to help me brainstorm what to say to Stanley, what to leave out. I would have to convince everyone that I wasn't dating or hiding Landon, and also that Landon was innocent. I would have to call Jeanine, who would probably not pick up, and leave her a voicemail, warning her.

I pushed open my apartment door, my arms swimming in the baggy arms of the stadium guard's jacket, made of the noisy material of a cheap windbreaker.

"Laura?" I called.

It was dark in the apartment, quiet. I worried she'd already left for Columbus, too sick of me to wait for my return. I called her name again as I peeked into my bedroom, switched on the hallway light.

When I reached the end of the hallway I saw Bobby in his long camel hair coat, standing in my living room, feet planted wide on my rug. On the sofa next to him sat Laura, duct tape stretched over the lower half of her beautiful face, hands behind her back. She was as gray and limp as overcooked asparagus.

I opened my mouth, but nothing came out. It took a moment for me to realize that Bobby had a gun in his hands, and it was pointed at me.

I crossed my arms over my stomach. A second ago I'd let myself think Stanley could get me out of this. I'd believed that strongly in his infallibility, his control over other people's behavior. Stanley was an old man! What could he do if Bobby decided he wanted to kill me?

"What the hell is Laura doing here?" said Bobby, jerking the gun toward her. "I thought she lived in Ohio? This is not what I want. I don't want your sister here. I want to talk to you. Stop walking toward me!"

I stopped. I hadn't even realized I was moving.

"Put up your hands!" said Bobby, and I did.

Handguns were hard to aim, Sharrice had said. It was hard to hit what you wanted. It was the noise I was scared of most, I realized. I was scared of blowing out my eardrums, and being startled, and not knowing what to do.

Bobby thrust the gun toward me sloppily. He had his other hand on Laura's shoulder.

"If you thought pulling up your skirt like some silly cow meant I wouldn't figure out what a conniving, lying whore you've been—"

"Bobby, please—"

"Stanley let you think you're untouchable. You're not untouchable. You think your dead dad makes you untouchable? *He* wasn't even untouchable. I'm allowed to kill you for what you've done, you stupid bitch. I said stop walking!"

I bent over and put my hands on my knees, to make my legs stop moving without my permission.

"I said hands up!" said Bobby. "No more cat and mouse. I want Landon Maher. And I want Jeanine's body. Give me those two things, and I won't throw your sister out the fucking window."

"Bobby, I don't know—"

"Don't you dare fucking say to me that you don't know," yelled Bobby. He still had his hand gripped on Laura's shoulder, as if to press her into the couch. "You were just with him, you fucking idiot. You think I don't know? I *know*."

"Stop touching her," I said.

His eyes widened, mocking me, and he placed his hand flat on my sister's head. Laura's breathing grew quick and labored through her nose.

"Stop it!" I screamed.

I wanted to burn that hand with my gaze, like sending sunlight through a magnifying glass. I wanted to see that hand start smoking. He gripped my sister's head and shook it. Her eyes squeezed shut.

"Stop it! Bobby, I'll get you Landon. Okay? I'll get you Landon, I'll—I'll call him. See? I'm calling."

"Tell him you want to meet him. Tell him calmly."

I tried the number Landon had used to call me after we drank at the Foundry, knowing he wouldn't pick up, because he was gone, and Jeanine was gone, everyone was gone, gone—

"He's not answering," I stammered.

" 'He's not answering,' " he mimicked. "How much time do you think this is going to buy you? If he won't answer, you take me to him. Take me to his hideout."

"I'm trying, I'll *try*," I said.

I sank to my knees on the living room rug and called again. And again. The recorded voice repeated that the person I was trying to reach was not available, and I had to clench my teeth together to keep from screaming.

Desperate, I called the number Jeanine had used to text me in Columbus. It rang and rang and of course she did not pick up.

Hands shaking, I texted:

Bobby has a gun in my apartment.

Help me.

"I'm a reasonable guy," said Bobby. He pointed the gun at Laura's leg. "Tell me how we find Landon, or I take out a knee. I'm being more than fair."

I was gripping my phone so hard I was sure it would shatter in my hands.

"We'll go, okay?" I shouted. "Get away from her. I'll take you to Landon."

"See how simple life can be," he said.

He ordered me to drag over a chair from the kitchen table. He pushed Laura onto it, then handed me the duct tape. I wept as I circled it around her ankles, taping her to the chair legs, while Bobby stood over me with the gun. "You'll be okay, you'll be okay," I chanted. Laura's eyes were vacant, focused on the wall behind me.

"You don't have to leave her like that," I gasped as Bobby grabbed my arm and pulled me to my feet. "She'll be good. She'll stay quiet."

"Why don't you let me decide," he said, "what needs to be done."

BOBBY UNLOCKED THE BMW parked out front and pushed me into the passenger seat. My body started having some kind of reaction as he climbed into the driver's side. My skin was crawling, itchy with disgust; I wanted to claw my way out of it. I looked for an object I could use to smash the windshield and saw only used tissues in the cupholder, an empty beer can on the floor. I should have screamed in the hallway, so my neighbors would hear—what was wrong with me? Why couldn't I think?

"Where are we going?" I said.

"Where are we going? *You* tell me where we're going."

The blood drained from my face and pooled in my feet. For a moment I worried I would pass out.

If I didn't bring him Landon, Bobby would kill me, and Laura. No one could help me. Jeanine couldn't help me. She could be across the Canadian border by now. She could be anywhere.

Behind Bobby's head, the driver's window darkened with a presence. My throat seared, and a scream erupted in the car—my scream, I was screaming.

"Fuck—" shouted Bobby, twisting around.

We both froze, while the BMW made the mysterious ticking noises that cars make in the cold. The specter gazed through the condensation, then raised a shadowy hand to tap on the glass. Bobby rolled the window down.

"What the fuck is going on in here?" said Antweiler.

"I'll make you pay," said Bobby. "I'll make you and Maher pay for what you did to her."

Antweiler leaned forward to stick his head between the front seats. "Stanley doesn't want you near this, kid," he said to Bobby. "Let me drop you at the Neapolitan, and I'll take the girl and the car."

"You're not leaving me out of this," said Bobby. "This is my operation."

"There's no operation. You've got bodies turning up for the police to find, you got your shit scattered all over the city. You got a cheerleader hostage in your car." Antweiler gave Bobby a weary shake of his head. "Stan never liked this dirty business. This is exactly the kind of bullshit he was trying to avoid."

"He's certainly happy to enjoy the money that comes in from it. Money *I* come up with," Bobby snapped. "Let her take us to Maher. Let her take us to Jeanine's body. You're not elbowing me out. I wanna be there. Don't call my dad. Don't even text him."

Antweiler sighed. He turned to me.

"So, honey. Where are we going?"

LAURA HAD BEEN tied up for at least twenty minutes by now, and the only way I was getting back to her was to bring them to Landon.

I started listing places.

We drove first up to Black Rock, to the Foundry. Antweiler went inside while Bobby and I waited in the car. When Landon wasn't there, I suggested the tavern where I'd dropped him off after the Pink Fountain, adding another unbearable twenty minutes to the time Laura would spend tied up. Again, Antweiler went inside while Bobby and I waited in the car.

Bobby had a nosebleed. I pointed it out, and he swiped at it with his sleeve.

"Are you one of those people who thinks he drives better high?" I said, my desires split between hoping he would attract cops and also not wanting to get killed.

Chapter 35

"WE ALL GO crazy with love from time to time," said Antweiler from the backseat of Bobby's car. "I feel a certain sense of responsibility. You needed more guidance growing up, more male role models. If Stanley had been around more, or even I—"

"My dad gave her whatever she wanted," Bobby spat, swinging the wheel around as he drove us careening into the night. "How much more could he give her?"

"But the fact is, honey," Antweiler went on, calm as a judge, "Landon Maher's got nothing to offer you but trouble. He's put your family in danger. He's put *you* in danger. We need to know what he *knows,* sweetheart. Do you see what I'm saying? It's not punitive. It's a *conversation*. We don't want to hurt your boyfriend. Forget Romeo up there. I'm not going to let Landon get hurt. I just want to talk to him."

"Did you and Maher work together to take her out of the picture?" said Bobby. "Is that what happened?"

"I don't know where he *is,*" I said. "I've called and called." I showed my phone as proof. "Please let me go back and untie my sister. She has nothing to do with any of this."

"Every place this guy's been hiding, you've been seen with him there," said Antweiler. "We know you know where he is."

"Let me worry about the car, and the road," he said.

My stomach was burning with fear and rage. By now Laura was probably getting thirsty. I pictured her lying on her side, the chair tipped over from her struggle, cheek pressed against my living room rug. She probably couldn't breathe properly the way he had her taped up. I tugged furtively at the door handle, but he had the child lock on. The only sound was the heat coming from the vents.

"You know, you shouldn't have toyed with me like that," said Bobby into the silence.

"Bobby . . ." I rubbed my eyes furiously, forgetting my makeup until I saw the soot of mascara stuck to my fingertips.

"You don't get to do whatever you want just because you bop around in that little skirt."

I wiped at the makeup under my eyes. I couldn't begin to explain to him how little I was able to do what I wanted, or even locate what I wanted, or how often the question of want didn't even come into the picture.

"Well, I don't care how short your skirt is or how big a fatherly hard-on Stanley has for you," Bobby said. "You think sentimentality will save you? It never saved anyone. If you fuck up, you get dealt with. Your dad fucked up and got dealt with."

My hands fell to my lap.

"What do you mean 'dealt with'?" I said.

"Ask old Ant. He'll tell you."

My heartbeat traveled up into my ears. Bobby was clearly pleased he was getting a reaction. He raised a hand to his nose and inhaled deeply.

"You're just trying to scare me," I said.

"Awful young to have a heart attack, that's all I'm saying. Don't think you're exempt. No one who fucks up this bad is exempt."

Antweiler pulled open the backseat door, shaking his head.

"Should've known this was another bullshit location," he muttered, shuffling his huge bulk inside.

He waited for me to name the next destination, but I found myself unable to form words. I could not believe what Bobby was suggesting, and I would not believe it. Stanley had been crazy about my father. It was not possible that Antweiler could have hurt my father on Stanley's watch. But it was also not possible that I was trapped in this car with Bobby and Antweiler, or that Laura was tied up in my apartment, and yet, I was in the car, and Laura was tied up, and I wasn't waking up; no matter how often I blinked, I never woke up.

Antweiler tapped at my headrest, and I jumped.

"Hello? You in there? Where are we going next?"

I swallowed and suggested Brittany's house.

"I've *been* there," said Antweiler. "He's not there."

"The Pink Fountain?" I said.

"Are you asking or telling me?" said Antweiler.

"I'm not driving all the way out to the Pink Fountain so you can buy time," said Bobby. "No more fucking around. I want a real destination. I want Maher. Ask Antweiler here what'll happen if you send us to one more bullshit garbage-dump hole in this city that's not where Jeanine or Landon is. Ask Ant what he does to people who cause problems. Ask him about your dad."

"Watch your mouth, kid," said Antweiler sharply.

"What does he mean?" I whispered.

"Don't listen to this asshole," said Antweiler. "Your father was my friend. It broke my heart when he died, like it broke Stanley's. Like you're breaking Stanley's heart now. You want to make it up to Stanley? Give us Maher, and we can get on with life."

"I don't know where he is." My voice was small with fear.

"And Jeanine!" yelled Bobby. "I want Jeanine."

"I don't know what to give you, I can't give you—"

But then I thought of something.

"What are we doing?" I said. "This is stupid. You want Jason. The man who died—Frank something, right? Jason killed him. It was all Jason. You've got the wrong fucking person."

"Jason—you mean Morley?" said Antweiler.

"Yes, Jason Morley. He shot your guy in the head. He's the one you want."

"I don't believe it," said Bobby. "I've never had a single problem with Jason Morley. She's making shit up."

"Now, wait a minute," said Antweiler.

"Oh, for fuck's sake," said Bobby.

"I told you before—I never liked Landon Maher for this." Antweiler shrugged and held out his hands. "You want my opinion, that's my opinion. He didn't have enough shit, he didn't have enough money, he didn't have enough stake. He's small. Give him a partner, a bigger guy—it makes more sense."

"She's covering for Landon. She'll say any name she can think of. You want to knock on Jason Morley's door and embarrass yourself? You want to waste hours tracking him down while Maher has time to get away?"

"Jason's got a warehouse," I said. "On Tonawanda Island. Where her car was found."

In the rearview mirror, I could see Antweiler's eyebrows shoot up with interest.

"What warehouse?" said Bobby. "Jason's business is in Lackawanna."

"It's his dad's old warehouse on Tonawanda Island. Maybe Jason's name isn't on it. But it's his warehouse. I think."

"Is her body buried on Tonawanda Island?" said Bobby. "Is that what you're trying to tell me?"

Bobby was right that I would say anything to get out of this car, away from these people who spoke about my father as if they had any right to say his name or to tie people up or lock them in cars. After a lifetime on its outskirts, I had entered the world of people who did exactly those things they had no right to do, and nothing ever happened to them as a result. They got away with it.

"Well, I for one," said Antweiler loudly, "would like to know about this fucking warehouse."

BOBBY KILLED THE headlights as he steered the car into a little semicircle of gravel on the eastern side of the PanAtlantic warehouse. A copse of trees shielded the patch of gravel and the car from the gaze of anyone who might be looking out the warehouse windows, about thirty feet away.

Antweiler slipped out of the car and pulled out a pair of binoculars. Beyond the warehouse was the black expanse of the river. This had been a bad idea. There was no one here to hear me if I called out. Bobby and Antweiler could torture me and dump my body in the river and no one would stop them.

Bobby rolled down his window, letting in the cold air. He brought his palm to his nose again and inhaled.

"There's movement," whispered Antweiler. "Someone pulling something, looks like a dolly. There's a pickup truck. Looks like—" He lowered the binoculars. "Man alive."

"What?" said Bobby. He jumped out of the car to stand by Antweiler. I pulled fruitlessly on the door handle. I had to get the courage to scream, I had to run, run to the bridge, yelling my head off the whole way—

"Your girlfriend isn't dead. She's right there pulling a fucking dolly, you stupid shit," said Antweiler as he pushed the binoculars into Bobby's chest.

I clawed at the buckle of my seatbelt. I had led them right to her. I had given her up.

"Baby," said Bobby, binoculars held to his face. "Jeanine, baby—I've got to talk to her."

"No one does shit," hissed Antweiler.

He was crunching through the gravel to my side of the car. I'd barely gotten my seatbelt undone when the door swung open. He gripped my upper arm and yanked me out of the car.

"This fucking girl is back from the dead," Antweiler said, "pulling shit from this fucking warehouse we don't know about—this is not good. This is not normal. We need to get a bucket around this water. There are way too many people involved. We need backup. I'm calling Stanley."

"No," said Bobby. "No Stanley."

"Sit there on the ground," Antweiler said to me. "You did good, delivering this. We'll talk to Stanley. Everything will be okay."

He pushed me onto the ground by the driver's front tire. Cold, wet soil seeped into the scant fabric of my uniform bottom. My ears were numb. I didn't feel afraid, but I sensed a huge bubble of fear approaching, rising from the ground below, preparing to encircle me. A whine of surprise escaped my throat as he slid a zip tie around my wrists.

"Have you forgotten who pays who?" Bobby said. "Have you forgotten who calls the shots? It's not you, you fucking dinosaur. We don't make any calls until I talk to her. We don't do anything until—"

Antweiler made a movement, swift and nearly imperceptible, and Bobby fell backward. I heard his head smack against the car and gasped.

"I fucking hate these kids," said Antweiler. Bobby jerked around on the ground while Antweiler tied his hands behind his back with plastic zip ties. "Stupid cracked-out little shitheads. I didn't get into this to be your babysitter. I'm not your daddy."

"Uncalled for," Bobby spat through blood, as Antweiler pushed him into a seated position against the car, next to me.

Antweiler made like he was going to kick Bobby in the face. Bobby yelped and pitched sideways. Antweiler laughed.

"See? Babysitters, that's what these kids need."

"What's going to happen?" I said, with growing hopelessness. "I didn't know she was here. You want Jason, not her."

"Honey, I don't know how you know about this place, I don't know how deep this clusterfuck of a situation goes, but you don't get to say who we want. You don't get to say what happens next. You sit on the ground while the grown-ups take care of it."

He extended an index finger and seemed about to tell me exactly how things were going to go, but before he could, he collapsed.

I gasped. In the spot where Antweiler had been standing only a moment before—was Ray.

Ray, with a rock in his hands.

"Are you all right, Virginia? Are you damaged?" he said to me.

"Who the fuck is this?" said Bobby.

But Ray was already moving toward him. I squeezed my eyes shut with panic, and when I opened them, I saw that Ray had pushed Bobby facedown in the dirt.

"Ray—" I said, drawing my knees to my chest.

My mouth opened and closed, but nothing more came out. Ray dug in Antweiler's waistband and pulled out his gun. Then he found more of those plastic ties in Antweiler's pockets and began the business of rolling the big, semiconscious man onto his stomach, pulling his hands behind his back. Meanwhile, Bobby growled and moaned, facedown, legs kicking for purchase in the dirt.

"What the fuck is going on?" Bobby slurred, hands still tied behind his back, voice muffled in the leaves.

"If you'll allow me," said Ray, showing me the pocketknife in his palm.

"You have to get out of here, Ray," I whispered, my hands shaking as Ray cut the ties around my wrists, the cold steel gentle against the backs of my hands. "Before he sees you."

"I'm not leaving you," Ray said, pulling me to my feet. He handed me the gun he'd pulled off Antweiler. "I'll protect you. Do you have a phone? Please, call the police."

"No one is calling the police," I said.

Bobby had maneuvered his knees beneath him, so his hips swayed in the air, unsteadily, his face and shoulders still pressed in the dirt.

"Who the hell is there?" he growled. "Jeanine! Get me Jeanine!"

"You have to get out of here!" I shouted at Ray. I felt, childishly, that all of this was his fault, that Ray, in his stupid Bills jacket that was never warm enough for the weather, had caused everything that had brought me to this moment. My gratitude was gone. I reached for the rock Ray had dropped after hitting Antweiler but grabbed only a handful of leaves and dirt, which I hurled at Ray. He jumped back, elbows raised in front of his face, and I felt for all the world like I was throwing rocks at a sad stray dog. I remembered the gun was in my other hand—my left hand, stupidly—and I pointed it at him.

"They will kill you. Do you understand me? You weren't here. You never followed me."

"But you need help." Ray's chin tightened with tears, and I wanted to hit him for not understanding.

"Get out!" I said, my voice ugly and raw.

Ray began a stumbling, slump-shouldered retreat into the trees, leaving me in the terrible quiet, broken only by the distant hum of warehouses. I wished he were back, if only to provide some direction to my fear. I didn't know what to do with a gun in my hand and two men on the ground. Bobby was rocking in the dirt, still on his stomach. Antweiler was frighteningly still.

I backed away, the gun dangling from my hand.

"Get me Jeanine!" Bobby slurred in the dirt. "I want Jeanine!"

I stumbled backward, into the patch of trees surrounding the car. Just before the branches blocked my view, I saw Antweiler stirring, his great form rolling in the dirt. I turned and ran toward the closest shelter I could find.

When I reached the warehouse I texted the last number I'd used to try to reach Jeanine, fingers shaking.

I'm outside, I wrote. **By a green door. Can you let me in?**

I waited, heart in my throat, staring at the green door atop a short set of stairs surrounded by yellow posts. After a moment, Jeanine opened it.

"Oh my God," she said.

Chapter 36

"Go around," Jeanine insisted. "Go *around*."

Through the gap in the door, I could make out the wood-paneled walls of what looked like an office behind her, but she insisted I enter the warehouse through the garage doors around the corner. I hurried over and squeezed past a huge red Toyota Tacoma backed into the open garage door of the loading bay, my nostrils filled with the smell of wet asphalt and the metallic, fishy scent of the river.

Inside was a massive, open room, dimly illuminated by flickering fluorescent bars: a wide expanse of cement floor, boxes stacked along the walls, wooden pallets and dollies, and one forklift in the corner.

Jeanine stood among the pallets, her hands up.

"Okay, Virginia, calm down. Take it easy."

I looked down and saw Antweiler's gun still in my fist.

"Oh, God." I held out the gun. "I don't want this."

"Put the safety on. Like—yeah, pull that thingy. Now put it down. Good."

She exhaled as I set the gun down on the gritty concrete floor and kicked it under a pallet. Her forehead was shiny with sweat, the split ends of her terrible hair zinging out from her face.

"You did it again," she said. "*Again*? How did you find me? How do you know about this place?"

"Google," I snapped. "I googled it. What are you doing here, Jeanine? What were you *thinking*? We had a plan! After everything I went through to find you, you run out on me and come—here?"

I didn't know what I'd been expecting to find inside the warehouse, but it wasn't this. Stacked on the pallets were towers of grocery store items, drums of cooking oil and olives, and boxes of grains. On the nearest pallet, big plastic-wrapped boxes containing bags of polenta.

"*You* had a plan," said Jeanine. "I thought about it, and I didn't like the plan. If I go crawling back to Bobby now, I will spend the rest of my life looking over my shoulder, praying he and Stanley never figure out what I did, hoping everyone thinks I'm a good little girl who never had a thought in her head except tagging along after her boyfriend who's too coked up to know he's losing money—no, fucking forget it. If that's my only option, then I'll take this. I won't live like that. I have to protect what I have left."

"Which is—what?"

I gestured to the stacks of polenta and oil around us. Jeanine was taking deep breaths through her nose to calm down. The buzzing of the fluorescent lights above drowned out the sound of the water lapping in the darkness. I realized, with a burst of unease, that something else was bothering me, a nagging feeling I'd had ever since I'd seen the Tacoma.

"I know that truck," I said. "That's Jason Morley's truck. Is Jason here?"

"Of course not."

"Then what's his truck doing here?"

"He parked it here."

"I'm not getting in a truck with Jason Morley."

"He's not *here,* I said." Jeanine pushed her hair back from her forehead and appeared to regroup. "Okay. Change of plans. You have to stay with me. I can't get rid of you anyway. We're in this together now. If you want to be here, you have to help."

"Help?"

"I need what's left of the stash house stuff, but I can't *find* it," said Jeanine. "I don't know what Jason did with it. There's enough here to make one more big sale to Gabe in Columbus so I can start up somewhere new. I'm not losing any more money."

"You need *more* money?" I said.

"I don't have anywhere to go!" she shouted. "I have to set up a whole other life! Don't you fucking get it? I'm taking everything!"

She hurried around with renewed purpose, knocking over boxes, ripping into the film wrap around the boxed polenta. How long had Laura been tied up? An hour? Two hours? And Bobby and Antweiler—how had they not burst in on us by now? Surely they were regrouping in the trees. They'd found a way to contact Stanley. If they saw me helping Jeanine look for drugs, they would—what would they do to us?

"Jeanine," I said in despair. "Stop."

She dropped the box she was holding. "Wait—while I look . . . you need to hide your car. In a better place than where I hid my Mazda. Where did you park? Let's move it. Or maybe—we can caravan? But I'd rather stick together."

I was at a loss for words. I could not think of a good answer to this question.

"Where's your car?" said Jeanine, with increasing panic. "How did you get here?"

As if on cue, through the open garage door, the quality of the light changed—first the swoop of white headlights sliding across the trees, a car pulling into the gravel by the warehouse. And then the bounce of red and blue lights.

Jeanine and I faced each other, our mouths open.

"Did you call them?" she said.

"I didn't. I swear."

"Stay here," she whispered. "Let me look out the window."

She hurried into the depths of the warehouse, swerving between boxes. Ray had probably called the cops. In his position, I certainly would have. Terrified of being left alone, I padded along the route

Jeanine had taken, squeezing between pallets and plastic-wrapped cases of olive jars.

She had shut herself behind a plain white door with a silver knob, which I opened to find a tiny office. It was a box of a room: wood paneling, a desk made of fake wood, peeling linoleum floor. Shoved against the wall was a dirty plaid couch, sandwiched between green filing cabinets. Jeanine was standing on the couch, face pressed against the tiny rectangle of a window. She turned with a start.

"Virginia! Don't come in here!"

But I had already seen what was in the corner.

I realized I was on the floor only by the feel of grit scraping my elbows. My mouth was open, and my throat ached; I was screaming. I slammed my palms against the floor, leaving sweaty handprints all over the linoleum.

My ears were ringing, but through the buzz I heard: "V, shut up, shut up!"

Jason was slumped in the corner, smooshed next to one of the filing cabinets, his empty eyes staring and his cheek pressed against the wall. And there was blood—a horrible spatter of red on the paneled walls.

I felt Jeanine's arms circle my torso and yank me up. I fell back to the floor, pulling her with me, the room swinging. There was a faint smell, like burnt soot, which I realized was the smell of a recently discharged gun. Jeanine groaned, pulling me again to my feet.

"Virginia, it's okay!" she said. "Just don't look. Don't look at it."

She pushed me so I faced the wall, my nose brushing the wood panels, like I'd been sent to a time-out. I panted, my breath hot against the wall, and stared into the whorls in the pattern, praying they would erase the sight of Jason from my mind. Behind me, I heard the squeak of the couch's springs as Jeanine climbed back onto it.

"The cops are in the trees over there, looking around. I don't think they heard you scream. They're not coming this way."

Another squeak, as she jumped to the floor. I stared harder into a spiral swirl in the wood, imagining I could crawl through it to a different dimension, a different world where none of this was happening.

"We can make it." Her hand was on my elbow, pulling me out of the wood pattern. "We're going to get out of here. Just march ahead, out the door. Don't turn around. Forget you saw it. It doesn't matter."

I marched. The rusty smell of the river, which flowed beyond the open garage door, hit me with renewed power. There was a dead body behind me. How could I ever explain why I was in this warehouse with a dead man? I worried about my heart beating this hard for so long—I couldn't afford to pass out at a time like this, and yet all I wanted was to be unconscious, and for it to be six hours ago, so I could wake up in bed next to Laura and do everything differently this time.

"Listen to me." Jeanine gripped my shoulders and shook me. "You need to keep it together. You can tell yourself any story about this you want. Think whatever you have to think to turn this into a situation you can stand. You're saving me. That's the story you wanted, right? This is you saving my life."

"We should check," I said. "We should check to see if he's alive."

"He's not alive."

"Maybe we can . . . can explain—"

"Virginia," Jeanine said as she grabbed my hand. "You can't go back. You see that, right? You can never go back."

Chapter 37

"We go out that window," said Jeanine, pulling me by the arm. She pointed at a narrow, rectangular window above the cab of the forklift. "Once you drop to the ground outside, stay close to me. I'll get us out of here."

"We can't go out there. Where will we go?"

Jeanine didn't answer. She climbed onto the forklift, pulling herself up onto the top of the cab. She dug her fingers into the side of the dusty pane and yanked it sideways. With a shriek that made us both grimace, the window slid open. I watched as Jeanine hoisted herself through the narrow opening and disappeared.

I followed, climbing up the same way she had. Adrenaline started to take over, dissipating the fog. I felt drugged. Jason's slumped form flashed in front of my eyes. It would be in my mind forever, to carry around, to see when I closed my eyes at night. Jason had been shot. Shot by Jeanine. Jeanine had killed someone.

I scraped my way out the window, too panicked to control my landing, and hit the concrete hip-first. I scrambled upright.

I could barely see Jeanine slinking along the length of the warehouse, her back pressed against the corrugated steel wall. Heart pounding in my throat, I scurried behind her, keeping close to the wall. We were on the opposite side of the warehouse from the parking lot where the cops had pulled up, and the copse of trees where I'd left Bobby and Antweiler. The lights from the warehouse gave us just enough dusky orange light to see. To our left, across a length of grass and gravel about twenty feet wide, I could make out the grubby shrubs and trees that lined the riverbank.

Jeanine halted, back still pressed against the wall. She took my hand and squeezed, and I surprised myself by squeezing back.

"We're running that way—" she whispered, indicating vaguely north. "Keep the river on your left. It's not far."

"*What's* not far?"

But she was gone—running, bent over in an approximation of a soldier, into the darkness. I remained frozen against the wall, my ribs expanding and contracting with quick breaths like a rabbit's, the cold metal pressing through the windbreaker the stadium guard had given me. I waited for an eruption of sirens, but there was only the sound of the wind. The silence, and my aloneness, felt far more terrifying than wherever Jeanine was leading me to in the darkness. I started after her.

I kept my eyes trained on my boots, my shoulders hunched with fear. The ground beneath my feet changed from gravel to grass. I heard voices floating behind me, and peeked over my shoulder to see the headlights of two cop cars parked outside the warehouse, illuminating the outline of two figures, their flashlights flickering, making their way toward the building, where there was a body.

I ran. I followed the ghostly tuft of Jeanine's bleached hair down and up a drainage ditch, across a scrappy stretch of grass, down an alleyway between two big white warehouses. We ran until we reached the unmarked two-lane road, then we ran in the gravel alongside it. Long, low buildings loomed out of the darkness on my right and left; a snarled chain-link fence sprouted, then was devoured by ivy. The deathly silence was pierced only by my gasping breath. At the end of the chain-link fence stood a boat supply store, a big beige box of corrugated walls, the surrounding boatyard scattered with covered boats, like a herd of great sleeping pachyderms in the grass.

We scurried between the boats until we reached the other side of the supply store, which faced the back channel. There was a large parking lot and a little marina I had not seen when I'd first driven to the island. Jeanine made a beeline across the asphalt to the floating docks. The moon broke out of the clouds and lit up the water, illuminating her as she darted between the rows of docked boats. It felt like a million miles of darkness separated us from the warehouse, though in truth we couldn't have been more than a quarter mile away. If the cops began to search the island in their cars, we'd be found in minutes.

I caught up to Jeanine on the dock, where she was inspecting the boats furiously.

"Jason has a boat," she said. "It's got a green stripe. Look for a green stripe."

"A boat?"

"Yes! This one!" She began yanking at the ropes.

It was a deck boat, sleek and pointed, the inside lined with enough cushioned seats for maybe ten people, and a steering wheel like a car's. It was the kind of boat I didn't understand owning—all you could do was sit on it and get your hair messed up. I didn't want to get inside it.

"Do you know how to drive this?" I said.

"What do you mean? It's a fucking boat."

Having dispensed with the ropes, she slung a leg over. "Get in. Come *on*!"

She pulled me over the side with her, and I stumbled aboard.

"Where are we going?"

"It doesn't matter!" She collapsed in a rush into the seat behind the wheel. "Cops don't patrol the waterways. They're back at the warehouse, they're fucking busy. We're safer on a boat. Help me turn this on. I have his keys."

At the thought of Jeanine pawing through Jason's pockets while his head was reduced to a splatter on the wall, I felt a wave of dizziness. I knelt over a cushioned seat and gripped the side of the boat.

"Here we go." Jeanine found the ignition, and the engine roared to life with a terrifying growl, then settled into the bubbly purr of burning diesel. "See!" Her eyes were wild. "I told you I would get us out!"

JEANINE DID NOT know how to drive the boat. It took a few tries for her to figure out that the bow moved in the opposite direction the wheel turned, but eventually we made it out into the channel, heading south. The roar of the engine seemed impossibly loud, but there was no movement on the shore, no explosion of lights and sirens, no helicopter descending to stop us. Jeanine pushed the boat faster. We passed under the bridge, cleared the edges of Tonawanda Island, and then we were out of the back channel, in the Niagara River.

The air was freezing. Jeanine kept bursting out in strange gasps of laughter, like she was trying to swallow her own excitement. The engine growled and rattled. In the darkness, amplified by the water, came the sound of sirens. I twisted in my seat to look toward the shore and saw red and blue lights zooming north along the river, toward Tonawanda Island. More police, speeding to a murder scene.

I was filled with a dread so acute it was difficult to register as an emotion—it felt like teetering over a very large pit. The water was black and terrifying and flat, like we were hurtling through space. Every time I blinked I saw the outline of Jason Morley slumped against the wall. The cold made everything more hopeless. I was certain I'd be cold forever.

"Where are we going?" I said. "Canada?"

"That's Grand Island over there," said Jeanine. "Still America."

This was not an answer. If we kept going south, we'd pass under the Peace Bridge and be spat out into the massive dark expanse of Lake Erie, wide as an ocean, waiting to gulp us up and swallow us whole. The thought made me want to throw up with fear.

"So how does this work?" I said, gripping my elbows. "Do I get a new identity, too? Is there another Jills donor who will buy me a car, give me her name?"

Jeanine pulled a lever to slow the boat, and the engine quieted a bit.

"This is important," she said. "Did you mention the name Olena Rossi to anyone else?"

I said, "No," though Sharrice knew it, and Ray. I figured this was not the time for honesty.

"Then we'll be all right," she said. "I can't explain it right now, but that name is how I survive. It's how I'm able to disappear. Now it'll protect both of us."

"That woman helps you wash the money, doesn't she?" I said. "You give the cash to her, and she donates it to the Jills. Is that right? But you have to get it back somehow. That's how laundering works." I tried to remember how my dad had explained what happened to money that went to charities. "Does Olena Rossi get a big tax write-off for the donations? And she sends you . . . her tax refund? Or she uses it to pay for your car, your house in Ohio?"

"I'll handle all that stuff. Don't worry about it."

"Is Olena going to help us? Can you contact her? Where's the cash we packed up in Columbus?"

"*I'll* take care of us. I'll figure everything out. Here." She took off her coat and handed it to me. Beneath, she wore the same slacks she'd been wearing when she'd left me in the house on Como Ave, along with a gray sweatshirt.

"But you'll be cold," I said.

"We'll trade. Take it for a while."

Too cold to argue, I shed the stadium windbreaker and handed it to her, after sliding my phone out of the pocket. I pulled her coat on over my uniform. It was warm from the heat of her body.

"I did try to save Landon," said Jeanine, drawing the jacket tight across her body.

"What?" I blinked, and there again was Jason Morley, in that horrible position.

"I knew he'd gotten ahold of some drugs that might tie him to that murder. The day before I left town, I asked him to meet me. I was praying he hadn't sold them yet, or at least hadn't sold them all. I was going to take them to Ohio with me. So he wouldn't be implicated, and he'd be safe. But he'd already found someone to sell them to, so it was too late."

"Oh," I said.

"So you see. I'm ruthless, but I'm not a monster." She gave me a hopeful smile.

"You gave him the drugs in the first place, Jeanine. You set him up."

She was quiet for a moment.

"I tried to save him," she repeated.

She pushed the lever forward, bringing the boat back to full speed, the engine drowning out any reply I might have made. I looked over the side of the boat into the inky water.

Had Jeanine said this to me because she needed me to believe she was a good person? Was that the safety I offered her: the unfailing reassurance that she was right, and she was good, and anything she did could be fixed, and I would help her fix it? Framing Landon, selling drugs to my sister, killing Jason—she'd *killed* someone. Was I going to help her justify all that? Was I that desperate to be needed?

We were both trapped, I realized. Jeanine had built a cage and trapped herself inside it, and I'd fought tooth and nail to get inside the cage with her, because I was too terrified to be left on the outside on my own. We were never going to escape. Like Landon, like Jason, I'd become an obstacle to be disposed of, or fodder to be tossed into the line of fire. Things were not going to get better, wherever we were headed. They were about to become infinitely more desperate. And whatever the situation required, Jeanine could justify it to herself. If destroying me helped her get through another day, she could say to herself: *It's what Virginia wanted.*

I had to get the hell out of there. I had to get back to Laura. Laura, who didn't want to use me like this. Who wouldn't let me get away with destroying myself under the guise of helping her anymore.

I reached over the side to dip my fingers into the water sliding along beneath us, and shuddered. I gauged the distance to land. It wasn't that far—maybe the length of two swimming pools at the gym. That was one lap. I could swim a lap.

I slid along the cushioned seats to the stern. The fear in my stomach loomed and deepened. There was a short platform off the back of the boat with a metal ladder, so people could more easily jump in and climb out of the water. I lowered myself the six inches onto the platform, backward, so I could keep an eye on Jeanine. *I'm sorry,* I thought. *I'm sorry, I'm sorry.* I sank to my knees and gripped the ladder to steady myself. The ladder was to the left of the propeller; I'd have to launch myself away to avoid hitting it when I jumped in. I put a foot on the first rung, trying to breathe normally, as if I were lowering myself into a pool. Jeanine turned around. Our eyes locked.

She had a gun in her hand—Sharrice's gun. The same gun, I assumed, she'd used to kill Jason. She pointed it at me. We both went still. Time seemed to stretch. Then, her face hardened with resolve, she pushed the gun back into her waistband, abandoned the steering wheel, and lunged toward me.

I let go of the railing, but she caught me, hooking her hands under my armpits.

"No," I chanted. She wrapped her arms around me. "No, no, no, no."

We fought on the edge of the boat. She gripped the coat she'd lent me and pulled. But I was stronger than she was. I stayed on that ladder. I punched at her shoulders, her arms still twined around me, clawing for purchase. I screamed, not from fear this time but from sheer animal outrage. The boat dragged us wildly forward. And all at once, Jeanine let out a long, despairing cry and released me. I fell backward into the water, where everything was black.

Chapter 38

I STUMBLED, STILL DRIPPING, into a blindingly bright 7-Eleven on Niagara Street.

The small man at the cash register behind a pane of plastic looked up from his phone, startled. After I'd crawled onto the banks of the river and stumbled, numb, across the grassy stretch of waterfront, then clambered over the wire guardrail of the two-lane road, I'd nearly burst into tears at the sight of the sign. It had loomed ahead like a mirage, drifting farther away the faster I careened toward it on rubber legs, until all of a sudden I was upon it, a 7-Eleven gas station in a depressing little shopping plaza squeezed between a closed liquor store and a nail place.

I was shaking so hard I was certain that if I stopped moving, I would die. I staggered toward the cashier.

"Can I use your phone?" I said. The fluorescent lights seemed to be screaming at me.

The man behind the plastic barrier looked me up and down.

"Are you okay, miss?" he said.

"Can I please, please make a call?"

He handed me his phone.

"I'm just going to take it to the bathroom," I said.

Before he could stop me, I shut myself inside the reeking single-occupancy women's room, yanking off Jeanine's sopping coat as I locked the door. I turned on the hand dryer and sat under the weak stream of warm air, knees drawn to my chest, the coat dripping in a heap on the floor next to me.

My own phone had fallen somewhere in the Niagara River. But like Jeanine, I, too, had phone numbers memorized—two of them. The first was Laura's old number, from before she went into rehab and deactivated it. And the second was one of the first numbers I'd memorized in childhood.

"Stanley?" I whispered, my voice caught in my throat. The hand dryer shut off over my head.

"My God," he said. "Where are you? What happened?"

"Before I say anything else, I need you, please, please, to go to my apartment. Laura is in there, and she's been—"

"I've got Laura," he said. "Laura's fine. Where are *you*?"

Dopamine flooded my system, and for a second I almost felt warm. "She's okay? Where is she?"

"Laura's safe. Are you in a safe place? I'll come get you."

"Stanley, you may have a problem on Tonawanda Island," I said, trying to stop my teeth from chattering. "There's a warehouse, and—and Bobby and Antweiler—"

"Stop," he said. "Not on the phone. Just tell me where you are."

"I'm at a 7-Eleven on Niagara Street. In Tonawanda."

"Don't move," he said.

Stanley hung up.

There was a knock at the door. I shakily got to my feet and opened it a crack.

"Have you finished with my phone?" said the gas station attendant.

"Yes, sorry." I handed it to him.

"You shouldn't be wet," said the attendant. "It's very cold."

He handed me a T-shirt, taken from the small rack of shirts near the register. It was a child's size large and featured a cartoon car with flames exploding from the wheels over the words NEED FOR SPEED.

"Put this on," he said. "And maybe these can help get your hair dry." He held up a half-used roll of paper towels.

I gripped them gratefully. Having kindly dispensed his items, the attendant took a step back to regard me with concern.

"Hey," he said, pointing at my Jills uniform. He offered a shy thumbs up. "Go Bills."

STANLEY ARRIVED ABOUT twenty minutes later, in a sleek nondescript black car, not one of his usual refurbished models.

I had warmed up a bit under the hand dryer. I dropped into the passenger seat, wearing the NEED FOR SPEED shirt over my uniform, Jeanine's wet coat still in my arms.

The road swung around through the windshield as Stanley turned south on Niagara. The car was silent in the way only very expensive cars are silent. Under his wool coat, Stanley wore a bright white T-shirt. I had never seen Stanley in a T-shirt before.

"You're wet," he said.

"I had to jump off a boat." I wiped my nose.

"I believe—" Stanley stopped, considered, then tried again: "I believe I might have been mistaken about— Well, to be honest, I don't understand what's going on, and I would like you to explain it to me."

"I'm not sure where to start."

"Did you know Jeanine was going to be at the warehouse tonight?"

"No."

"Where is she now?"

"I don't know," I said.

"Then where is Landon Maher? He's the last person we need to account for. I can make sure he doesn't get hurt if you tell me where he is."

"I don't know where Landon is. I'm not in love with Landon. Landon took the drugs from the stash house without knowing where they came from. He was set up. He has no idea what's going on. Jason killed that other man, Frank. Jeanine killed Jason. I don't know what else to say."

"Jeanine," said Stanley carefully, "killed Jason. Jason . . . and Jeanine."

Fatigue was catching up with me. My limbs were rubbery and weak, my arms prickling and clammy. I began to shake again.

"I'm sorry the cops showed up," I said. "I'm sorry Jason is dead. I'm sorry if this causes a lot of trouble for you."

Hearing the quake in my voice, Stanley turned up the heater and adjusted the vents so they faced me. He was quiet for a few moments, glancing over every so often to see if I was warming up.

"Scott and Bobby got away from the area on foot before the cops showed up," he said finally. "They had to leave the BMW, which is a problem, though not an unsolvable one, since it's a company car and not in Bobby's name. The police were apparently responding to a call from some hysterical person claiming a cheerleader was being held hostage. This person was not able to describe the kidnappers with any specificity, which is exceedingly lucky. That part, we seem to have under control."

"Oh," I said, my jaw tight from shivering. The Paladinos, it seemed, were always able to get away.

"As for Jason, it's obviously very sad that he's dead. But beyond some importing and building materials he coordinated for my son, we have very little connection to him. Whatever he was doing in that warehouse cannot be tied in any capacity to my son's business ventures or my own. Correct?"

"Yes," I said automatically.

"Okay, then. My biggest problem, as far as I can see, is Jeanine."

This was my opportunity to pretend that Jeanine was as big a victim in all of this as I was. I felt nothing at the arrival of this moment. It arose, along with a handful of dark spots in front of my eyes, and dissolved just as quickly.

"Jeanine is on a boat going south," I said. "I can't protect her. I can't control what happens to her. She's probably in the middle of Lake Erie by now, or climbing onto the shore of Canada. You'll find her or you won't. I have nothing else to offer."

I couldn't say any more, I was shaking so hard.

"You okay, kiddo? There's a blanket in the back," he said, reaching behind him to pull up a fleece blanket with the Bills logo on it.

"I don't feel cold," I said as I pulled it around my shoulders. "But I'm shaking like I'm cold."

"You're probably in shock," he said. "Hold on a little longer." He pressed harder on the gas pedal.

After a few long minutes my shaking began to dissipate. Prickles blossomed up and down my arms. "I think I'm okay," I said. Stanley let out a breath but did not slow the car. Looking out the window, I realized with a start where we were: Suzanna's neighborhood, in East Aurora. The street ended in a cul-de-sac, Suzanna's massive, boxy house perched at the crest.

Stanley pulled into the driveway. He looked me in the eye for the first time since I'd gotten into the car.

"You're all right?" he said. "I'd like to say one more thing to you before you go inside. I want you to understand that Bobby was acting entirely on his own tonight. He should not have done that to Laura. Scott was operating under the assumption that you were protecting Landon Maher, who we both understood to be a reckless drug dealer and a potential murderer. I did not want you to be scared or threatened. But you kept things from me. I did the best I could with the information I had. So, kiddo, before you leave this car, I need you to swear to me, on your father's life, that you've told me everything you know."

"What's my father's life worth to you, Stanley?"

His eyes flickered. I was surprised that I'd had the boldness to say this to him. I faced him, blanket gripped around my shoulders. He refused to break my gaze.

He said, "I loved your father like a brother. I have loved you like my own daughter."

The backs of my eyes prickled with tears. This did not answer the question. Out of the corner of my eye, through the windshield, I saw the front door swing open. Suzanna stepped out onto the porch, pulling her bathrobe tight.

"Go," said Stanley. "I'll finish cleaning everything up."

"LAURA IS HERE," Suzanna whispered as she closed the door behind me. "Sleeping upstairs."

I'd been to Suzanna's house before; at the start of each season, she hosted a catered barbecue luncheon for the Jills. I was shocked by its size the first time I saw it. The furniture, counters, drawers—everything was long and thin and modern. She favored steely gray fabrics with one pop of bright color. It was stylish and austere, a difficult place to feel welcome, despite the number of sofas and bedrooms. I remembered eating with great caution at the barbecue, the practice of chewing made obscenely carnal in this place of clean lines and ninety-degree angles.

Suzanna led me to one of her many immaculate bathrooms. I draped Jeanine's coat on one of the hooks, peeled off my filthy uniform, and stood under the hot water in the shower for a long time. Suzanna had left a clean tank top and silk shorts on the counter next to the sink, along with a fresh toothbrush. She had put up plenty of Jills over the years, when they broke up with boyfriends, lost apartments, changed jobs. This big house waited, empty and ready, for girls to need it.

When I emerged, Suzanna was waiting outside in the carpeted hallway, a glass of water in hand. My uniform and Jeanine's coat were bundled in my arms.

"Leave your uniform in the hamper. My cleaners might be able to save it. I'll take your coat. It should be fine in the dryer on low heat."

"Okay," I agreed numbly.

In the guest bedroom, I sank into the pillows as Suzanna smoothed the fluffy white comforter over me.

"No one's going to bother you here," Suzanna said. "It's a safe place."

I was so tired, but as soon as Suzanna shut the door behind her my brain lit up like a lamp. I wanted Laura. I wanted only Laura.

Then, as though I'd willed it, the bedroom door creaked open. Laura padded in, in identical silk shorts, smelling like coconut oil. She got under the covers and we looked at each other in the dark, shy and sad.

"I'm so sorry," I said, or tried to say. I started to cry, and the words collapsed in my throat. "It's all my fault. It's all my fault."

"I'm okay," she said. "I'm right here."

"I left her, Laura. I gave her up."

"That's good. You did good."

My face grew tight with tears, my lips pulling back to bare my teeth. "I can't do it again, Laura."

"Do what?" she whispered.

"If I have to do it again, I think it will kill me. I can't stand it. I don't want to keep letting go of people. I want it to stop."

"People go," she said, stroking my damp hair. "Sometimes you have them for a long time, sometimes just a little, but they always, eventually, go."

"I want everyone to stay. I want Dad."

"I know. Me, too."

I put my head on Laura's chest, and she wrapped her arms around me.

"I am not going to go," she said firmly, her arms tightening. "I'm the one who stays."

I wiped my eyes and sniffed. Laura petted my hair, her breathing steady. I could feel her keeping watch on the guest room door as she held me. I suspected she might be shooting Reiki energy into me, but I was too tired, and it felt too good to be bothered by it. I couldn't believe she was here—and still here, and still here. The darkness of a deep sleep, ancient and alluring, crept up around me, and I would have been scared to let myself sink into it had my sister not been there to protect me.

Chapter 39

"You're where?" said our mother on speakerphone.

"East Aurora," Laura repeated. "We need a ride."

We sat at the massive island in Suzanna's kitchen, talking to our mom on Laura's phone. By the time we'd woken up, Suzanna was already gone. She'd left us a box of pastries and extensive written instructions for how to use her French press, signed with a flourished *S* that took up the whole bottom half of the notepaper.

Laura had been brought to Suzanna's house the night before in a car sent by Stanley. It turned out she had been tied up in my apartment for about forty minutes. Sharrice had driven over after I failed to answer her texts asking if I'd gotten home from the stadium. She let herself in with the key I'd given her to watch the cat.

She untied Laura, who'd convinced her not to call the police. Instead, Laura called Stanley.

"We've had kind of a rough night," Laura explained to our mom. "We don't have our cars. Can you come get us?"

"East Aurora? I didn't know you were back in town all of a sudden, Laura. I wish you'd call me when you visit. Who do you know out in East Aurora?"

Laura glanced at me.

"Um, it's— Well, we're at . . . we're at Suzanna's house, but we weren't here to see *her.*"

There was a long silence.

"Mom?" I said.

"You come to town without telling me, and go to Suzanna's house? She's the one you want to see? You want to stay at her house? You can stay at her house."

"It's not like that—" Laura began.

"You need a ride? Why don't you ask *Suzanna*?" she said, and hung up.

Laura looked up at the ceiling. She'd slept in her contacts, and her eyes were red.

"Do you think she could ever once, just once—actually help us?" she said.

The Jills roster and contact list was, helpfully, hung on Suzanna's fridge, aligned perfectly with the edge of the fridge door. I gestured for Laura to hand me her phone. "I hate to ask Sharrice for one more thing, but . . ."

Sharrice of course agreed to get us. She took an early lunch break and zoomed into Suzanna's driveway in her sky-blue Volkswagen Beetle.

"Thank God you called me," she said, as she tumbled out of the car, pulling me into her arms, then Laura. "I didn't sleep last night, even after Suzanna texted me that you'd made it to her house. You scared the crap out of me."

On the drive she tried to convince us to press charges, her voice shrill with relief and concern.

"It doesn't *matter* that you know the guy who tied you up," she said to Laura, addressing her in the rearview mirror. "Just like it doesn't matter that you know the guy who harassed you at the stadium," she said to me. "Most women do know their attackers. That guy could come back and do it again. Get him in the system. Put what he did on record."

"Sharrice, it's really, really hard to explain our family situation," said Laura. "Thank you, genuinely, but we're going to handle this in the family. Stanley will take care of it. Honestly, he can control everyone involved better than the police can."

"Clearly *not,*" said Sharrice. "You could file charges for kidnapping," she said to me. "That's basically what happened to you. What did Bobby do after you left with him? Where did he take you?"

"Sharrice, I'm okay," I said. I pulled at the sleeves of Jeanine's coat, which I'd found hanging in the bathroom when I woke up. I wore it over my NEED FOR SPEED shirt and some velvet tracksuit pants Suzanna had left out for me. "He just drove me around. He thought I knew where Jeanine was. He was really high and . . . hallucinating or something."

"God, that's awful. That's terrifying. Please change your minds and file a report. I can advise you. Us women have to make the law work for *us.*"

She huffed and put on her large aviator sunglasses. In her work suit, hair pulled back in a sleek professional bun—so different from the bouncy curls she maintained for her Jills look—she seemed impenetrable, ruthlessly sensible. I felt a wave of love for her.

"By the way," said Sharrice, "I heard some news around the office this morning. It's about that drug-related murder investigation I told you about last week—the one that Landon Maher was tied to. Do you want to hear it or wait? I don't want to overwhelm you."

"I want to hear it," I said.

She proceeded to explain that there'd been a shooting last night, in a warehouse on Tonawanda Island, of all places, around the same place Jeanine's car had been found. The man who got shot was a guy named Morley. The police pulled his fingerprints to identify him, and to their shock—

"The prints matched the ones that were found at the site where the drug murder took place. The police have totally shifted focus. They're searching Morley's homes and businesses for a murder weapon. So we'll see. The office is buzzing about it."

I glanced back at Laura. I had told her earlier that morning about Jason, and she had not known how to react. Now she simply stared ahead, and gave me a little nod to show she was okay.

"Obviously, this is not public news—I just wanted you to know they're not pursuing Landon anymore," said Sharrice. "I never heard any follow-up about the search warrant, so I doubt they found much on him they could use."

"Thanks for telling me, Sharrice," I said.

"I don't know what to think about all this activity on Tonawanda Island. It's so spooky how this happened near where Jeanine's car was abandoned. But I can't figure out what they have to do with each other? Is it just a coincidence?"

I made a noncommittal noise. Laura reached up to squeeze my shoulder. I burrowed deeper in Jeanine's coat, which was mostly dry from a cycle through Suzanna's dryer. My arms occupied the sleeves that had held her arms. I slipped my hands into the pockets that had held her hands.

In the left pocket, my fingers closed around a hard metal object. A key. I drew it out and studied it on my lap. It was small, too small for a door, the right size for a lockbox or cashbox.

"Oh wait—Virginia!" The Beetle wavered a bit as Sharrice's hands gripped the wheel. I slipped the key hurriedly back into my pocket. "There's something else. I should have told you straight off."

"What's wrong?" I said, thinking, *What now?*

"After I went to your apartment and found Laura—after the car picked her up, I cleaned your place up a bit and I realized . . . I'm not sure when it happened, or if it was me who let him out, but—your cat is gone."

"Oh," I said weakly. "Sharrice, it's okay."

"I feel responsible. You did leave him in my care."

"It's really okay." And it was, in terms of Sharrice being at fault, which she certainly wasn't. But it wasn't okay at all, not really, the thought of Jeanine's cat in the street, in the cold.

If that's the worst thing, I thought, pulling Jeanine's coat tight, touching the little key once again. But actually, it did seem like a very sad thing.

LAURA STAYED WITH me one more night before heading back to Columbus. I wouldn't have minded if she stayed forever, but she had a life: massage classes, yoga clinics, NA meetings. I managed to keep it together as we hugged goodbye in front of her car. "It won't be long," Laura whispered in my ear, and what she referred to was unclear: not long until we would be together, or until I would feel better. After her car disappeared around the corner, I went back upstairs to my empty apartment and cried on the couch for a long time.

I was still wearing Jeanine's coat, which I'd slipped on when I walked Laura to her car. The little key was still inside the pocket. I took it out and held it aloft.

I sniffed and wiped my eyes while I studied it. It was thin and flimsy, which meant it probably didn't open a safe. It was the right size and shape for a mailbox key. I had a copy of Jeanine's key for her mailbox in Buffalo, and the two didn't match. The house on Como Ave had a typical mailbox out front, with no lock on it. A PO box, then. Perhaps.

I wondered if she needed it, wherever she was.

"You've got to be done with this," I said aloud in my empty apartment, looking at the key. "People are dead. You've got to be done."

But I put the key on the kitchen counter, by the fruit bowl, where I could see it.

THE REST OF November passed in a strange fog.

I got a new phone, after which Suzanna was able to contact me to let me know I was terminated from the Jills, effective immediately, though she insisted I re-audition in April. I told her I understood. I pictured the Jills dancing far away, encased in a gentle golden mist through which I could never again penetrate.

The other Jills sent me supportive texts, but Sharrice was the one who came over about twice a week to make sure I was eating. She helped me make salads and broil salmon and was content to watch episodes of old sitcoms with me to fill the scary, empty evening hours. I told her a version of Ohio that seemed safe enough for her to hear: that someone matching Jeanine's description had been seen in Columbus by some people my sister knew, but I hadn't been able to figure out any more details. When I found it hard to talk, I helped Sharrice with her LSAT practice tests, checking her multiple-choice answers, listening as she worked her way through the maze of logic problems, filling my living room with inscrutable good sense.

All the while, Jeanine's key sat out on the counter. To Sharrice it was simply part of the kitchen's clutter, but I was constantly aware of its presence.

I went nowhere except to the grocery store and the gym, determined to maintain a normal schedule. I talked to Laura on the phone every night before we went to sleep. For Thanksgiving, I brought a rotisserie chicken and roasted Brussels sprouts to my mom's condo, which we picked at quietly, Mom softening the wounded distance she'd assumed after our stay at Suzanna's house after a couple vodkas.

Throughout this period, the days slid by, substance-less. Every so often I was seized by a sense of urgency with no source or outlet. When this happened, I walked the block, looking for the cat, and pictured all the places Jeanine could be. She could be in a bad motel in Canada. She could be at the bottom of Lake Erie. She could be dead from exposure or drowned, washed up on a wooded shore. She could be at a party, hair dyed red, seducing someone into sex or friendship. She could be in the bed of a wealthy man, explaining that she was on the run from an abusive ex, while he ordered his butler to bring more champagne. And if Stanley had caught up to her . . . if Stanley caught up to her, I might never know what happened to her.

Over time, my urgency solidified. I tried to pretend I didn't care what the key was for, because it didn't matter anymore. This was a lie. I had a theory. At times my eyes flew open in the middle of the night, my whole body alive with the urgency to test it.

In my dreams I fell off the boat and into the river again and again, the weight of the coat dragging me downward, my limbs turned to stone from the cold, the dim light of the shore a million miles away in the blackness. I dreamt that I was on the phone with Jeanine, but no matter how loud I screamed, she couldn't hear what I was saying. *Are you there?* her voice said. *Hello? Hello?*"

I DID ONE other thing after Laura left: I searched the papers on my kitchen counter until I found the scrap where I'd written down a phone number, the one with a Rochester area code that Landon had called Brittany from.

I dialed it. Marianne picked up.

"Hey, it's me," I said. "The teeth girl. I got a new number. Is there any chance you can pass it on to Landon? I think it's safe for him to come home now."

Chapter 40

A DAY CAME WHEN I had no classes or clients and I felt remarkably capable. I woke up and made breakfast, asking myself, *Are you really going to do this?*

I decided I was going to do it. This was my last chance, I told myself, to be a crazy person. I had to do this one thing—then I'd put it to bed forever.

I made the drive to Columbus once again, to the post office at the address Ray had so carefully written out for me in his cramped print. It was on High Street in Clintonville, about a mile north of the house on Como Ave. I walked over to the wall of tiny boxes, without making eye contact with anyone, and followed the numbers until I found the PO box number matching one listed on the Junior Jills donor spreadsheet for Olena Rossi.

The key slid right in.

There was only one item in the box: a long, thin envelope. I grabbed it and hurried outside, fearing, irrationally, that a postal worker would scream that I was not Olena Rossi and tear the envelope from my hands.

On the steps outside, I got a good look at the return label. It was a Buffalo address. I ripped open the envelope.

Inside was a check for thirteen grand, made out to Olena Rossi, from the Junior Jills Cheerleading Scholarship Fund.

I sat on the steps of the post office and stared at it. It was a long time before I was able to draw a breath and return the check to the envelope.

My first wild thought was that I now knew how the donated money came back *out* of the Junior Jills program: through scholarship checks that Suzanna wrote. That *Suzanna* wrote. The obviousness of it stunned me. Suzanna kept an iron grip on every facet of the Jills organization. How could I have thought for a moment that she wasn't aware of every dime moving in and out of the Junior Jills program?

A second thought, more urgent, arose and swallowed the first. If Jeanine had managed to get off that boat to some safe shore, she would contact the person who was helping her with money. The person who'd given her a name to use, who'd bought her a car, who helped her move great chunks of money under the radar.

I slid the check into my coat's inner chest pocket and stood up. My anger, my sense of purpose, began to sputter back to life, like an old engine, revived to mercifully drive away my sadness.

IT TOOK FIFTY minutes to drive from Columbus to the ear, nose, and throat office in Springfield where Olena Rossi worked. Throughout the drive, my anger shook and vibrated in the pit of my stomach, throwing sparks. I cradled and fed it, relieved to once again have a secret around which to focus my life. Every so often, I felt in my pocket for the check.

The door gave a pleasant *ding* as I entered. Behind the reception desk in the lavender waiting room sat a woman who matched the picture on the office website. Her hair was full of product that had turned its texture both stiff and damp, and her dark roots peeked out beneath her honey-blond dye job. She was a bit heavyset and pretty, with a thick layer of expertly applied makeup. Her nameplate said RECEPTION: OLENA.

She smiled and asked with thinned midwestern vowels, "Name and appointment time?"

I pulled out the check and slid it across the desk.

"What is this?" she said. "What is Junior Jills? Is this a prize?"

"It's from Jeanine," I said. "Your scholarship."

"I don't know who that is."

"Jeanine," I repeated. "Jeanine Chanowitz. Though she also goes by the name Olena Rossi?"

It gave me some satisfaction when the woman blanched. She stood up.

"Go around back," she whispered. "I'll be out in a second."

I waited on a patch of grass at the back of the building, half-expecting to see Olena in a car peeling out of the parking lot. But after five minutes she came out, coat clutched against the cold, her stiff hair lifted like branches in the wind.

"I made myself very clear," she said. "I don't want to be involved with this Calhoun business. How do you know where I work? Who gave you my information? I will get a lawyer if I have to. This is against the law. This is harassment."

"The Calhoun Clinic?" I said.

"Did she send you?" She pointed at my chest, at the pocket from which I'd pulled the check. "I never asked to be contacted. I didn't ask for her files or her information. I thought I made that perfectly plain. I should have used a fake name when I went to Calhoun. I should have given her a different one. Then no one would have found me."

I understood what she was saying before I knew I understood it. The realization crept toward me, bit by bit. The phrase *dawning realization* seemed abundantly appropriate: the slow advancement of light, of clarity.

"She has the same name as you," I ventured, holding up the check.

Olena closed her eyes. "I didn't know what else to put down. I thought I had to give her a name right away. The doctors were so pushy. You're allowed to wait, but I didn't know that. I didn't even give birth at the Calhoun Clinic. I just dropped her off there. I wasn't supposed to know anything about her, or what her new parents named her, or where she went. She wasn't supposed to know about me. I don't understand why you're bothering me." She opened her eyes. "Oh my God—you're not a reporter, are you? Or a private detective? You have to tell me if you are."

"No," I said. "I'm a friend—a friend of Olena's. Or Jeanine's."

"Is that check even real? You shouldn't trick people like that."

It began to sink in who I was bothering, who I was dragging into this.

Olena Rossi, the original Olena Rossi, hadn't deposited a single check, hadn't given Jeanine a car, hadn't even wanted to meet Jeanine. The only thing she'd done was drop a baby, whom she'd named after herself, at a clinic, then drive away. The name Jeanine had been using was her first identity—her given name, discovered, perhaps, on an original birth certificate sent by Linda Sulzener.

Olena was not a middleman whom Jeanine used to wash money. Jeanine had done it all on her own.

"It's my right to address these things in my own way," Olena said. "I'm not being allowed to do it my way."

"You're absolutely right," I said. "I made a mistake. I won't bother you again."

She jutted out her chin in a feeble attempt at finality. It seemed we were finished, but for a moment she hesitated, on the verge of turning back to the building.

"Obviously, I'm glad she's okay," she said. "I want to see her doing well. I just don't understand—I mean, what do you people *want*?"

Chapter 41

I KNEW SUZANNA SPENT Saturdays in her office at the Kmart. I knocked on the locked double doors until she heard me and came to open them.

In her office she gestured for me to sit, and though I'd intended to remain standing, I obeyed.

"I'm happy to see you," she said, opening a Diet Coke with a crack. "I hope this time off from the squad has been restorative. Obviously I hope to see you back next season. I suggest you start strategizing for auditions as early as possible. If you like, we can—"

I dropped the pay stub from the check on her desk, and she fell silent. The check, I'd kept for myself. Suzanna leaned forward, frowning at it, then sat back, waiting. She was perfectly composed.

There were a million questions I could ask, like how long had she been helping Jeanine wash her money, and was it her idea or Jeanine's to use the Junior Jills organization, and did she know where Jeanine's money was coming from? There were, I now saw, a dozen ways for Suzanna to get the money back to Jeanine after she made a donation, depending on the size of the transaction. Suzanna could pay Jeanine a salary as a Junior Jills "staff member," she could pay Jeanine appearance fees for fundraisers that never happened, she could ask Jeanine to "consult," and every transaction would have an invoice, a justification. And when they had to move larger sums, they could use the accounts Jeanine had set up using her identity as Olena: for scholarship funds.

But there was no reason for Suzanna to explain all this to me, and in truth, these details didn't matter. I was here for the same reason I'd gone to Olena Rossi in Springfield: I wanted to know if there was anyone left to whom Jeanine could reach out, to ask for help, to indicate where she was and if she was safe—if there was anyone who could tell me what fate I'd abandoned her to when I'd jumped off the boat.

"Have you heard from her?" I said.

"Who?"

"You know who."

Suzanna didn't respond.

"Are you in contact with her?" I said. "Can you get a message to her?"

"Some of our need-based scholarship recipients prefer to remain anonymous to the public."

"I won't tell Stanley you were helping Jeanine like this, if you tell me where she is and if she's safe."

Suzanna's "presence" was often discussed among the Jills, and right now it manifested as an almost physical wall of ice between us. Behind her head, a gallery of younger Suzannas smiled at me from their frames.

"Are you attempting to blackmail me?" she said.

I crossed my legs. I refused to be intimidated.

"Let's speak plainly," said Suzanna. "Women are socially conditioned to pretend they know less than they do. So I'll do you the courtesy of being direct. You do not want to blackmail me, and you do not want to disrupt the Junior Jills program."

I said nothing, letting her warning hang in the air. She waited for me to ask her to clarify, and when I didn't, she barreled on.

"You are perfectly aware that the Paladinos are among the many generous donors who contribute to this program. Obviously my little charity plays an insignificant role in the vast currents of wealth moving through that family's accounts, but it's a very good system and it benefits everyone. They have their own interests in the continuation and success of the program. And I have mine. I hope you won't ruin it for them, or me, or any other people you purport to care about."

"Surely you must get something out of it, too?" I said. "What's your cut?"

"You're in no position to be flippant. All the work I do, in every capacity, is a form of protection. I protect people, through carefully constructed systems, through financial support. It was your father's job to protect people, too, but you, like your father, are not careful. You are shortsighted and emotional, you operate on urges and not reason, because you were not taught how the world works. And because you think nothing can happen to you as long as you're Stanley Paladino's adorable girl, you make messes for other people to clean up. You waving around this pay stub like a trophy is the perfect example of your complete lack of understanding—"

"What do you know about my father, Suzanna?"

The question echoed around our heads; I'd nearly shouted it. Suzanna drew back. The air in the room hardened and grew still. It was now or never. I would never be in a room with Suzanna again if I could help it. This was the most important question I might ever ask. Beneath my anger was a need, a great swirling need to know. And beneath that need was more terror than I'd ever felt in my life, more than I'd felt when I'd run for my life from that warehouse.

"Tell me about my father," I said.

"That's an entirely separate conversation," said Suzanna. She looked concerned.

"Did Stanley do it?"

The room blurred as tears filled my eyes. Suzanna studied me. It was clear that she understood what I was asking, and this chilled me.

"What happened to my dad?" I said. "Don't tell me you don't know. You know. Everyone seems to know except me. I don't want to be exempt anymore. I want to know, too."

Suzanna paused to consider this shift in the conversation.

"All right." She folded her hands on her desk. "At the time I met your father, he was on every upper he could find and had progressed to crack cocaine. He was reckless, and he was causing problems. Whether he met his end thanks to his own choices or with encouragement from outside sources is a question neither you nor I will ever be able to answer. Only one man can answer, and he never will. I'll say this: the distinction is only as important as you make it. The way your father was living, he was not going to be alive much longer. It's not an easy thing to say, but it's true. The people who live a long time in this world are killers. The others get killed or kill themselves. Frankly, the path your father was taking, I don't think you would have wanted to know him."

I could have struck her. Of course I wanted to know him. At any cost. I wanted my father like I wanted my sister and Jeanine—I wanted them all. I wanted to love them and never lose them. They were not disposable. No one was disposable.

"I'm telling you to be careful," said Suzanna. "Your relationship with Stanley isn't shatterproof. It's already shaken."

"Meaning what? I might end up like my dad?"

"I just said I don't know how your father died."

I stood up. I pointed to the pay stub. "You can keep that. No one knows I've seen it except you. But you know that I know."

"Virginia, what can you use this information for? Who are you trying to hurt? The fact is, I can't send money to Olena Rossi anymore. We both know whose fault that is."

Before the door closed behind me, she called, "Even if I could get a message to her—what on earth do you have to say?"

Chapter 42

I DROVE AWAY FROM the Kmart for what I was sure would be the last time.

I knew more now but still did not understand. Knowing the mechanism through which Jeanine had supported herself did not tell me what drove her to do what she did. All I could figure was that she, and Suzanna, and Jason, and Stanley, and Bobby had all been infected with the same illness. They were chasing some fatally elusive, ever-morphing specter of accumulation and power and control, things that promised pleasure but never gave it, because it was not a pleasure to have power unless it was the power to make choices on your own behalf. They constructed their lives and identities around this aspiration and called it ambition and, even worse, success.

I knocked on the door of Paladino's Steakhouse until the bartender let me in. "Stanley's in the back," he said cheerfully. "I'll let him know you're here." The bartender knew nothing of the events of the last few weeks. He still lived in the time before I found Jeanine, before Bobby told me to ask Antweiler what happened to my father, and I envied him this version of reality.

Stanley was surprised to see me. "What are you doing here?" he asked, a question never before posed to me inside a Paladino establishment.

"I don't know," I said.

I sat at the bar. Stanley lowered himself onto the stool beside me and asked the bartender to bring out a grenache blend and two glasses. The bartender, seeming to sense the heaviness in the air, poured the wine and then retreated to the kitchen. Stanley cleared his throat, swirling the liquid in his glass.

"Looks like you've been keeping yourself out of trouble," he said finally.

"I guess," I said. "Everything still okay with you?"

"Oh, I carry on."

"How's Bobby?"

"I've shipped him out to Saratoga Springs to clear his head." He tapped a finger to his sinuses pointedly. "I give him a long leash. But even he knows who really runs the show."

I watched the liquid spin in Stanley's glass. I couldn't think of a single thing to say. Here was the closest thing to a father I was going to get for the rest of my life. My heart ached with this awareness—with grief and grief's twin, love. Suzanna was right that even if I asked Stanley directly, I would never be sure how my father had died. I would never know if the love Stanley had given me over the years was due to a terrible, unpayable debt he owed for having failed to save my father, or for having taken my father away from me. Whatever the case, he had given me that love, and now I didn't know what to do with it.

Stanley cleared his throat again. "Did you, uh—need something, kiddo?"

"I just wanted to sit with you for a minute," I said. "I guess I'll go."

"Oh—all right."

"Sorry you wasted the wine."

"It's not a waste." He walked me to the door, but when we reached it, he held out an arm to stop me.

"You should know," he said, "despite everything that has been said and done the past several weeks, I am still yours."

My body shivered with a rush of emotion I couldn't name.

"Virginia—" he said, but I had already pushed past him.

Leaving Paladino's, I walked out another door I might never reenter. The sensation was one of leaving home but not arriving anywhere—like if you exited a door and walked through a dim, gray hallway, many, many miles, only to turn around and see the door still right there behind you, open, its interior now unfamiliar and unknowable and terrifying to consider. I had gone to Paladino's, I now understood, to confirm that Stanley was still mine. What I didn't know was whether I could still be his.

I DROVE HOME in a hurry; Sharrice had made plans to eat dinner with me at my apartment, and I was a few minutes late. She stood at the covered entrance of my building, gripping what looked like a black bag. She was smiling hugely.

"I think this is yours?" she said.

The bundle in her arms revealed itself, as I got closer, to be a small black cat.

"He was in the bushes in front of your building," she said.

I could not believe it. The cat's eyes were wide and frightened. I reached for him, his fur freezing cold in my hands. I fell to my knees on the front stoop.

"Oh—Virginia," Sharrice exclaimed.

I was sobbing. The crying seemed to be happening not to me, exactly, but everywhere—the crying was here in front of my building, where I happened to be also. The cat was tense as a board in my hands, but he didn't claw, and he didn't try to run away. After a while, the crying receded as quickly as it had come. I wiped my face on the fur of his back and stood up. I apologized to Sharrice.

"That's okay, hon," she said.

She followed me up the stairs to my apartment and continued to watch me, guardedly, as I retrieved the cat's food and water bowls from under the kitchen sink. I filled the bowls for him and watched him eat, feeling an almost manic level of relief and satisfaction. He was my cat now. Jeanine had left him, and now he was mine.

ON DECEMBER 13, her birthday, I drove to Columbus to keep myself busy.

The length of the drive didn't bother me. Time spent in the car was both empty and full of purpose, a tranquilizing combination.

I checked the PO box again. Inside was a notice from the city that the white Hyundai had been towed and had accumulated a fee of $485.

Beneath that, a short stack of flyers. They were from hardware stores, mattress companies, and Internet providers, all advertising deals for your new home. I flipped through them slowly. These sorts of flyers usually came when you filled out a change of address form, when you got a new apartment. I placed them back inside, unsure if they meant what I thought they meant. If she was still using the name.

Atop the flyers, I placed the check from the Junior Jills Scholarship Fund. Here, at least, I knew where it was and that it was safe. It was evidence, though I did not yet know of what.

Leaving the post office, I got a call from an unknown number.

"Hey," said a familiar voice. "You know what today is?"

"Landon?"

"Yeah, still alive. How are you doing? Sorry it took me so long to call. Hard to believe the coast is clear. What are you doing right now?"

I looked over my shoulder at the steps of the post office, where I'd just left the check. There was so much to explain.

"I'm staying tonight with my sister, Laura."

"The one you drove three hundred miles for? Hey, that's great."

"A lot has happened the past few weeks," I said.

"Yeah, no shit." There was a pause, warm but also full; it was clear we each had a lot we wanted to say.

"Well, when you get back, do you want to grab a drink or something?" he said.

Chapter 43

I MET LANDON AT the Foundry, in the booth where we'd drunk together what felt like a million years ago.

We looked at each other shyly, each clearly more fragile than we'd been when we last met.

"Where are you staying?" I asked.

"I'm at Marianne's again. I'm still working up the nerve to go back to my apartment."

"I think you're really all right, Landon."

He shrugged hopefully. "What about you? You okay?"

"Not really."

"Yeah, me neither." He looked at the wall behind my head. "It's sort of slowly been dawning on me that she set me up with that shit on purpose," he said.

I nodded.

"What do you think is wrong with us that we nearly ruined our lives for Jeanine?" he said.

I closed my eyes. I understood that this question was crucial, that I had to do whatever was required of me to answer it, or at least try.

But how could I even begin to answer this question, when I had so many questions of my own? Like: What was I supposed to do with all those good memories, with the gratitude I'd felt? Those things didn't just up and die. They didn't get canceled out. I carried them around, stumbling and uncertain, praying for a place to put them down. People helped you and hurt you. How did you forgive somebody to whom you were also indebted, who'd made it possible for you to live?

My cheeks grew cold as my tears dried on them, but I still didn't open my eyes.

"Could I hold your hand?" said Landon.

"Yeah," I said.

I felt his hand. My sternum began to split, right down the middle. The miracle of it was, after all this: there were still people. Landon, Laura, Sharrice.

I opened my eyes. Landon was wiping his own face with his free hand. He laughed, embarrassed, and I did, too.

We sipped at our glasses and began to talk of other things. Landon had gotten into UB early decision, he said. Because he was a first-generation college student, they'd awarded him significant financial aid, with a scholarship on top. He would hardly pay a dime. He'd signed up to retake his gen ed English class at Erie Community College in the spring semester, since he hadn't been able to finish after going on the run. I congratulated him, and we repeated the word *exciting* back and forth to each other. I was going to have to get something like that, I thought: school, a business, a life of my own design.

As we talked, I could see that Landon was afraid. I was afraid, too. We drew deep breaths before nearly every sentence, to steel ourselves for whatever might come out. We glanced at each other for reassurance, and were excessively grateful to find encouragement in the other's face. Neither of us knew who we were without her. We were starting from scratch. I was comforted to know that someone else was as confused as I was.

In the windowless bar, time halted and stretched. Once we finished this drink, I would have to get up and start the rest of my life. Let's order another, I suggested. I'm not counting calories anymore, I joked. Just one more. And one for the bartender, too. Just a little longer in the warmth of the bar before we had to walk each other to the door.

AFTER WEEKS OF falling off the boat every night in my sleep, my dreams began to shift. I dreamt I was running from the warehouse, following Jeanine through the darkness. We are moving impossibly fast. I catch up to her and take her hand. In the dream, she does not let go. Her hand closes around mine. We run. We run until the concrete under our feet turns to dirt and grass and leaves. There is music playing. My heart is pounding several feet above my head. I can hear her gasping beside me. We are elated, because we are finally free. In the dream, we don't stop running. We don't get anywhere; there's nowhere to go. The lights suddenly brighten all around us, blurring out the trees and buildings beyond. We are surrounded by light. We are holding hands, suspended in wild triumph and escape. Somehow we made it, we made it. The dream does not go on from there. That is where we remain. Running. Everything else is gone.

ON THE TWENTY-THIRD of December I left again for Ohio. Last Christmas Laura and I hadn't been speaking to each other, and now I would stay in her little apartment, where I'd bake cranberry orange bread in her kitchen and help her study for her massage certification exam. I was happy to discover that within the surging mess of emotions I'd endured since abandoning Jeanine on the river, I had room for nervous, elated anticipation. It was bright and sunny and unseasonably warm as I drove.

I planned to check the PO box before I went to Laura's house. This would be my last visit to the post office for a while, I'd decided. Since the night at the warehouse, I'd snipped three articles from *The Buffalo News*.

The first was the news article tying Jason Morley to Frank Vicente's death, with the headline "TONAWANDA ISLAND SHOOTING VICTIM TIED TO OCTOBER SLAYING."

The second article was an update on Jeanine's missing person case with the headline "MISSING CHEERLEADER PUZZLES POLICE." It was a short, perfunctory follow-up to the original article reporting her disappearance, stating only that the police had found no signs of foul play (though they were still "pursuing every lead"). Suzanna was quoted as saying, "The Jills are grateful to law enforcement for their efforts. We want Jeanine to know, wherever she is, that she is loved."

The third was an announcement that Bobby's real estate company had completed construction of its newest residential building. There was a picture of Bobby Paladino cutting a ribbon strung across the entrance, surrounded by smiling people in suits. He was flanked by two Jills, Carmen and Kenzie, their hands parted in mid-clap. The new units, the article said, were renting for four to five thousand a month.

I'd shoved these clippings into a folder, then into the file organizer I kept in my closet. What was I doing, collecting little souvenirs of this period of my life? Reveling in the useless despair of it? I didn't even have a copy of my father's obituary. I did not want my life to be a museum of things I'd lost.

But I'd kept the articles, for weeks.

Of course, they were not reminders for myself. They were things I wanted Jeanine to know. The articles said, *Look what you've done.* Or what you didn't manage to do. They asked what any of it meant. Tell me, please, what it all meant.

I had them next to me now, in my purse on the passenger seat. They were my driving company.

At the post office, I ascended the concrete steps and went to box 1031. I swung the little door open, and my breath caught in my throat.

It was empty. So empty it seemed to echo, as wide and yawning as a cave. Everything, including the check, was gone.

She'd come and cleared it out.

Around me, people stood in line, gripping packages, last-minute holiday gifts to ship. None of them knew that sometime in the last ten days, Jeanine had been to this PO box. Jeanine had stood in this exact spot, her feet lined up with my own, and opened this box to collect her things.

Almost on autopilot, I slipped the newspaper clippings out of my purse and placed them inside the box. I slammed it shut. I would never come back, not even to see if she'd gotten the message. I'd let it go. This was my final act, and it was done.

Three blocks from Laura's place, I pulled over and turned around. I went back to the post office and opened the box one more time.

I pulled out the clippings and crumpled them into my purse. There was nothing to say. I had lost Jeanine. She had done what she'd done, and the rest of my life was mine. But still, Jeanine was lost. I had to begin there. I could not stuff her into an angry, dark section of my heart. Whatever she was doing now to survive—it had nothing to do with me.

I DON'T UNDERSTAND love. I'd told almost every girl I'd ever cheered with that I loved her, and I had, but I don't know what that comes to. I'd said it to a few boys. I don't understand what it requires or what actions are appropriate to communicate love or how far it should be taken or what happens when the beloved no longer exists. I don't understand what death does to it.

Ghost, on a light dose of cat Valium for the drive, was beginning to stir in his crate in the backseat.

Next to the cat was a large poinsettia Stanley had sent me to bring to Laura. It shook and bounced happily in my rearview mirror. You can't choose the love life gives you. For New Year's Eve, I would have Sharrice and Gina and Ashlee over, and we would dance into the night. Every time I'd thought I couldn't stand to walk from one end of the day to the other, I'd been saved by girls.

Maybe I do understand love. I carried my cat and poinsettia up the walkway to Laura's apartment. Laura opened the door for me, smiling wide in the silvery dusk of Ohio winter, and welcomed me inside.

Author's Note

The Jills is a work of fiction based on a real cheerleading organization. The Buffalo Jills were formed in 1967 and were owned by the Buffalo Bills until the mid-1980s, when management of the Jills passed to a series of third-party contractors. In 1995, the Jills voted to unionize, forming the first (and only) cheerleaders' union in the country. The union was short-lived: the Jills' management company ceased operations within months of the vote, and the squad was reinstated, union-free, under new management the following year.

Then, in April 2014, five former Jills filed a lawsuit against the Buffalo Bills and the Jills' current and former management companies. The suit argued that the Jills were incorrectly classified as "independent contractors," violating state minimum-wage and other labor laws, and included allegations of degrading treatment, withheld gratuities, and delayed compensation, among other complaints. At the time, the Buffalo Bills were valued at just shy of $1 billion. The company managing the Jills promptly suspended all activities, citing the lawsuit as the reason, and the Jills were disbanded.

This book is not about the lawsuit. But it was the lawsuit that first brought the Jills, and the financial plight of NFL cheerleaders, to my attention. Like a lot of people, I assumed that cheerleaders had no other duties except to dance on the sidelines at games, and that they received a salary from the NFL to do so. Then in 2016, I came across an article by Michael Powell in *The New York Times* titled "Buffalo Bills Cheerleaders' Routine: No Wages and No Respect," which corrected this assumption.

I was instantly fascinated, and proceeded to read every article about the subject I could find. There were a lot of them: the Jills' suit was one of a nationwide wave of lawsuits filed in the mid-2010s by NFL cheerleaders demanding fair pay.

Though I started this book focused primarily on the financial disparities cheerleaders face (and money remains a key thread holding the plot of the book together), over time I grew more interested in the deep camaraderie that cheerleading makes possible: the sisterhood, the shared accountability, and the mutual support in the face of immense pressure and general disregard from the culture at-large. While interviewing former Jills, I found myself longing for the intense bonds these women described. The Jills had provided them with lifelong friendships, an emotional support network they could lean on, and group solidarity from having lived through a high-intensity and adrenaline-rich experience.

As I worked on this project, I came to understand that the motivations for pursuing cheerleading are complex and, at times, deeply personal and paradoxical. Through research and interviews, I learned that the cheerleaders' struggles to attain financial security in pursuit of their passion was not unlike my own efforts to earn a living as a writer. Taking a closer look at the Jills has pushed me to reconfigure my ingrained definitions of value, obligation, commitment, and care.

In 2022, the Jills participating in the 2014 lawsuit reached a $7.5 million settlement. At the time of writing this, the Jills have never been reinstated.

Karen Parkman
January 2025

Acknowledgments

This book owes an enormous debt to a number of former cheerleaders who generously took time to speak with me about their experiences. Heartfelt thanks to Dana Segal, Lisa O'Connor, Alyssa Kragor, and Lisa Grimaldi for sharing your stories with me.

Thank you to the NBA dancers who spoke to me and helped me understand the rigors and demands of dancing for a major sports organization: Sara Haley, Holly Reimer, and especially Athenia Elie Williams for your warmth and support over multiple conversations.

I am grateful for the knowledge I gained from the memoirs *It's Not About the Pom-Poms* by Laura Vikmanis with Amy Sohn, and *Deep in the Heart of Texas: Reflections of Former Dallas Cowboys Cheerleaders* by Suzette Scholz, Stephanie Scholz, and Sheri Scholz.

The Jills takes place in approximately the 2011–2012 football season, but some of the details that appear in the book—pay rates, scheduling, practice locations and rituals, etc.—are lightly fictionalized or borrowed from other seasons and cheerleading organizations. All accuracies in the book are thanks to the amazing sources above. All inaccuracies and liberties are entirely my own.

Immense gratitude to the many people who helped me fall in love with the city of Buffalo while working on this book: to Spencer Williams for taking me out to the downtown and Allentown bars. To Josh Voorhees and Leah Vonderheide for a madcap tour of Buffalo, from Orchard Park to Niagara Falls, from Thirsty Buffalo to Salvatore's. Special thanks to the amazing people who welcomed me into their homes or showed me around: Mary Scalzi, Tom Scalzi, Laura and Nick Schiro, Tori Greco, and Joe Santa Maria.

I am so fortunate to have dear brilliant friends who read drafts of this book and gave feedback: Maria Kuznetsova, Liam O'Brien, Kevin Smith, and Keenan Walsh.

I owe a tremendous thanks to so many people for their friendship and support throughout the writing of this book. To Alice Bolin and Dan Hornsby, Maggie Dimmick, Bri Ditzler, Rachel Huffman, Jessica Saint Jean, Ryan White, and Katie Kelly. To Ethan Canin and Margot Livesey for teaching me. To Charlie D'Ambrosio for the detective fiction seminar that made me believe I could write a book like this. To all my writing communities in Boston, Iowa City, Minneapolis, and Knoxville: you make life as a writer possible.

To my sister, Kate Thompson: thank you for being my champion and my ideal reader, always. And thank you for reading this book (twice!) and believing in it so completely.

To my parents, Ross and Anna: I will never be able to thank you enough for trusting and supporting me, and for believing in me as a writer.

Thank you from the bottom of my heart to the people who made my greatest dream come true: to my brilliant agent, Dorian Karchmar, who gave me the courage to go deeper and dream bigger. To my editor, Hilary Teeman, who saw straight into the heart of this story and helped it find its final form. To Sophia Bark, Carolina Beltran, Nicole Weinroth, Aren Barnes, and Albin Shibu at WME. To Elsa Richardson-Bach and everyone at Ballantine who helped make this book a reality.

And finally, to Connor White, my best reader and fiercest advocate, who read countless drafts and stayed up late before deadlines holding my hand: thank you for building the life of my dreams with me.

About the Author

KAREN PARKMAN is an Iowa Writers' Workshop graduate based in Knoxville. *The Jills* has been supported by MacDowell and Yaddo fellowships, the Sozopol Fiction Seminars, and the Vermont Studio Center. Parkman's stories have appeared in *Michigan Quarterly Review, Joyland,* and other outlets.

About the Type

This book was set in Sabon, a typeface designed by the well-known German typographer Jan Tschichold (1902–74). Sabon's design is based upon the original letter forms of sixteenth-century French type designer Claude Garamond and was created specifically to be used for three sources: foundry type for hand composition, Linotype, and Monotype. Tschichold named his typeface for the famous Frankfurt typefounder Jacques Sabon (c. 1520–80).